FAYE KELLERMAN

Cold Case

D0293085

HARPER

Harper
An imprint of HarperCollins*Publishers*
1 London Bridge Street, London SE1 9GF

www.harpercollins.co.uk

This paperback edition 2009

1

First published in Great Britain by HarperCollins*Publishers* 2008

A catalogue record for this book
is available from the British Library

ISBN-13 978-0-00-724325-9

Typeset in Meridien by Palimpsest Book Production Limited,
Grangemouth, Stirlingshire

Printed and bound in Great Britain

For Jonathan—for now and forever

And welcome to Lila

1

Twenty-five years ago, they were called nerds.

Today, they're called billionaires.

Even among outcasts, Genoa Greeves suffered more than most. Saddled with a weird name—her parents' love for Italy produced two other children, Pisa and Roma—and a gawky frame, Genoa spent her adolescence in retreat. She talked if spoken to, but that was the extent of her social interaction. Her teenage years were spent in a self-imposed exile. Even the oddest of girls would have nothing to do with her, and the boys acted as if she'd been stricken by the plague. She remained an island to herself: utterly alone.

Her parents had been concerned about her isolation. They had taken her through an endless parade of shrinks who offered multiple diagnoses: depression, anxiety disorder, Asperger's syndrome, autism, schizoid personality disorder, all of the above in comorbidity. Medication was prescribed: psychotherapy was five days a week. The shrinks said the right things, but they couldn't change the school situation. No amount of ego bolstering or self-esteem-enhancing exercises could possibly counteract the cruelty of being so profoundly different. When she was sixteen, she fell into a deep depression. Medication began to fail. It was Genoa's firm opinion that she would have been institutionalized had it not been for two entirely unrelated incidents.

As a woman, Genoa had definitely been born without feminine wiles, or any attributes that made girls desirable sexual beings. But if she wasn't born with the *right* female qualities, at least Genoa did have the extremely good fortune to be born at the *right* time.

That is, the computer age.

High tech and the personal computer proved to be Genoa's manna from heaven: chips and motherboards were her only friends. When she spoke to a computer—mainframes at first and then the omnipresent desktops that followed—she found at last that she and an inanimate object were communicating in a language that only the blessed few could readily understand. Technology beckoned, and she answered the summons like a siren's call. Her mind, the primary organ of her initial betrayal, became her most welcome asset.

As for her body, well, in Silicon Valley, who cared about that? The world that Genoa eventually inhabited was one of ingenuity and ideas, of bytes and megabytes and brilliance. Bodies were merely skeletons to support that great thinking machine above the neck.

But even growing up at the cutting edge of the computer age wasn't a guaranteed passport to success. Achievement was surely destined to elude Genoa had it not been for one individual—other than her parents—who believed in her.

Dr. Ben—Bennett Alston Little—was the coolest teacher in high school. His specialty was history with a strong emphasis on political science, but he had been so much more than just an educator, a guidance counselor and the boys' vice principal. Handsome, tall, and athletic, he had made the girls swoon and had garnered the boys' respect by being tough but fair. He knew everything about everything and had been universally loved by the twenty-five hundred high school students he had served. All that was good and fine, but virtually meaningless to Genoa until that fateful day when she passed him in the hallway.

He had smiled at her and said, "Hi, Genoa, how's it going?"

She had been so stunned she hadn't answered, running away, her face burning as she thought, *Why would Dr. Ben know my name?*

The second time she passed him, she still didn't answer back when he asked "how's it going?" but at least she didn't exactly run away. It was more like a fast step that converted into a trot once he was safely down the hall.

The third time, she looked down and mumbled something.

By the sixth time, she managed to mumble a "hi" back, although she still couldn't make eye contact without her cheeks turning bright red.

Their first, last, and only actual face-to-face conversation happened when she was a junior. Genoa had been called into his office. She had been so nervous that she felt her bladder leaking into her cotton underwear. She wore thick baggy jeans and a sweatshirt, and her frizzy hair had been pulled back into a thick, unwieldy ponytail.

"Sit down, Genoa," he told her. "How are you doing today?"

She couldn't answer. He looked serious, and she was too anxiety ridden to ask what she did wrong.

"I just wanted to tell you that we got your scores back from the PSAT."

She managed a nod, and he said, "I'm sure by now that you know that you're a phenomenal student. I'm thrilled to report that you got the highest score in the school. You got the highest score, period. A perfect 1600."

She was still too frightened to talk. Her heart was pumping out of her chest, and her face felt as if it had been burned by a thousand heat lamps. Sweat was pouring off her forehead, dripping down her nose. She quickly wiped away the drops and hoped he didn't notice. But of course, he probably did.

"Do you know how unusual that is?" Little went on.

Genoa knew it was unusual. She was painfully aware of how unusual she was.

"I just called you in today because I wanted to say congratulations in person. I expect big things from you, young lady."

Genoa had a vague recollection of muttering a thank-you.

Dr. Ben had smiled at her. It had been a big smile with big white teeth. He raked back his sandy blond hair and tried to make eye contact with her, his eyes so perfectly blue that she couldn't look at them without being breathless. He said, "People are all different, Genoa. Some are short, some are tall, some are musical, some are artistic, and the rarefied few like you are endowed with incredible brainpower. That head of yours is going to carry you through life, young lady. It's like the old tortoise and the hare story. You're going to get there, Genoa. You're going to get there, and I firmly believe you're going to surpass all your classmates because you have the one organ that can't be fixed by plastic surgery."

No comment. His words fell into dead air.

Little said, "You're going to get there, Genoa. You just have to wait for the world to catch up to you."

Dr. Ben stood up.

"Congratulations again. We at North Valley High are all very proud of you. You can tell your parents, but please keep it quiet until the official scores are mailed."

Genoa stood and nodded.

Little smiled again. "You can go now."

Ten years later, from her cushy office on the fourteenth floor looking over Silicon Valley, about to take her morning hot cocoa, Genoa Greeves opened the *San Jose Mercury News* and read about Dr. Ben's horrific, execution-style homicide. If she would have been capable of crying, she would have done so. His words, the only encouraging words she had received in high school, rang through her brain.

She followed the story closely.

The articles that followed emphasized that Bennett Alston Little didn't appear to have an enemy in the world. Progress on the case, slow even in the beginning, seemed to grind to a halt six months later. There were a few "persons of interest"—it should have been "people of interest," Genoa thought—but nothing significant ever advanced the case toward conclusion. The homicide went from being a front-page story to obscurity, the single exception a note on the anniversary of the homicide. After that, the files became an ice-cold case sitting somewhere within the monolith of what was called LAPD storage.

Fifteen years came and went. And then, quite by happenstance, Genoa picked up a copy of the *Los Angeles Times* and read about a homicide with overtones of Dr. Ben's murder. When she saw the article, she was sitting in the president's chair, located in the CEO's office of Timespace, which was housed on the fifteen through the twentieth stories of the Greeves Building in Cupertino. But unlike Dr. Ben's murder, suspects had been arrested for this carjacking.

She wondered . . .

Then she picked up the phone and called up LAPD. It took a while to get through to the right person, but when she did, she knew she was talking to someone with authority. Though Genoa didn't demand that the Little case be reopened, her intent was crystal. It was true that she had money to hire a battalion of private detectives to investigate the murder herself, but she didn't want to step on anyone's toes—and why should she shell out money when she paid an exorbitant amount of California state taxes? Surely the cash that she would have had to expend in private investigations could be put to better use in LAPD, aiding the homicide detectives in their investigation.

Lots of money, in fact, should the department decide to reopen the Ben Little homicide and actually *solve* it.

The inspector listened to her plaints, sounding appropriately eager and maybe just a tad sycophantic.

Genoa wanted to reopen the case to do right by Bennett Alston Little.

Genoa wanted to reopen the case because the more recent homicide brought to mind the Little case and she thought about a connection.

Genoa wanted to reopen the case to bring a murderer to justice.

Genoa wanted to reopen the case to bring peace and solace to all of the victims' friends and families.

Genoa wanted to reopen the case because at this stage in her life, and sitting on 1.3 billion dollars, she could do whatever the hell she pleased.

2

"The conversation went like this: 'The case is fifteen years old,' I say. Then Mackinerny responds, 'Strapp, I don't give a solitary fuck if it's from the Jurassic era; there's a seven-figure endowment riding on this solve, and you're going to make it happen.' I respond, 'Not a problem, sir.'"

"Good comeback."

"I thought so."

Lieutenant Peter Decker regarded Strapp, who within the last ten minutes seemed to have gained a few more wrinkles from frowning. He was turning sixty this year, but still had the bull frame of a weightlifter. The man had a steel-trap mind and a matching metallic personality. "I'll do what I can, Captain."

"That's the idea, Lieutenant. *You'll* do what you can. I want you to handle this personally, Decker, not pass it off to someone in Homicide."

"My homicide squad is more up to date on the latest techniques and forensics. They'd probably do a better job since most of my time is spent doing psychotherapy and scheduling vacations."

"Horseshit!" Strapp rubbed his eyes. "Last summer you spent way more time in the field than in your office, judging from the amount of overtime you racked up flying Southwest to San Jose and to Santa Fe. Surely you got a couple of free trips out of that."

"We cleared two homicides."

"One of which was twenty-five years old, so this one should be a snap. We've got a hell of lot riding on this solve."

A potential seven-figure gift could lift LAPD into state of the art. Equipping the department with the newest in forensic machinery could potentially put more felons behind bars. Still, Decker has found that in the end, it was always the human factor: men and women sweating hours on end to extract confessions, noticing a detail that was overlooked, doing just one more interview.

Not that technology didn't have its place. And with a big endowment . . .

Money talks, etc.

"What prompted the call?" Decker asked Strapp.

"She read about the Primo Ekerling carjacking in Hollywood and it reminded her of the unfinished business with the Little case."

"Doesn't Hollywood have a few cholos in custody for that one?"

"It does, but that's not the point. The parallels

were similar enough to strike a chord in her very wealthy mind."

"What's her connection to Little other than the fact that he was her guidance counselor?"

"I think it's as simple as that. She told Mackinerny that Little was the only one who had been kind to her during her awkward years, and now she has enough money to get people to jump," Strapp said. "We were both in Foothill when the Little murder happened. From what I remember, he was a good guy."

Decker hadn't followed the details closely. He did recall that the case had occupied space in the local newspapers. "How soon do you want me on this?"

"How does yesterday sound, Lieutenant? Top priority. Got it?"

"Got it, and over and out."

Though he couldn't delegate the thinking, Decker could certainly dole out the grunt work. He assigned one of the newest detectives the necessary but excruciatingly frustrating task of driving from the West Valley to downtown to pick up the Little file. In morning rush-hour traffic that was a heavy one- to two-hour commute, depending on the amount of Sigalerts on L.A.'s arteries. In the meantime, Decker went over his current assignments, clearing most of his paperwork to devote his attention to the Little case.

The department had detectives who worked

cold cases routinely, and why they didn't pick this one up was anyone's guess. Decker suspected that if West Valley got the solve, a substantial slab of the coveted cash would be directed to Strapp. Also, it was logical that the local detectives might have better luck concluding a case that happened in their own backyard.

By the time Decker could actually turn his attention to the six boxes that had been checked out from storage, it was after six in the evening. Too many miscreants had occupied the day, and if he was to get anywhere, he needed solitude to read and think. He decided to work from his home office, and though it wasn't proper procedure to carry out official material, it happened all the time.

The drive to his house took less than fifteen minutes, down Devonshire Boulevard to his ranch-style wood-sided house. Decker's property was over a third of an acre, not nearly as big as the ranch he had owned when the Little case broke through to the media, but the space was large enough for him to spread out his workbench on a lovely spring day and play with his tools. The grounds had become a feast for the eyes since Rina had taken up gardening about two years ago. She had turned what had been a boring sheet of green lawn into lush gardens with riotous colors. Last spring, it had made the L.A. Garden list of places to visit. One entire Sunday had been taken up by troupes of gardening aficionados traipsing through his property oohing and aahing and congratulating Rina on a job well done.

Upon arriving home, Decker could smell garlic coming from the kitchen. His wife's cooking skills even surpassed her eminent prowess as a landscaper. Balancing three of the boxes while fiddling with the front door key, he managed to make an entrance, place the boxes on his dining room table, and not fall on his ass. It was a good sign.

Rina emerged from the kitchen, her hair maddeningly black without a hint of gray even though the woman was in her forties. Her lack of aging never ceased to painfully remind Decker that he was in his fifties and had a head streaked with silver. The follicles that retained the most of Decker's original carrot red coloring were embedded in his mustache. The facial hair was maybe a bit out of style, but Rina claimed it made him look very masculine and handsome, and she was the only one he was still trying to impress.

Rina wiped her hands on a dish towel. She pointed to the boxes. "What's all that about?"

"I got saddled with another cold case, only this one needs a quick solve."

"See what happens when you're too successful?"

Decker smiled. "Aren't you my good friend. What smells so good?"

"Chicken cacciatore over pasta. I've loaded it with garlic trying to stave off the current flu bug. My plan is to make it uncomfortable for anyone to get too close to us. But we'll be okay with each other because we'll both eat the same entrée."

"What about our progeny? Will she be able to come close?"

"Hannah is irrelevant since I basically haven't seen her in three days—the consequence of a driver's license. She's at Lilly's studying for a chemistry test."

Decker brightened. "So we're all alone?"

"Yes. How about if you clear off the table and I'll open the wine. I've picked out a Sangiovese that I found on KosherWine.com."

"Sounds wonderful but just a single glass for me, darlin'. I've got to work."

"Hence the boxes."

"There are still three more in the car."

"Yikes. Can I help?"

"No, just leave these on the table for a moment, and I'll drag everything into the office. Then we can have dinner before I plow my way into ancient history. How's your day been?"

Rina's eyes twinkled flashes of blue. "The same as always. I try to teach resentful kids something that they have no interest in learning."

"Charming. For what they pay you, you can walk away."

"I could . . ." Again she smiled. "But then life wouldn't hold any challenges. As much as I love gardening, a plant is no substitute for a surly teenager. And honestly, I really do like the kids."

"The cold case I'm working on was a teacher."

14

Rina turned serious. "Who?"

"It happened fifteen years ago. A history teacher at North Valley."

"Bennett Little. Found in the trunk of his Mercedes, shot execution style."

"What a memory."

"It was a big case. You were still at Foothill and we were living at your old ranch." She smiled. "I miss the ranch sometimes, even though it was a two-and-a-half-mile walk to shul."

"I miss the ranch, too, although I do not miss cleaning horse stables. My hands are dirty enough as is. I'm really impressed with your memory, although it makes sense. At your age, I had a pretty good memory as well."

"I know, Peter, you're ready for the glue factory."

"What else do you recall about the Little case?"

"In the end, the ruling was that it was probably a carjacking." She frowned. "Am I wrong or isn't there a current Hollywood case similar to Little that actually *is* a carjacking?"

"Indeed there is. Two sixteen-year-old punks have been arrested."

"Are the two related?"

"Fifteen years apart?" Decker shrugged. "Doubt it, but without knowing the specifics of either case, I can't say."

"Did they open the Little case because of the Hollywood case?"

"Indirectly, yes." Decker blew out air. "I'll explain

it over dinner. Let me get those other boxes inside. Then I'll clear the table and we can eat. I'm starving."

"Are you sure I can't do anything else for you, Peter?"

"You can bring out the candles. As far as I know, a little atmosphere and romance never hindered anyone's investigation. And I suppose you can make a strong pot of coffee. I'm going to need it tonight."

3

The dry facts of the homicide played out like this. After a full day of work, Little left his office and headed to the school parking lot. Before he reached his three-year-old silver 350SL Mercedes-Benz, he was cornered by a group of six students. The pupils described the interchange as jocular. They chatted with Dr. Ben until Little checked his watch and excused himself, saying he was late for a meeting. According to the kids, Little left the parking lot around four-thirty.

The meeting consisted of a local group of residents and Connie Kritz, a member of the L.A. Board of Supervisors. They were talking about community shelters for the homeless—a hot-button issue in the nineties.

Not that the homeless weren't just as needy today. But having gone through years of dealing with civic issues, Decker knew that there was only so much room for star status. The unwashed schizophrenics seemed to have been supplanted by global warming.

According to records, Dr. Ben had called his home number from his car phone at 4:52 P.M. Melinda Little, Ben's wife of fifteen years, said that the conversation was brief because the car phone's reception was full of static. Ben stated that he expected to be home around seven.

When the clock struck eight, Melinda started to grow concerned. She called his car phone but no one answered. She paged him on his beeper but he didn't call back. Still, she wasn't really worried, figuring that Little had turned off his beeper and was deep in debate. Passions ran high when dealing with the homeless. When her cuckoo clock struck nine and there was still no word from Ben, Melinda told her sons that she was going out for a few minutes.

Melinda drove to Civic Auditorium only to find it empty. With shaking hands, she drove back home, locked herself in the bedroom, and started going through a roster of community numbers until she managed to secure the home phone listing for Connie Kritz. The supervisor was surprised that Melinda hadn't heard from Ben. Connie told her that the homeless meeting had finished up around seven-thirty. She thought that Ben had left with the rest of the group.

It was now close to ten.

Melinda called the police, only to be told that an adult isn't considered officially missing until he or she has been gone for at least forty-eight hours. She told them how unusual it was for Ben to be late, but the sergeant wasn't interested. He suggested some other possibilities.

Maybe he was with a friend.

Maybe he was with a girlfriend.

Maybe he stopped off to get some dinner.

Maybe he stopped off at a bar.

Maybe he took a drive.

Maybe he was having a midlife crisis and needed some time to think.

Whatever the situation was, the sergeant suggested that she go to bed and the situation would probably resolve itself by morning.

Melinda would have none of that. She knew that if Ben had gotten waylaid, he would have called on the car phone. That's what the damn thing was for. Emergencies.

At eleven-thirty that evening, the boys knocked on the bedroom door and asked why their mother had been locked in her bedroom for the past hour and a half. Not wanting to alarm them, Melinda said she was helping a friend in crisis.

"Where's Dad?" asked the youngest.

"Out helping someone else."

The sons had no problem believing the story. Ben was *always* helping someone.

Melinda told her sons to go to bed and began making more phone calls. An hour later, when Melinda still hadn't heard from Ben, her closest friends came over to stay with her until this ordeal resolved. Their corresponding husbands had been sent out to look for Ben and/or his car.

The dreaded call came in at three-thirty in the morning. Ben Little's Mercedes had been spotted—the sole vehicle in a paved lot at Clearwater Park. The police had been called. Two squad cars eventually arrived at the location.

The interior of the Mercedes was empty and there was no sign of Ben anywhere. As the group decided on their next move, a particularly alert officer noticed that the back of the Benz was sagging, and something was dripping from the rear of the car. Gloving up, one of the uniforms fiddled with the lock until the trunk popped open.

Bennett Alston Little was fully clothed. His hands and feet had been tightly bound by generic shoelaces, and a blindfold had been placed over his eyes. He had been shot three times in the back of the head.

Again Melinda found herself talking to the police.

This time they had taken her very seriously.

The first thing Decker did was sort through photographs. In cases where he wasn't the original primary detective, he liked to have clear mental images. The premortem snapshots showed that Ben Little had been a very handsome man: sharp light eyes, a wide, bright smile, a strong chin, and an athletic build. The file contained two head shots and one with Ben and his family.

In contrast, the postmortem shots showed the hapless teacher in the fetal position with his knees bent and touching his forehead—an odd position to take after death. Ben's head was resting in a big pool of blood. Decker continued to read the crime scene report until he found what he was looking for. Several bullet shells had been found inside the trunk, which probably meant that the trunk was the original crime scene. Ben had been living when he had been placed inside and had instinctively curled up in a defensive position. Then he had been executed.

There was something otherworldly about reading original case notes. It transformed a corpse into a living, breathing human being. The two original homicide investigators—Arnold Lamar and Calvin Vitton—seemed to have worked hard, and the file was complete. The resurrection of Ben Little would demand that Decker have a long chat with Lamar and Vitton, but he wanted to form his own opinions first.

Slowly, Little emerged as a complete and complex person. He had his idiosyncrasies—knuckle cracking, a braying laugh, and compulsive list making—but he didn't seem to have any overt or dangerous vices. According to Melinda Little, her husband was a man of boundless energy, involved with the school, with the faculty, with the troubled students, with the honor students, with community clubs and civic duties, and—not to be neglected—with his family. Once in a blue moon, he'd wear out and come down with a cold or flu, and when this happened, Ben reverted, "as most men do, to a complete baby."

Melinda claimed that she was more than happy to wait on him hand and foot, to give back because he was always giving to others. As far as she knew, there were no other women.

"When would he have time?"

He was always leaving her schedules, addresses, and phone numbers of his meetings in case of an emergency. And the few times she had to locate him, he was always where he said he would be.

He didn't drink, and he didn't take drugs. They had money in the bank, a retirement plan, life insurance, and college plans for both the boys. If Ben was spending money on a vice, he wasn't taking anything out of their savings account. The house didn't have a secret second mortgage, the car payments were timely, there was always money for birthday and Christmas presents, and he and Melinda always made a point to get away alone at least once a year. Ben was kind and thoughtful, and if he had one fault, it was his overextension. A few times, he had missed the boys' play-off games and a couple of their school plays, but wasn't that the case with most working husbands?

When pressed, Melinda admitted that Ben had occasional down periods. There had been a student who had died in a car accident, another who died of an overdose. A promising girl had gotten pregnant. Those kinds of things made him blue, but his favored way of coping was to throw himself into another project. He didn't dwell on what was out of his control.

At the time of Ben's death, his sons, Nicolas Frank and Jared Eliot, had been fifteen and thirteen, respectively. They'd be thirty and twenty-eight by now. Decker wondered about the boys' perceptions now that they were adults. They needed to be interviewed.

By the time Decker was done with the file, it was three in the morning. His eyes were shot, his back hurt, and his shoulders felt the crushing weight of obligation. He tiptoed into his bedroom and slipped under the covers of his bed, taking precautions not to wake up his wife. As soon as Rina felt the shifting of the mattress, she nestled closer to her husband.

"Everything okay?" she asked.

"Fine."

"Love you."

"Love you, too." Decker was exhausted, but even so it took him a little time to fall asleep. His dreams were disturbing, but when he woke up the next morning, he couldn't remember them, only a hollowness somewhere in the recesses of his heart.

4

Tooling through the Santa Monica canyons with the windows opened provided Decker with a blast of misty brine in his face, a welcome change from the hotter and drier climate of his work and residence. Here in the Palisades was the California dream: multimillion-dollar houses cut into rocky hillsides with landscaping that was far too green to thrive without the help of additional irrigation. Towering eucalyptus and ficus stood like sentries on either side of the asphalt. The sun was breaking through the fog, patches of cobalt peeking through the gray clouds. The temperature was mild, and at ten in the morning, the day was shaping up to be a good one.

Decker pushed his hunk of junk Crown Vic upward, straining with each twist and turn of the road. The address put him on the top ledge of a prominence where parking was limited but at least the street was flat. The house that corresponded to the numbers was modern, fashioned from wood, glass, and concrete.

Melinda Little Warren answered the door before he even rang the bell. She invited him in and offered him a seat on a white sailcloth sofa. No small talk; the woman was all business.

"After all these years . . . why now?" Melinda wanted to know.

Decker gave the question some thought while looking out the window at a commanding view of the Pacific blue. "I could tell you it's because your late husband, Ben, was a good man and the open case has always bothered a lot of people. And that would be true. But the real reason is someone offered LAPD a big endowment if the case gets solved."

The woman must have been in her midfifties, but she looked younger with her dark flashing eyes, a mane of blond hair, and legs that wouldn't quit. She wore olive drab capri pants and a white linen blouse and had sandals on her feet.

"It's always about money, isn't it?" She raked long fingernails through miles of ash-colored tresses. "I suppose I should have thought about that myself. Of course, I did hire a private detective after the case went cold. It cost me a lot of money and a lot of heartache."

Taking out a notepad and a pencil, Decker said, "Did he have any success?"

"Certainly nothing that cracked the case."

"Do you remember his name?"

"Phil Shriner. I haven't talked to him in years."

"I'll check him out."

"Fine if you do, fine if you don't." She shook her head. "When I think about what Mike took on when he married me . . . my rock-bottom finances, and my needy boys . . . admiration for the man just grows logarithmically."

Mike was Michael K. Warren of Warren Communications. His techno specialty was voice activation. He and Melinda had lived in this piece of paradise for ten years. The interior had natural wood floors, a two-story fireplace, and walls of glass. The furnishings were white and spare, but the place didn't blow a frosty attitude. Maybe it was all the knickknacks—the tchotchkes, as Rina would say.

"Logarithmically," Decker said. "You must have been a math teacher?"

She smiled. "And you must be a detective."

"That's how Ben and you met."

"Right again." Her eyes misted. "I've had so much misfortune in my life, but I've also been overly fortunate in the relationship department. I guess you can't have it all."

Decker wondered what her other misfortunes were.

Melinda said, "May I ask who offered to donate the money?"

"Genoa Greeves. She's the CEO of Timespace."

"I've heard of Timespace. What was her connection to Ben?"

"She was his student in the early eighties. She describes herself as a typical geek, and according

26

to her, your husband was the only person other than her parents who ever gave her a word of encouragement. Smart people have long memories."

She raised an eyebrow and said nothing.

"Do you remember her?" Decker asked.

"Not at all, but her words don't surprise me. Ben was always doing things for other people. I've never met a more altruistic man in my entire life. Sometimes I almost wish I had discovered a drug habit or a mistress. It would have made him more human. By now, the man has reached Godlike stature in my eyes. Everyone falls short. Although I adore Mike, he can never . . ." Tears rolled down her cheeks. "I'm sorry. This is very painful."

"I'm sure it is, but if I'm going to do this case correctly, I have to start from the beginning."

She dabbed her tears with a Kleenex. "I'm afraid I don't have anything new to tell."

"It would be helpful if you went over the incident for me."

A heavy sigh. "Why not? I've only told the story about a million times. Ben said he'd be home around seven. When he wasn't home by ten, I started to worry. I got in the car and went down to Civic Auditorium, trying to find someone from the meeting. Everyone was gone. I drove back home and called the police. They told me to call back in forty-eight hours. A grown man missing is no big deal."

"Do you remember who you spoke to on the phone?"

"Wendell Festes. He wound up apologizing to me for his flippant attitude, but then started saying things like 'you gotta understand what usually happens.'" Melinda clenched her teeth. "I really didn't give a damn about what usually happens. The man was rude, and I told the captain that when I spoke to him."

Decker nodded. "So what did you do after speaking to Festes?"

"A few of my friends came over to the house to keep me company. Their husbands went out searching for Ben. They found his car and called the police, and the police found Ben." She sat down on a leather club chair and made a swipe at the tears in her eyes. "That's really all I can recall . . . I'm sorry."

"What do you think might have happened that night?" Decker asked.

Melinda shook her head. "I thought about it endlessly for years. His car was all alone at Clearwater Park. Maybe he got a last-minute phone call and was meeting someone there, although his car phone records didn't indicate that. But he could have made a call from a phone booth. The cell phones back then weren't reliable."

"Who would he have met?"

"If he was meeting anyone, it was a student in trouble. I suggested that to the detectives at the time, but that went nowhere."

"What do you mean?"

"You know how teenagers are, especially the

boys. Risk takers. They do stupid stuff and usually get caught. Doing something idiotic doesn't mean that the kid is a sociopath. Ben was their best advocate. He went the extra mile for them the *first* time."

"And the second time?"

"Their pleas fell on deaf ears. Ben had a sense of fairness and justice. If you didn't prove yourself to be trustworthy, you didn't get trusted."

"So it is possible that Ben might have angered the repeat offenders."

"The chronic troublemakers would have gotten expelled, anyway, regardless of what Ben might have told the administration. You can't sell pot continually to your fellow students and expect not to be expelled."

"Do you have a specific kid in mind?"

"Darnell Arlington . . . a real charmer. One of the few kids who fooled Ben in a big way, but I must tell you, the police checked him out thoroughly. Darnell had moved to Ohio to live with his grandmother. The night of Ben's murder, he was playing in a basketball game at the local high school. About a hundred people saw him.

"From what I was led to believe, Darnell was turning his life around. His grandmother was a no-nonsense person. But check him out if you want."

"Do you remember any other wayward students?"

"Not specifically, but there could have been

others. I do remember Ben being upset about Darnell even after he moved. For some reason, the kid tugged at his heartstrings."

"Did Darnell ever come to the house?"

"No, not on your life. Ben kept his students away from his family. He never gave out his home phone number or his car phone number."

"What about his pager?"

"From what I recall, no one had paged Ben that evening."

Her memory was correct. No activity was recorded on Ben's pager on the evening of his demise. Still, Decker didn't have Ben's pager records for the previous morning and afternoon. It was possible that someone had paged him earlier in the day and Ben used a public phone to return the call that evening. Maybe a hasty meeting was set up. That would explain why Ben was at Clearwater Park, but it wouldn't shed any light on why Ben hadn't called his wife.

"Was Ben familiar with Clearwater Park?"

"We'd been there before for cookouts when the boys were little."

"So Ben had driven the roads around that area before."

"Why do you ask?"

"If you were going to Clearwater Park from Civic Auditorium, you'd have to take some small roads and at night. If Ben wasn't familiar with the park, it would indicate to me that he was driven there by his abductors. If he knew the park well, maybe he was meeting someone."

"We'd been there a few times. That's all I can tell you." She shrugged.

"The primary detectives interviewed scores of people, including quite a few students. What did you think of the detectives?"

"That's an odd question."

Decker didn't respond.

"Arnie Lamar and Cal Vitton." She smiled, but it lacked mirth. "I suppose they were nice enough; they just didn't get anywhere. It was always Arnie's contention that it was a carjacking. That didn't make sense to me."

"How so?"

"First of all, Ben wasn't a fool. If someone wanted the car, he would have handed over the keys. The other option is that they stole the car and purposely put Ben in the trunk while they went on a joyride." She made a face. "I don't see kids driving a stolen car with a dead man in the trunk."

"There's a case in Hollywood right now that's similar to Ben's case: a body was discovered in the trunk of his Mercedes. Two teens are currently in custody."

Melinda's hands flew to her mouth. "Do you think they're connected?"

"The boys that were arrested weren't even alive when Ben was murdered," Decker said. "It's the boys' contention that they didn't know the body was in the trunk when they stole the car for a joyride. But that would be the logical thing to say. The victim's name was Primo Ekerling. Does the name sound familiar?"

She thought a moment. "No . . . no, not at all."

"He was around forty. The papers listed him as an independent music producer and an entrepreneur."

"That's L.A. speak for a slacker."

"I must admit that nonspecific occupations tweak my antennas. But the case isn't mine, and Hollywood has plenty of well-trained homicide detectives. I'm sure they have their reasons for arresting the punks."

"I'm sure they do."

"Still, now that I've been assigned your husband's case, I'd like to know more about the Hollywood carjacking. If I'm going to get anywhere, I can't just cover old ground."

"I agree."

"I'm glad you do because there were people who were not interviewed the first time around that I'd like to talk to. Your sons, for instance."

"My boys?" Melinda was taken aback. "They were just kids."

"Kids have memories, Mrs. Warren. They see things, they hear things, they experience things. Oftentimes, they won't volunteer any information because that road has gotten them into trouble before. But many times if you ask them a question point-blank, they're not likely to lie. Your sons are adults now, so I don't need your permission to contact them. However, it would help if I had your cooperation."

Her mouth frowned although her forehead remained smooth— Botox. "Let me call them up and get back to you. I'm sure they won't mind talking. Ten years of therapy has taught them how to talk to anyone."

5

When homicide detectives were a hair shy of a solve, the last thing they needed was a hotshot from some other substation messing around with their cases. Two similar felonies fifteen years apart did not a criminal pattern make, and while Decker had no intention of gumming up anyone's finely oiled conviction machine, he did feel it was incumbent to review the files of the recent Hollywood carjacking/homicide, *just in case*. To make the cold call to the detectives was an unpleasant prospect.

Lucky for him that he had an in, and that brought a smile to his face. He had done umpteen favors for his daughter and that was to be expected because he was the parent. This little assignment would give Cindy a chance to reciprocate.

From the winding roads of Sunset, Decker hooked onto the 405 heading north into his home turf of the San Fernando Valley. Morning clouds had given way to full sun, necessitating air-conditioning. Although the car was old, it valiantly sputtered a stream of Freon-laden air, which felt good on Decker's sweaty face. He loosened his tie and waited for phone reception as the Vic chugged through the mountain pass. When he reached the top of the hill, he used his voice-activated earpiece to talk hands-free. Cindy picked up on the third ring.

"Are you busy?" he said without introduction.

"Just sitting down to a vegetarian club salad."

Decker checked his watch. It was eleven-thirty. "Early lunch?"

"Joe's hungry and the timing works. What's up?"

"I'd like to talk to you for a few minutes. It would be helpful if you had some privacy."

"Hold on." Decker heard Cindy talking to her partner. Several moments later, she was back on the line. "Is everything okay?"

"Just fine. Did I make you nervous?"

"Of course you did. You never call me during working hours."

"That's because the call is business. Sorry if I scared you. I need a favor, Cin."

"A favor, huh?" A pause. "Well, now I know I've arrived."

"Weren't you involved in the car recovery of the Primo Ekerling case?"

"Initially Joe and I were assigned to the case until we popped the trunk and discovered the body. Then it immediately went over to Homicide."

"So the car was reported as stolen?"

"Yes, but the vehicle wasn't the main issue.

35

Ekerling's girlfriend reported that he, along with the car, went missing. About a week later, a traffic officer was about to write a ticket on the Mercedes when he noticed that the car already had a ticket on the windshield. The car was parked on Prince right off Hollywood Boulevard."

"That's a residential area, isn't it?"

"Yes, it is. The car was being ticketed because it was parked on the wrong side on a street cleaning day. The first ticket was for the same violation. The car had been sitting there for at least a week."

"And no one called it in?"

"It was a brand-new Mercedes. I suppose it didn't look out of place. The miracle was that no one vandalized or stole it, especially with all the bars in the area. Lots of bars mean lots of drunks doing stupid things."

"That is often the case."

"Anyway, the officer ran the plates and the car came back hot. Joe and I caught the call. When we got to the location, we peeked inside the vehicle. Something just didn't look right. Just as important, something didn't smell right. Joe jimmied the lock on the trunk and the rest is history."

"And no one complained about the smell?"

"It wasn't that strong, and you know how it is in L.A. No one really walks and you'd have to pass by to notice an odor."

"Most of the gas and bloat was gone?"

"Most of it, yes, but we got a whiff of something funky as soon as we got close enough."

"Was the body in the open or was it wrapped up in garbage bags?"

"It was curled up in the trunk." A pause. "Daddy, I have to get back to my lunch or Joe's going to get suspicious. Can we talk about this later?"

"I need the file."

"And you don't want to just call up Homicide and ask for it."

"Exactly. They've got suspects in custody, and I don't want to inject something new unless there's good reason."

There was a long pause. "We should talk later. I never fully bought into the carjacking/murder theory. How soon do you want it?"

"As soon as possible, but a day or two won't make a difference. Do you remember the name of Ekerling's girlfriend?"

"Marilyn Eustis. I'd like to hear the details of what you're working on. Can we meet for dinner?"

"Love to."

"I'll call you up when I get the file and we'll have a date. How about Italian?"

"You get the file, princess, I'll take you anywhere you want. I'll even pay."

"You always pay, Daddy."

"I do, don't I." Decker smiled. "See how much your father loves you?"

*　　*　　*

Taking on the cold case didn't mean that Decker's paperwork didn't pile up. As soon as he hit the squad room, he became the lieutenant in charge and was bombarded with questions, comments, and complaints. Lucky for him he had a few genuine allies that he now considered close friends.

Marge Dunn in specific.

Dunn had worked for or with Decker for over twenty years, starting out as a rookie detective under his tutelage in Juvenile and Sex Crimes for the Foothill Division of the LAPD. He had brought Marge with him to Homicide in West Valley because of her insights and work ethic. A winning personality made her a gem among dross. The woman was tall and big boned with light brown hair that had grown blonder since her involvement with Will Barnes, a former Berkeley detective who had moved to Santa Barbara to be within commuting distance. It was wonderful to see Marge happy, not only from a friendship point of view but also because Marge worked better when she was in good spirits.

Who didn't?

Dunn had filtered out all the nonsense, leaving Decker with the nuts and bolts of what needed to be dealt with to successfully run the detective's squad room. She sat in his office as he rummaged through a forest's worth of phone messages.

She said, "FYI, I went over the list of the current faculty at North Valley High and found a few old-timers who remember Ben Little."

Decker looked up from his pile of pink slips.

Today Marge was wearing a magenta cotton blouse tucked into beige slacks. "Did you get a chance to talk to anyone?"

"No, I had a court case to deal with and an emergency scheduling issue. Besides, I thought you told me that Strapp wanted you to do the interviewing personally."

"Well, that's not going to happen."

"It's rotten of Strapp to put this kind of pressure on you."

"I'll survive. Did you have a chance to look up when Christopher Donatti came to L.A. as a student?"

"Bad boy Chris came to Central West High a year after Little's murder. He never attended North Valley, although the schools are only six miles apart. If you want, I can delve a little further. The Little murder looked like a professional hit, and Donatti was . . . is a professional killer."

Decker nodded. "Actually, I might even give him a call. Guys like him are always paranoid and hyperaware, so he may have heard something."

"You can't be serious!" When Decker shrugged, Marge said, "The son of a bitch shot you."

"It wasn't personal."

"You're crazy!"

"Maybe so, but a lot is riding on a solve for a fifteen-year-old case, and I'll take any help I can get. So who's still teaching at North Valley High from the Little days?"

Marge handed him the list—two teachers

from the humanities, two from math and science, and the boys' gym coach. "If you allow me to bring Oliver in, we could probably rip these interviews off in a couple of days. He would also be helpful because Scott was in Homicide at Devonshire when Little was murdered."

"Have you talked to him about the Little case?"

"I don't do anything without your okay, boss, but I'm sure if he read the file, a lot would come back to him. I did ask him about Arnie Lamar and Cal Vitton."

"And?"

"He said they were all right . . . not corrupt as far as he knew. They were old-timers, although he was quick to point out that they were probably the same age as he is now. Then as he thought about it, he slipped into one of his famous funks. As you well know, it's unpleasant dealing with Scott Oliver when he's moping."

"Did he wonder why you were asking about Lamar and Vitton?"

"I think he guessed, Pete. They've become synonymous with Ben Little's murder."

Decker handed her a slip of paper. "The first name—Phil Shriner—was the private detective that Melinda Little Warren hired to look into her husband's murder. He wasn't successful, even though Melinda said that she paid him a fortune."

"Do you know if he's still practicing?"

"No idea."

"I'll check him out." She wrote down the name in her notepad. "Who's Darnell Arlington?"

"A pet project of Ben Little. The first time Darnell was expelled, Ben went to bat for him and the school gave the kid a reprieve. The second time, Darnell got the boot and Ben backed up the school. Arlington was in Ohio when the murder happened, and Ben's widow had heard that the kid turned his life around. Cal Vitton talked to him at the time of the murder, but he's worth a second look."

"Consider it done." Marge wrote down Arlington's name and gave the slip back to Decker. "So I can bring Oliver into the fold?"

Decker thought about it. "All right, let's include Oliver. Strapp knows that I can't do this all by my lonesome, but he doesn't want it getting back to the big boys that I've farmed it out. With all his faults, Scott can keep a confidence."

"That is true."

"And who knows? Maybe a special assignment will snap him out of his funk."

Marge shrugged. "One can hope, and yet one will probably be disappointed."

6

Calvin Vitton and Arnie Lamar had turned in their guns and shields shortly after the Little murder, but neither had left town. Silent Cal—as he was known—had an address in Simi Valley, a mountainous community northwest of L.A. The area had wide streets, big skies, and lots of undeveloped land that sat atop granite and bedrock. Many working cops called Simi home, and an equal amount of vets retired to small ranches carved from the hillsides. When Vitton didn't pick up the house phone, Decker left a message on his machine, asking him to please call back at his convenience.

Arnie Lamar lived in Sylmar northeast of L.A. The neighborhood was noted more for its honor farms and detention centers than it was for its natural scenery. It was rugged country: some mountains but also dusty flat areas that were perfect for Lamar's passions of auto building and racing, and climbing up hillsides in one of his ATVs.

When Decker phoned, Arnie was just about to go to the track, testing one of his newest vehicles, something that he had cobbled together using parts from a Viper, a Lamborghini, an old Jag XKE, and a small engine jet. They decided to meet at three in the afternoon.

Decker showed up on time. Upon arrival, he took note of Arnie's four-car garage, the door to one of its stalls yawning wide open. A chimerical, cherry red vehicle was parked in the driveway with a pair of denim legs sticking out from the undercarriage.

"Hello," Decker called out.

"In a minute," was the response.

The lieutenant used the downtime to look around. Lamar seemed to have a nice-sized spread, similar to Decker's old homestead except there weren't any stables. The front yard was bereft of green, a brown square of hardscrabble dirt spotted with shreds of rubber, discarded chrome, and rusting steel. The house was one story and wood sided and if it had any style, Decker would call it California ranch. It wasn't exactly dilapidated, but upkeep wasn't Lamar's forte.

The body slid out from underneath the red hunk of metal. Lamar was on his back, resting on a block of oak on wheels. He had on oil-stained overalls and a gray T-shirt. His feet were housed in sneakers. He rolled over to his side and hoisted his frame up until he was erect. Lamar was a short man and slight in build, bald with a white mustache, dark coffee eyes, and knobby fingers that clutched a wrench. "Three o'clock already?"

"By my watch, it is."

"Sheez, I get under there, I forget about everything." His face was streaked with dirt and grease. He wiped his hands on an oil-stained rag. "I'd like to clean up. It won't take longer than ten minutes. You want something to drink. It's hot today."

"Water would be nice."

"How 'bout a beer?"

"I'm working."

Lamar smiled with yellowed teeth. "I won't tell."

Decker smiled. "Water is fine, thanks."

"Suit yourself." The retired detective opened the door and led Decker inside.

The interior was surprisingly clean: floors swept, shelves dusted, and the furnishings simple and old. The dining table and chairs looked handmade, the work good but not professional. Pictures adorned the walls and tabletops: one special woman and children at various ages until they were grown with children of their own. At present, there was no sign of the special woman anywhere.

The house was on the dark side even with the blinds open. Decker sat down on a faded floral sofa. The only other seating was a cracked leather lounge chair that had a bird's-eye view of the television—no doubt Lamar's special seat. His *makom hakevuah,* Rina would have called it, using the

44

Hebrew term for an honored place. At home, Decker had a blue leather armchair and ottoman.

Ten minutes later, Lamar made his appearance, pink cheeked and wearing clean denims and a black T-shirt. He was carrying a plastic cup of water and a can of Coors Light. After giving the cup to Decker, he pop-topped the beer and took a long swig.

"That's good drinks." Lamar plopped down in his chair. "I used to hate diet beer. Now I've gotten so used to the light taste that the dark brew seems way too strong."

"It's amazing how we adjust our attitudes to rationalize things."

Lamar said, "So who decided to reopen the Ben Little homicide?"

"It seems one of his fans from his teaching days struck it big in technology up in Silicon Valley. There's a hefty endowment riding on the success of the case."

Lamar nodded. "Good luck to you, then."

"You don't harbor much hope?"

"Nothing would make me happier than a solve. The damn thing was always a thorn in my side. There seemed to be no reason for it other than bad luck. You know as well as I do . . . you see homicides and each one of them is ugly. But some . . . drug dealers, hookers, thieves, gangbangers . . . now no one deserves to die by violence. But if you're gonna put yourself in harm's way, shit happens. But this guy . . .

nothing I dug up indicated that he was anything else except Joe Model Citizen."

"How deep did you manage to dig?"

"We didn't get any interference if that's what you mean." Lamar thought about the question. "We started with the wife and when we hit a wall, we branched out to friends, coworkers, students, and community people. There was an insurance policy, but at that point, the widow hadn't bought herself a new car or a flashy diamond ring. There was money in a college fund for her boys. She also took a job."

"What kind of work?"

"I think the school hired her as a secretary or a teacher and used his seniority so she could keep the benefits." He finished off his beer. "We scoured through Little's desk, his files, his old floppy disks and the computer, his credit cards, his phone records, his bank account. When I tell you nothing was awry, I mean it."

Decker nodded, although something struck him as odd. "I spoke to the widow. She married very well."

Lamar took a moment to digest that. "Good for her."

"She also told me that she had gone into debt, hiring a private detective named Phil Shriner, trying to get a lead on the case."

"Hmm . . ." Lamar crushed his beer can. "Did she get anywhere?"

"Nothing that she wanted to tell me about. But

when you checked out her account, she was solvent."

"She must have gone into debt after I retired."

"So you don't know anything about the private detective?"

"Didn't even know he had a name until you told it to me. Have you checked him out?"

"I have someone going down that avenue," Decker told him. "Right after you retired and I came on, one of my first assignments was dealing with a murder of a coed at Central West Valley High."

"Central West . . ." Lamar wiped his mouth on his hand. "Cheryl Diggs, was it?"

"Exactly. Her boyfriend at the time was a guy named Christopher Whitman. He's now Christopher Donatti."

"Whitman . . ." He looked confused. "Why does that name sound familiar?"

"Because we originally brought him in for the Diggs murder. It turned out he was innocent, but as a side note, we discovered that the boy was totally mobbed up."

Lamar frowned. "As in New York mob?"

Decker nodded. "He worked as a hit man for his uncle—a real goombah named Joey Donatti. After Joey died, Chris inherited his money as well as his enterprises. What Chris didn't inherit, he made on his own by running numbers, operating brothels, and peddling subscriptions to Internet porn sites. He took his unreported cash and now he owns a chunk of Manhattan real estate between Harlem and Washington Heights. His registration dates put him at Central West after Little was murdered, but he could have been here before the official date of enrollment. I just was wondering if you had any dealings with him before I came on."

Lamar shook his head no. "I don't recall talking to him as part of the Little investigation. Look in the notes and see if I interviewed him."

"I did and you didn't."

Lamar shrugged as if to say, "So there you have it." "As far as I know, his name never came up. But neither Cal nor I bothered to look into people from Central West."

"I have one more guy I want to run by you. A kid named Darnell Arlington."

"Darnell Arlington . . ." Lamar scrunched his eyes. "I remember him . . . a black kid . . . troubled. I think we ruled him out. How 'bout refreshing my memory."

"You're right. Darnell was a troubled kid. When he was threatened with expulsion, Ben went to bat for him and got him a second chance. Darnell blew that opportunity, and the boy was finally kicked out of North Valley for good. That happened about six months before Little was murdered. The second time, by the way, Ben sided with the school."

Lamar didn't talk for a moment. "I never did talk to the boy, when his name came up. As I'm remembering it, he wasn't even in the state when Little was killed."

"Little's widow told me that he was in Ohio, playing in a school basketball game."

"Yeah, it's coming back." Lamar nodded. "Cal was the one who interviewed Darnell. The kid was back east playing in a game, witnessed by about one hundred people. From what I recall, the kid was broken up about Little's death." A pause. "You're looking at a revenge thing?"

"I'm considering everything."

"Like I said, Cal checked him out. He could tell you more than I could about Darnell."

"When I talk to Cal, I'll ask about Darnell. Do you still keep in contact with your old partner?"

"We see each other every now and then. For all that we went through together, once that whole thing ended, we found out that we didn't have too much in common. I'm a doer, Cal's a brooder. Sometimes it worries me, but I'm tired of mothering the man. Eventually he needs to figure it out on his own."

"I've left a message. I trust he'll call me back."

"Oh yeah, he'll do that. Little bothered him as much as the case bothered me. Let me know if you make any headway. Be nice to see someone in custody before I die. That's not too much to ask of the Good Lord, right?"

Decker agreed that it wasn't too much to *ask*. But when it came to results, the GL always seemed to have other ideas.

7

By six in the evening, most of the detectives had checked out on the whiteboard, leaving the squad room hauntingly quiet. When Decker listened hard enough—carefully enough—he could hear wounded voices speaking to him through the blue-covered murder books. He often got his best insights by being receptive. Focused and wired on coffee, he cleared about half his desk when the knock on the door frame broke his concentration.

Marge Dunn and Scott Oliver looked as if the day had dragged on too long. Marge's hair was wilting, and Oliver's royal blue tie was askew. His formerly starched white shirt was limp, and he was carrying his suit jacket.

Marge said, "Ben Little should be nominated for sainthood."

Oliver kicked out a chair with his foot and sat down, stretching his legs in front of him. "He'd give Mother Teresa a run for her money. Not a speck of dirt to dig up, but I'm still not convinced. No one can be that good."

"I agree with Oliver," Marge said. "How can a guy that dynamic and active not have at least one skeleton in his closet?"

Oliver said, "I remember the cops being frustrated about that. I think we all would have been more comfortable dealing with the whack if the vic had some bad habits."

"Interesting that you say that," Decker said. "Arnie Lamar remarked that the Little homicide was particularly sad because he was such a nice guy." His eyes drifted to Oliver's. "What did you think of Homicide's handling of the case?"

"They worked it pretty hard for about six months. Then it just froze. I recall that Arnie and Cal kept at it from time to time, but this wasn't a case with a lot of forensics. There was some ballistic evidence, a couple of prints that Arnie would run from time to time. And DNA? Pshaw, my friend, pshaw." Oliver waved his hand in the air and chanted, "Ice, ice, baby."

"What did you think of Cal and Arnie?" Decker asked.

Oliver gave the questions some thought. "They were competent. I liked Arnie more than Silent Cal, but that doesn't mean that Cal was a bad Dee. Have you talked to Vitton yet?"

Decker shook his head no. "Just Lamar."

"What'd you think of him?" Marge asked.

"He's all right . . . seemed to care." To Oliver,

Decker said, "Did you ever work with either of them on any homicide case?"

"Sure, on the homicides that we worked in teams of five. They were competent if not inspiring. They seemed like a tight twosome."

"Lamar said he rarely talks to Vitton now that they're both retired. Cal's apparently a brooder."

"I can see that," Oliver said. "I think he went through a bad divorce."

Decker said, "Did you ask any of Little's colleagues about Darnell Arlington?"

Marge flipped through her notes. "Marianne Seagraves from the English Department remembered him—and I quote—as a big black boy with a big chip on his shoulder. Darnell didn't have a father and his mother had a drug problem. Marianne said that Little tried his best with Darnell—after-school tutoring, lunch off campus, lots of heart-to-hearts, Christmas presents—but no one was surprised when Arlington was expelled."

"Any history of violence?" Decker asked.

"Darnell had his fair share of fights. No weapons other than his fists as far as Marianne can remember."

"Did you locate him?"

"I found a high school gym coach named Darnell Arlington who lives near Akron, Ohio, but I haven't verified that it's the same Darnell Arlington."

Oliver said, "How many Darnell Arlingtons are out there?"

"According to Find-it Yellow Pages, there are four: one in Texas, one in Louisiana, one in Wisconsin, and one in Ohio."

"That's the problem with these search engines," Oliver griped. "They bring up all this irrelevant information."

"Yes, but they bring up relevant information as well," Marge told him. "Like my grandfather used to say, you take the good with the bad."

The phone call came at nine in the evening on the cell. Decker had been working at home in his pajamas, scouring through the Little file, trying to find a scintilla of an overlooked clue. He regarded the number and realized it was Vitton.

"Thanks so much for calling me back, Detective. At your convenience, I'd like to meet with you for an hour or so regarding the Bennett Little homicide—"

"You can stop right there, Lieutenant. Arnie called me up and told me you were at his place on some kind of a mission. I'll tell you what you already know. If I would have thought of something new, I would have told someone a long time ago."

"I realize that, Detective. I don't expect a breakthrough. Just your thoughts and insights—"

"No new thoughts. Definitely no new insights. You taking time out to talk to me would be a total waste because I don't have anything to tell you."

"Sometimes just by talking, new things pop up."

"We're talking now. Nothing new is popping up."

Decker gritted his teeth. "Still, if you can give me an hour, I'd appreciate it."

"Why?" Vitton's voice had tightened even further. "I already told you, I got nothing to say."

"Okay, then let me spell it out for you. I was ordered to reopen the case. That means I have to talk to everyone involved. If there's a definite reason why you don't *want* to talk to me, I'd like to hear it."

Silent Cal was silent. Decker waited him out.

"I just don't have anything new to say to you. Arnie and I never found a good suspect, and we went through them all."

"Who did you interview?"

"Just read the goddamn file."

Again, Decker felt his jaw clench. "I have the file in front of me. I was wondering if there were people who didn't make it into the file."

"Everyone I interviewed should be in the file."

"Who came closest as a suspect?"

"No one. The man didn't have any enemies!"

"He must have had one."

"No, he didn't. He had bad luck."

"You think it was a random carjacking?"

"He drove a Mercedes. A car like that would be a good score to a couple of punk boosters."

"But they didn't steal the car."

"Maybe Ben came out and surprised them . . . that has always been my theory . . . that the punks panicked, threw him into the trunk, and drove

54

to Clearwater Park. Once there, they whacked him."

Decker gave Cal's ideas brief consideration. Immediately the question arose: How did the punks escape from the park? It could be the punks just walked away. The file had recorded lots of shoe prints on the grass by the car lot, but none of them led anywhere, and fifteen years later, that was probably a dead end.

"That's one explanation," Decker told Vitton. "I'd like to talk to you in person and consider other theories."

Another round of silence.

Decker said, "Look, Cal, if I didn't have to talk to you, I wouldn't bother. But I need to do this. So help me out and make it as painless as possible. The quicker we do this, the quicker I'm out of your hair."

"I used that line many times when I was at LAPD, and I know that it's a truckload of shit. This is only the beginning."

"What time can you meet me tomorrow?"

"Come at nine in the morning."

"I'll be there. This is the address I have for you." Decker read off the numbers. "Is it current?"

"Yeah, it's current."

"So I'll see you at nine."

"Fine. I'll meet with you. But don't expect a hot pot of coffee waiting for you. This ain't a social call."

8

The numbers written on Decker's notepaper matched a small stucco house in a development of modest homes. The street was wide—typical of most streets in Simi Valley—and ended in a cul-de-sac. If lawns were classified like eye color, the patches would have been designated as hazel, a mixture of green grass with russet, sun-bleached weeds. The sidewalk trees were stalks with bushy, untrimmed canopies, resembling adolescent boys with a 'fro. Mixed flowers offered some color, as did the blue sky, but most of the surrounding rocky terrain was brown and dusty.

Both of Decker's stepsons and his younger daughter had taken their driver's license examinations in Simi. It was a good place to learn because the roadways were broad and there were assigned left-hand turn lanes complete with arrows. With Hannah now driving, Decker was left to ponder how fast his life had come at him. He felt active and vigorous, but that didn't change the years. Was retirement a theoretical concept or an inevitable reality of the near future?

After parking the car, he checked his watch. At precisely nine o'clock, he got out of the cruiser and ambled up the walkway, climbing two steps to reach the door. He gave the wood a firm knock, the type of rap that told a cop that another cop had arrived and there was serious talking to be done.

When no one answered right away. Decker was peeved. He rang the bell and waited, feeling uneasy when silence answered him back.

He glanced over his shoulder, as if he expected Cal to materialize; then he looked upward at the cloudless cerulean ether. No Cal in the sky, either, just the fluttering of black ravens along with harsh cawing. The late spring morning was still cool enough to be comfortable, but the warmth from the sun was attracting bugs—bees, gnats, flies, and the ever pesky mosquitoes.

He knocked again, tried the door handle, which, not surprisingly, was locked.

His watch now read 9:10.

Vitton's driveway was empty.

Who the hell did he think he was, avoiding the police? Cal must have been an idiot to think that an amateurish dodge would discourage Decker. With an angry scrawl, he wrote on the back of his business card that he'd be in touch! He dotted the exclamation point angrily and was two steps away from his car when something tickled his brain.

The house had a one-car garage sealed with a plank door that contained a glass inset. Decker turned around, walked up the empty driveway, and peeked through the window. Inside sat an old black pickup next to a workbench area.

Would a guy like Vitton own two vehicles?

He looked at the gray cement driveway. Although it wasn't pristine, it wasn't spotted with oil stains or fluid leaks.

Again he glanced around, biding his time while his brain fired ideas.

Someone could have come by and picked up the old man.

Cal could have gone out for a walk.

But Decker was bothered. Cal was first and foremost a cop. Career detectives didn't miss appointments without explanations. If Vitton hadn't wanted him to come, he would have phoned Decker and told him so. And if there had been an emergency, Cal would have left a note or a message on Decker's cell. No-shows were irresponsible. More than that, they were cowardly, and Calvin Vitton didn't impress Decker as a coward.

There was a six-foot wooden gate that separated the front and back yards. Decker peered over the top and noticed that the gate was secured by a bolt lock. He called out and when nothing answered him back, Decker decided to jump the fence. He found a purchase for his foot on a low cinder-block wall, but his hands still had to do the majority of hoisting up his big frame.

Up and over.

He landed awkwardly on his right foot, but shook it off with a couple of steps.

Vitton's backyard was small and dry and backed up against a spillway that was fenced off by cyclone wires. As Decker peered through the metal, he noticed a few shallow pools of stagnant water basking in the heat of the spring. They were green with algae and white with mosquito larvae. He made a note to himself to call County Pest Control or the area was going to have an infestation.

The back door to the house was also locked. Decker knocked hard, but the noise elicited no response. He checked the windows. The shades were down. Nothing seemed awry: no broken glass, no locks that seemed jimmied, and no signs of forced entry.

He gave himself a moment to think.

The sun was climbing higher. Decker could feel the heat on the back of his neck. Competing with the ravens' calls was the buzzing of insects: the hum of dozens of gnats, the drone of bees foraging for pollen, the high-pitched whine of mosquitoes. And the flies . . . lots of flies.

He swatted the pests away from his face and regarded his surroundings. A splintered chaise longue with a faded cushion sat on a patch of crabgrass. A few small trees languished around the fence of Vitton's property. There was a Weber barbecue that looked in pretty good shape. A white plastic table and chairs were off to one side.

The top of the table was thick with dirt and bird droppings.

When Decker returned his attention to the house, he noticed that a heavy funnel of flies had congregated near one of the back windows.

That was *not* a good sign. Investigating further, Decker was hit with a strong whiff of decay, violently sparking his olfactory nerve.

He exhaled forcibly while holding back a gag.

He knew why Cal hadn't answered the door.

He called 911.

The rule was by no means foolproof, but generally women took pills and men ate the gun.

Calvin Vitton had done both.

The shot had, among other things, taken out the old cop's eye. His mouth was agape, and his other eye was wide open. An open vial of oxycodone was spilling its contents onto the blue bedroom carpet. Near the pills lay a half-dozen empty beer bottles. His right hand had been singed with powder burns and blood spatter. The .32-caliber Smith & Wesson handgun was lodged between the bed frame and the wall and had landed about two inches from Cal's knee. Blood had turned the white sheets red and was still dripping crimson onto the carpet.

The old man had thin gray hair with blue eyes, although the remaining one looked black because the pupil was dilated and fixed. He had been wearing a white shirt and a pair of jeans. His feet were bare. Rigor had set in; lividity was pronounced. Although a warm temperature could speed up the biological processes—and it had been sweltering inside when the Simi Valley cops had busted inside—Decker had a sense that the deed had been done shortly after the phone call.

Two coroner's office investigators—a woman and a man—were about ready to wrap the stiff body in plastic. The crime scene photographer had done his job. A tech was dusting for fingerprints, but almost everyone agreed that it looked like suicide. Cal had taken booze and pills to self-anesthetize. Before Cal totally passed out, he put a gun to his head . . . more to his face. Or maybe his hands slipped and that's how he took out his eye. There were powder burns around the affected area, but there was also powder scatter. The investigators thought that the nose of the gun had been fired from about a half foot away.

Simi Valley was an incorporated city of Ventura County, and although it contracted out to the county for fire, the city was patrolled by its own police department. The detective assigned to the case, named Shirley Redkin, was a pixieish woman in her fifties with short black hair and round dark eyes. Suicide was worked under a homicide detail until the coroner made his ruling. She flipped over the cover on her notebook, and then pointed to the open vial. "First the pills, and when that didn't happen, he went for the gun."

Decker said, "It looks kind of staged."

"Yeah, there is something a little overly dramatic about it with the pills *and* the booze *and* the gun. But killing yourself is a very dramatic act."

"Of course."

"Can we go over the phone call one more time?" she asked Decker. "I keep feeling I'm missing something."

"Join the club," Decker told her. "I never got a sense that the guy was ready to pop himself. More angry than upset."

"Angry about what?"

"That I wanted to go over the Bennett Little case with him." He explained the details to her. "It had been cold for a number of years. I think it was a personal affront to the man."

"But every homicide cop has a number of cold cases."

"This one was very public . . . played out in the papers. To a guy like Vitton, maybe it represented failure."

"Why would he shoot himself now?"

"Maybe he didn't want to feel humiliated if the case got solved."

"Was he obstructionistic?" Shirley asked.

"He clearly wasn't interested in digging up bones. Maybe he was more involved than he was letting on."

"Meaning?"

Decker threw up his hands. "Cal was known as a guy who played it close to the vest. His own partner said it was hard to tell what he was thinking. Maybe someone paid him off not to look too carefully into the homicide. If his dirt got exposed . . . that might drive a lonely man to pull the trigger."

"Anyone specific in mind for the payoff—if there was a payoff?"

"No, just talking in generalities. I'll look a little deeper into Cal's life, starting with his ex-partner, Arnold Lamar."

"He sounds like someone I should talk to."

Decker gave Shirley Redkin his phone number. She said, "How close are the two of them?"

"I think they were very close once, but they each went their separate ways. But he needs to be told. I'd like to call him up after you're done with me. Do you mind if I break the news to him?"

"Go ahead. What I'd like is for him to come down to the station for a chat."

"I'll set it up. This afternoon sound okay, Detective?"

"That sounds fine, Lieutenant."

"Mind if I sit in?"

"Fine with me. Maybe we'll both learn something." Shirley closed her notebook. "The cold case must be very important for a detective lieutenant to devote so much time to it."

Decker smiled enigmatically. "I do my job; I've got no complaints. Life is good for some of us. Then there are guys like Cal Vitton who harbor different opinions."

9

"*What?*" Marge shrieked.

"You heard right." Decker was sitting in the cruiser, parked two blocks away from the crime/suicide scene. The air-conditioning was going full blast, but because the car wasn't in motion, it wasn't as cool as it could be. He was sweating under the collar. Talking to Marge over the line, he was trying to keep his voice even, cop style, and then he wondered why. The tragedy of the situation demanded emotion, yet after all these years on the job, it was somehow respectable to be blunted.

"Oh my!" Marge was still registering shock. "And it looks like suicide to you?"

"The gun was fired at close range. He dulled his senses with drugs and booze. The big question is how and if it's related to the Bennett Little case. I'm meeting with Arnie Lamar at Simi Valley headquarters this afternoon to get a better feel for Vitton."

"Well, this certainly changes the complexion of the investigation."

"It adds another layer. What's on your agenda?"

"Oliver and I have arranged a lunchtime meeting with Phil Shriner. That way it doesn't take too much out of our working day."

"Was he cooperative?"

"Not bad. We'll know more once we talk to him. I do have a question for you. I've located the correct Darnell Arlington and he's willing to talk to me about his high school experiences and Bennett Little. Now I can do a phone interview, but it would probably be better to do it in person. Since I'm not supposed to officially be working on the case, is there a way that you can get funding for the trip?"

Decker said, "Set it up, Marge, and I'll figure something out."

"You're sure?"

"Not a problem. One of Rina's inherited paintings recently sold at auction for big bucks. We're feeling flush."

"You shouldn't be spending your good luck on departmental obligations."

"I have no intention of doing that. I'm just saying having the extra money has made us feel a little cockier. Rina teaches because she wants to, and I work because I want to. If Strapp starts to protest too much, I'm outta here. That's what money does. It allows me to pass the buck and let some other schmuck squirm in front of the brass."

*   *   *

Phil Shriner lived with his wife of fifty years in a retirement home called Golden Estates, not too far from where Calvin Vitton blew his head off. The acreage was beautifully planted, with living quarters consisting of an apartment complex and public areas. There were also small, detached bungalows set around winding walkways.

The community had an on-site cafeteria, two restaurants, a recreation room, a gym, and a movie theater. The grounds included two swimming pools with accompanying Jacuzzis, two tennis courts, a nine-hole golf course, and a massage room. It could have been a resort, but most hotels didn't include a wing of hospital rooms as well as an emergency facility that was manned 24/7 by a rotating team of doctors, EMTs, and nurses.

Shriner and his wife lived in bungalow 58 off the putting green. His wife had gone to her daily exercise class, Phil explained to Marge and Oliver, so he could spare them around an hour. The house's interior was light and airy with hardwood floors and a fireplace. It was also crammed with furniture.

"We just moved in a few months ago," Shriner explained. "We've downsized our living space and we didn't have time to sell all of our furniture. Sit anywhere you like."

Their options were three couches, four big stuffed armchairs, or two ottomans. Marge chose a chair while Oliver opted for one of the sofas. Shriner was of average size and weight, and had thinning silver hair, a liver-spotted complexion, and dark eyes. He wore a blue polo shirt and brown slacks, his wiry arms still sculpted with defined musculature. Orthopedic sandals were on his feet.

He folded his arms in front of his chest, his butt just barely touching the edge of the seat. "So what's going on?"

Defensive posture, Marge noted. "LAPD is reopening the Bennett Little case. The cops never got too far, and we understand that Melinda Little hired you to look into what happened to her husband. We're wondering what you remember about it?"

The arms folded tighter across his chest. "Melinda called me, said you might be coming down."

Marge glanced at Oliver and tried to hide her surprise. "I didn't know the two of you were still in contact."

"Haven't spoken to her for nearly fourteen years."

"Why did she call you?" Oliver asked.

"She wanted me to lie." His jaw tightened. "I'm older, I have enough retirement money, I'm sick of games. But mainly, I told her I wasn't going to do it because it was going to come out sooner or later."

"You two had an affair," Oliver suggested.

"I wish." He sank back into the chair. "The story was she hired me to look into her husband's death.

I didn't work too hard on it because she was barely paying me. I suppose you want an explanation for that."

"It would be nice," Marge told him.

"I'm a compulsive gambler. Nothing that I thought I couldn't handle until that fateful day when it hit me that I was over my head and if I didn't get out of debt real soon, I was going to lose everything. So I turned to GA."

Gamblers Anonymous. "Good call," Oliver told him.

"It was my only call. The first thing they taught me to do was to admit to my family that I fucked up. Once I did that, my mom, God bless her, bailed me out. It took me time to pay her back, but eight years later, I was all caught up and then some. I had a lot of business. I took on a few employees to help me out."

"Melinda Little?" Oliver asked.

"No, I met Melinda way before," Shriner said. "We used to frequent the same casinos."

"She had a gambling problem." Marge tried to keep her voice even.

"She did. I was the one who talked her into going to GA before she hit the skids. She was reluctant to admit it, but once she did, she went with the program. The hardest part was confession. She just couldn't bring herself to admit to her folks that she'd been gambling away her dead husband's insurance money. We worked out a plan. She'd say that she spent the money on hiring a private investigator—the reason why she was low on funds. Her parents bought the story and helped her out. She was ashamed, but swore she'd never go near a table again."

"I was told that she had money in the bank when Ben died," Marge said. "When did she start gambling?"

Shriner shrugged. "I met her about six months after the tragedy. She was hitting the tables pretty often: her game was blackjack. I do know that some of her husband's insurance went to the boys for an educational fund that she couldn't touch. That was probably a very good thing. We compulsive gamblers don't have a good stop mechanism."

"She was very forthright giving us your name," Oliver told him.

"She didn't know I was going to blow her cover. Otherwise she might not have."

"How'd she react to that?"

"She wasn't pleased, but she didn't try to talk me out of it. Part of the GA philosophy is to come clean with your lies and excuses. I thought it would be therapeutic for us if we told the truth. She's not ready for confession, but she had no right to tell me how to run my own life. She knows that you'll be contacting her again."

Oliver said, "Do you think it's possible that she had something to do with her husband's murder?"

"Anything's possible, but I'd say no."

Oliver said, "Why?"

"I could just tell that the woman was in pain."

"She may have felt bad about his death, but that doesn't mean she didn't cause it, especially if she had a habit to support."

"It was my understanding that she started gambling after the murder. At least, I don't remember seeing her until after it happened."

"She could have gambled elsewhere."

Shriner said, "Look. I'm not saying that she didn't have the urge. I'm not saying that she didn't indulge from time to time. But it was my understanding from being in the group with her that the problems started on a large scale after her husband was murdered. The woman appeared despondent. She was lonely, she was ashamed, and she was in an altered state of mind. Unless you've been there, it's hard to imagine how quickly you can go from 'I'm okay, I can handle it' to 'I'm totally out of control.'"

"So you think she hid her compulsion until after he died?" Oliver was skeptical.

"I betcha that her husband knew about her tendencies. He probably was able to rein her in. Once he was gone, and she had this sudden windfall of cash . . . that's a deadly combination. The whole point of my confession is that I don't want you to see me as incompetent. I was a very good private investigator, and I did what I could for Melinda, but I wasn't going to go the full nine yards for her because I had my own troubles."

"So we're back to my first question, what do you remember about the case?"

"Little seemed to be well liked and admired. The way it laid out, it seemed like a professional hit, but I couldn't find a reason why someone would have wanted to off him."

Oliver said, "That brings us back to his wife . . ."

Shriner said, "If she was in deep, deep trouble, she had resources other than murder."

"Did you know if she owed anyone cash?"

Shriner said, "Not to my knowledge."

"What did you investigate?" Marge asked.

"The usual. His friends, his relatives, his colleagues, some of his students."

"Does the name Darnell Arlington mean anything to you?"

"The black kid who was kicked out of school. Yeah, I talked to him over the phone. By the time Little was murdered, he'd moved away. I remember that he seemed broken up about Little. Why? Does the kid have a record?"

"He teaches physical education at a high school in Ohio."

"Good to hear that he straightened himself out."

"So you never suspected him?" Oliver asked.

"Of course I suspected him. I ruled him out early on because he had a good alibi, although it skips my mind at the moment."

"Supposedly he was playing sports in front of an audience."

"Yeah, that was it. Hard to be in two places at one time, and he didn't seem angry enough to hire a hit six months later. But check him out.

Like I said, I didn't spend an abundance of time on the case."

"Have you ever heard of a man named Primo Ekerling?" Marge asked him.

For the first time, the private detective gave the question some thought. "He sounds vaguely familiar."

"He was a music producer," Marge said. "A few weeks ago, he was murdered, stuffed into the trunk of his Mercedes-Benz. Hollywood has a couple of cholos in custody, although they're denying the charge. They admitted to boosting the car, but not to the murder."

"Could be I read about him in the papers . . ."

"You don't recall Ekerling's name in your mini-investigation of Little?"

"Mini-investigation . . ." Shriner smiled. "That's a good term for it. I might have heard the name. If he turns out to be a lead, let me know. In the meantime, I've got a date with my golf clubs. It's not as exciting as PI work, but it keeps me out of trouble."

Decker had just finished eating his bag lunch when Marge called, recapping the interview with Phil Shriner. When she was done, he said, "Exactly how *bad* of a gambling problem?"

Marge said, "That's what we're trying to figure out. I'm sure that Melinda Little is expecting your call any minute. I think you should pounce on it, Pete, before she starts thinking of some very clever excuses."

"I'm still in Simi Valley." Decker shifted the phone to his other ear. "Besides, I've got the interview with Arnie Lamar in fifteen minutes at the police station. What's your afternoon like?"

"I have some free time."

"Oliver and you need to pay her a visit."

"What if she lawyers up?" Marge asked.

"Then that'll tell us something." Another call was coming through the line. A private number. "Someone's breaking in, Marge. Set something up with Melinda and let me know, okay?"

"Will do. Good luck."

Decker hung up and took the private call. "Decker."

"What do you want?"

The low, smooth voice was instantly recognizable and made Decker sit up in the cruiser and grab his pencil and notepad. Normally, he would have thanked Donatti for calling back, but there was no such thing as chitchat with Chris. "What do you know about the Bennett Little murder?"

A long silence over the line. "You suspect me?"

"So far as I can tell, you were fifteen and in New York when it happened. Am I wrong?"

"Then why are you calling?"

"You were in L.A. when the murder was still fresh. You're a good listener. Maybe you heard something."

Another pause. "It was a long time ago, and I have a substance abuse problem. If I ever had any long-term memory, it's gone by now."

"But you remember the case."

"A guy gets hit, you're wondering who's working the territory."

"You think it was a hit?"

A small laugh came over the line. "Uh, yeah."

"But no idea who?"

"Before my time. Is that all?"

"Speaking of abuse problems, I heard that Little's wife had a secret of her own."

Another pause. "She gambled. What was her name? Rhoda, Melinda?"

"Melinda. Where'd you know her from?"

"My uncle was a silent partner in several card houses in Gardenia." A beat. "This was a long time ago. Joey let go of the casinos ten years ago. He's dead, you know."

"I do know."

"Good riddance."

"What can you tell me about Melinda Little."

"I was sixteen. The woman was a MILF."

"A MILF?"

Mother I'd Like to Fuck. Red hot. What does she look like now?"

"She's still hot. Did her hotness get her into trouble back then?"

"Not with me, unfortunately."

"Could there have been someone else?"

"There always could be someone else, but nothing I remember."

"Did she owe your uncle money?"

"Decker, I didn't keep track of her. I had just

moved out to L.A. and had my own problems. If she was in hock big-time, I never knew about it."

"How about a cop named Calvin Vitton?"

A pause. "Vaguely familiar."

"He worked the Little case. He just blew his head off this morning."

"If I were you, I'd look into that."

Decker made a face, although Donatti couldn't see it. "Thanks for the advice. Can you tell me anything about Vitton?"

"I recall that he was an old guy . . ." Another pause. "Let me think about him."

"Fair enough. How about a guy named Primo Ekerling."

"He's a music producer," Donatti told him. "What'd he do?"

"Someone whacked him and stuffed him into the trunk of his Mercedes in a manner reminiscent of Bennett Little's murder."

"This happen recently?"

"About two weeks ago."

"Hmmm . . . can't keep up with everything. You might want to look into his case, too. Maybe Ekerling and the cop and Little share a common link."

"And what might that be?"

Another small laugh. "You expect me to do your work for you?"

"You owe me one for plugging me."

"No, no, no. I settled the score with that one, pal. If anyone owes, you owe me."

"Bullshit. That one doesn't count."

"Ask your sons if it doesn't count."

Silence. Then Decker said, "Call me if you think of something."

"Why would I do that?"

"Just because you would."

"Why don't *you* call *me* if you think of something? 'Cause from where I'm sitting you're not only barking up the wrong tree, you don't even have a stump to piss on."

10

Melinda Little Warren was not surprised by the detectives at her door. "You should have called first. I'm about to go out."

As the inscrutable Colonel Dunn would have said: the woman was a cool cookie. Even her blond hair was more ice than amber. She wore a kelly green silk blouse and a pair of chino pants. Her feet were housed in rhinestone sandals. Marge said, "How about giving us a few minutes?"

"If I thought this would only take a few minutes, I would let you come in. And if I thought it would help Ben's case, I'd let you come in. But I know what it's about because you've probably talked to the bastard."

"The bastard?" Oliver asked.

"Don't play coy with me!" She was red with anger. "That man is a liar!"

"So tell us your side, because right now all we've heard is his story."

"Like you give a solitary damn . . . oh fuck!"

She threw open the door and walked away. The detectives took it as a sign to continue the conversation indoors.

The view from inside was lovely, but Melinda didn't notice. She was too busy pacing back and forth. "The fact that I may have had a little problem a long time ago does not impact upon what I told that tall detective. And it has *zero* to do with my husband's murder. But of course, you always have to look at the grieving widow, don't you? I stood to gain the most from Ben's death. No matter that I was total train wreck. No matter that I was suicidal. No, you have to look at the widow!"

Marge said, "Why did you call Phil Shriner a bastard?"

"Because that's what he is! I hired him to keep confidences, not to break them!"

"He claims you didn't hire him at all. That he was your excuse for gambling away insurance money—"

"That's a lie!" Melinda pivoted around. "I had a problem, okay? I met Phil from those problem days. The one *good* thing he did was to get me into GA meetings, but he only did that because he wanted to get into my pants."

"Did he?" Oliver asked.

"Don't insult me!" Melinda hissed. "I was a compulsive gambler, not a drunk! I was clearheaded and Shriner was a pig."

Oliver held up the palms of his hands. "We're

trying to get a handle on your husband's murder. We're on the same side."

"That's what the police told me fifteen years ago and I don't believe you any more than I believed them." Melinda melted into her white sofa. "Incompetent idiots!"

Oliver had no answer for that. He looked to Marge for backup. She exhaled softly and sat next to Melinda on the sofa. "I'm sorry to be opening up old wounds, Mrs. Warren. It must be very painful for you."

Melinda glared at Marge with moist eyes. "Spare me the amateur psychobabble. I've been to enough therapists to know the empty words from the real thing, okay?"

The room fell silent. Oliver busied himself by staring at the view. Melinda said, "I keep waiting . . . wondering . . . when can I move on?" Her eyes softened as tears spilled down her cheeks. "Aren't I entitled to a little happiness?"

"If I were in your shoes, I'd kick us out, saying talk to my lawyer." Marge shrugged. "I hope you don't do that, though. If we want to find Dr. Little's murderer, we've got to talk to you about Phil Shriner and your gambling problem."

Oliver felt it was safe to chime in. "We'd like to hear what you have to say since you and Shriner seem to be at odds."

Marge treaded lightly. "Phil implied that you'd gambled away insurance money and you were too embarrassed to admit it to your folks. So instead you told them that you spent money on a private investigator. Shriner agreed to be your cover."

Oliver added, "He was quick to admit that he was also a compulsive gambler. *And* he also implied that it was probably your husband's death that drove you to gambling."

"Of course his death drove me to gambling!" Melinda cried out. "It did all sorts of weird things to my psyche. Do you think I made it a habit to gamble when Ben was alive?"

Marge said, "So when did gambling become a problem for you?"

"About six months after . . ." Melinda pulled a box of tissues onto her lap and yanked one from the slot. She blotted her tears. "You have to remember that it wasn't just loneliness, it was fear! The police had no idea who killed Ben, and I kept thinking that there was someone out there who wanted to finish the job by killing my boys and me. I was petrified. I sold the house and moved in with my parents, but that got old very soon. I started going to casinos just to get out. My dad taught me poker when I was five. I was good at it. At first I won money. That was my downfall. If I would have lost right away, I probably wouldn't have returned."

"How long before you knew that your gambling was out of control?"

"I don't know what Phil told you, but I was never broke. I still had some savings."

She reached for her purse, pulled out a compact

and began to reapply her makeup: powder, blush, lipstick. When she was done, the traces of her tears had vanished.

"But it was embarrassing . . . throwing away money like that. Phil and I reached a mutually beneficial plan. He would cover for me but only if I threw some money his way to look into Ben's murder. Phil jumped at the agreement. He was in hock up to his eyeballs and was grasping at anything green."

Marge said, "We'll need to go over your bank records at the time of your husband's murder. If we have your written permission, it'll be easier."

She was quiet for a while. "If it'll get you off my back, go ahead."

"To verify that you didn't have gambling problems before your husband's murder."

Melinda licked her lips. "*Not problems.* Ben and I went to Vegas, sure. We'd see the shows, we'd gamble . . . sometimes I'd win, sometime I'd lose. I always enjoyed it, but I didn't feel any compulsion to keep doing it."

"And once again, you're telling us that the problems happened after the murder."

"Absolutely. I was a psychological wreck and was given this sudden windfall. I wish insurance wouldn't have been so forthcoming. Time might have helped me be more discerning."

"Why do you think Shriner suddenly decided to blow your cover?" Oliver asked her.

"Because you're reinvestigating the case and he didn't want to look like a boob to the cops."

The stories jibed . . . maybe too well. Marge said, "You said that he agreed to cover to your folks, but only after you agreed to pay him some money. To me, that sounds like blackmail."

For the first time, Melinda smiled. "I wouldn't go that far . . . I . . . he needed money and I was thoroughly disgusted with the police. It would have been nice if he had investigated Ben's murder with a little more zeal, but . . ." A sigh. "I didn't pay him much. Frankly, I don't see why I should have had to pay him at all. The police should have done their job."

"How well did you know the primary investigators?" Oliver wanted to know.

"I called a lot at the beginning. Less after Phil started hunting around. In the end, they retired and the case went cold. By the time I recovered from my gambling and my fears and my infinite psychiatric bills, I just wanted to move on with my life."

"When you called up the investigators, who did you talk to?" Marge asked.

The question momentarily stumped her. Then Melinda said, "Mostly Detective Lamar, I think. I found him more congenial than Detective Vitton." She looked at her watch. "I'm late to a luncheon and the honoree is a very dear friend. I'd like to go."

Oliver said, "What would you say if I told you—"

Marge said, "Thank you so much for your time, Mrs. Warren."

"Not a problem. But please next time, do call."

Marge stood and signaled Oliver to the door. "We will. Good-bye now."

As soon as they were outside, Oliver turned on his partner. "Why'd you interrupt me mid-sentence?"

"Because I didn't want you to tell her about Vitton's suicide until we know more."

"But *I* wanted to see how the Ice Queen would react! I haven't ruled her out as a suspect. The murder looked like a hit, and she *has* a gambling problem. How do you know she didn't whack him for insurance? Or maybe she hired Shriner for the hit—or Vitton and that's why he killed himself."

"Exactly why I want to dig up more information on her and on Vitton before we drop the news. Things like: What kind of funds did she have before her husband was murdered? Did any money go out shortly after Little's death? Did she know Cal Vitton before Ben died? Let's say we find something on her. The suicide would be a perfect excuse to come back and talk to her. And if we don't find anything on her, why put the woman through more pain by mentioning the suicide?"

Oliver still looked miffed. "I don't like being muscled out of my comfort zone even if you do outrank me."

"Would it help if I bought you some cookies?"

"Fuck you," Oliver snapped.

"It was a serious offer." Marge looked wounded.

"Mrs. Grich's. Macadamia nut, white chocolate and coconut. But suit yourself, bud."

"You think you can mollify me through my stomach?"

"It always worked in the past."

There was a long pause. "I like dark chocolate."

"Anything you want, sweetheart."

Retired detective Arnold Lamar showed up as if he were dressed for a funeral: ill-fitting black suit meant for a bigger man, skinny black tie, and white shirt. His feet were stuffed into scuffed oxfords. His face was drawn, and his eyes were glazed as they scuttled back and forth between Decker and Detective Shirley Redkin from the Simi Valley Police Department. Finally Lamar's eyes landed on Decker, staring at him from across the interview table. "What'd you say to him?"

"What do you mean?"

"Did you set him off or anything?"

Decker didn't take offense. "I told Detective Vitton the same thing I told you. That I wanted to talk to him about the Bennett Little case and get his impressions. If he found that offensive, then I plead guilty."

Silence.

"I wasn't threatening, just insistent. Can you think of a reason why he'd kill himself?"

"No."

"You called Vitton before I got hold of him. He told me that much. What was his state of mind?"

"He was Cal." Lamar shook his head. "Grumpy. After he retired, he didn't want anything to do with LAPD except to cash his pension check. For a while, we kept in contact, but then that fizzled. He didn't give me any indication that he was desperate, but I'm no psychiatrist or anything."

"What was *your* conversation about?"

"I told him that LAPD reopened the Little case and you'd be calling him."

"What did he say to that?"

"He asked what they expected from him. I told him I didn't think they expected anything. They just wanted to hear about the investigation. He grumped and said something like it's a little late in the game for this. In short, he was just being Cal. If I would've thought that there was something wrong, I would have . . ." He blinked back tears. "Cal hasn't been happy for a while."

"Women problems?" suggested Shirley Redkin.

Lamar made a conscious effort to shift his eyes from Decker's face to hers. He thought she looked like an Aztec Indian. "The divorce was years ago. At the time, it was a bad one, although at their son's wedding, they were on speaking terms. Two children . . . both live out of town."

"Where?" Shirley asked.

"One's in San Francisco, the other lives in Nashville."

"What do they do?" Decker wanted to know.

"Not police work." He shook his head. "The Nashville son, Freddy, is a producer of country songs, whatever that means. Cal Junior . . . well, what can I say. He bats for the other side."

"Do you mean he's gay?" Shirley asked.

Lamar nodded painfully. "After Cal J came out, Big Cal was never the same."

"How long ago was this?"

Lamar had to think about it. "Ten years ago, maybe."

Decker said, "So it wasn't a recent thing that pushed Vitton over the edge?"

"It wasn't recent, but that don't mean it didn't push him over."

"So why now?" Shirley asked.

"I've been thinking about that nonstop. Maybe it was a combination of things. Reopening a case that was our biggest failure, his son being gay, no steady work, no women in his life. After a while, everything adds up."

Decker said, "Enough to get him to eat his gun?"

"Cal hadn't been happy for a long time," Lamar repeated.

"Who is Cal's ex?" Shirley asked him.

"Francine Vitton. Don't ask me where she lives, I have no idea."

"What about the boys? Do you have a telephone number for them?"

"No, but I'm sure the number's in Cal's directory. He kept in touch with his boys . . . mostly Freddy, but he was on speaking terms with Cal J. That wasn't always the case."

"No?"

"Well, you know how it is. When Cal first told his dad, Big Cal wanted nothing to do with him. Cooler heads prevailed later on. They reconciled. I'm sure the boys could tell you where their mother lives."

Shirley said, "Are you being completely open with us, Detective Lamar? There isn't something in Cal's life that could have driven him to kill himself?"

"If there was, I didn't know about it."

"Did Cal feel that he gave the Little case one hundred percent?" Decker asked.

Lamar bristled. "That's a loaded question, Lieutenant. When the case remains open, you always feel that there's something more that you can do. But sometimes you just fail. And as you both know, that ain't a good feeling."

11

A nugget popped into Decker's mind.

When he had asked Arnie Lamar about Calvin Vitton's sons, the retired detective had responded: *The Nashville son, Freddy, is a producer of country songs, whatever that means.* Earlier in the day when he had talked to Donatti and asked him about Primo Ekerling, he had said, *He's a music producer. What'd he do?*

There were tens of thousands of people in the recording industry. It wasn't *much* of a coincidence, but Decker was alone in an ocean, grabbing at any log that happened to be floating by. As soon as he got into his office, he phoned Lamar. "It's Pete Decker again."

"What's going on?"

"A quick question about Cal's boys. How old would they be?"

"Freddy's around thirty-five, Cal J's a few years younger. Why are you asking?"

"I like to have a mental picture before I do interviews."

Lamar paused. "There's more to it than you're lettin' on."

"Then please tell me what I'm holding back. I can use all the help I can get."

"Say hello to the Vitton boys for me."

He cut the line before Decker had a chance to respond. Just as he set the phone down, Marge knocked on the doorjamb. She was with Oliver, and Decker motioned them in. Their mission was to bring him up to date on Melinda Little Warren.

"We want to go over her finances at the time of the murder," Oliver said. "See if there was any money coming in or out before Little died."

Marge added, "We know the original detectives went through her bank accounts, but we need to make sure that nothing was overlooked."

Decker said, "Sounds reasonable enough, but I don't know how much luck you'll have with fifteen-year-old records."

"We know where she banked," Oliver said. "Everything was computerized fifteen years ago. I don't think we'll have any problem with it."

"Did you get her permission?"

"She said she'd sign something."

"And you still suspect her?" Decker asked.

Oliver said, "She's a compulsive gambler: Little had insurance. If she was in the hole . . ."

Decker looked at Marge.

"Haven't ruled her out," she told him.

"How did she react to Cal Vitton's suicide?" Decker asked.

Oliver cocked a thumb in Marge's direction. "She cut me off. The sergeant wants to use the suicide as an excuse in case we want to come back and question her again."

"Oh . . ." Decker nodded. "That's good thinking."

Oliver snapped, "To me, it made more sense to lay it out and see how she reacted."

"A case could be made for that. But if you're looking through her financials and something comes up, it will be a convenient excuse to see her again. Then as long as you're there, you can ask her about any bank discrepancies."

Marge grinned. "Oliver, you're not only outranked, you're outvoted."

Decker said, "I want one of you to look into a couple of things." He explained to his detectives the weak relationship between Primo Ekerling and Freddy Vitton. "It would be interesting if they knew each other."

"And what would that prove?" Oliver asked.

"Two men dead within two weeks and both have some kind of tangential association to the Little case."

"Loo, we don't know that Ekerling has a connection to the Little case."

"I have to go with Oliver on this one," Marge said. "I don't see it leading anywhere."

"At the moment, I'm just like a computer. I amass

data and spit back facts, but I offer no opinion." Decker shrugged. "Just peck around."

Oliver said, "Doesn't Hollywood have someone in custody on the carjacking?"

"Yes, they do. Two people actually."

"So what justification do we have throwing in new theories and fucking up their solve?"

"We don't have any justification and yet, I still want to look at the file."

"So call up your daughter and get it on the sly."

Decker rolled his eyes. "Good idea, Oliver, I wish I had thought of that."

The house had turned into a jewel box: a perfect little bungalow. Converting eight hundred square feet into twelve hundred fifty had produced a two-bedroom, two-and-a-half-bath house with a small nook off the living room that could be sleeping quarters or a TV watching area—its current use. The kids had gone with a Mission turn-of-the-century look that was in keeping with the geography of old L.A. The area was filled with hundred-year-old bungalows as well as a few Victorians. There were also remakes and redos: housing from the fifties to the present.

The best part of the remodel was a new and improved patio overlooking the hillside chock-ablock with houses cut into the granite. On warm days, the landscape gave the feel of Southern Italy or Spain. It was on this very patio that Decker sat with Cindy, enjoying the spring weather, drinking espresso while taking in the view.

Cindy stretched and looked outward. "It don't get much better than this."

"No, it does not." He smiled at his daughter. Her wild red hair was tied back in a ponytail holder, and her skin was smooth and pale with just a hint of blush at the cheeks. She wore cutoff jeans and a baggy T-shirt with flip-flops on her feet. It was a pleasure to see his daughter so relaxed. He said, "The rose garden is spectacular."

"It's the one thing that Koby insisted that we leave untouched and how right he was."

"The remodel is just perfect, princess. I know it was a hassle but it couldn't have turned out better."

"Thanks for all your help, Daddy. We couldn't have done it without you."

"You're welcome, although I didn't do much."

"First of all, you put us in contact with Mike Hollander. That was ninety percent of it. Second, you did most of the finished tile work. It came out beautifully."

"I'm glad you like it." He finished his espresso. "So now we're even. I tiled the backsplash in your kitchen, you got me the Ekerling file."

"It's not quid pro quo, Dad."

"Yeah, you had the harder job."

"That might be true." Cindy smiled. "Luckily I inherited your ability to lie glibly and seamlessly."

He didn't deny the obvious. "What lie did you tell them?"

"It really wasn't a stretch. Being as I was the initial detective on the scene, I just told them that I needed a copy for my records. They weren't even a tad suspicious."

"Who're the detectives on the case?"

"Rip Garrett and Tito Diaz. Diaz gave me the file. It took me over a half hour to copy it, and the pictures didn't come out so great, but I did the best I could. Anyway, the original file is back where it belongs and you have your copy."

"I'm grateful to you, Detective Kutiel. It wouldn't be cool to inject myself into their case without a reason." Decker picked up his coffee to drink and remembered he finished it.

"Would you like another?" Cindy offered.

"Actually, I don't have intentions of sleeping, so why not?"

"Come inside and I'll hand over the file. You can also watch me use my new nifty espresso machine."

He followed her inside to a petite kitchen, which included a farm sink and an old-fashioned stove. "Wow, this came out great."

"You say that every time."

"At least I'm consistent. And it's true. This is simply charming. Unfortunately for me, Rina's getting ideas."

"Uh-oh." Cindy put the coffee into the machine.

"Although she has a point. The kitchen is a little dated."

"It wouldn't take much."

"Not to you."

Cindy smiled. "Just tell her it doesn't matter about the shape of the kitchen, what matters is the cook, and in that regard, she has me beat by a mile."

"You're a good cook."

"No one is like Rina."

Decker didn't have a comeback to that. "Would you like to come over Friday night for Shabbos?"

"Uh, what day is it? Tuesday?"

"Yep."

"I think it would work for me. Let me ask Koby and I'll get back to you." The coffee started to brew, the steam roaring as it forced the water through the grounds. "Did you clear this with Rina?"

"You've got an open invitation, but I'll clear it with her."

Cindy handed her father another shot of espresso. "I love this machine. I can even steam milk. It saves a bundle on my outside coffee bills."

"Yeah, what do they charge now for designer coffee? Something like five dollars for an amount the size of a thimble?" Decker held up the file. "Thanks so much for this. It really, really helps."

Cindy sized up her father. "I keep waiting for you to lose passion about your cases. It never happens."

"Some cases get more attention than others. This one has a lot of money riding on a solve."

"And you think Ekerling has something to do with a fifteen-year-old murder case?"

Decker simply shrugged. He finished his espresso and wiped his mouth on a napkin. "I can't put it off much longer. Traffic's going to be horrible, so I might as well bite the bullet."

"I'd ask you to stay for dinner, but I think we're meeting some friends tonight."

"No, I have to get back to my wife and your sister, although Hannah's never around anymore. But Rina still loves me."

"I'm sure Hannah loves you as well."

"Yeah, I'm sure she does, but at her age, she has a funny way of showing it."

12

After writing copious notes on two packs' worth of index cards, Decker had a neat summary of the Primo Ekerling case. He had come away with the following account.

At five-thirty in the afternoon, Ekerling and his brand-new silver 550S Mercedes sedan left his office on San Vicente Boulevard and disappeared into the ether. His initial absence from the world was noticed by his girlfriend, Marilyn Eustis, when she failed to reach Ekerling by phone. She left messages but wasn't particularly wary when he didn't return the calls. He had an eight o'clock dinner meeting that night, and Marilyn figured that they'd meet up at the designated restaurant. Primo could be lax with phone calls, but he was always punctual with his fellow associates and this evening mixed business with pleasure.

At nine in the evening, Ekerling was still a no-show. His associates were miffed, and although Marilyn was concerned, she kept it to herself and made excuses. She knew that Primo must be very much indisposed because this gathering was important. Song-sharing sites had just about rendered multitrack CDs obsolete, and because of this, the state of the recording industry had turned dismal. Companies were loath to record more than a single song per artist, which greatly reduced time in the studio, which in turn greatly reduced the need for record producers. Among the few survivors, the competition was fierce. This particular group of people represented an up-and-coming hip-hop band, and they were reinterviewing Primo for the position of producer for their newest release. The money wasn't terrific but the exposure was, and Marilyn Eustis felt that Ekerling would have prioritized this meeting. At the very least, had he not been able to make it, he would have called.

Still, the show went on. Marilyn mollified egos in the producer's absence and treated the gang on her tab. The wine flowed, the food kept on coming, and when they emptied out of the restaurant at a little past eleven, she felt that a good time had been had by all.

For her part, Eustis hardly ate a thing.

She drove to Primo's condo and let herself in with her key. As usual, the space was tidy with no signs of disturbance. Marilyn checked the development's gated parking lot and was quick to note that Primo's Mercedes wasn't in its allotted slot.

Her initial calls were to the police and highway

patrol inquiring about accidents. When that turned into a goose egg, thank God, she called the police a second time to report Ekerling as a missing person.

The police were unimpressed by the urgency in her voice. She'd have to wait until Primo was missing for a longer period before they'd send someone to look into the disappearance. When it became clear that Primo wasn't going to show up on his own accord, the police sent a detective named Marsden Holly to talk to Marilyn.

Holly, upon hearing what Primo did for a living, offered alternative scenarios, most of them variations on his cutting town or being with another woman. Marilyn was insistent that neither was plausible. The detective took down the model, make, and license plate of the Mercedes and called it in. Ekerling remained a mystery until a cop noticed a ticketed Mercedes. When the vehicle turned up as hot, he reported the crime to GTA— grand theft auto.

Detective Cynthia Kutiel—Decker allowed himself a bit of pride here—noticed a sagging trunk. When the lid was popped, detectives discovered the partially decomposed body curled into the fetal position. The victim had been shot in the head execution style, his hands and feet bound tightly.

Homicide detectives were called in along with the coroner investigators.

They were followed by the techs and a police photographer.

Evidence was collected, pictures were taken, and fingerprints were lifted. The good news was that the fingerprints secured at the crime scene matched two low-life petty criminals named Geraldo Perry and Travis Martel. Both teens had priors, although up to now, they had managed to eschew violence. Detectives Rip Garrett and Tito Diaz pointed out a trend of escalating crime in the boys' rap sheets and felt that they had finally crossed that line.

The teens were brought in and grilled in separate interview rooms. Both boys recited the same story and used the same defense. At around ten in the evening, the boys had wandered into Jonas Park—a known drug spot—looking to score weed. Instead they had found the lone Mercedes in an empty parking lot near the park. Both freely admitted to stealing the car, but neither confessed to killing Ekerling. They claimed they took the car joyriding: cruising Santa Monica Boulevard, then racing down Sunset at three in the morning, eventually abandoning the car in the Hollywood hills after the engine started to smoke.

Both were adamant about their innocence. They claimed they had no idea that Ekerling had been stuffed inside the trunk and was moldering in his own private coffin.

"Where'd you go after you abandoned the car?" Rip Garrett asked Travis Martel.

"We was hungry, man. We needed eats, nomasayin'? We went to Mel's, had some waffles. They was good. Then we called up some buds and axed them to pick us up."

"And why would your buds pick you up, forty miles away from your house?"

"'Cause we told them we boosted a Benz and would give them the navigation system and the stereo for twenty bucks and a ride home. They said okay."

"So then what happened?"

"They come to Mel's and order some waffles, too. I was still hungry, so I ordered a club with extra bacon. Then when we all was finished we went by the Benz and drove it into the hills where it was real quiet. We left the nav, but we boosted the stereo. It had took about five minutes."

"When did you leave Hollywood?"

"Like four o'clock. Me and Gerry was tired."

Rip and Tito didn't believe the jokers. They theorized that the bad boys were attempting to jack the Mercedes when Ekerling confronted them. Shots were fired, Primo was murdered. The kids stuffed the dead man into the trunk, drove the car forty miles away from the crime scene, and left the Mercedes in the Hollywood hills.

The buds of Travis and Geraldo—two dudes named Tyron and Leo—confirmed the teens' stories. The waitress at Mel's remembered all four boys. But the detectives remained unconvinced. So did the D.A. and a grand jury. Travis Martel and Geraldo Perry were arraigned for the crimes of carjacking and murder. Bail was denied. The teens were languishing in jail.

Decker regarded the photographs.

Geraldo Perry was five eight and 120 pounds,

a thin teen with a scrawny mustache and a soul patch. His eyes were droopy and his shoulders were narrow. He looked like a hype.

Travis Martel was black but not the typical African American. He had wavy hair, mocha-colored skin, thick lips, an angular nose, and upward-slanted brown eyes. He was also five eight, thicker in build but not any sort of a muscleman. In his mug shot, the eyes engaged and challenged.

Primo Ekerling was six one, a solid two hundred pounds if Decker had to make a guess. He had a thick head of curly hair, dark brown eyes, and a jutting, cleft chin.

Decker was struck by some similarities between the Ekerling and Bennett Alston Little cases: same make of the cars, bodies stuffed in the trunk, public dump spots for the vehicles. But if Decker was to get anywhere, he needed to ramp up the connections. As it stood, there was nothing Decker could hang his hat on.

He put down the case file and googled Primo Ekerling; over a thousand references flashed across the monitor. The first few pages dealt with his shooting, but after those thinned, most of the articles had to do with his business as a producer and then his youthful stint as a punk rock star. It was interesting to note how a person could be almost a complete unknown and still have so many references.

Primo Ekerling had his backers. But he also had

a number of detractors as evidenced by all of his lawsuits.

He was suing a band that he had produced for back payment.

He was suing a record company that had hired him for back payment.

He was suing a former member of his own defunct band—the Doodoo Sluts—for royalties from their "best of" CDs.

He was also suing a number of other record producers for back payment.

Decker read the articles carefully, trying to find Freddy Vitton's name, but that came up empty. Decker did notice that one of the many producers whom Ekerling was suing had also been a band member of the former Doodoo Sluts—a guy named Rudy Banks.

He picked up the Ekerling file, looked for Rudy's name but didn't find it anywhere. Not surprising because Martel and Perry had been arrested almost immediately, so why bother? And it wasn't a smart thing to start calling up Ekerling's critics and asking pointed questions. Someone might get pissed. Someone might call up Detective Rip Garrett or Detective Tito Diaz and start complaining about a nosy lieutenant from West Valley. And if they mentioned the name Decker, not only would he be in a tight spot, that lieutenant would also put his daughter in an even tighter spot.

Especially because two suspects were currently in custody and those two suspects had been in diapers or nonexistent when Bennett Alston Little had been murdered.

No, no, no, it would be an unwise thing to talk to Ekerling's adversaries. What Decker needed was one of Primo's allies.

He wrote himself a reminder to call Marilyn Eustis tomorrow morning.

13

While the morning coffee was brewing, Decker turned on the family laptop. It was clogged with a plethora of different sites and icons and was ancient in a rapidly moving techno world. However, it still worked.

The Doodoo Sluts had gone through several transformations, but in its heyday eighteen years ago, it consisted of a quartet: Elvis Costello look-alikes who were, in turn, Buddy Holly look-alikes—four white boys in black suits, white shirts, thin black ties, and big round black-rimmed glasses. Their most successful track was entitled "Bang Me" and climbed its way to number eight on the Top 100 hit list. The song wasn't available in any routine download format.

Decker was still searching for the song or a "best of" CD that contained the song when Hannah walked into the kitchen. The teen was dressed in a full blue skirt and a white-collared polo top, the preferred uniform of the school. With her red hair, she could have doubled as the American flag. Decker closed the computer, convincing himself that he was spending some quality time with his elusive daughter. That usually translated into making her eggs and pouring her orange juice.

"How's it going?" he said cheerfully.

"You're taking me to school?"

"Is that okay?"

"I love your company, but your car doesn't have satellite radio. Can we listen to my CD mix?"

"Absolutely."

"Thanks." She plopped down on a kitchen chair, her eyes still full of sleep. "I'm not hungry, Abba. I'll eat later at school."

"All they serve is sugar cereal and that's a terrible thing to eat in the morning. You get a blood sugar rush, and then you crash. You need protein."

"I need another twenty hours of sleep."

"What time did you get to bed?"

"It doesn't matter when I get to bed. It's when I wake up."

"Well, if you get to bed earlier, it might be easier to wake up earlier." He was sounding preachy this morning. "How about some scrambled eggs?"

"If you insist."

Decker took out a pan and three eggs. She liked only one yolk and the rest egg whites. He gave the eggs more substance by adding a little milk and cheese. "I need your professional help."

Hannah looked up. "*My* help?"

"What do you know about the punk scene?"

"You mean the real punk scene or the retro punk scene."

"The original period. I'm interested in a group called the Doodoo Sluts. They peaked in the late eighties."

Hannah's smile was genuine. "And the name's for real?"

"Would I lie?"

"Yes, but probably not about this. I've never heard of them, Abba. Personally, I never got punk rock, but I am sorry I missed the grunge scene."

"That's too bad. I never understood Nirvana's appeal. Jake loved them."

"They're not my favorite. I'm talking about Pearl Jam, Soundgarden, and Alice in Chains. But I digress. I have a friend who's a maven on original punk rock. What do you want to know?"

"Anything he or she can tell me about the Doodoo Sluts."

"It's a he—Ari Fieger. He's a bit of a nerd and overly pompous, but he knows his stuff."

Decker spooned the scrambled eggs onto a plate. "Here you go."

"You're too good to me, Abba. And all I ever do is give you attitude."

"You're a terrific daughter."

"Now you're lying."

"I'm telling the one-hundred-percent truth." His cell phone rang: it was Marge. "Excuse me, sweetie. Yo."

"I'm at the airport waiting for Continental to tell us how long we will be delayed. So far, it's an hour."

"That doesn't sound good."

"Weather, they say. It's always weather."

"When in doubt, blame it on the weather. When is your interview with Darnell Arlington?"

"Not until eight in the evening. So far we're okay because I've built in an airline delay factor."

"Marge, do you have your computer with you?"

"I do."

"Does the wireless work?"

"It does. What do you need?"

"Everything you can find on the Doodoo Sluts. Spelled just like it sounds." He heard her laughing on the other end. "Primo Ekerling was a member of the group. He was suing another former member named Rudy Banks. Ekerling is also involved in another suit with Banks . . . something about a record they coproduced and Banks withheld money."

"Great. It'll give me something to do. Or should I say doodoo."

Decker smiled. "I'll talk to you later." He discontinued the call. "Ready?"

"Not really, but what's my choice other than malingering."

"That won't get you anywhere. You'll just have to make up the work." Decker hoisted her backpack. "What's in here? Lead?"

"Meaningless and out-of-date textbooks that you and Eema paid a fortune for."

"You're going to hurt yourself carrying all this weight."

Hannah hugged her father's arm. "That's why I need a big, strong abba."

The building was four stories of chrome and glass, a stone's throw away from where Suge Knight had set up offices for the notorious Death Row Records, the premier label of L.A. gangsta rap. While investigating a case years ago, Decker used to pass some of Suge's billboards perched atop the office building: people sitting on toilets and other offensive images. Now Tupac was dead and Suge was in jail. Ah, the fleeting phantom of fame.

Ekerling's office was on the second floor, sandwiched between an insurance agent and a guru named Om Chacra who sported a degree in Far Eastern and holistic medicine. The door was locked and there was no bell, so Decker knocked. The door opened but only a crack because it was bolted by a chain.

"Yes?"

"Lieutenant Decker of LAPD. I'm looking for Marilyn Eustis?"

"You found her. ID, please?"

Decker slipped his badge into the allotted space and waited. A moment later, the door opened and a slim, leggy blonde with a cigarette was giving him a quick once-over. She returned his billfold. "Can't be too sure nowadays. Come in. The place is a mess, so watch your step."

She turned her back, and Decker followed her swaying hair and rear until she pointed to an empty folding chair. "Have a seat. I'll be back in a moment."

Decker complied and studied Marilyn. She was dressed in black, and although she was attractive, she emitted nothing but nervous energy. Her blue eyes quivered as if they were bathing in adrenaline.

He looked around. It was a small room in utter chaos: papers and boxes everywhere with lots of shelves of CDs, most of which were jewel-box demos. A single pot of coffee sat by itself in a corner, looking forlorn. He saw her dragging over a chair and got up to help. "Are you in the process of moving?"

"Just cleaning out Primo's shit." She plopped down. "Seeing if there was any money due. He seemed to be current. He was a lousy housekeeper, but pretty good with the bills." She rubbed her neck. "So why are you here? I thought the police had the punks in custody."

"They do."

"So I repeat, why are you here?"

Decker leaned toward her. "This, in no way, is a reflection on the detectives involved in Mr. Ekerling's case. I'm sure that the perpetrators in custody did it. I'm here because Primo Ekerling's murder was similar to one that happened over fifteen years ago involving a man named Bennett Alston Little." He waited for the name to register. When it didn't, he said, "The case has been reopened. I'm in charge and I just want to make sure that the coincidences are merely that—coincidences."

Marilyn crossed and uncrossed her slender legs. She was wearing a tight black skirt that showed lots of skin. "What kind of coincidences?"

Decker told her about the cars and the bodies in the trunks plus the fact that both cases involved public parks after dark.

She continued to stare. "You're thinking like a serial killer?"

"The murders were fifteen years apart."

"A choosy serial killer."

Decker didn't dare smile, but her black sense of humor was better than bitterness. "I'm trying to see if there was a direct link to the two men, and so far I haven't come up with anything. So I'd like to get a little background on Primo. What can you tell me about him?"

She shrugged. "Primo was born in New York. I met him in New York. I know that he spent some time out here when he was involved with the punk music scene in the late eighties to the early nineties."

"The Doodoo Sluts."

"You've done your homework."

"Not completely but while looking up Primo on the Internet, I noticed he was involved in several lawsuits with a man named Rudy Banks who was also in the Doodoo Sluts. What can you tell me about that?"

"You suspect Rudy?"

"I don't even know Rudy enough to suspect him. But I can do basic math. If Mr. Ekerling and Rudy were out in the L.A. scene in the late eighties to early nineties, that would be right around the time that Ben Little was murdered."

She puffed on her cigarette, but blew the smoke the other way. "And?"

"I have no *and*, Ms. Eustis. I'm just trying to gather information."

"Rudy can be summed up with a single word. Schmuck! Now if *he* would have been murdered, no one would have been surprised. The man only had enemies."

"Why's that?"

"Because he rips off people habitually. He makes compilations. He steals songs but won't pay royalties. He also plagiarizes songs that other people write and won't pay them for it. Sometimes he actually makes money legitimately. Primo and Rudy co-produced a retrospective on the L.A. punk scene with current artists doing old favorites. The CD album made a little money—one of the cuts even made it to iTunes for a brief period of time—but Rudy took all the profits."

"How does he get away with it?"

"When people complain, he says sue me. Some do, but most don't."

"Where does Rudy get the money for legal work?"

"The son of a bitch is smart. Ten years ago, right

111

after the group broke up, Rudy went to law school. One of those nighttime rip-off deals where none of the students ever pass the bar. Guess what?"

"He passed the bar."

"He specialized in intellectual property. He knows the ins and outs. Let me tell you something, Lieutenant, it's hard to get a judge to even listen to your case. Ninety-nine percent of these cases get thrown out on the first round. Primo let Rudy have a free ride for years just because it wasn't worth it."

"So what changed his mind?"

"Rudy put out a retrospective CD of the Doodoo Sluts without giving Primo, Liam, and Ryan—the other guys in the band—any money whatsoever. The three of them got together and sued. It stopped the release of the CD—at least temporarily—and so far, no one has made a penny except Rudy."

"So what would happen if all three members died? Would Rudy get all the profits, or would it go to the estates of the members?"

"I have no idea." She paused and smoked her cigarette. "Rudy is always suing someone or someone is suing him. It's a way of life for him. Still, I don't see him as having anything to do with Primo's death."

Another pause.

"Although I'm not quite sure that I buy the carjacking gone wrong thing." She shook her head and regarded Decker's eyes. "You don't buy it, either. That's why you're here."

"I'm just gathering information. Why don't you buy it?"

"The death seemed calculated. I saw the interview tape of the punk . . . I guess he's one of the punks. The kid sounded as if he couldn't plan a fart after eating beans."

"Do you remember the name of the interviewee you saw?"

"No. He was black."

"Travis Martel."

"Yeah, that's it." Marilyn finished her cigarette and lit another. "But what do I know? In the meantime, I'm careful. If it wasn't those jackasses, then maybe it was something more personal. So then maybe I should be looking over my shoulder."

"Anyone specifically in mind?"

"No, and that's why I'm nervous. The recording business attracts a whole lot of psychos. Some even have talent. It's all marketing these days. What you sound like is irrelevant. It's how you present."

"I'm sure that's true. How did Rudy meet Primo?"

"I don't really know. I came into Primo's life long after the split of the Doodoo Sluts. We met at AA. I've been sober for over five years. Primo, so far as I know, had been sober for a little longer, but who knows?"

"You think that Primo might have slipped up?"

She blew out smoke. "When I heard that this punk carjacked the Mercedes from Jonas Park, my first thought was: what the hell was Primo doing in a park in southeast L.A. alone at night. Almost immediately I answered my own question. He was probably sucking on a bottle or getting high."

"Did you ask the coroner if he had alcohol or drugs in his blood?"

"Why would I bother doing that?" She stared at him. "It wasn't what killed him . . . directly."

"It would be interesting to know."

"Yeah, it would explain why he gave up without a fight. If he was drunk or stoned, he probably didn't know what was flying. As a sober guy, he could take care of himself."

Decker wondered if a comprehensive toxic screen had been ordered at autopsy. He made a note to check it out.

"He was a really good producer. Not that anyone cared. The entire industry is in the throes of a shake-up. The CD is a dinosaur. Everything is downloaded from song-sharing sites. And lots of new groups are bypassing traditional producers and selling their own shit on the Internet. Primo's jobs were fewer and fewer. If he had succumbed to drinking, I wouldn't have been surprised."

"And you said he would have probably resisted if he wasn't drunk?"

"I didn't know Primo when he drank. I don't know if he was a mean drunk or not. As a man, I can tell you he was a good guy." She blinked back tears. "If you find anything new, let me know."

"I will. And I'd appreciate your keeping the conversation quiet. The detectives assigned to Primo's murder wouldn't like me butting my nose into their business." He paused. "You wouldn't happen to have Rudy Banks's phone number."

"Do I have it?" She laughed derisively. "I must have called it a thousand times. Sometimes he even answers."

"Thanks. That would save me some work. And just so I don't overfocus on Rudy Banks, is there anyone else who might have had a stake in hurting Primo?"

She took a deep drag on her cigarette. "Who knows? In this business, you make enemies without even knowing it."

14

The message popped onto the machine after ten rings, giving the caller adequate time to hang up. If the male voice was that of Rudy Banks, his tonal quality was raspy, as if he had a chronic case of laryngitis. Decker left his name, rank, and phone number. From past history, intuition, and experience, he was going to have to chase the sucker down. He hung up and began to sort through a falling tower of pink message slips when Oliver came into the office and sat down.

Decker barely glanced up, but his eyes had enough time to take in Scott's jaunty outfit, a glen plaid jacket over olive pants. "You're looking very English today."

"Fifty bucks for the jacket." Oliver smoothed the lapel. "Brand new. I found out about Ben and Melinda Little's finances. They were in good shape."

The way Oliver spoke made Decker wonder. "Do you mean good shape or *very* good shape?"

"I mean outstanding shape."

"As in way too good for a teacher?"

"As in skirting the boundaries of what would be logical," Oliver told him. "And that got me thinking. How did a guy on a teacher's salary without a working wife afford such a nice house and an expensive car?"

"I thought he was also a vice principal . . . which probably meant he had a little more lunch money."

"At the time, he was making forty-one thou a year plus health and benefits, which was pretty good back then, but it doesn't explain how he amassed personal savings *and* the Mercedes *and* the kids' college funds, *and*, I found out, he was also making payments on a motorboat. Not a big one, but still. *And* he also had a trailer and a camper to tow it."

"Nice stash. Did you ask Melinda Little about it?"

"Yes, yes, yes. Melinda told me that Ben loved to camp and spend weekends at Lake Mead. She stopped paying for the boat after he died, and the company repossessed it. The trailer she sold for a discount— they're worth next to nothing on the resale market—and basically broke even. If I was looking for an infusion of cash from the sales of the vehicles to fund her burgeoning gambling habit, I didn't find it."

Decker nodded. "But the question you asked is a good one. Where did he get all the money?"

"Melinda claimed that Ben took care of the finances, and she never questioned where the money came from. She was provided for, the kids were provided for, and that was good enough for her."

"Do we know if Ben had other jobs?"

"Like what?"

"My kids go to religious day school. Their Hebrew studies are in the morning and the English studies are in the afternoon. A few of their secular studies teachers are public school instructors who moonlight for a little extra spending cash."

"That might explain the car *or* the boat *or* the camper, but not the car *and* the boat *and* the camper."

"What did his bank deposits look like?"

"Nothing out of the ordinary. Most of the money was direct deposit from work."

"If he owned the camper and the trailer, how did he pay for them?"

"My next step."

"And what about the Mercedes? Was he making payments on that as well?"

"Melinda was pretty sure that the Benz was paid off."

"And she wasn't suspicious of where the money was coming from?" Decker asked him.

"I don't think she cared. When I hinted that Ben might have been involved in illegal activities, she thought the suggestion was ludicrous."

"How vigorously did she defend her late husband's honor?"

"Not as adamantly as one might have expected, but maybe she's just tired. She *was* quick to point out that no one has ever had a bad word to say about Ben."

"Maybe we haven't talked to the right people."

"Anyone in mind?"

"We've only talked to 'Fans of Ben.' We haven't delved into the bad kids at North Valley during Little's reign. Maybe Marge's interview with Darnell Arlington can shed some light on the kids that Ben didn't reach."

"If she ever gets to Ohio."

"Yeah, with the way current airline travel is going, someone should bring back the Pony Express."

Decker was surprised to find a live voice on the line. "You're *still* in LAX?"

"I'm on board and they're about to close the cabin doors," Marge told him. "That means I should land about fifteen minutes before the appointed interview time. I already told Arlington I'll be late. He was cool with that."

"I have a few questions I want you to ask him." He quickly recapped his conversation with Oliver. "Maybe Little and Arlington were doing something on the side and Ben nudged Arlington out."

"But Arlington was thousands of miles away the night of the murder."

"He didn't kill him—that we know—but maybe he has an idea who did. How's it going with the Doodoo Sluts?"

"I was going to write all my notes up on the

119

plane and e-mail them to you when I land, but as long as you called, I'll give you a quick recap.

"Primo Ekerling started the group with a guy named Rudy Banks. Ekerling and Banks are both music producers, and they were involved in a number of lawsuits regarding royalties and back payments."

"I know that. What about the other members?"

"The group went through a lot of changes, but the final incarnation included Ekerling, Banks, Liam 'Mad Irish' O'Dell, and Ryan 'Mudderfudder' Goldberg. They had several albums that sold decently. Their biggest hit was a lofty aria entitled 'Bang Me.' Banks distributed a 'best of' CD two years ago, apparently without sharing any of the profits with the band. Ekerling, O'Dell, and Goldberg had the CD stopped and are currently in litigation to get what was rightfully theirs. Banks is also involved in a lot of lawsuits."

"I've left Rudy Banks a few messages, but he hasn't called back. If I have to, I'll hunt him down."

"And when you do, ask Banks about his high school experiences. Although Ekerling went to school in Baltimore, Banks is a local boy—North Valley, to be exact."

Decker sat up. "When did he graduate?"

"I've got your attention, I can hear it in your voice. He dropped out when he was seventeen—a good four to five years before Ben Little was murdered—but it does open up all sorts of possibilities. Hold on . . ." Muddled noise in the

120

background. "We're pushing back, Pete, I've got to turn off the cell."

Decker dialed Banks again, and when he got the same message, he gently placed the phone back in the cradle. He pulled out a phone book and found what he was looking for in a matter of minutes. Rudy Banks had an address in the phone book. It could have been a residence or an office. It was time to do some legwork.

If Rudy was making money from his litigious adventures, he wasn't spending it on the outer trappings of success. His place was in old Hollywood about thirty blocks from downtown. The apartment was on the fourth floor of a French Normandy–style building that had probably reached its glory days ninety years ago. Since then it had gone through some serious decay, including peeling plaster on the outside and an interior smell of mold. There was a small, stuffy red lobby with terrazzo floors and no attendant. An ancient nonoperative elevator was on the right and appeared as if it hadn't been working for a very long time. The staircase was to the left of the entrance, and Decker trekked up the four flights. The building had no air-conditioning, and by the time he reached Banks's door, he was sweating.

He rang the bell several times, then loudly knocked on the door, but there was no response. Decker fished around in his billfold for his official card, hearing the *clop, clop, clop* of some other soul traipsing up the steps. The sound stopped at the fourth floor, and when Decker looked up, a man was approaching. He seemed to be in his late thirties or early forties, tall and thin. He wore tight jeans and a black short-sleeved T-shirt, his arms festooned with tattoos of all shapes and colors. Pointed lizard-skin cowboy boots projected from the hem of his denim. His face was clenched and he kept pounding a fist into an open palm. He stopped in front of Banks's apartment.

"Bastard's not in?"

"Looks that way."

"Did you bang hard?"

"I did." Decker sized up the man. "You look like you're out to settle a score."

The eyes narrowed. "Who are you?"

Decker showed the man his badge and gave him his card. "And you are?"

"I've been called all sorts of names, so take your pick." The man had hazel eyes haloed by red rims, but there was intelligence behind the windows to his soul. He focused on Decker's face and then pocketed the card. "My mum still calls me Liam."

His voice sang with a slight brogue. Decker said, "As in Liam 'Mad Irish' O'Dell."

Liam smiled, showing a mouth of brown teeth. "You're a fan, eh?" Decker smiled enigmatically. "Let me tell you something, mate. Rudy is not only a prick and an asshole, but a sellout as well. Have you heard the shit he's been producing?"

15

The storefront was old but spotless with Formica tubular tables and matching chairs that probably dated back to the fifties. The menu hosted a variety of entrées inspired by exotic regions of the globe, with tofu playacting in everything from shrimp cocktail to moo shoo pork. The server was a beefy fellow with a buzzed haircut, a neatly trimmed soul patch, and a diamond stud in one earlobe, a conservative boy by today's standards. O'Dell ordered the usual. Decker decided on the Cobb salad, figuring there wasn't much the kitchen could do to ruin raw vegetables.

O'Dell gulped tap water. He was an easy talker. "I did it for Mudd, you know."

Mudd was Ryan "Mudderfudder" Goldberg, the lead guitarist of the group. "You sued Rudy for Mudd's sake?"

"Right-o. Me? I'm doing fine. I get lots of me meals comped for performing acoustic versions of some of the Sluts' big ones. I usually do Tuesday and Thursday here at Millie's. The weekends I'm at a small place in Venice. I live right near the café two blocks from the beach. I don't have much money, but I don't need a lot."

"You sound like a happy man."

"I know luck when it bites you in the arse. And I still get the chicks. Young ones." He sat up. "Still got the bike and the bad boy image. The simple ones really go for that."

"So being a bad boy is an image?"

Mad Irish grinned. "Sometimes yes and sometimes no, and I'd be bloody daft to explain meself any further." Meaning he still indulged in illegal substances. "I'm doing fine, Primo *was* doing fine, but it's Rudy who's livin' the vida loca." His eyes darkened. "Mudd wasn't so lucky."

"Why's that?"

"Dunno. Maybe he started believing all that rot about us being with the devil. He was lead guitar: the most talented, the most sensitive, and the most gullible. I think the voices started before he joined us, but we all figured it was the drugs."

Decker nodded.

"But it kept going . . . the voices. They got more evil, too, telling Mudd to do crazy things. He was always a bit crackers, but then he started cuttin' himself—his arms, his legs, between his legs." Mad Irish winced. "His mum had no choice but to get him committed."

"When was he hospitalized?"

"Ten years ago. In the beginning, I visited. He was

His eyes narrowed. "Unless you think that Banks . . . ?" The idea of Rudy as a killer struck O'Dell as hilarious. His laughter sounded like dry hacking. "It'd be grand to pin Primo's murder on Rudy, but I think you're looking the wrong way. Banks doesn't have the balls for it." O'Dell's eyes clouded. "Didn't they arrest the fuckers who wiped Primo?"

Decker mopped up his brow. "It's really hot here. You said you're about to eat lunch. How about we do that and I'll buy."

O'Dell grinned. "You really are a fan, eh? Or maybe you're one of those sneaky-arse reporters who'll do anything to get the inside story of the Sluts."

"No, I'm a cop. I saw a coffee shop down the street. How does that sound?"

"Bert's? You ever eaten there, mate?"

"Can't say that I have."

"The grease is so thick it drips off the ceiling."

"Thanks for the tip. I'll stay clear of Bert's. Do you have a suggestion?"

"How about Millie's?"

"Sure," Decker said. "Where is it?"

"Three blocks away. We can walk it."

"Great. What kind of a place does Millie run?"

"It's vegan."

Decker stifled a smile. "O'Dell, I'm a cop and a good detective, but I would have never figured you for a vegan."

Mad Irish flashed another maniacal grin. "How d'ya think I keep my girlish figure?"

"Pretty bad, huh?"

"That's the master of the understatement. Luckily the fans have spoken. His new CD tanked." O'Dell shrugged. "I was in the area. Thought I'd give it a go before lunch. You know even if he was there, he wouldn't answer. He knows the wolves are after him. How much does he owe you, mate?"

Decker said, "Actually nothing . . ."

"How'd you manage that?" The hazel eyes widened. "Don't tell me you're here to arrest him? A fuckin' all right! Can I watch?"

"I'm sorry to dash your hopes, sir, but I just came to talk."

His face fell. "Not as sorry as I am. I'll make a bet with you. I bet you won't be able to talk to Rudy more than five minutes without wanting to murder the son of a bitch."

"I've heard similar sentiments," Decker said. "I've also heard that he's making money doing the 'best of' albums." He looked pointedly at O'Dell. "Including the *Best of the Doodoo Sluts*."

"I'm dealing with it legally."

"Then this visit was for *what* purpose?"

"The bastard was trying to nick us blind," Liam said. "Just a friendly talk before lunch."

Decker didn't answer.

O'Dell said, "It was actually Primo's idea to fight back." He paused. "Poor Primo. You must have heard about that one."

"One of the reasons I'm here."

"Why talk to Banks about Primo? They're at war."

123

and Thursday here at Millie's. The weekends I'm at a small place in Venice. I live right near the café two blocks from the beach. I don't have much money, but I don't need a lot."

"You sound like a happy man."

"I know luck when it bites you in the arse. And I still get the chicks. Young ones." He sat up. "Still got the bike and the bad boy image. The simple ones really go for that."

"So being a bad boy is an image?"

Mad Irish grinned. "Sometimes yes and sometimes no, and I'd be bloody daft to explain meself any further." Meaning he still indulged in illegal substances. "I'm doing fine, Primo *was* doing fine, but it's Rudy who's livin' the vida loca." His eyes darkened. "Mudd wasn't so lucky."

"Why's that?"

"Dunno. Maybe he started believing all that rot about us being with the devil. He was lead guitar: the most talented, the most sensitive, and the most gullible. I think the voices started before he joined us, but we all figured it was the drugs."

Decker nodded.

"But it kept going . . . the voices. They got more evil, too, telling Mudd to do crazy things. He was always a bit crackers, but then he started cuttin' himself—his arms, his legs, between his legs." Mad Irish winced. "His mum had no choice but to get him committed."

"When was he hospitalized?"

"Ten years ago. In the beginning, I visited. He was

"Pretty bad, huh?"

"That's the master of the understatement. Luckily the fans have spoken. His new CD tanked." O'Dell shrugged. "I was in the area. Thought I'd give it a go before lunch. You know even if he was there, he wouldn't answer. He knows the wolves are after him. How much does he owe you, mate?"

Decker said, "Actually nothing . . ."

"How'd you manage that?" The hazel eyes widened. "Don't tell me you're here to arrest him? A fuckin' all right! Can I watch?"

"I'm sorry to dash your hopes, sir, but I just came to talk."

His face fell. "Not as sorry as I am. I'll make a bet with you. I bet you won't be able to talk to Rudy more than five minutes without wanting to murder the son of a bitch."

"I've heard similar sentiments," Decker said. "I've also heard that he's making money doing the 'best of' albums." He looked pointedly at O'Dell. "Including the *Best of the Doodoo Sluts.*"

"I'm dealing with it legally."

"Then this visit was for *what* purpose?"

"The bastard was trying to nick us blind," Liam said. "Just a friendly talk before lunch."

Decker didn't answer.

O'Dell said, "It was actually Primo's idea to fight back." He paused. "Poor Primo. You must have heard about that one."

"One of the reasons I'm here."

"Why talk to Banks about Primo? They're at war."

His eyes narrowed. "Unless you think that Banks . . . ?" The idea of Rudy as a killer struck O'Dell as hilarious. His laughter sounded like dry hacking. "It'd be grand to pin Primo's murder on Rudy, but I think you're looking the wrong way. Banks doesn't have the balls for it." O'Dell's eyes clouded. "Didn't they arrest the fuckers who wiped Primo?"

Decker mopped up his brow. "It's really hot here. You said you're about to eat lunch. How about we do that and I'll buy."

O'Dell grinned. "You really are a fan, eh? Or maybe you're one of those sneaky-arse reporters who'll do anything to get the inside story of the Sluts."

"No, I'm a cop. I saw a coffee shop down the street. How does that sound?"

"Bert's? You ever eaten there, mate?"

"Can't say that I have."

"The grease is so thick it drips off the ceiling."

"Thanks for the tip. I'll stay clear of Bert's. Do you have a suggestion?"

"How about Millie's?"

"Sure," Decker said. "Where is it?"

"Three blocks away. We can walk it."

"Great. What kind of a place does Millie run?"

"It's vegan."

Decker stifled a smile. "O'Dell, I'm a cop and a good detective, but I would have never figured you for a vegan."

Mad Irish flashed another maniacal grin. "How d'ya think I keep my girlish figure?"

15

The storefront was old but spotless with Formica tubular tables and matching chairs that probably dated back to the fifties. The menu hosted a variety of entrées inspired by exotic regions of the globe, with tofu playacting in everything from shrimp cocktail to moo shoo pork. The server was a beefy fellow with a buzzed haircut, a neatly trimmed soul patch, and a diamond stud in one earlobe, a conservative boy by today's standards. O'Dell ordered the usual. Decker decided on the Cobb salad, figuring there wasn't much the kitchen could do to ruin raw vegetables.

O'Dell gulped tap water. He was an easy talk "I did it for Mudd, you know."

Mudd was Ryan "Mudderfudder" Goldberg, lead guitarist of the group. "You sued Rud Mudd's sake?"

"Right-o. Me? I'm doing fine. I get lots meals comped for performing acoustic ver some of the Sluts' big ones. I usually do doped up with Thorazine twenty-four/seven. He couldn't even talk, much less carry on a conversation. Then he began to get these weirdo tics and started drooling." O'Dell shuddered. "I stopped going. It wasn't very big of me, but he sure as bloody hell wasn't the Mudd that I remembered. That Mudd was disappearing—bit by bit by bit by bit."

"It's hard to watch someone you care about deteriorate."

"Bloody painful. I'd visit and then I'd be depressed for days. Me girl said to give it a rest and once I did, I never went back."

"Like you said, he probably wouldn't have known the difference, anyway."

O'Dell seemed grateful for the reprieve. The food came, and Decker watched him chow down in silence. Halfway through his veggie curry, he said, "About a year, year and a half ago, his mum called me out of nowhere. Mudd was out of the hospital, living in a halfway house on disability. She told me where. She didn't say go visit him, but that's what she wanted. So . . . I went to see him."

"How was it?"

"Not nearly as bad as I expected. Mudd was always a big guy, but he had gained about two hundred pounds. His brain wasn't totally scrambled. He recognized me instantly . . . hugged me." O'Dell's eyes watered. "He was so bloody happy that I came by to say hi."

"You did a good thing."

"I did what was right. Which brings us back to Banks. About six months before my visit, Rudy started peddling his *Best of the Doodoo Sluts* over these sleazy cable stations. When Primo first mentioned that we should sue, I thought what the fuck do I need it for? But then, after I saw Mudd, I said to meself: I don't need it, but balls if I would let Rudy steal Mudd's money. So I called up Primo and that's how it all came about."

His jaw tightened. "If Banks would have given us something, if he would have given *Mudd* something, all this lawyer nonsense could have been avoided. But Rudy is Rudy and a skunk can't change his stink. If I could kill that bastard and get away with it, I would."

"Let's hope for your sake, he doesn't show up dead."

O'Dell rolled his eyes. "How's your food?"

"Very good actually," Decker said. "Where's Mudd living now?"

"Still at the halfway house." O'Dell gave him the address. "If you go by, tell him Mad Irish says hello."

"I'll do that." Decker placed the slip of paper in his wallet. "How'd you wind up hooking up with Banks, Liam?"

"Banks and Primo had been doing this punk thing for a while. They brought me in because they needed a drummer, even though my first love is guitar. That's how it works. You play whatever the band needs, and they needed a drummer."

"When did you hook up with the band?"

"Late eighties. I was twenty-three. Primo and Mudd were a bit older, but Rudy was younger than I was. Made it hard for us to get booze in the places we played. Most of the time, we'd nick it. The bartender looked the other way."

"How did Mudd come into the band?"

"That was Banks, too. He's a bastard, but he had a good ear. Mudd was with another group, his talent wasted. With Mudd on guitar and Primo on bass, Banks started playing keyboard and the band just clicked. Banks, being a master of self-promotion, got us a record deal almost immediately. We put out an album. It made the charts. We made money. We partied. We had pussy coming out of our ears. We were perpetually wasted. We never thought it would end, but it did. Primo and Banks became producers. I managed to find some paying gig. I knew the big time was over. I keep it all in perspective, but Mudd couldn't handle it—the crash. In the recording business, there's always a 'next big thing' breathing down the neck."

"Did you write your own songs?"

O'Dell laughed. "You think a cut like 'Bang Me' came from Harold Arlen?"

Decker smiled. "You know your music, Mad Irish."

"I like Harold Arlen. I wish I woulda written 'Over the Rainbow.' I'd be set up for life."

"Who wrote the band's songs?"

"Mostly Banks and Primo."

"So they got most of the royalties if someone did a remake of the band's numbers?"

"A-right about that. And over the years a lot of artists have covered our songs. I'm not claiming a piece of that. That battle's between Banks and Primo. What burns my arse is Banks remastering and selling a *Best of the Doodoo Sluts* CD without giving us a bloody red cent in royalties. It's my vocals on those songs. It's Mudd's vocals. What gives that arsehole the bloody right to take silver from our pockets?"

"So let me ask you this, O'Dell. What were you going to say to Banks if you would have found him this morning?"

Mad Irish hesitated. "I'd worked meself up real good when you saw me. I suppose it was a good thing he wasn't there."

"You should stay away from him, Liam. Let your lawyer do the talking."

"That's what I was doing. I really was. I said to meself that it isn't worth getting meself in a mess over. But now with Primo gone, who's gonna fight for Mudd? I don't have the kinda money to support a lawyer. And Mudd *needs* money."

"Threatening Banks isn't going to do you any good."

"I don't *threaten*, mate."

"Liam, think about it. If something happens to Banks, guess who I'll be going after?"

"If something happens to Banks, I wouldn't

130

want to be in your shoes, mate. Rudy only has enemies, and over the years, he's made hundreds of them."

The Hollywood Terrace sat on a side street about a mile from the Hollywood Police station, around three miles from where Primo Ekerling sat moldering in the trunk of his car. The building was a bunker, run-down and a step away from the wrecking ball. No plants in front to soften the gray stucco, just a few occupied parking spaces in a chunky asphalt lot. The glass door to the lobby was locked, the individual apartments listed on the wall with a button after each name. Ryan Goldberg lived in unit E.

Decker pushed the buzzer, and a moment later the door clicked open. The lobby was the size of a jail cell with yellowed linoleum floors and a cottage-cheese-sprayed ceiling. There was one long, dimly lit hallway, and when Decker found unit E, he knocked on the door. He could hear the electronic noise in the background. When a heavyset man opened the door, the television volume boomed in Decker's ears.

"Mr. Goldberg?"

The man had wilting brown eyes that blinked constantly. His facial features seemed small and piggish, but his skin was baby smooth. He wore sagging pants without a belt and a flannel shirt. Slippers on his feet. "Who're you?"

"I'm Lieutenant Detective Peter Decker of LAPD,

131

but I'm also a friend of Liam O'Dell's. He gave me your address. I'd like to talk to you if that's okay."

Goldberg just stared. Decker knew immediately that he'd given him too much information at one time. He started over. "I'm a friend of Liam's."

"Oh . . ." Blink, blink, blink. "Okay."

"Can I come in?"

"Okay."

But Goldberg didn't move aside. Decker had to skirt around him. "Mind if I lower the volume on the TV?"

"Okay."

Decker noticed that the man's hands shook, and he wondered why he had come to see him. Just what was he hoping to find out? He looked around, surprised that the studio was free of trash and dirt. There was a flat-screen television on a scarred chest of drawers opposite a deflated sofa. Several TV trays were folded and leaning against the wall. The place had a fridge and a hot plate. It didn't smell great, but nothing reeked. He told Goldberg that he could sit down if he wanted.

Mudd said, "My brother's a doctor."

Decker nodded. "Really."

"A lung doctor."

"That's impressive."

"I used to smoke. I don't anymore."

"That's good."

"My brother helped me quit smoking. He's a lung doctor."

"He sounds like a nice man."

"He's a good brother. He's a doctor."

Decker nodded. "Does your friend Liam O'Dell ever visit you?"

"Call me Mudd. Everyone calls me Mudd. Even my brother. He's a doctor."

"Okay, Mudd, does your friend Liam O'Dell ever visit you?"

"Yes, he does. Liam's a good friend. He buys me things."

"What kind of things?"

"He bought me that . . ." Mudd pointed to the flat screen. "My old TV was a piece of shit, that's what Liam said. It was a piece of shit."

"So Liam bought you the new television?"

"Yes, sir."

Mudd was still standing. Decker said, "You can sit if you want, Mudd."

The request momentarily stumped him. Mudd kept blinking until he shook his head no. "I'm okay. It's good to stand up and walk around. Otherwise you can get blood clots in the leg. That's what my brother told me. He's a doctor."

"He's right about that." Decker held back a sigh. "Do you still play guitar, Mudd?"

"Oh yes, I do." He smiled. "I still play guitar. But I can't play loud. It disturbs my neighbors. I can't disturb my neighbors."

"Do you have an acoustic guitar?"

"I have a Martin. Want to see it?"

"Please."

Mudd went to a kitchen cabinet and took out

something wrapped in a blanket. Carefully, he took off the wrapping and presented him with a Martin Dreadnought. Decker wasn't an expert on guitars but his son, Jake, had a passion for them. This one was in pristine condition. "Can I see it for a moment?"

Without any hesitation, he gave it to Decker, who looked at the label and memorized the serial number. Decker handed it back. "Can you play for me?"

A smile went on the big man's face. "Yes, I can." He sat down on the sagging couch and began to finger a few rifts. Within minutes, he was playing like the professional that Liam claimed he was. The transformation was otherworldly. Tension melted off his face, his tic had all but disappeared. Decker listened to him for the better part of an hour without saying a word. Finally he knew he had to leave.

"That was beautiful, Mudd."

"Want me to play more?"

"Uh, you can, but I have to leave. I have to go back to work." With effort, Mudd stood up, gingerly wrapped the guitar back in the blanket and stowed it back in the kitchen. "Thanks for visiting."

"You're welcome. Your guitar is very expensive—"

"It's a Martin."

"I know that. Don't tell anyone you own it, okay? Some not nice people might try to steal it."

"That's what my brother says."

"Your brother is right."

"All right. I won't tell anyone else except my brother."

"Good. Take care of yourself, Mudd."

"Oh, I will take care of myself." The big man nodded. "I promised my brother I will take care. He's a doctor."

16

Marge landed with a half hour to spare, just about enough time to rent a car, check the maps, and arrive at Darnell Arlington's house on time if traffic wasn't a problem. And from the looks of the town, it appeared that traffic was never a problem. An empty highway passed through a commercial area that was gone in a heartbeat, and then it split through a residential neighborhood of modest houses composed of brick and stone.

In the dark, Marge could see that Arlington's two-story home was set on a patch of lawn, the lane shrouded in the shadows of lacy elms. Street lighting was minimal. Perhaps crime was so low that L.A.-style klieg lights weren't necessary. She parked in front of the address, walked up a cement pathway, and rang the bell. The woman who answered the door had a baby on her right hip and a toddler on her left clutching the hem of the woman's skirt. Both children appeared to be girls. "Sergeant Dunn?"

"Yes, that's me." She showed the woman her badge. "Mrs. Arlington?"

"Yes. Call me Tish. Please come in."

"Thank you, Tish."

She nudged the toddler. "Crystal, get out of the way." The little girl didn't move. Tish then scooped the girl up until both babies were in her arms. She managed to hold the load with an erect spine. "Come in."

The house was tidy and furnished conservatively: flowered sofa with a matching chair, coffee and end tables with lamps and magazines, a fireplace with family photos. There was also a large playpen filled with toys. Tish lowered both girls inside the cage. "Y'all be good, you hear?" She turned to Marge. "Coffee?"

"Please."

She disappeared into the kitchen but continued to talk. "How long have you been in town?"

"About twenty-five minutes," Marge answered while looking at the framed snapshots. Arlington was almost a foot taller than his wife, and Tish seemed around five four. His complexion was also much darker than that of his wife. Tish's hair was tied in a ponytail, and her eyes were light brown. Her face was long, and she had a slender figure. "Can I help with anything?"

"If you could keep an eye on the babies. Crystal's a good girl, but she's only nineteen months. She loves Moisha, but sometimes she loves her too much."

"They're doing fine," Marge told her.

"Let's keep our fingers crossed." A few minutes later, Tish brought out a coffee tray. "Darnell is running just a little late. The team made regional finals and practice sessions have become longer."

"Congratulations."

"Darnell has really turned it all around. We moved here five years ago and Polk High was a joke." She sat down and handed Marge a coffee cup. "I don't know how you take it. Help yourself."

"Thank you." Marge doused the coffee with cream and sweetener. "Where'd you move from?"

Tish said. "I'm originally from North Carolina, but I met Darnell in Cleveland. Big cities have their advantages and disadvantages. I don't miss the noise, the crime, and the traffic, but I do miss having a black community. Kensington has been very welcoming to us, but I can still feel eyes on the back of my head."

"It's a good thing that Darnell turned the team around."

"Yes, he's a local hero."

"Has he experienced any racism?"

"Nothing overt, but until Darnell proved himself we didn't receive a lot of invitations to the neighborhood barbecues. That's changed, but you wonder what if the team starts losing."

"You're only as good as your last victory."

"Exactly." Tish sipped coffee. "Oh, I think I hear him. I'm going to warm up dinner. Do you mind keeping an eye on the kids again?"

"Not at all."

Marge heard the keys slip into the door, and within seconds, Darnell filled the doorway. "Sergeant Dunn?"

"Yes, sir."

"I'm sorry I'm late."

"Take your time." In the background, Crystal was shrieking "Dada, Dada, Dada." Arlington went over to the pen and lifted both girls in a single motion. He kissed both of them on the forehead. "Hey, little women." He gave Marge a cursory smile. "Excuse me for a minute."

From the kitchen, Marge heard low noises. No one was arguing, but there was conversation. Then one of the girls started to cry. Five minutes passed; then Tish emerged and was hip-carrying the girls. Crystal was babbling "ba-ba," which in Marge's ear could have been bye-bye or bottle. Moisha was wailing, her face beet red. "Time for baths and bed."

"Have a good night, girls."

Tish scurried up the stairs. A few moments later, Darnell came out of the kitchen, holding a plate while wolfing down a sandwich. He was tall and broad but stoop shouldered with a round face and long limbs. He wore a button-down shirt and a pair of slacks—probably the required dress for his school. He repeated his apologies for being late.

"Hey, enjoy your dinner."

"Are you hungry?"

"I'm fine."

Arlington sat down on the chair and liberated the footrest. "Excuse my casualness. It's been a long day. For you, too, I bet. When did you get in?"

"About a half hour ago, but I'm fine."

"If you want anything . . ."

"No, I'm fine."

"So . . ." Arlington polished off the sandwich and took a long gulp of a Bud. "You're reopening Dr. Ben's murder?"

"Yes."

"So . . . anything new?"

"We always find out new things. Whether it's relevant or not . . ." She took out her notebook. "What can you tell me about Dr. Ben?"

Arlington's eyes went down to the empty plate. "He was a great man. I was very sorry when I heard the news."

"I understand that on the night of the murder, you were playing basketball in front of a hundred people."

The eyes lifted and fell back on his lap. "I didn't hear about it until later. A friend from North Valley called and told me." His eyes met Marge's. "I was crushed."

"Why's that? From what I understand, he was instrumental in getting you kicked out of North Valley."

Arlington shook his head. "No, that isn't right. *I* was instrumental in getting me kicked out. *I* screwed up. That wasn't Dr. Ben's fault."

"Still, you must have been pretty angry."

"Leaving L.A. was the best thing that ever happened to me."

"Did you feel that way at the time?"

"No," Arlington admitted. "When I got expelled, I was furious." He looked straight into Marge's eyes. "I was an angry young man with a ginormous chip on my shoulder. No daddy, and I lived with a drug-addicted mother. My brother and I were left to fend for ourselves. I started smoking weed and graduated to booze and X by the time I was eleven. Dr. Ben tried, but he couldn't babysit me twenty-four/seven. Every time he turned his back, I messed up. If it hadn't been for my nana, I'd be doing hard time."

"How'd you come to be in your grandmother's care?"

"After I got expelled, she sued for custody. My mother was overjoyed to get rid of me and my brother. Nana straightened us both out."

Marge said, "So even though you were angry at Dr. Ben, you felt crushed when he died?"

"Yes, I did. I got kicked out about a year before he died. There was part of me wanted to come back to him and say, 'I tole you so.' I wanted to show him and everyone else that they were wrong. After Dr. Ben died . . ." He shook his head. "I don't know . . . I just felt so . . . so bad!"

"You hung out with a pretty rough crowd in high school?"

Arlington continued to shake his head. "We was

just a bunch of bums . . . boozing and dropping X and other stuff and just being bums."

"How about crime, Darnell?"

"That, too: shoplifting, breaking and entering, vandalism and graffiti." He regarded Marge. "Not good stuff, but I wasn't violent. I never mugged no one. I didn't get into guns, neither. I've always been afraid of guns, Sergeant. I saw my uncle shot when I was eight." He held his hand an inch away from his nose. "Right in front of my face. Blood splattered everywhere, including on me. I didn't want nothin' to do with guns.

"When I think about how lucky I was to get out . . ." He blew out air. "I go to church every Sunday. That's where I met my wife—in the church choir. Thank you, Jesus, for giving me a good voice."

Marge said, "Let's talk about some of your North Valley friends. How'd they feel about Dr. Ben?"

He hung his head. "We all thought the school administration was a bunch of idiots. We was just too cool, know what I mean?"

"But you didn't drop out. Why's that?"

He cleared his throat. "There was parts of school I really liked. I liked being on the basketball team and the football team. I liked orchestra, jazz ensemble, and chorus. And I liked Dr. Ben." A chuckle. "I just hated everything academic. I didn't see any purpose to learning, and I had no study habits. In my family, who's gonna teach me how to study?"

"What got you kicked out of school?"

"The first time that Dr. Ben went to bat for me, I got in trouble for spray painting the library. I swore I'd never do it again, I repainted the walls, and that was that. I tried to stay clean, but I had no guidance and I had no money. Of course, there's always ways of getting money, know what I'm saying?"

"You sold drugs?"

His face darkened with shame. "Dr. Ben couldn't save me from gettin' expelled, but he did save me from gettin' busted. I was so damn lucky that he was on my side. And I think also that the school preferred to keep everything quiet. I was real fortunate." He looked up. "Thank you, Jesus."

"How long had you been selling drugs?"

"Maybe a year or so. I was makin' money. I was livin' it up. After I got busted . . . that's when my nana sued for child custody." Again his face had darkened, but this time it appeared from anger. Sweat rolled down his brow. Then he composed himself. "Best thing that ever happened to me."

But he still sounded resentful. Marge said, "What about your former peeps? Did any of them have contact with Dr. Ben?"

"Sure. We all did when we got into trouble. But if you're thinking that they had anything to do with his murder, you're going in the wrong direction. None of them gave a damn about Dr. Ben."

Marge said, "What are your old-time buds doing now?"

Arlington let out a gust of air. "I lost contact with most of them. Our lives went in different directions."

"How so?" Marge pressed.

"Some are doing hard time, some are dead, maybe one or two is doing okay."

"Can you give me a list of their names?"

"I will, but I'm telling you, they had nothing to do with Dr. Ben's death. They didn't care enough to kill him."

"Someone cared enough to kill him."

"From what everyone told me, he was in the wrong place at the wrong time."

"He was at a local civic meeting and was supposed to come directly home. That was the last anyone heard. What do you think happened?"

"Wrong place at the wrong time. He got 'jacked. He drove a nice car."

"How'd a guy like Dr. Ben afford such a nice car?"

Arlington shrugged. "I wouldn't know."

Too glib? Maybe it was Marge's imagination. "Did anyone speak to you about the murder?"

"Yeah, friends told me about it."

"Do the names Calvin Vitton or Arnie Lamar sound familiar?"

"I can't say . . ." A pause. "Who are they?"

"Cops involved with the murder of Dr. Ben. I'm surprised they don't sound familiar. Detective Vitton called you up and asked you questions about the murder."

"He probably spoke to my nana."

"He did. His records also indicated that he spoke to you."

Arlington stiffened. "I'm sorry, I don't remember."

"You don't remember being interviewed?"

"It was a long time ago, Sergeant. I was stunned. If you said he spoke to me, I'm sure he did, but I don't remember."

"Do you know a man named Primo Ekerling?"

Arlington paused, then shook his head no. "No, don't know the man."

"What about a man named Rudy Banks?"

A beat before he spoke. "Now he sounds vaguely familiar." He stroked his chin meaningfully. "Someone in high school . . . maybe he was in chorus with me."

"He's a music producer."

"Okay . . . so maybe it *was* chorus."

"Rudy Banks and Primo Ekerling were in a punk group called the Doodoo Sluts."

"Punk . . ." Arlington was pensive. "I wasn't into punk much—white-boy rebellion. Not my thing."

"What is your thing?"

"R & B. Hip-hop. I play bass. That's what I played in orchestra. Later on, I switched to electric bass."

"Do you still play music?"

"Once in a while, I'll fill in a spot in the school orchestra. The kids get a kick outta that. Every so often I think about getting another band together, but with my own kids and my job, there's no time left over."

"You've played in bands?"

Arlington looked down and smiled. "Sure, before I got married." He laughed. "Singing and playing was always a good way to get the girls. When I first moved in with Nana, she made me join the church choir. I didn't want to sing in no church choir. I was resentful. But after a while . . . I really liked it. Being musical separates you from the crowd."

"Did you have a band when you lived in L.A.?"

"Nah, my peeps were more into rap. Wanna know what's funny? I had more talent than any of them. If anyone could have made it in rap, it woulda been me. Nana hated rap. She called it idiotic doggerel and told me I was too good for that stuff. I still like rap, but now as a parent, I see her point."

"But your nana let you play in a band."

"Nana loves R & B. She's got good taste."

"By the way, Rudy Banks went to North Valley High."

Arlington smiled. "So that's why I remember him from chorus. The other one . . . Ekermen—"

"Ekerling."

"Did he go to North Valley?"

"No, he grew up back east."

"So that's why he don't sound familiar and Rudy does."

Marge nodded.

But the ages didn't match up. Marge would check it again, but she had thought that Rudy had dropped out by the time Arlington was a freshman. If there was a reason to reinterview him, Marge would point out the inconsistency at that time.

The only reason Decker heard his cell was because it was still in his jacket hanging up in the bedroom closet. Once again, he'd forgotten to plug it into the charger. But this time it was fortunate. He slipped out of bed carefully, so as not to wake up his wife, and barely made it to the cell before the message machine kicked in. He closed the door to the closet and said hello.

"What do you want from me *this* time?"

It took a moment for Decker to wipe the sleep from his brain. The smooth, albeit irritated voice was instantly recognizable. "What time is it?"

"Your time or my time?"

"On either time, you're up late."

"It must be the drugs."

"What do you know about a guy named Rudy Banks?"

A small laugh over the phone. "You throw names at me like I know every sleazeball in the world."

"Take it as a compliment. Besides, how do you know he's a sleazeball?"

"Who else would you be asking me about?"

"He's a music producer. A former partner of Primo Ekerling."

"The guy stuffed in the Benz."

"Good memory."

"My brain may be swimming in booze, but alcohol is a wonderful preservative."

"Ekerling and Banks were in a punk group called the Doodoo Sluts in the late eighties."

"I was twelve, Decker."

"You're a musician."

"Classical musician."

"Ever heard of the group?"

"Rings a tiny bell. What do you want with Banks?"

"Banks isn't returning my phone calls."

"Maybe he doesn't like you."

"You have any suggestions as to how I might get his attention?"

"No."

"Do you have any relative in the recording industry that might evoke some reaction in the man?"

Donatti laughed. "I have friends everywhere. Watch your back."

"I could give you the same suggestion. How about a name?"

Silence over the line. Decker waited him out. "Sal Crane."

"Sal Crane," Decker said as he wrote it down. "What does Sal do?"

"Sal does a lot of things."

"In the music business?"

"How should I put this?" A long pause. "Sal works in . . . compensation. For instance, if a group covers a song, Sal makes sure that the original artists get royalties."

"Using his name might be helpful then. Would he mind if I used his name?"

"No, he wouldn't like it at all. But if you mention him to Banks, I'm betting that he wouldn't call Sal to verify that you're a friend. And even if he did, Sal wouldn't take his call. Sal doesn't like to be bothered by the little folk. It makes him irritated."

"Sal's got a temper?"

"Don't we all."

17

Rina poured the coffee. "Who were you talking to in the closet last night?"

Decker hid his face behind the newspaper. "What are you talking about?"

"I heard you get up, close the closet door, and speak in low tones."

Busted. "A snitch."

Rina grinned. "Sure you weren't playing virtual life behind my back?"

"Check my computer," Decker said. "If there's anything racier on it than the Porsche Turbo convertible, I plead guilty."

Rina sat down. "First of all, why would *you* be speaking to a snitch? And second, why was your snitch calling you so late?"

"In answer to your first question, I'm working on an actual homicide instead of doing paperwork like a normal lieutenant. A lot is riding on a solve and I need help. Second answer is, snitches don't keep banker's hours." He looked at her and smiled. "Any other questions, Ms. Curious?"

"Just one. Do I have to be careful?"

Decker looked at his wife's face—a mask of concern. "About what?"

"About weird people showing up on our doorstep."

"No. The snitch lives three thousand miles away, and there's not a chance in the world that he'll hurt you."

"Oh . . ." A pause. "Him." Rina tried to appear calm, although she wasn't. She couldn't imagine why he'd be using Donatti as a source of information. She changed the subject. "Cindy called. They're coming over for Shabbos. She also said for you to phone her when you get a chance."

"Like in right away?"

"Like in when you get a chance . . . which could mean right away."

He checked his watch. "Do you mind if I give her a buzz now? Maybe I can get her before she starts work."

"Of course not. I'll wake up Sleeping Beauty. Can you take her to school?"

"Sure. If you have time for lunch, I could probably get away for an hour."

"I think that's a go." She stood on her tiptoes and gave her husband a peck on the cheek. "Give me a call if you don't get swamped with work. And please, please, please, be careful. Your snitch may be able to provide you with a wealth of information, but it also means you're swimming with a great white."

Decker didn't answer right away. Rina was swift in the logic department, but then again how many sources did he have three thousand miles away? "I'm always careful," he reiterated. "I know whom—or what—I'm dealing with."

"I hope so." She bit her lip. "Just make sure that if anyone is chopped-up chum, it's him and not you."

Decker gave her a confident thumbs-up. As soon as she left the kitchen, he dialed his elder daughter's cell. "Hey, I heard you called."

"I did. Hold on." The line went quiet but not dead. In the background was the roar of traffic. "Can you hear me?"

"You're outside. Are you at the station house?"

"Yes, so I'll make this quick. Rip Garrett got wind of your poking around the Ekerling case. He and Tito are grumbling. Thought you might like to know."

"Are you getting flack?"

"No, because I'm acting like I'm on their side. When they pointedly asked me what was going on—and you knew that I was going to be called on this—I immediately offered to call you up and ask what you were doing. Of course, I knew what you're doing. Later I told Rip and Tito that you said you were working on a cold case, but you were playing it close to the vest. Then I said something like 'That's my dad's style, sticking his nose into everything. Is there anything you'd like me to say to him?' And then they said something like, 'Tell him if he has questions to give us a call and stop hotdogging it.' Hence the call."

"There's nothing in the file that I couldn't have gotten from Marilyn Eustis."

"Who, by the way, is the one responsible for your grief. She contacted Rip and told him you were looking at suspects other than Geraldo Perry and Travis Martel. She wanted to know what was going on. It didn't settle well with him."

"I'll call Garrett and Diaz to let them know what I'm doing. Thanks for the heads-up. I'm sorry I got you involved in this mess. I'll take it from here."

"I sure hope so. I've got to work with these guys. If some sleazeball holds a gun to my head, I don't want to wonder if my partner likes me or not."

Marge was nothing if not efficient, having downloaded her notes from the airport in Ohio at six in the morning EDT. By the time she arrived at Decker's office, he had already read them twice and had made his own marginal notes. He looked at his favorite sergeant clad in a blue jacket, vanilla top, brown slacks, and flats. Her face was clean and bright, and she appeared downright perky for someone who had been up since one in the morning PDT.

"I slept on the plane," she explained. "I took

two Benadryls as soon as we took off and didn't wake up until we were landing. Drugs have their purpose . . . legal ones." She pointed to the notes. "What do you think?"

"Several things come to mind."

"Shoot."

"Why did Darnell say that he was in the school's chorus with Rudy Banks when their time in high school didn't overlap?"

"An obvious blip in the man's honesty radar or a simple mistake."

"And you're sure your dates are correct?"

"No, I'm not positive, so I'm rechecking everything. As it stands, Rudy dropped out a year before Darnell entered high school."

"Is it possible that they were in a community choir together?"

"Darnell didn't mention anything about a community choir. The second thing that mars Mr. Arlington's good citizenship record is a little white lie. How could he not remember Cal Vitton?"

"And it's a really stupid lie because the interview is in the case files."

"Clearly, he wants to really distance himself from the murder." Marge scribbled some figures. "According to my math, Ben Little was murdered about five years after Rudy dropped out. At that time, Arlington was a senior, living in Ohio, and Rudy and Primo were in L.A. cutting albums as the Doodoo Sluts."

Decker said, "If Darnell said Rudy Banks's name

sounds familiar, he damn well knows the guy. Being in high school chorus was the first thing Darnell could think of. So we've got to ask ourselves how the two really are connected and what, if anything, it has to do with Little's murder."

"Maybe music, maybe drugs, and maybe both," Marge said. "Arlington admits selling drugs. Maybe he was a runner for the industry and that's how he met Rudy."

"But where's the connection to Little?"

"Little knew Darnell was pushing. Maybe Little was going to expose the operation, leaving Rudy without his main supplier. So Banks had Little whacked."

"Arlington was already gone when Little was whacked. Surely Rudy could have found another source."

Marge mulled over the words. "Okay, how about this? Darnell was the pusher at North Valley, which is why he didn't drop out of school. Let's say Darnell got busted. Little managed to hush up the bust and get Darnell out of the picture. But then let's say a few months later, Rudy takes over Darnell's former turf and starts selling. Little finds out and gets in the way of Rudy's operation."

"That's a leap—from buyer to seller."

"Not really," Marge said. "From what we've found out, Rudy's pretty damn entrepreneurial."

"Okay. For argument's sake, let's say you're right. That would explain a connection between

Banks and Arlington. How does Primo Ekerling fit in?"

"Maybe Ekerling and Banks were in it together. Maybe eventually conscience caught up with Ekerling. He hated Banks. Maybe he finally decided to do the right thing and report Rudy. So Rudy whacked him as well."

"Fifteen years later?"

"Yeah, that doesn't make any sense at all. Nor does it explain why Cal Vitton decided to commit suicide right after you called him up to ask about the Little case."

Decker said, "While you were gone, Oliver's been working on Little's financials."

"And?"

"He owned a lot of toys—a Mercedes, a small boat, a trailer, a camper . . . plus, he had a little money in the bank and there was a college fund for each of the boys. That might have come from insurance . . . or from other sources."

"Ah . . ." She digested the new information. "So you're thinking that maybe Little was running drugs?"

"We have no indication that he was anything but a straight shooter."

"But we do know that his wife developed a big gambling problem after he died . . . meaning she probably had a little gambling problem before he died. Maybe Little needed some disposable income. A few hundred here or there can add up, especially since the income is unreported."

"Who would he be selling to?" Decker asked. "I'm sure Little was smart enough not to foul his own nest."

"Maybe Little got drugs from Darnell and sold them to Banks and his punk musician crowd. That's why when Darnell was busted, Ben Little went to bat for him."

Decker began to draw some diagrams. "Okay. This is what we have. We have a clear connection between Arlington and Little. And it feels like there's some kind of connection between Arlington and Banks."

"We also have a link between Arlington and Cal Vitton. Cal interviewed him."

"Yeah, Arlington does seem to have a few fingers pointing at him." Decker drew arrows. "We have Arlington and Little, Arlington and Banks maybe— and Arlington and Cal Vitton. Nothing so far between Arlington and Primo Ekerling."

"We have Banks and Ekerling, Banks and Little, and maybe Banks and Arlington. But not Banks and Vitton." Marge thought a moment. "And let me add something more to the mix. When Darnell was in high school, he hung out with a bum crowd. He gave me a list of his old peeps. His two best friends had hopes of becoming rappers." She consulted her notes. "Jervis Wenderhole, who went by the name of A-Tack, and Leroy Josephson, who became Jo-King. I found out that Josephson died. I don't know where Wenderhole is, but I do know that he cut a couple of demos. He wasn't very successful, but Rudy wasn't a very successful music producer."

"I'll look into it." Decker shrugged. "I think we need to explore this Banks and Arlington link. At least those two are still alive. Now Banks isn't returning my phone calls. I've got one more secret weapon. If that fails, I'll start hitting the streets."

18

Although Decker had never met Rip Garrett, he recognized him by the look: overworked, underpaid, and pissed off. Physically the detective appeared to be in his thirties, medium height, medium weight, with a full head of dark hair and light brown eyes. He wore a tan suit, a white shirt with a wrinkled collar, and a red tie. Decker introduced himself, and the two shook hands. As soon as both men were seated at a corner booth and the waitress had taken their orders, Decker explained the situation and began in earnest to eat a few bites of crow.

"I should have called in the beginning. I wanted to see what I could find on my own before I bothered you."

Rip Garrett looked him over. There was still anger in his voice. "Doesn't look like you're any farther along than when you started."

"No, I'm farther along: I've now got a dead cop to contend with." Decker gave a shrug. "He took a lethal dose of sleeping medication and had powder burns on his right hand. But I'm waiting for the official report. The fact that it's taking a while makes me suspicious . . . that someone could have done it for him postmortem."

"And why would you think that?"

"The timing. It gives me a bad feeling when I call up and arrange an appointment to talk to the guy about a fifteen-year-old case and he turns up dead."

Garrett said, "Must be your karma."

Decker was tiring of his persnickety attitude. "And how long have you worked Homicide?" When Garrett didn't answer, he glared at the young man. "You agreed to meet with me because (a) I outrank you and you don't say no to a detective lieutenant with over thirty years of experience because someday you may be working under me, (b) you're curious to see what the hell I'm up to, and (c) if you've got a modicum of intuition about homicide cases, deep down inside those arrests don't sit right with you; two stupid punks jacking and offing Ekerling, stuffing him in the trunk, then joyriding around in a flashy Mercedes."

"Stupid is the operative word," Garrett shot back.

"It's bullshit. Something's off but *you* don't know what it is. Right now you know you've got a sure solve with the two lowlifes holed up in the cage, each of them with sheets longer than a roll of toilet paper. Even if they didn't do Ekerling, you're not too concerned with a miscarriage of justice. Sooner or later, both of them would have ended up doing hard time."

Garrett started to speak but thought better of it.

Decker pulled back. "Normally, I'm not such a rude motherfucker, but I'm getting a lot of pressure from the brass. In the end, Garrett, I'll do you way more good than harm. I have a very long memory, and that works both ways."

The waitress appeared at the table, serving Garrett a club and placing a cottage cheese and fruit plate in front of Decker. The watermelon was fresh, but the rest had come from a fruit cocktail can. Decker stabbed a wedge of pineapple but didn't put it in his mouth. "It's more than just a cold case now. I've got a dead cop on my conscience. I pressed Cal Vitton for an interview about Little and Vitton balked. Flash-forward twelve hours, the man is dead."

"You still haven't told me what Cal Vitton has to do with Primo Ekerling?"

"I don't know yet."

"And what's the connection between Ben Little and Primo Ekerling other than a similar MO?"

For the first time since meeting him, Decker saw true curiosity in Garrett's eyes. "I don't know that, either." He made a swirl in his cottage cheese. "What do you know about Martel and Perry?"

"Long sheets—DUIs, drug possession, shoplifting, illegal possession of firearms, burglary, car theft—"

"Assaults?"

"Don't recall right away."

"Batteries?"

"Don't recall that, either."

"So you don't remember anything violent."

"You carry a firearm, you've got the potential for violence."

"No argument there." Decker put down his fork and leaned over the table. "I am looking into a guy who knew Ekerling very well and might have known Little. He's a music producer with a Hollywood address. His name is Rudy Banks."

Garrett thought a moment, then shook his head no.

"Twenty years ago, Banks and Ekerling were in a punk band called the Doodoo Sluts. More recently, Banks and Ekerling have been clashing legally. Also, Banks went to North Valley High where Ben Little taught. So far he's my only common denominator."

"Kinda weak."

"I've got to start somewhere, and Rudy's a good place. Ekerling's girlfriend thinks he's a total scumbag. Everyone I've talked to seems to have the same sentiment. I'd like to form my own opinions except Rudy's not returning my phone calls."

"Why would he do that?"

"Indeed you are right, Detective, ignoring me is a good plan on his part. Because normally I'd be swamped and disinclined to pursue weak links. But a lot of money is riding on this solve, and the potential donor has been making calls to my captain. I left Rudy an urgent message. If he doesn't call back, I'm going to start being concerned."

"Want me to ask around about Banks?"

"If you don't mind, you can ask about Banks, Ekerling, Little, as well as the two thugs you have locked up. Any information you give me would be appreciated."

"All you had to do was call me up, Lieutenant."

"It's Decker, and I should have called personally. Sometimes I get busy and forget my manners. And while I'm thinking about it, I'd love to have a copy of the Ekerling file."

"You don't have it?"

"No, I don't have it," Decker lied smoothly, hoping the fib would extract Cindy from the mess he created. "Would I have asked if I had it?"

Garrett sized him up. "I can get you a copy of the file."

"Thank you."

"Rudy Banks . . . what kind of music does he produce?"

"From what I can tell, he mostly does old compilations of has-been groups like his own. From what I could glean on the Web, he's also tried contemporary groups—lots of hip-hop and rap."

Garrett said, "Martel listed his occupation as an aspiring rapper. That's not unusual. The cage is full of rappers in the making."

"Good call, Garrett, it's worth checking out," Decker told him. "FYI, Ekerling was also a music producer. Matter of fact, he had a scheduled dinner with an up-and-coming hip-hop, R & B group. He was hoping to produce their album."

"Yeah, I know. How'd you find that out if you didn't have the file?"

"I interviewed Ekerling's girlfriend, Marilyn Eustis, the one who called you up and got you in an uproar when she asked about my poking around. Not that I would have reacted differently. I don't like my feet stepped on, either. If Travis Martel was an aspiring rapper and Ekerling turned him down, it could be a working motive for Martel whacking Ekerling."

"How would that connect to your Little case?"

"I don't know. I'm just blurting out ideas as I think of them. I'm giving you the benefit of my years of experience."

Garrett smiled and finished his sandwich. "You don't look happy with your lunch, Decker. You on a diet or something?"

"Not really, although I could take off a couple of pounds." Decker drank up his coffee. "You know how it is, Rip. Sometimes it's just not a cottage cheese kind of day."

The cell phone went off at five in the afternoon. The window told Decker that the number was private. The man on the line was screaming. "Who the fuck is this?"

Decker took a few moments to gather his thoughts. "Lieutenant Detective Peter Decker of the LAPD. Who's this?"

164

"A lieutenant? Sal Crane's got a lieutenant in his pocket? Well, I'll be damned!"

"I repeat. Who is this?"

"Rudolph Banks. Did you know that on my phone plan I have to pay for incoming as well as outgoing calls?"

Decker wanted to say: *Then you could have saved a few bucks by answering my calls the first time, buddy.* Instead he said, "First of all, I'm not in anyone's pocket, let alone Sal Crane. I used the name to get your attention because you hadn't returned any of my numerous calls."

"I haven't returned anyone's calls because I've been on fuckin' jury duty for the last five days. As an alternate! Do you believe that shit! I have to sit through some bullshit trial that was a total waste of *my* taxpayer time and *my* taxpayer money and I can't even be part of saying whether the son of a bitch is guilty or not guilty. No, no, no, I have to park my ass on a rock-hard bench outside the courtroom waiting for those twelve mother-fuckers to render a verdict just in case one of them happens to keel over. And for this privilege, I get paid fifteen big ones a day plus fifty-three cents a mile gas *one way.*"

"You're doing your civic duty."

"No, it's them who did their doodie on me. Thank God it's over. What do you want, Lieutenant?"

"Thanks for asking. I'm currently working Homicide, Mr. Banks—"

"So what do you want with me? Whoever got whacked, I didn't have anything to do with it."

"I'd like to talk to you about Primo Ekerling—"

"They caught the bastards. It was in all the papers, Lieutenant. If you give me your e-mail address, I'll send over the articles."

"I have a few questions that you might be able to help me out with."

"So ask."

"These kinds of questions are better asked in person."

"I didn't whack him. End of conversation."

"His murder was remarkably similar to another individual who died fifteen years ago. A teacher named Bennett Alston Little. I understand you went to North Valley High where Dr. Little taught history, civics, social studies . . ."

The slight pause was very telling.

"I went to North Valley. So did thousands of other teens. I dropped out in eleventh grade way before he died. What's that gotta do with me?"

"Mr. Banks, it's really in both of our interests if we get together and talk. When can I meet you?"

"Do you know how far behind I am on my work?"

"Sir, this really is in your interest. And the sooner we talk, the sooner you'll be rid of me."

Another slight pause. Decker heard the man take a breath. "I'll call you in a week."

"No, that's too long, Mr. Banks. I guarantee you,

it won't take more than an hour of your time. I can even meet you, tonight if you want—"

"No, I don't want, goddamnit. I know what you're going to ask. You're going to ask about Primo. Yes, I knew Primo. Yes, we were suing the shit out of each other. Yes, we've been going at it for a while. No, I did not murder him.

"As far as your victim, I don't remember him, but I vaguely remember the murder. I was living in L.A. when it happened. That's all I can tell you. At the time, I was not only fucking every girl I could get my hands on, I was perpetually stoned. Jesus, I could use a good doobie now."

"How about if we meet some time tomorrow?"

"Why are you putting the screws on my balls?"

"Just a few simple questions, Mr. Banks. I can come to your place in Hollywood. I've already been there. I left you my card—"

"All right already. Fine. Come tomorrow at three. If I'm in, I'll talk to you. Don't bother ringing the bell, it's broken. And if you knock, no guarantees that I'll answer. Three in the afternoon is my low period. Sometimes I doze off, and when I do, I'm a sound sleeper. You come at your own risk."

"I'll expect you to be in, sir."

"Expect? Just because you expect, I have to jump? Let me tell you something, Lieutenant, I *expect* lots of things. But I don't always get what I expect. Instead what I get is a lot of fuckin' a-holes breathing down my neck. What I get is ingrates suing me for no goddamn reason other than greed. What I get is jury duty as a fucking alternate. What I get, Lieutenant, is a bagful of disappointments because the hard truth is people are liars, hypocrites, and thieves. I know damn well that life is basically a tall mound of shit, but I'll be a cocksucker before you or anyone else is gonna make me step in it!"

19

The elevator still wasn't working, and the stairwell hadn't gotten any cooler. Decker was steaming, but not from the heat and the humidity in Banks's hallway. Ten minutes of red-knuckle knocking passed without a response. Decker's impulse was to kick in the door, but instead, he took a deep breath and tried to figure out his next move. Normally he'd wait around, but it was Friday and his religious observance prevented him from doing evening surveillance.

Maybe Marge or Oliver would be willing . . .

There were footsteps in the stairwell. The door opened, and Liam O'Dell ambled toward Decker as casual as denim. "Hey, mate."

Decker was nonplussed but tried to hide it. "Fancy meeting you here."

"Just come back from Millie's. You should try the enchilada special. It's tasty."

"What are you doing here, Liam?"

"Same thing as you, mate, and that would be

lookin' for Rudy." He reached in his pocket and handed Decker a crumpled piece of paper. "You must rate. The bugger took the time to write."

Smoothing out the paper, Decker read:

Emergency situation. Monday, same time, same place. Don't bother to call, I won't call back.

"Bastard!" Decker whispered.

"You're first discoverin' it?"

"He could have called." Decker shoved the note back into his pocket. "Now I've got to deal with rush-hour traffic back to the Valley."

"If that's the only way he's screwed you, consider yourself lucky, mate."

Decker regarded O'Dell. Today he chose to wear cutoff shorts and a Hawaiian shirt. Tattoos had been inked on every limb. "Do you stop by every day, O'Dell?"

"I thought I'd try one more time before heading back to Venice." He smiled at Decker with stained teeth. "'Fraid I did the bastard in? You can kick in the friggin' door and we can both see what's going on."

"I can't kick in the door unless there's suspicion that harm has come to Mr. Banks." He gave O'Dell a meaningful look. "Is there a reason why you think Mr. Banks has met with harm?"

"I can't say for sure, but eventually some harm is comin' his way. You can't be a bastard for *that* long to that many people and not suffer consequences." He stared back at Decker. "If you're concerned, kick in the door."

"No need." He took a pick from his key ring and played with the tumblers until the lock popped open.

O'Dell was round eyed with surprise. "You're a handy gent."

Decker said, "Stay back. If you step inside, I'll have you arrested for trespassing."

"You call the shots, mate, I'm just a bystander."

"I'm serious, O'Dell." Decker stepped over the threshold and was immediately blasted with a waft of heat. The place had no air-conditioning. "Mr. Banks?"

No response.

The living room was blanketed in shade because the drapes were drawn. The area was nicely decorated, deco in style. There were oil paintings on the walls, and most of them were nudes.

"Mr. Banks?"

Quickly, he moved through the unit: two bedrooms, two bathrooms, a kitchen, and a laundry room with a trash chute.

"Mr. Banks?"

Decker opened and shut closet doors. He lifted the trapdoor to the rubbish shaft and looked inside. It smelled of ripe garbage but nothing more sinister.

"Mr. Banks?"

Though the place wasn't compulsively clean, it was orderly. Satisfied that nothing was awry, Decker shut the self-locking door. O'Dell was sitting in the hallway, listening to an iPod, his eyes closed, his body swaying to an unheard beat. Decker walked over and tapped him on the shoulder. O'Dell's eyes flipped open and he bounded to his feet. "All clear, mate?"

"All clear." Decker regarded him. "Why'd you take my note, Liam?"

"I was a bad boy." O'Dell wiped sweaty hands on his shorts. "I thought I might stick around and see who it was for. Then I saw you . . ." He smiled. "I coulda kept it."

"Thanks, buddy, for your consideration. Any idea what the emergency was?"

"With Rudy, an emergency could be anything. Mostly the emergency happens when he wants to get out of something."

"You shouldn't come around here so often, Liam, especially if you think something's going to happen to him." Decker smiled. "See, that would make you a suspect."

"Ooh, a suspect! Can I play meself in the movie?"

"I'm serious."

"Yeah, I know you're trying to do the right thing, Lieutenant." O'Dell looked at his watch. "It's going on three-thirty. If I was you, I'd leave soon. Traffic is going to be a real bitch if you wait much longer."

Decker held open the door to the stairs. "After you, Liam."

"If you insist."

172

"I insist." He waited for O'Dell a little longer than he should have. Finally, when Liam was in the stairwell and in front of him, Decker let the door close. They went down to the first floor without talking, drowned out by the clops of the shoes banging on steel steps.

What Decker had pictured in his mind was an almost forty-year-old rock star gone to seed—overweight and with a puffy face from alcohol and drug abuse. But as recently as a year ago, Rudy Banks was a good-looking man—a lean jaw with an aquiline nose, clear blue eyes, a clean white smile, and a cleft chin. He had dark curly hair, a couple days' worth of beard growth, and his mug could have been on Page Six in the *New York Post*, the caption saying he was an up-and-coming actor.

The man's image was so out of sync with his rotten personality that Decker checked several "find a face" search engines just to make sure he had the right guy. What had happened in this person's life to turn someone that handsome into such a bitter, crude, and rude human being?

Maybe it was precisely because he had been good-looking. Being Mr. Adonis often led to failure to thrive; it simply wasn't necessary to develop more substantial attributes.

Decker felt a presence over his shoulder and looked up from the screen and into the eyes of his elder daughter.

"Very nice," she remarked.

"No, actually, he isn't at all."

"What did he do?"

"So far nothing." Decker gave Cindy a peck on the cheek. "When did you get here?"

"About ten minutes ago."

He smiled at his detective daughter. She wore a simple black dress and black heels. Her hair was aglow with the colors of a raging fire. "You look lovely."

"I try."

"Where's my man Koby?"

"He's coming later." She pulled up a chair next to him. "So who's the guy?"

"Rudy Banks. He was a founding member of a punk band called the Doodoo Sluts. So was Primo Ekerling."

"Aha." She peered at the computer and started reading the text. "I heard that you and Rip Garrett reached a semi-rapprochement."

"It's always better to have cooperation than animosity. And why semi?"

"Rip and Tito still aren't thrilled by your inter-ference. But at least they don't *glare* at me anymore."

"Father knows best."

"Father is what got me on the hot seat in the first place." She stood up. "Why don't you print out some of Rudy's articles and we can go over them after dinner. Right now I'd like to help Rina in the kitchen. Not that she needs my help. She seems to have everything under control—like always."

Decker pressed the print button. "I can help Rina. Why don't you go spend some time with Hannah? She seems to prefer you to me."

"That's because I let her have free rein in my closet."

"Whatever the reason, she smiles when she sees you. It's the only time I ever get to see her teeth."

Cindy laughed. "Was I that surly?"

"You might have been, but you didn't live with me. I think your mother got the brunt of your teenage sulkiness."

"And the woman still speaks to me. What a saint!" She stood up from the chair. "I promised Rina I'd help with the salad. You find out all you can on Banks and we'll talk later. After all, Primo Ekerling was originally my case."

"The GTA was originally your case. As far as I know, you're currently not working Homicide."

"Correct about that, Lieutenant, but a girl can dream."

Around the table, everybody was scrubbed clean and garbed in fresh clothes for the Sabbath. Rina had curbed her culinary largesse, deciding on just a single meat entrée of turkey with rice stuffing and fresh cranberry sauce with a side of steamed asparagus. Preceding the bird were two appetizers: carrot ginger soup followed by an arugula and grapefruit salad. Grilled pineapple and peaches rounded out dessert.

"Too much food," Decker told her after he downed

the last little bit of warm, sweet fruit. "As usual, I was a total glutton."

"I as well," Koby said.

Decker looked at his son-in-law, six two but rail thin. Maybe it was all those years of food shortages in Ethiopia. For the Sabbath, Koby had on his usual white short-sleeved shirt and black slacks. Sandals were on his feet, and that was a concession. Koby hated shoes.

"Everything was delicious," Cindy said. "Really light if you didn't stuff your face."

"Thanks for noticing," Rina answered. "I'm trying to cook a little healthier. Hannah made the soup."

"It wasn't a big deal." Hannah shrugged.

"It was delicious, and I believe the proper response is 'thank you.'"

Hannah smiled. "Thank you, Eema, I'm glad you liked the soup."

"Did I detect coconut milk?" Koby asked her.

"You did," Hannah answered.

"Good touch, Hans," Cindy told her.

"Thank you times two," Hannah said.

"Please let me clear the dishes," Decker implored. "I need to move."

"No argument from me," Rina told him. "I will gladly leave you the mess while I read the paper."

"I'll help you, Daddy," Cindy said.

Hannah brightened. "Are you two going to talk shop?"

"Maybe," Cindy answered. "Why? Are you interested in the intricacies of police work?"

"Au contraire, I believe it would be inappropriate for me to hear your discussions. As such, I'd like to be excused from KP—please."

Rina shot her daughter a look. "Surely you can weasel out with a better excuse than that?"

Cindy smiled. "Even if we don't talk shop, I would pick up your slack, Hannah, provided your mother approves."

Hannah's eyes went to her mother's face.

Rina wagged a finger. "Next time you make the chicken as well."

"Deal!" She hugged Cindy. "You're the best sister in the entire world!"

"Perhaps you're right," Cindy agreed.

Hannah now turned her attention to her brother-in-law. "Can you walk me over to a friend's house?"

Decker said, "I told you I'd do it when I was done with the dishes."

"I'm sure Koby won't mind."

"I'm sure he won't, but that's not the point."

Hannah let go with a deep sigh. Her body was at the dinner table, but her mind was already with her school chums. Koby came to her rescue. "If it's all right with you, Peter, I would not mind a little walk." He regarded his father-in-law. "It's up to you."

Decker threw up his hands. "The girl is an expert manipulator."

"I prefer to think of it as efficient. So it's a go?"

"This time," Decker said. "Thanks, Koby."

"Yeah, thanks." She bounced up from the table. "I'll go pack."

Rina caught her by the arm. "We didn't bench."

"Oh . . ." She sat back down. "Sorry." She rushed through grace after meals, leaving before the rest of the table was done, flying out of her chair and into her room, slamming the door.

"She hates us," Decker said when he was done with his prayers.

"She loves us," Rina told him. "She just doesn't want to be with us. We're boring."

"How would she even know?" Decker complained. "She never talks to us."

Cindy patted her father's arm. "It'll change, Daddy. Look at me. I thought you and Mom were the lamest people on earth—"

"You did?" Decker said. "How was I lame?"

"Daddy, it wasn't about *what* you were, it was about *who* you were. Parents are lame. And on top of that, you were this big, hulking cop. By extension everyone was afraid of me."

"You had friends," Decker protested. "You had boyfriends."

"A testament to my charm and charisma."

Koby cleared his throat and raised his eyes to the ceiling. Cindy hit his shoulder. They spoke about childhood for another thirty seconds until Hannah returned with her suitcase in hand. "Ready."

"That was fast," Koby told her.

"She prepacked days ago," Decker told him. "She can't wait to get out of here."

Hannah put the suitcase down and threw her arms around her father's neck. "Abba, you are the best! I love you very much and always will. But a girl's gotta do what a girl's gotta do." She smiled at Koby. "I'm all set."

"Be careful, Koby." Cindy's voice was uncertain. "Maybe you should take my gun."

"That is not a smart idea," Koby said. "If the neighbors see a black man with a weapon, I will create more harm than good for myself."

Rina said, "I'll go with you two. I could use a walk myself."

"No need, Rina, I'm sure I will not be lynched. If I am, at least the remodel of the house is done and Cindy can relax."

"That's not funny," Cindy said.

Rina said, "Honestly, Koby, I'd like to take a walk."

"Can we just go?" Hannah said testily.

Rina kissed Decker. "We'll be back in a half hour."

Koby added, "And if we're not, call the cops."

20

They cleared the table, piling the china and silver into a tub of warm, soapy water. Cindy donned an apron and rolled up her sleeves. "Do I wash or rinse or what?"

"Just rinse them off and place them on the towel. I'll load the dishwasher. It's not only Shabbos ready but programmed to go off at three in the morning."

"Don't you just love that? You wake up the next morning and everything's sparkling clean. I'm still so thrilled with the kitchen. Mike Hollander did a fabulous job. I think he went the extra mile because I was your daughter. Or maybe it was because you made him feel like a detective again."

"He was a detective again. He found the technology that led to identifying Beth Hernandez. Even though he's retired, Mike's a handy guy to have in reserves. You can't put a price on all those years of experience."

Cindy lifted up a bundle of silver and gave it to Decker. "So what specifically is it about Mr. Banks that spoils his good looks?"

"Well, he's foulmouthed, he's involved in a number of lawsuits, he's been accused by several people of ripping them off, he breaks appointments, and he seems entirely unreliable in all capacities. But it is not for me to judge, only to interview, and I've had a rough time getting hold of him."

"And why do you want to interview him with regard to Primo Ekerling's death?"

"Ekerling was the push behind the Doodoo Sluts lawsuit. He claims that Rudy Banks released the 'best of' CD without paying his ex-bandmates."

"So who's taking over the lawsuit now that Ekerling is dead?"

"I'm not sure. I've met the two other members. The drummer, Liam O'Dell, absolutely detests Banks. The other member, Ryan Goldberg, is nonfunctional. Mental problems. Ekerling was still producing records—still in the business—so I suppose it made sense for Ekerling to initiate legal action."

"And you think Rudy finally had enough and either killed Ekerling himself or hired Geraldo Perry and Travis Martel to kill Ekerling?"

"I'm not saying Banks did anything to Ekerling. I'm just saying that Ekerling was behind a couple of lawsuits against Banks."

"Okay. So I can understand Banks possibly being

involved with Ekerling. But what does he have to do with your cold case?"

"Banks was a student at North Valley High when Ben Little taught there."

"Aha. Any contact between the two?"

"Still to be determined. I'm interested because the two murders have similar MOs. Both victims were stuffed in the trunk of their own Mercedes."

Cindy said, "I don't think that L.A. is overrun with cases involving dead bodies in trunks, but it's not unheard of."

"In almost all cases where the crime scene differs from the body drop, the body is transported in a motor vehicle to the dump spot. And most of the time, the felon will use the trunk to transport the body. But to find a car with the body still inside— and an intact body at that, one that hasn't been dismembered or burnt or disfigured for ID purposes—that's a little different."

"What about the teens they have in custody? Are you totally comfortable with eliminating Perry and Martel as suspects?"

"Not at all. Their fingerprints were lifted from Ekerling's car. If they were the *only* ones behind Ekerling's murder, Little and Ekerling aren't going to be related. But let's assume for the sake of argument that their story was true."

"Okay, let's assume that Perry and Martel went to Jonas Park, looking for drugs, and happened upon the Mercedes with the keys in the ignition and a body in the trunk."

Decker smiled. Stated succinctly, the tale sounded far-fetched. "If you murdered someone and stuffed the body in the trunk of his or her own car, you'd want to get the car away from the crime scene and in a place where a parked car might not stand out so brazenly. The parking lot of a public park sounds like a good idea. It's usually an isolated area at night and no one's around to watch your movements."

"Yes, but then there's a flip side. How does the murderer get away? Not a lot of public transportation."

"There had to be more than one person—or the murderer called up someone to ask for a lift. Now we know that Perry and Martel dumped the car and called up buddies for a ride back to the 'hood. But they called in from a restaurant on the Strip, not from a tower near the park area."

Cindy nodded.

Decker groused. "So if we're assuming that Perry and Martel really did find the Mercedes at the park, then Ekerling's killer may have left in a second vehicle. If Rip Garrett and Tito Diaz had bothered to check out the story, maybe they might have found not only tire tracks from Ekerling's Mercedes but also another set of tire prints from the getaway car. As it stands now, what has it been . . . three weeks ago? The original scene has been violated if not obliterated."

Cindy gave his words some thought. "Okay, so even if someone besides the teens killed Ekerling, why do you suspect Rudy Banks? Was the lawsuit between Banks and Ekerling particularly nasty?"

"I don't know. From what I understand, Banks is involved in a lot of lawsuits."

"So why would you suspect that he's made the jump from suing people to murder?"

"I don't suspect anything. I just want to talk to the dude."

"Nonsense, Daddy, you wouldn't waste your time just 'talking' to him unless you were going for something more sinister."

Decker bent down and rearranged the china to fit more plates into the dishwasher. When he was done, he stood up and stretched. "I suppose I'm stirring up the pot to see if anything rises to the top."

"Surely you're investigating more avenues that just Banks."

"Of course. I have a guy named Darnell Arlington. He was Bennett Little's charity case, but eventually Little kicked him out of school when Arlington was caught drug dealing. The problem with Darnell is that he was over fifteen hundred miles away when Little's murder went down. We're checking out the possibility of murder for hire because Arlington had some thuggish friends."

"How's that going?"

"Just found out the names. Unlike TV, we just don't cut to the next scene. Locating people takes a while. Also, I had a retired cop who *might* have helped me with the Little case, only now he's dead—like on-purpose dead. Suicide."

Cindy stopped working. "Who's that?"

"An LAPD detective named Calvin Vitton. He originally worked the Little case. I had an appointment to talk to him and when I showed up at his house, he appeared to have killed himself. Empty pill vials, then a gunshot to the head."

"So why do you say he *appeared* to have killed himself?"

"Because I haven't gotten the final path report. I got the feeling that if Cal were going to kill himself, he'd do it like a man. Just aim and shoot— no pills for him to soften the act. So I'm thinking cause and effect. I bring up Ben Little to Cal Vitton, and the next thing I know is that he's dead. It's not inconceivable that Cal called someone who came over, knocked him out with pills, shot him, and then staged the scene."

"Did Cal have residue on his hands?"

"Yes, but someone could have wrapped the gun around his own hand and pulled the trigger for him. And if he did kill himself to hide something, what's the secret?"

"More important for Hollywood Homicide and me: What do Vitton's suicide and Little's murder have to do with Primo Ekerling?"

"That's legitimate. I don't know that they have anything to do with it."

Cindy cocked her hip. "I understand why you think Vitton's suicide is related to the Little homicide. It's not just a coincidence. But I don't see what Vitton or Little have to do with Ekerling's murder."

Decker began to wipe down the counter, busying his hands while his brain fired—or misfired—ideas. Maybe he should stop trying to shove the two cases under the same umbrella. "The connection is Banks, and it's tenuous. In the back of my mind I'm thinking that if I find out who really killed Ekerling, it might shed some light on Ben Little's murder. I need to find out more about Banks, especially because Marge thinks that there may be a connection between Banks and Darnell Arlington."

"The suspect that was over fifteen hundred miles away when Little was murdered with the thuggie friends that you're looking for."

"Exactly. Marge flew to Ohio to interview Arlington about Little."

"And?"

Decker stopped cleaning the tile and sat down on a kitchen chair. "And when Margie asked about Rudy Banks, Arlington acted edgy. Darnell remembered Banks as an upperclassman and being in choir with him except the two boys weren't in North Valley at the same time."

"Maybe Darnell knew Banks from just hanging around."

"If that's the case, why not just say, 'Hey, I knew him from hanging around.'"

"Because people get nervous and are afraid to say things because they don't know how their words will be twisted around."

"I take offense. I do not twist people's words."

"Okay, not twist. Misunderstood."

Decker gave her a sour look. "All I'm saying is that there's a definite connection between Arlington and Little, and a *possible* connection between Banks and Arlington. Furthermore, there's a connection between Arlington and Cal Vitton."

Cindy perked up. "Really?"

"Vitton interviewed Arlington over the phone. That's right there in the charts. But Darnell claims he doesn't remember the interview or the cop who talked to him."

"That's a bunch of bullsh . . . malarkey. You don't forget those kinds of incidences or names."

"Do you have any thoughts?"

"I still think there's a good chance that Ekerling and Little are unrelated, unless . . ." Abruptly, Cindy flushed with excitement. "What about Banks and Vitton, Daddy? Cal Vitton was still an active detective when Banks was in high school, right? Rudy didn't become a bad boy overnight. I bet he had run-ins with the police when he was in his teens. Maybe even with Vitton."

Mentally, Decker hit his forehead. He leaned over and kissed his daughter's cheek. "Good call, Cin; hold that thought. I may need you to retrieve it for me as soon as Shabbos is over."

"Yeah, wouldn't it be great if you found out that Vitton arrested Banks for possession or—" Cindy stopped abruptly. "If Banks was arrested in high school, wouldn't his juvenile records be sealed?"

"Not always. Sometimes they're not."

"Or maybe he got arrested as an adult."

"That I have checked out. Banks was hauled in for disturbing the peace, drunk and disorderly, and a DUI when he was in the Doodoo Sluts. The incidents took place in West Hollywood and out of town. Nothing he did went down in our district, so Vitton wouldn't have dealt with Banks on those charges."

"Too bad."

"I'm still thinking about what Banks could have done as a teenager . . ." Decker drummed his fingers on the kitchen table. "It's true that Banks's juvenile records might be sealed. But even if the records are sealed, memories aren't. Vitton's partner, Arnie Lamar, is still alive—at least for the time being."

Cindy made a face.

"I meant it as a joke, but maybe I'm a little worried about him. Anyway, it certainly wouldn't hurt to pay Lamar a visit on Sunday and tell him my concerns. And while I'm there, I'll ask if a guy named Rudy Banks ever showed up on their radar."

21

The shell of a 240Z took up valuable driveway space. It had no tires, no seats, and no interior to speak of except for the dash and steering wheel—both original and in surprisingly good shape. The chassis had been lifted upward and was resting on a set of bricks. The Datsun had several generous dents, and the silver paint job was faded and pocked with orange rust stains. But even so, it was a good-looking car—streamlined and way ahead of its time. There was a toolbox nearby, but no feet were sticking out from underneath the car's carriage. The doors to the four-car garage were closed.

Decker scanned the yard for signs of Arnie Lamar, but came up empty. The ground had been baked from the recent heat wave, turning stone hard with sizable cracks. Red ants were scampering in and out of the fissures. The metal scrap strewn and spangled across the front area reflected blinding sunlight.

Walking up to the front door, Decker got a hinky twinge when he saw that it was wide open, although the screen was closed and locked. He knocked on the doorjamb, gently at first, then louder when he didn't get a response.

This was not promising.

Looking through the mesh, Decker could make out Arnie's tidy but dimly lit living room. He could hear a whirring fan and feel a tepid draft blowing out the door.

What to do?

The day was hot enough to burn away the smog, leaving behind a languid blue sky shimmering in the heavens. The ground was smoking, waves undulating off the black asphalt. Dark funnels of gnats swirled around a vortex in hurricane fashion. Flies dive-bombed his face. Sweat had darkened circles under Decker's armpits and had drenched his back. He had the complexion of a typical redhead and couldn't walk for more than a hundred feet in full sunlight without his skin beginning to burn. The whine of a mosquito pierced his ear and he slapped at his cheek.

Torpor began to set in, a sodden blanket draping over his shoulders. His head began to pound and his eyes felt itchy.

He checked his watch: 2:10.

The appointment had been set for two. He longed to slide back into his Porsche, crank up the AC, and drive away. He was hot and grumpy, but maybe it was because of his reticence to stumble upon another body. He swore to himself, glanced longingly at his car, but pressed on.

The garage had sealed off the backyard from the front yard on the left side, but there was a gate adjacent to the right of the house. It was six feet high and secured with a padlock. Since he cleared the height by four inches, he peered over and looked around. The backyard was just as brown and vegetation free as the front, but there was no sign of Arnie anywhere.

"Lamar?" He jumped up to get a better view. "Arnie, are you there? It's Pete Decker."

Nothing.

A distant dog was barking so hard, it wheezed. Birds chattered from a neighboring fifty-foot magnolia studded with white flowers as big as dinner plates. He went back to the front and knocked his knuckles sore. He mashed his nose to the screen and yelled out, "Yo, Arnie, it's Pete Decker." He checked his watch. "It's a quarter after two . . ." A hard knock. "Lamar, are you there?"

He exhaled forcibly and yelled out, "I don't like the looks of this, Lamar, especially after Cal. I'm coming in."

It didn't take more than a single pop with a credit card to open the screen. The living room validated his first impression; it seemed unbothered by its lack of occupants and there was nothing to suggest nefarious activities. An industrial-sized fan blasted g-force wind onto his face, a bit annoying with his hair blowing around, but it felt good.

The living room led into a dining area and then the kitchen—around ten feet by ten feet and as dark as a bunker with the blinds drawn. Scratched laminate cabinets lined the walls and the old linoleum flooring had buckled in several spots. The fridge was newer, as was the stove. There were no dishes in the sink. On impulse, he opened the refrigerator. There wasn't anything rotten inside—several six-packs of beer and a fresh salad. A steak was defrosting on the countertop.

"Lamar?" Decker called out.

He went on to check the bedrooms. In the master—if you could call it that—the bed had been made. Lamar had used redwood burl tree stumps for nightstands. Opposite the bed was a home-made pine armoire with an old-fashioned TV on the top shelf. No cable box or DVD player in sight. Then Decker remembered that there was an antenna on the roof.

Free TV: now there was an old-fashioned concept.

"Arnie?"

Silence.

Down the hallway was the spare bedroom, its door shut tight. Decker became aware of his racing heart and his overactive sweat glands. No bad odor coming from the room, no telltale blackflies buzzing around the door. There was that one obnoxious horsefly relentlessly attacking his face, but that pesky critter had followed him from the outside. He swatted the air and pressed his ear to the door and heard electronic noise . . . a radio or a television that was suffering from lots of interference.

He gripped the knob and rotated it slowly. The door swung open, revealing a room that was dark and sweltering, without an ounce of circulation.

Decker choked back a cough, his eyes focused on Arnie Lamar slumped in a recliner chair, his bare feet propped up and crossed at the ankles. His head tilted back, his mouth wide open, drool was dripping down from the corners of his cracked lips. His face was bathed in moisture, his eyes shut tightly, and his arms drooped life-lessly at his sides.

He was snoring logs.

There was an empty can of beer on the table next to the chair, and a radio was playing fifties music over the constant crackle of static.

Decker went over to the retired detective and laid a solid hand squarely on his shoulder, a gesture that didn't register in Lamar's consciousness. An earthquake wouldn't have aroused the man.

"Hey, Arnie." Decker shook him forcefully and did it several times. Lamar began to stir. "Wake up!"

One eye popped open and immediately Lamar recognized the face. He bolted out of the chair, wiping his wet mouth on his forearm. "Lordy Lord, what time is it?"

"Twenty-five after two."

He rubbed his eyes. "Sorry." He made a grab for the beer can and brought it to his mouth.

When nothing came out, he crumpled it in his hand. "Man, it's hot in here."

"No shit."

"You want a beer?"

"You bet. Frankly, I'd rather pour it over my head, but if you insist on manners, I'll drink it instead."

"Come into the living room. I've got the fan going in there."

"Sounds good." Decker sat on the couch, in the indirect path of the turbo engine wind that was rustling the blinds. Lamar brought out two cold Buds and Decker downed half in an intake of breath and forced himself not to chug the other. "Cold . . . good."

Lamar took a sip from the bottle. "I've got plenty in the fridge."

"I noticed."

"You noticed?"

"I checked out the fridge before I went looking for you in the bedrooms. Just to see if the stuff in there was fresh."

"Thought I might be missing?"

"Missing or moldering in some hidden spot. After my experience with your partner, I was a little nervous."

"Well, I'm not missing or moldering, just plain hot and sweaty. I was working on the Z out there in the heat. All of a sudden, summer's here and I'm sweating and heaving and I just wanted to do one last little repair. I think I pushed myself."

"Not a good idea."

"No, but after thirty years of being a detective, you learn to do that. Just try one more thing, just check out that one last lead. I started feeling a little faint and decided to take a break. I guess I was way more tired than I thought."

Decker smiled. "Well, Arnie, it's good to see you alive."

Lamar smiled back, took another swig, and leaned back in the chair. "Cal's gonna have a memorial next week. Did anyone call you?"

"No, but give me the time and place. I'll be there."

"I'm not telling you this to make you feel obligated. But Cal's sons . . . you mentioned something about wanting an interview. They'll both be there."

"And willing to speak with me?"

"I think so."

"How are they doing?"

"Well, they're both a bit shook up. I think it's harder on Cal. Maybe he thinks it's his fault that Big Cal ate his gun."

"And that's the official ruling?" Decker asked him. "That Cal ate his gun?"

"I just assumed . . ." Lamar leaned forward. "It isn't?"

"I don't know. Last I heard, the toxicologist report hadn't come in, so the pathologist hadn't come back with an official ruling. Let me ask you something, Arnie. Was Cal suffering from major pain—like back pain or neck pain or . . ."

"He was old like I am. I'm sure he had some kind of pain somewhere."

"He had an open bottle of oxycodone at his bedside. It was his name on the prescription, but it had expired over a year ago. Any reason why he'd have it in the first place?"

He thought for a while. "When we were partners, Cal had kidney stones. Maybe he had one recently."

"Oh, okay. That explains the oxycodone. But you don't know if Cal took pain medication regularly?"

"I suppose if the bottle was over a year old, it wouldn't look like he did. What are you driving at, Decker?"

"I don't know, Arnie." He tried to organize his thoughts. "The medicine was over a year old and the bottle was almost full. I would think that Cal might have forgotten about it. I just don't see him medicating himself before he took the gun. But you would know better than I would. What do you think?"

Lamar stared but didn't speak.

Decker said, "You know what I'm getting at. I want to make sure that Cal didn't get help in killing himself."

Lamar nodded. "And who might have helped him?"

"I was going to ask you that."

"I don't have a clue. I don't think Cal had much in the way of friends. But I don't think he had anything in the way of enemies. He kept to himself."

Decker took out a notepad. "When the Little murder happened, was it a particularly hard time in Cal's life? Is there something associated with the case that would have set Cal off?"

Lamar thought about it. "I don't remember. It was a long time ago. A lot of water under the bridge."

"You said that Cal J might have felt guilty about the death."

"Just speculating."

"Where did the Vitton boys go to high school?"

"North Valley, but both of them had graduated before the Little murder."

"How long before?"

"Four, five years."

"Did they know Dr. Little?"

"Yes, they did. We talked to the boys about Dr. Little, and like the rest of the community, both had positive things to say about him. Cal J was especially fond of Little. Cal J was having problems with some boys at school and I think Little intervened and diffused the situation."

"What kind of problems? Bullying?"

"What else?"

"Cal J was the target of homosexual bashers?"

"That was the rumor."

"So his classmates probably knew he was gay," Decker said. "What about Big Cal? Did he know?"

"If he knew, he wasn't admitting it."

"Who was responsible for the bullying?"

"I don't have any idea, but I think Cal J is comfortable enough that if you ask him about it, he'd tell you."

"When did Cal J come out?"

"Way after the murder. About ten years ago."

"So he was about in his late twenties?"

"About. Him being gay had nothing to do with Little. Like I said, Cal J was fond of Dr. Ben . . . that's what he called him. Dr. Ben."

"So Cal J graduated about five years before Dr. Little was murdered?"

"It all blurs, Decker. Like I said, you can direct these questions to the boys. First of all, they're a hell of a lot younger than I am and their memories are much better. Second, you're asking about their business, and they're alive to tell you about it if they want to."

"Just their business as it relates to Big Cal's suicide. Did he have personal problems at that time?"

"I don't remember Cal being upset personally, only by our failure to come up with a decent suspect. It's not for not trying. Did you read our report cover to cover?"

"Absolutely."

"So you see how many people we interviewed."

"We're rechecking as many as we can. One of my sergeants just went to Ohio to interview Darnell Arlington."

"Yeah, Arlington definitely made the cut, but

he was miles away. We thought about a murder for hire, but where would the kid come up with the money?"

"He was dealing drugs."

"He was selling dime bags of pot, which barely supported his own habit. He wasn't big-time, Decker, if that's what you're wondering. Little couldn't have kept the bust a secret if it had been a serious dealer."

"Still, it's amazing that someone expunged the drug charge. It had to be someone pretty important to make that call."

"Had to be, but it wasn't me."

"And it wasn't Cal?"

"We were working Homicide, not Narcotics."

"Have you ever worked anything in West Valley other than Homicide?"

"Of course . . . GTA, Burglary, Sex Crimes . . ." Lamar shrugged.

"I worked Sex Crimes in Foothill. Did you have Sex Crimes and Juvenile under the same detail?"

"Yep."

Decker felt his heart thump. "So if there were bad boys in the district, you'd know about them?"

"We did when we worked the detail."

"Did you ever have experience with Arlington in Juvey before the murder?"

Lamar drained his beer can. "This is going back some. I don't recall ever running the boy in and that would make sense. Kid would have been about ten when we left Sex Crimes and went into

Homicide. I do recall, when we worked the Little case, talking to several of Arlington's buddies: one kid in particular—Leroy Josephson. He had the usual list of offenses—D and Ds, B and Es, vandalism, petty theft, misdemeanor battery, underage drinking—nothing over-the-top violent but he was going in the wrong direction. We ruled him out right away."

"Do you remember why?"

"His alibi checked out as I recall. I remember him only because someone from South Central contacted me about five years after Little's murder. Leroy was in the wrong area at the wrong time and caught a big one right through the neck that damn near decapitated him." Lamar shook his head. "He was all of twenty-one."

Decker was scribbling notes. "When you worked Juvenile, did you ever pull in a kid named Rudy Banks?"

"Rudy Banks?" A big grin opened up Arnie's face. "Now if there was ever a pisshead, that would be Rudy. Foulmouthed little turd."

Decker was trying to hide his excitement. "Want to tell me about him?"

"The kid had a voice of an angel. He had the face of an angel. But his soul . . ." A chuckle along with a shake of the head. "I tell you, he was one with Satan."

"Where'd you hear him sing?"

"In the school choir. In church. He was a tenor . . . a voice that was clear and beautiful. And with those big blue eyes . . . looked like an English altar boy. He cussed like a sailor."

"What did you haul him in for?"

"Stealing. All kinds of stealing. Purse snatching, breaking and entering, shoplifting. I think he even stole from the church. And all this before he reached high school. I heard he became a rock star in one of those punk bands that spit and curse at the audience."

"I don't know if you'd call him a star. He was in a punk band called the Doodoo Sluts."

Lamar smiled. "That seems consistent with Rudy's style."

"He doesn't have much of a record as an adult unless it's the recording kind of record." Decker brought Lamar up to date with Rudy's current occupation and his numerous lawsuits. "So you remember Rudy very well."

Lamar shrugged. "Yes, I do."

"Would Cal Vitton have known and remembered him as well?"

"Oh yeah. Matter of fact . . . it's coming back to me. Cal had a real hard-on for Rudy."

"Like a personal vendetta?"

"I wouldn't go that far, but he detested the boy. He was a real wiseass."

Decker tried to stay focused. "A wiseass and maybe a bully?"

Lamar took in Decker's eyes. "Are you asking me if Rudy bullied Cal J?"

"I believe I am."

"I don't know. Cal J didn't talk about his problems with me, or with his dad for that matter. But now that you mention it, Rudy was in school the same time as the Vitton boys. If anyone would be bullying Cal J, it would be Rudy Banks."

"So maybe that's why Vitton hated Rudy."

"Pete, it's safe to say that everyone hated Rudy . . . except for maybe a few stupid girls who liked a pretty face. What was so ironic was the kid had talent. He probably could have made a lot of money by singing if he was just an itty-bitty bit nicer, but it wasn't in his makeup. That kid was a bad egg."

"And you're pretty sure that Cal J and Rudy attended high school at the same time."

"No, I'm not positive, but that wouldn't be hard to verify." Lamar got up and wiped his face with a cloth. "Man, it's a scorcher. Want another beer?"

"Water would be great."

"All I have is lukewarm tap."

"Bud it is."

Lamar returned a few minutes later with a couple of cold ones. "So you're gonna talk to Rudy?"

"If I can find him." Decker popped the top and drank with gusto. "He seems to be avoiding me. I only talked to him once over the phone, and as you said, he was foulmouthed."

"Primo Ekerling was also found in a car trunk like Ben Little?"

"Yes."

"And you want to talk to Rudy about the Ekerling murder since Primo and Rudy were in a long-standing lawsuit?"

"Yes."

"Even though Hollywood already has a couple of carjackers in custody. They don't mind you nosing around the case?"

"They're not happy about it, but we've reached a cold war understanding."

Lamar looked at his watch. "I'd like to catch a little more sunlight out there. Do you mind?"

"Not at all."

"Keep me posted, Decker, and I'll do the same for you. My memory isn't too good, but if you jog it here and there, it just might get up and take a nice long run."

22

Banks's cell had gone immediately to voice mail. It was probably a waste of time and police resources to trek over the hill for the appointment, but Decker made the plunge, sitting in wall-to-wall traffic for over an hour. It didn't surprise him that his peevish knock went unanswered. This time Banks didn't bother to leave a note, so Decker left a note of his own.

He was about to leave when he saw the door to the stairwell open. A neatly dressed man in his twenties emerged. He had a trimmed goatee, and his dark hair was buzzed short. He wore a white T-shirt, cutoff jean shorts, and sandals and carried a bag from L.A. Art Supplies. He was attempting to act disinterested in Decker's six-foot-four, 220-pounds-of-muscle frame, but his eyes flitted like a hummingbird. He stopped across from Banks's door and when he took out a set of keys, Decker saw his hand tremble.

"Excuse me, sir." The man looked up. "I'm

Lieutenant Decker from Los Angeles Police. Can I talk to you for a second?"

The man paused. "What about?"

"Your neighbor, Rudolph Banks." Decker took out his badge.

The man said nothing, but his eyes fell upon the open billfold. Decker said, "I had an appointment with Mr. Banks this afternoon. He doesn't seem to be home now and from my dealings with him, he isn't home a lot."

"I didn't have much to do with him. He wasn't very friendly."

"I've heard he's a bastard."

"Yeah . . . I'd agree with that." The man put down the bag of art supplies. "He moved out over the weekend."

Decker felt his jaw clench. "When?"

"On Saturday."

Decker exhaled. "I don't suppose you'd know his forwarding address."

The man shook his head. "You're right. He wasn't home a lot. But you could always tell when he *was* home. This is an old building with old, thick walls, but even with the insulation, I could always hear him screaming and swearing. No one on the floor liked him."

"Did you see Mr. Banks on Saturday?"

The young man pressed his thin lips together. "Actually, I didn't. But I talked to the movers." He gave a fleeting smile. "I remember telling one of them that I hoped Rudy was moving far away."

"What did he say to that?"

"That he was only hired help. But now that you mention it, it was odd that Rudy wasn't around directing things."

Decker smoothed his mustache. "Could he have been around when you weren't home?"

"I was home most of Saturday. I did go out for brunch for a few hours. It's possible I missed him."

The notebook came out of Decker's pocket. "Do you remember the name of the moving company?"

The man faltered. "No . . . no, I don't remember."

"Were the movers dressed in any kind of a uniform?"

"Pardon?"

"You know, usually movers wear shirts with the name of the company embroidered over the pockets."

He thought about the question. "I don't remember the name of the company, but they were dressed in a single color—matching shirts and pants in dark gray. Three of them. One big guy with tattoos, another was a little guy with like . . . geez, sort of a mullet, Hispanic or Italian looking; the third was also darker complexioned . . . buzz cut. Tough-looking dudes."

"Do you recall any names?"

"Sorry, no. I'm good with images, not words."

"You're helping me a great deal. Do you remember what time it was when you spoke to Mr. Banks's mover?"

"About one in the afternoon . . . what's going on?"

"Mr. Banks and I arranged an appointment for this Monday. He never mentioned anything about moving, and I can't reach him on his cell. Could I get your name, sir?"

"Baker Culbertson. Do you think something happened to Rudy?"

"I don't know. Does the apartment complex have a manager?"

"Not in the building, no."

"So who do you call when there's a problem?"

"Imry Keric. If you hold on a minute, I'll give you his number." Culbertson opened the door just wide enough for him to fit through and closed it in Decker's face. The gesture probably came more out of suspiciousness than rudeness. Decker was filling in his notes when Baker returned with a slip of paper. "This is his work number and this is his cell."

"Thank you very much, Mr. Culbertson. I'd also like to get your phone number if you wouldn't mind."

"Why do you need my number?"

"In case I think of additional questions for you."

He paused a long time, but in the end he recited a string of digits. "I don't know why you'd want to talk to me again. I told you everything I know."

"Just in case something comes to mind." Decker flipped the cover of his notepad and tucked it into his pocket. He handed Culbertson a card. "And here's my number if you feel the need to call."

"I don't know why I would. I barely knew the man."

"You knew him enough not to like him."

Another hint of a smile. "True. It was hate at first sight."

The bartender poured another shot, and Oliver pushed it in front of Nick Little. They were drinking at a bar—not some gussied-up, pussied-up travesty of a saloon that peddled apple martinis and frozen strawberry daiquiris, but a bar's bar. Dark inside with an old-fashioned box TV playing sports. Sawdust on the floor, barstools with red Naugahyde seats, and a polished wood bar top that had heard secrets as old as the Bible.

The neon in the window called the establishment Jackson's Hole, and Nick Little was a well-known patron. He was slugging back booze almost as fast as the barkeep could pour. It loosened his tongue. Within fifteen minutes, Oliver found out that Nick had been married and divorced twice, one kid with the first and one with the second. His ex-wives were bitches and whores and marriage was a cruel joke perpetrated on men by conniving women in order to screw their husbands out of their paychecks.

It didn't take much acting for Oliver to agree with him, although he and his ex could now be in the same room without fireworks discharging. He didn't actively hate his ex, but she did bring out the dyspeptic side of his personality.

Nick Little had manly features—a roman nose veined from alcohol and a big chin with a heavy shadow of stubble that darkened his face. His eyes were Christmas colored—kelly green and red-rimmed. Metal studs pierced his earlobes and climbed all the way up to the cartilage. He was big across the shoulders but thin at the hips. His arms were muscled and festooned with ink. By trade, he worked in a pit crew. When he wasn't servicing cars, he was racing them. He liked who he was and how he lived, and if anyone had a problem with that, they could eat his shit. He had packed a lot of living into his thirty years and intended to stuff even more life into his next thirty big ones if the guy upstairs permitted.

Oliver was trying to persuade him to talk about his mother, but Nick was too busy ragging on his exes to make the switch. He'd just have to wait Mr. Macho out. Eventually—and probably when Nick was drunk enough—he'd get around to talking about Melinda.

That happened about an hour later, although the man could sure hold his liquor. When he talked, he made eye contact and his hands were steady. "She tried the best she could." He licked his lips. "It sucked all the way around."

"How much do you remember?"

"I was fifteen, I remember everything. I liked my dad. He was a good guy. He might not have approved of how I live, but he would have supported my decisions. I'm financially independent and he would have liked that."

"And your mother?"

"Yes, there's Mom." His blinked several times. "Mom fell apart. When her world crashed, she couldn't handle her own shit, let alone ours."

"She was absent a lot?"

"A lot—as in all the time. I hated her for it, but now I understand it. Sometimes life turns you into this person that you don't want to be."

"She's doing okay now."

"Yeah, she married well. Good for her."

No bitterness there, Oliver thought. "How'd she meet her current husband?"

"Some kind of charity . . . at least, that's the cover story."

"And the real story is . . ."

"Probably in Vegas over one of the card tables."

"Yeah, I heard she had a problem."

"Had?" He smiled. "*Had* would imply that she no longer deals with the issue."

"She still gambles?"

"Does a bear still shit in the woods?"

"Where does she get the money?"

"I don't know, Detective; I don't follow the vices of my mother. We're not close. She doesn't approve of me—my externals. Still, I wish her well." He downed another shot. "No one's perfect."

"I could understand how she gets spending money now . . . Warren's a very wealthy man—"

"I'll drink to that." Little raised his shot glass.

"Where'd she get the money to indulge her hobby when she was married to your dad?"

"I don't know how much gambling she did when Dad was alive. He probably kept her in check. Why don't you ask her about it?"

"I did, and you nailed it. She said it wasn't a problem when your dad was alive . . . not much more than an occasional jaunt to Vegas."

Little appeared thoughtful. "I'm sure his death unleashed all sorts of hidden demons."

"Your father was well loved by everyone who knew him. Everyone said he was a straight shooter."

"That was the rumor." Little shot him a sneer. "What are you getting at?"

"He made a teacher's salary, Nick. Your mother didn't work. Your parents owned a lot of toys."

Little licked his lips but said nothing.

"I'm just wondering if you had any idea where the extra cash may have come from."

"I was fifteen."

"I'm betting that nothing got past you."

"I don't know anything about my father's extracurricular activities— or even if there were any extracurricular activities. Could he have been a hit man for the mob?" He shrugged. "Maybe."

"I was thinking much more low level, Nick."

Again the sneer. "What? Like he was stealing the kids' lunch money?"

"Drug pushing."

Nick laughed. "It sure wouldn't have fit my

image of Dad. All I know is that he was always there when I needed him. For a kid, that's all that counts."

"What happened to the toys—the boat, the trailer, the camper?"

Little furrowed his brow. "Good question. They just disappeared from my life, same as my father. My mom probably sold everything to make ends meet. It was a good thing that she couldn't touch our education fund, otherwise I could have never gone to an elite university and become the worthwhile citizen I am today." He smiled with dark-stained teeth. "Can't you tell?"

"I can actually," Oliver told him.

Little took in the words and scratched his cheek. "I thought I'd love college. Living away from home and away from the townspeople with their pitying looks. More than anything, I just wanted to get out." He nodded to the bartender, who poured another round. "Then I discovered that I liked chaos. It was fun . . . a real rush. Once I settled into the routine, I participated in every kind of protest known to mankind. Didn't matter what the cause was as long as I could yell about something. Duke sure as hell taught me how to drink."

"You went to Duke? That's pretty impressive."

Little belted back the shot. "I got in everywhere I applied: Harvard, Yale, Princeton, Dartmouth . . . all of them. My grades were okay, but I tested high. The key to my success was a murdered father.

You write an essay on that and on your mother's downhill spiral and how you hope for a second chance, blah, blah, blah. It's the type of shit that those bastions of bleeding hearts eat up. Plus, I wasn't a scholarship case thanks to my dad's foresight."

"The educational funds for your brother and you. Not to belabor the point, but where did that money come from?"

"I don't know." He took a sip. "I always thought it was my dad who put away the money for the funds. But I'm now thinking that it could have been my grandparents—my mother's parents."

"Are you in contact with them?"

"I used to get birthday and Christmas presents. After my father died . . . I don't know exactly what happened. There was a falling-out between my mother and them. It was probably over her gambling."

"What about your father's parents?"

"They were much older. They died when I was very young."

"And you're not the least bit curious about your living grandparents?"

"Not because I'm angry at them. I invited them to my wedding—the first one. They didn't come, but they did send a check, which was honestly way more appreciated than their presence." His eyes went to a faraway place. "The last time I remember seeing them was at Jared's graduation from Columbia—or maybe it was at his wedding.

Call Jared. He keeps in contact with them. He's a good guy. He came out much better than I did."

"What do you mean?"

"He made something of himself."

"What's wrong with working in a pit crew?"

Nick smiled. "Nothing. What I mean is that Jared's more conventionally successful. He's a real estate lawyer down in La Jolla."

"Lawyers get into trouble, too."

Nick laughed. "As far as I know, Jared's managed to avoid the pitfalls, but I don't know everything. He could be selling swamp land to little old ladies, but it wouldn't matter to me. He's my brother. I love him. End of story."

23

Imry Keric was a spectral figure. Decker could see veins through his translucent skin. Thick and blue, they coursed through his hands and sinewy arms and ran up his neck into his head. He looked as if he'd been wired for electricity.

Rudolph Banks had moved out three months shy of his lease, but he had left cash for the remaining sum in Keric's mailbox. As far as the building manager was concerned, Banks had been a model tenant because he paid on time and never had any wild parties.

"Neighbors say he used to scream a lot," Decker pointed out.

"Ech . . ." Keric waved his hand in the air. "Who doesn't scream?" He inserted the key into the lock and opened the door. "He didn't do damage. He left the place cleaner that my crew does. I don't do anything. You see for yourself."

Decker stepped inside and, indeed, the space

was bare and had been scrubbed down: bad odds for pulling up anything significant.

Bummer.

He started with the kitchen: Banks had been thorough. There wasn't anything in the cabinets, cupboards, or refrigerator. The shelves had been wiped down and were crumb free. The stove looked relatively hygienic. The walls had been coated with off-white semigloss enamel paint. In general, the hue yellowed as it aged, especially in the kitchen, where heat and fumes wreak havoc. But except for dings, the paint job appeared recent because the color was still fresh.

The living room had been done in a sage green, the paint as new as the kitchen judging by the amount of nicks and scratches. The nude pictures were gone, the nails the only indication that the walls had once been adorned. The wood flooring appeared recently refinished. Decker asked Keric about it.

"If he did it, he didn't ask my permission."

"So he didn't refinish the floors?"

"No, I say he did." Keric shrugged. "I don't complain, though. It looks nice." The manager pointed to an area in the corner. "There are some scratches."

"The movers probably did that."

"Maybe."

"Any idea why he'd refinish the floors?"

"No. He had good taste. Very . . . elegant."

"He wasn't a very elegant guy."

Keric shrugged. "He was always okay with me. Anything else?"

"Did Mr. Banks leave a forwarding address?"

"Maybe with post office, not with me."

Then there was no forwarding address. Decker had already called the local mail station while he was waiting for the manager to show up. "I'll just take a quick peek around the rest of the apartment."

"It will take long?"

"Not too long." He checked out the bathrooms: the counters and cabinets were empty. The bedrooms had been painted beige and brown, respectively. Tidy except for nail holes in the walls. "Are you going to repaint these rooms?"

"They look nice and clean to me. If no one complains, I just leave it as it is." Keric jingled the keys. "We go now?"

Decker eyed the wood in the bedrooms. Whereas the planks in the living room floor had been done in a central diamond pattern, these strips of oak had been arranged running board style. More important, the flooring was obviously original to the building and hadn't been touched in a number of years: dull finish and dirt in the open cracks. Not that it looked bad. It acquired a patina of its own, but if Rudy was going to do the floors in one room, why not just do the entire apartment?

"You are done, no?" Keric asked again.

"In a minute." Decker walked back into the living room, his eyes immediately focusing in on the baseboard and shoe molding. It was also semigloss and white in color. The electricity had been turned off. Although the room had some natural light, it wasn't enough illumination for details.

Decker took out a penlight. He squatted down at a corner and shined it in the area between the shoe molding and the floor. Carefully he went around the room, inspecting each millimeter of the crack. When he was finished scrutinizing the room, he stood up and repeated the process in the kitchen. It took up more time than Keric would have liked.

"Now we are done?"

There was a faint thread of hope in Keric's voice. Decker hated to dash it asunder, but it was what it was. "Not quite yet. If you can bear with me a little longer, I think we can wrap this up one way or the other."

"Wrap up . . . what is to wrap up?"

"I can tell you that just as soon as I do a small test with my kit."

"What is kit? You make powder on the walls."

"No, no." Decker had left the apartment and was bounding down the stairs. "I'm just going to swab a few areas with a Q-tip."

"What swab?" Keric was having trouble keeping up with him, so Decker slowed. "What do you mean, swab?"

Decker reached the lobby and went out to his car. From the glove compartment he retrieved a small cellophane package. "I found a few small stains between the shoe moldings and the floor in the living room and kitchen. This little packet is a presumptive blood test kit. It'll tell me whether the stains are blood or not."

Keric's ashen face turned grayer. "Why would there be blood?"

"I'm not saying there is." Keric was panting, and since Decker's CPR skills hadn't been tested for a long time, he walked at a more leisurely pace. The two men made it back up the stairs. By that time, Baker Culbertson had emerged from his warren and was lurking in the hallway.

"Is everything all right?"

Decker smiled and nodded. "I'm just about done."

"He tests for blood," Keric told the artist.

"*Blood?*" Culbertson was aghast. "Why would there be blood?"

"I'm not saying there is. Let's not draw any conclusions." Decker paused. "You didn't hear anything funny coming from Banks's apartment Friday night, did you?"

"No, everything was quiet," Culbertson insisted. "Not that I was home all of Friday evening. I have a life."

Decker gave him a hard smile. "It's probably best if you keep quiet about this. I wouldn't want to start a panic in the building." He turned to Keric. "That wouldn't be good for you."

"You here isn't good for me."

Decker kept his face flat. "Excuse me . . ." He went into Banks's place, squatted and swabbed a small blotch on the baseboard of the kitchen. The Q-tip turned blue.

"What is that?" Keric asked.

"It means that it's likely that the sample I took is blood." He stood up. "It could be human blood, but it also could be from raw chicken or a piece of meat. Or it could be horseradish or potatoes. They'll change the color as well."

"So why you do it?"

"Because the kitchen and living room paint jobs are new, but the entire apartment wasn't repainted. I'm wondering why." Decker went into the living room, found a few faded spots that he had spied earlier, and repeated the process. Again, the Q-tip turned blue on each trial.

"More blood?" Keric asked.

"Looks that way."

"Or potato?"

"Not so likely in a living room." Decker took out his cell phone. "I'm sorry to do this to you, Mr. Keric, but I'm going to call down some experts from the Crime Lab. They'll be able to tell me if it's horseradish or human blood."

"Why you look for human blood here? I get complaints that Rudy screams but none last weekend."

"Mr. Keric, that's what concerns me." Decker went through his cell directory and punched in the number for the Crime Lab. "That Rudy moved out and no one heard a peep."

*   *   *

The trouble with calling after hours was voice mail. Oliver resisted the urge to slam down the phone and tried to adopt a zen/yoga/pilates/tai chi kinda what-me-worry attitude as an anonymous voice said:

If you would like to be connected to Richard Poulson, press 1.

If you would like to be connected to Annette Delain, press 2.

If you would like to be connected to Cyril Bach, press 3.

If you would like to be connected to Jared Little, press 4.

Oliver pressed four.

The extension started to ring, and when a human voice answered, Oliver was momentarily thrown off.

"Mr. Little?"

"This is Jared Little. Who is this?"

"I'm Detective Scott Oliver from LAPD—"

"Yes, the detective. My brother said you'd be calling. He told me that you've reopened Dad's case."

"Actually, we've got several people on your father's case. Could I meet with you to talk about it?"

"Of course. I'd do anything for Dad."

"When would be a good time?"

"Name it."

"How about . . ." Oliver looked at his watch. It was a five-thirty. "Do you still live in La Jolla?"

"Yes."

221

"I could drive down tonight. I could probably be there by eight, eight-thirty."

"Tonight is my night out with my wife. I won't be back until about ten. It's going to be late to drive back to L.A. for you."

"I'm fine with driving back. Let me give you my phone number. I'll probably be in La Jolla around dinnertime. When you get home, give me a ring and I'll come over."

"That's a good idea. I wouldn't want you showing up, flashing the badge and putting Grandma in a panic."

"Grandma? Your mother is babysitting?"

"Hardly." A chuckle. "*My* grandparents. They're the resident babysitters. They love their great-grandson. It's a sweet deal all around."

"Your mother's parents?"

"Yes. My father's parents passed on a long time ago."

"You know, I'd love to talk to your grandparents. Would that be possible?"

The line fell silent. "I can call them and ask."

"It would be very helpful. I know that you remember a lot about that period, but you were only thirteen. Adults would have a different perspective." A long pause. "Your brother mentioned a falling-out between your mother and them."

"He oversimplified the situation," Jared told him. "It's more like: we all love Mom but she's difficult. Are you going to ask me prying questions about Mom?"

"I think prying is too strong a word." Even though it wasn't. "It's hard to talk about your dad without talking about your mom. I know she had problems with gambling in the past. I've heard she conquered her demons."

Another protracted silence. "More like a cold war. Anyway, I'll ask my grandparents and give you a call back."

"Thanks for being so helpful, Jared. It'll really help move the investigation along."

"No problem." A sigh. "I know you tend to idolize the dead, but my father was really a good guy. Nelson, my son, looks a lot like him. He's got the same winning personality, the same sparkle in his eyes, the same ability to command respect. I know that seems weird for me to be saying, but it's not just a proud parent talking. We just put him in preschool and the teacher said he's a natural-born leader."

"I'm sure she's right."

"It's uncanny, you know. The bastard took my dad away, but his genes live on."

Marge knocked on Decker's door frame and without waiting for a response, stepped into the office. "You wouldn't think a guy with the name of Jervis Wenderhole would be that hard to track down."

Decker pointed to a chair. "Remind me again . . . who is Jervis Wenderhole?"

"One of Darnell's ex-peeps."

"Right. A-Tack the rapper."

"Wenderhole holds a unique spot on Arlington's list," Marge said. "He's the only person who isn't in jail or isn't dead."

"But since you can't locate him, that's still an open question."

"I've run him through NCIC. He's got a record but hasn't been naughty for a long time. No death certificate found, so there's hope."

"He's not in the phone book?"

"Not in L.A. I've got a reverse directory for the Valley, but I'm looking for one in South Central. I found out that although Arlington went to North Valley, Darnell, Josephson, and Wenderhole were bused in from L.A.—a twenty-five-mile trip one way. I though mandatory busing was declared unconstitutional."

"Fifteen years ago, the program was voluntary. Lots of parents chose it because they thought their kids would get a better education at a whiter school."

"Yeah, that's right. Any other ideas on how you might track him down?"

"Didn't you say Wenderhole was a rapper?"

"Yes, I did. However, I haven't found any actual CD."

"So where'd you hear that from?"

"From one of the old buddies who is now in prison. Maybe Banks was his producer. Wouldn't that be convenient?"

"Banks's whereabouts would be convenient."

"He didn't leave any forwarding address?"

"No, but he did leave human blood behind in his apartment. We've got a positive on that."

"Oh my . . ." Marge sat down. "A lot of it?"

Decker said, "I found blood behind the shoe molding that dripped down to the baseboard and floor."

"Do we have any way to match it to Rudy Banks?"

"We're working on it, but I don't see how it could belong to Rudy. The paint job is new, but not that new. I talked to Rudy on Friday."

"It could be someone claiming to be Rudy," Marge said.

"I thought about that," Decker said. "Rudy mentioned to me over the phone that he'd been on jury duty. I checked it out and it was true. Banks had been impaneled at the L.A. courthouse as recently as Friday."

"So the question is, whose blood?" Marge said. "Primo Ekerling?"

"It's a thought."

Oliver popped his face through the open door. "I'm off to La Jolla." He looked at Marge. "You're here. Wanna come?"

"What's in La Jolla?"

"Jared Little and, as an added bonus, I'm interviewing Melinda Little's parents—Delia and Mark Defoe, who by the way are estranged from their daughter."

"That should be interesting." Marge stood up

and slung her purse over her shoulder. "A lot more interesting than what I had planned. Sure I'll come."

"What did you have planned, Margie?" Decker asked.

"Absolutely nothing. Will's on night shift, Vega's doing community service, tutoring inner-city kids on computers, and I'm a blank slate. Do you need me to follow up on the forensics at Banks's apartment?"

"No, I'll do it," Decker told her. "But thanks."

"What forensics?" Oliver asked.

"I'll fill you in while we're driving. I'm starving. Let's grab some sushi to go. We'll eat in the car."

Oliver shot her an incredulous look. "How am I going to eat sushi if I'm behind the wheel?"

"I'll feed you, Scotty." Marge shook her head. "I'll even wipe the soy sauce off your chin."

"You make me sound like a drooling, senile old fart."

She pinched his cheek. "Not at all. I'm just trying to help you . . . do you a service. Think of me as a geisha with a gun."

24

The sunset was on the right, a fiery ball spewing golden rays on a smooth slate surface. They were about ten miles from their destination, and while the traffic had been gnarly, the view had been pretty and the sushi had gone down smoothly except for the thirst factor. Oliver was on his second Diet Coke when he saw the off-ramp for La Jolla Village Drive.

"You turn right here," Marge told him. "Melinda's parents are Mark and Delia Defoe, correct?"

"Correct. As in *Treasure Island*."

"That was Robert Louis Stevenson," Marge said. "Defoe is *Robinson Crusoe*."

"Stop showing off."

"I'm not showing off, I'm just saying . . . never mind."

"Aren't you impressed that I even knew that Defoe wrote some South Sea shipwreck book?"

"Very impressed. Your literary Q has gone up a notch. Can we talk about the case?"

"Sure. Melinda's parents are babysitting their great-grandson. They're in their late seventies. Jared asked us to be gentle with them. What's the name of the development?"

"La Jolla Pines."

Oliver slowed the car. "What does that sign say?"

"That's La Jolla Woods."

He crept another mile. "How about that sign?"

"La Jolla Hills. Your directions say to go straight for three miles. It hasn't been three miles."

"What's that?"

"La Jolla Shores."

"They're not very original over here."

"Keep going . . ." They rode a minute in silence. Marge squinted in the dusk. "There's the turnoff to La Jolla Pines."

Oliver hung a left, which put them into a forested development of stucco and wood, two-story town houses, more or less Cape Cod in style. The homes were constructed almost identically but individualized by finishing material, plants, garden statues, fences, and gates. They drove through winding streets that gently rose and fell, the asphalt roads shadowed by mature eucalyptus and pines. Green lawns, lots of blooms, and a plethora of citrus trees. The air was wet and briny, the temperature around sixty-five degrees.

They parked in front of a white and brick house that was bedecked with multicolored impatiens. As soon as they got out of the car, the front yard lights came on and the door opened. An elderly woman stepped out onto the front porch. She was meticulously coiffed and dressed: white slacks, a white shirt, and a red blazer. Her teased salon-style hair was blond, her nails were long and painted pearlescent white, and large diamond rings adorned her knobby fingers.

Marge had her badge out as she introduced herself. "Mrs. Defoe?"

"Delia . . ." She walked a couple of steps and put her finger to her lips. "The old man fell asleep right on the living room couch. We can talk in the den."

The entrance hall was dark, but the living room had the lights on. The ceiling soared upward of fourteen feet, and a picture window provided a sparkling view of the illuminated hills of La Jolla. Beyond the lights was the afterglow of sun shimmering on the surface of the sea.

"This way," Delia whispered.

The den was dominated by a sixty-inch flat screen mounted on the wall. There were shelves of DVDs, CDs, and a few paperback books. The furniture was straight lines but comfortable and beige in color—as was the carpet. A corner chest was open and overflowed with toys.

"Sit anywhere you'd like. May I get you something to drink from the bar?"

Oliver looked around and saw a small closet with a half door. "I'd love a beer."

"Soda water for me, if you have it," Marge said.

"Coming right up!" She went into the closet/bar and opened a small refrigerator. She worked quickly and efficiently. The beer had frosted the glass, and the soda water bubbled in a crystal tumbler. "Here we go."

"Thanks so much," Marge said.

Oliver took a sip and sighed. Man, it was good. "So your grandson wore out your husband."

"Great-grandson," Delia corrected. "He's such a love. Most of the time we're here, he's asleep. Today Nelson got the wild notion to play hide-and-seek right before bedtime. It hyped up the little one and pooped out the big one. I had to read the little guy four books. The big guy didn't need any coaxing to sleep."

"Babysitting is fine as long as it's not your full-time job," Oliver said. "That's what I love about my grandchildren. Kiss them, spoil them, and then when they're all hyped up, you go home and sleep."

"How many grandchildren do you have, Detective Oliver?"

"Five . . . four boys and a little newborn girl. She's an oddball. I have three sons. We're over-loaded in the Y chromosome department."

"That's not too bad. I think boys are much easier than girls. At least that's been my experience. And you, Sergeant?"

"A daughter. She's in college."

Delia nodded and turned back to Oliver. "How old are your grandsons?"

"The oldest is going into high school. I don't know where the time has gone."

"It only gets worse the older you get. Time doesn't march, it does a steeplechase. I look in the mirror and I hardly recognize the face staring back at me."

It was a pleasant face, Marge thought. Kind brown eyes surrounded by skin that was a little smoother than it should have been. The plastic surgeon hadn't overdone it. "Thanks again for talking to us," Marge iterated. "We're trying to jump-start your late son-in-law's case."

"Poor Ben . . . what a gem he was. There wasn't anything that boy couldn't do. He was just so full of energy. We were all so . . ." A big sigh. "I was devastated. My husband was devastated. The kids were destroyed."

"And Melinda?" Marge asked.

The old woman's eyes were still far away. "Melinda?" They pulled back and focused in on Marge's face. "She fell apart, although she didn't need much of an excuse to do that. Melinda was always a delicate child. She was a beautiful little girl and because of that, she was indulged, mostly by her father. He just adored her. We've been estranged for a while. It's killing him."

"I'm sure it's hard on you as well," Marge said.

"I'm tougher than my husband." Her pained expression belied her bravado. "I understand her point of view, but she refuses to see our point of view. And no matter what we try to do or say, we're just mud in her eyes." The old woman was shaking her head. "But we just couldn't continue to fund her addiction."

"Were you aware of her gambling problem before Ben was murdered?"

"As soon as she turned twenty-one, we were both highly aware of it. So was Ben."

Marge said, "He married her even though he knew?"

"Melinda was very persistent. She chased him. Ben was very handsome and very charismatic. Why else would she go for a teacher? Melinda always wanted to marry money." A forced sigh. "Well, she got her wish with her second husband. I hope they're very happy."

"Do you like your current son-in-law?"

"I hardly know him!" Delia exclaimed. "It's all good and well. I adore Jared and Amy. We've very close."

"What about Nick?"

"I have nothing against Nick, but he's a little different. I've tried to get closer, but Nick has had his own problems. I send the children gifts at Christmas, and they write thank-you cards, but he doesn't call and I have to respect his privacy." Her voice dropped to a whisper. "We wouldn't have much in common, anyway, I don't think."

"I understand," Marge said, returning her whisper. "So Ben married your daughter even though she had a gambling problem."

"Yes."

"How'd he keep it in check?"

"With the purse strings. He watched her very carefully, and she didn't dare defy him. And he took her to Vegas every once in a while. It blew off a little bit of her steam."

"It didn't feed the addiction?"

"I suppose it did, but he was trying to be as kind as he could. As long as she couldn't touch the money, they were okay."

"What money? His?" Oliver asked.

"No, the money we put aside for Melinda. She had a trust fund. We had put in over a half-million dollars for her. It was for big things—a house, education, savings. Money that she might need as an adult, not money for the tables in Vegas."

"Of course," Marge said. "When was she to get the money?"

"It was in two stages. Half when she was twenty-five and half when she was thirty. But we could see the writing on the wall. It wasn't going to work." She lowered her head. "The trust provided us with a onetime spendthrift clause just for these kinds of problems. The clause meant we could take back the money from the trust and put it in our account at any time."

"I see where this is leading," Oliver said.

"She was furious. She threatened never to talk to us and that we'd never see our future grand-children." Delia's eyes welled up with tears. "It was a terrible scene! Thank God for Ben."

"What happened?"

Delia swallowed back a sob. "He offered us an alternative. We would give Melinda the money, but Ben would have full power to manage it."

Marge said, "And you didn't have a problem with having your son-in-law in charge of the money?"

"Whatever he'd do, it had to be better than what Melinda would have done. He promised to spend the money on things for the family—education for their future children; the boys weren't born yet. He said he'd use it for a life insurance policy and the occasional toy for the family like a boat or a car. He'd buy her jewelry so she felt like she would have something of her own. He promised that he'd manage her money and we could rest assured that it would be put to good use."

"And Melinda agreed to that?"

"It was either that or no money at all."

"So she agreed?"

"We had her put it in writing." She looked away and sighed. "And Ben, God bless him, kept his word. He consulted us with every purchase, even though he didn't have to. It was our idea to use it for the Mercedes. We wanted to reward him."

She hung her head.

"No one counted on him dying. Once he was gone, she ripped through all of it: their savings, her jewelry, the boat, the motor home, the cars, and his life insurance. It was just damn lucky that she couldn't touch the boys' educational funds.

She gave me this cock-and-bull story about hiring a private detective and that's where all the money went. For what she went through, she could have hired all of Pinkerton. It was so obvious, it was pathetic."

Marge said, "Maybe she was trying to save face."

"Or trying to get us to give her more money. We didn't fall for it. All of our financial support went for the care of the boys. We bought them clothing, we bought them computers, we paid for their health care, and we paid for their tuition to private schools. Each Christmas they got a box filled with the latest toys. Melinda got a five-hundred-dollar gift certificate to Saks."

"That's not too shabby," Marge said.

"Oh, but to her . . . she was seething, but what could she do? She couldn't support them on her own. She needed us."

"And after she remarried?"

"She dropped us like a hot potato." More tears. "After all we did for her, she just cut us off. And she wasn't much better to the boys. Lucky for us that they remained close . . . Jared did, anyway."

"And Nick?"

"As I said before, I'd be happy to welcome Nick into the fold. Nick and Jared talk a lot. Jared always makes sure to tell me that Nick says hi." She inhaled deeply and let it out. "You win some, you lose some. I'm closer to Jared than Melinda is . . . not that she cares much. Her true love is gambling. Mike is the best husband she'll ever find because he funds her. What does he care? He has millions. You think he'd give anything to his stepsons?"

Oliver said, "He doesn't share the wealth?"

Delia paused. "Actually, that's not fair. It could be that he has offered and they've refused." She wiped her eyes. "It's still such a shame. She's my only child. Of course, I love her. We love her. We'd love to have a relationship with her, but not if we have to be abused by her tantrums. I will no longer allow her to scream at us. I don't want to hear a litany of everything we've done wrong." She clasped her hands tightly. "God, I miss Ben. Please find out who did this."

"We're working hard on it," Oliver said.

Marge asked, "When the murder happened, what were some of the theories?"

"What do you mean? The police said it was a carjacking."

"I know that. But Ben was going home from a civic meeting. There were other people in the parking lot. How does a guy like that get carjacked?"

"I don't know, Sergeant," Delia said. "But a brand-new Mercedes might have attracted attention."

Oliver said, "Don't you think he would have noticed someone rushing up to the car. All he had to do was put his foot on the gas pedal and take off."

"Detective, sometimes you're just too close to notice things. I should have been suspicious when

Melinda wanted to learn poker from her father, but I just thought it was cute. I should have been suspicious when Mark taught her craps, but I just thought it was father-daughter bonding. I should have been suspicious the first time we took her to Vegas when she was twelve and she begged us to let her put a quarter in one of the slots. And we capitulated even though we could have gotten kicked out of the casino. I just thought she was enthusiastic. By the time I actually got a healthy dose of suspicion, it was too late. Maybe that's what happened to Bennett. By the time he actually noticed the monster, there was already a gun to his head."

Another late night. Decker pulled the car over a half block from home and made the call from there. He didn't want Rina to overhear because he knew what she'd say. He was prepared to leave a message and was surprised when Donatti answered. It was almost one in the morning back east.

"You're in bed."

"I wish. I haven't slept in twenty-four hours."

"Cut down on the uppers, Chris. They're bad for your liver, plus they'll turn your baby blues a nasty shade of red."

"What do you want now?"

"Rudy Banks is missing."

"And?"

"I thought you might be able to help out."

"Jesus, Decker, I barely know what's going on in my territory, let alone three thousand miles away. What do you expect me to do?"

"Just ask around, all right? We found blood in his apartment."

"Don't you have techs for that kind of thing?"

"Yes, we do. I think it's a crime scene, but I don't think it's Rudy's blood."

"If it's not Rudy, what do you care?"

"See, that's the problem. I do care. All you have to do is call up your ill-tempered producer friend Sal and have him ask around. At the very least, it would be handy to know if Banks is alive or dead."

"What am I getting out of it?"

"You get me as your father figure. Better than that demon seed who spawned you or the monster who raised you."

"It's true I haven't had luck with fathers. So why the fuck would I want you?"

"Because deep down, Chris, there's a little boy inside crying for help. Oh, wait. I forgot. Deep down inside, you're a stone-cold psychopath."

Donatti's comeback was to cut the line. Decker folded back his cell and stowed it in his pocket. He had a smile on his face.

25

Jared and Amy Little were home by 9:45. There were quick introductions, then Amy scurried upstairs while Delia woke her husband. The next fifteen minutes were devoted to Jared ushering his grandparents out of the door and walking them to their car. When he came back, he said, "Just give me a few minutes to change."

"Take your time." Oliver checked his watch. *Not too much time. It's already a little after ten.* When Jared was out of earshot, he turned to Marge. "What do you think?"

Marge said, "Delia's story explains Ben Little's toys."

"I could also see how the situation would build up resentment in Melinda."

"Man, ain't that the truth. His spending her money."

"In her mind, the agreement looked like collusion between Ben and her parents."

"Lots of resentment," Marge said. "But enough to murder?"

"I don't know," Oliver said. "I'm usually pretty good at reading women—for survival's sake—but Melinda's hard to decipher."

Marge said, "I'm just wondering how much Ben actually kept Melinda's gambling in check."

"I was thinking the same thing. What if Melinda was overspending, figuring that Ben would cover it with her own trust fund money? Then what if Ben suddenly cut off the access to their bank accounts? Did the resentment build to a breaking point? Or maybe she got herself in such a fix that Ben's life insurance policy was her only out."

"A life insurance policy is always a good motive for murder." Marge put her finger to her lips when she saw Jared bounding down the steps. The man had his mother's coloring—sandy blond hair and dark eyes—but his father's sharp features. He had changed into sweats and slippers. He plopped down on the couch and threw his head back. He closed his eyes and asked them how it went.

"Your grandmother was easy to talk to," Marge told him.

Oliver added, "Very forthright about everything."

He leaned forward, eyes open. "That means Mom, right? It's hard on Grandma . . . their estrangement. Did you get what you were after?"

Marge said, "The only thing we're after right

now is information . . . what was going in your parents' lives when your father was murdered."

"Also anything unusual going on in the marriage," Oliver said.

Marge said, "Sorry, but we needed to ask."

Jared said. "I was only thirteen. I paid way more attention to the Lakers than I did to my parents."

"If there's trouble, kids are astute about those kinds of things."

Oliver said, "And some parents make it obvious that things aren't going too well."

"Not mine," Jared countered. "I'm sure they argued, but they did it quietly."

"So as far as you know, things were peaceful?" Oliver asked. "It's important to the investigation."

Jared sat back in an armchair and directed a laser beam stare at Oliver. "It may be important to the investigation from your perspective, but the way I'm hearing things, it seems like you're implicating my mom."

Marge said, "No, that's not what we're doing."

Jared slowly turned his eyes in her direction. "Then explain it to me, Sergeant."

"I suppose I want to know if your mother was actively gambling. That could open up a lot of previously unconsidered avenues."

"Like my father's life insurance policy?" Jared snapped.

"I'd be lying if I said we're not thinking about that," Marge answered. "If your mother was gambling heavily, it would be a way to get hold of money. But I'm thinking more about some underworld figure going after your father because of your mother's unpaid debts. If I may be blunt, the murder was execution style."

Good cover, Dunn. Oliver chimed in. "Someone was trying to make a point. Like Sergeant Dunn said, sometimes kids hear things. Maybe you didn't because, like you said, they argued quietly. But we have to ask, Jared."

"It's a fifteen-year-old case," Marge said. "You were thirteen. You're not expected to remember everything."

"I can't even remember what I had for breakfast," Oliver said. "Anyway, if you want more neutral questions, can you remember anything about your dad that would have indicated he was worried or nervous about something?"

"My dad wasn't the nervous type. He was a doer."

"Yeah, that's why it would stand out if he was nervous."

"Well, he wasn't . . . not that I remember. Dad could always figure out a pathway of action. And if it didn't work, that was okay, too, as long as we learned from our mistakes."

"So as far as you saw it, nothing unusual was going on at the time?"

"No, I already told you that."

"Fine," Marge said. "Anything else you'd like to add that would help us along?"

Jared was still on the previous topic. "Did you ask Nick these questions?"

Oliver said, "I asked him some things. In light of what your grandmother said, I'll probably call him up again."

Marge said, "Maybe he'd remember more than you. He was older."

"Doubt it," Jared said softly. "Nick had a way of zoning out when . . ." He looked away.

"When what?" Marge asked. "When your parents fought? It's okay if they fought. It's okay if your father yelled. My father was a big yeller. He screamed more than he talked."

"My dad *rarely* raised his voice."

"I like the emphasis on the word *rarely*," Marge said. "So the couple of times he did raise his voice, I bet it made an impression on you."

"I have nothing to say to you."

Oliver shrugged. "It's certainly your prerogative not to talk."

Silence.

Marge stood up. "Jared, we've taken up enough of your time. Thanks for allowing us to come into your house and bring up painful topics."

Jared regarded her with suspicious eyes. "I went to law school. I did plenty of interrogation in my course work. By your line of questioning—the hit-and-miss quality—it's clear to me that you don't have a clue as to who did it."

Oliver smiled cryptically. "We have clues. Eventually we'll put them all together. And when we do, we'll have answers."

Marge held out her hand. "Good-night, Jared. Thanks again."

Jared waited a beat. "Are you going to be interviewing my mother again?"

"Most likely," Marge told him.

"So then you can ask her what they fought about."

"We already did," Oliver said. "Just like you, she said they rarely fought."

"More like they didn't fight at all," Marge said. "*That* I have a rough time believing."

Jared sighed. "It was money." Marge waited for more. "The *few* times I heard my parents arguing, it was about money. She was spending too much. And they weren't knock-down, blow-out rip-roaring fights. I just remember hearing my dad's voice in anger. And that was unusual."

"Thanks, Jared, for being candid."

"And isn't that what most couples fight about?" Jared said. "Money?"

"Money is definitely a flash point."

"Money as well as kids, the in-laws, and sex . . ." Jared shrugged. "I think you can sum up most of the flash points with those four topics."

Oliver said, "Money, the kids, sex, the in-laws, lack of attention, too much attention, not talking, talking too much, working too hard, not working hard enough, being a stick in the mud, being a good-time Charlie, being too risky, being too conservative, being too cultured, being a bore, being stuck-up, being white trash." He threw up his hands and gave him a pained smile. "My ex had an infinite list of topics to argue about."

The suit was clearly expensive. So were the shoes, the bag, and the jewelry. But the apparel just didn't sit right on the woman. The shoulders were too big, the purse was small, the skirt was too long, and the heels were too high. Now the jewelry . . .

The jewelry was nice.

She seemed lost. Marge wondered how she had gotten past the squad room secretary. She stood up from her desk and walked over. "Can I help you?"

"Help would be nice." Marge noticed that the woman's eyes had gone cold. "Originally, I came to see Captain Strapp."

"He's over on the other side of the building. I'll call his secretary and find out if he's in, if you want."

"Don't bother," the woman said. "He isn't. I'm not pleased." She reached in her clutch, pulled out a note, and gave it to Marge along with a hard stare. "I was told that this man was in charge?"

Marge read the note and glanced in the direction of Decker's office. "Uh, have a seat and I'll check to see if Lieutenant Decker's in."

"You're staring at an open door so it's obvious that he's in." She snapped her clutch shut. "It's good to know that someone is running the department. Apparently, your captain has an absentee problem."

Marge said, "Whom am I speaking to?"

"Genoa Greeves."

The name meant nothing to Marge. "If you'd just sit tight, Ms. Greeves, I'll go check if the lieutenant's in. Often his door is open, but he's somewhere else."

"Thank you." Genoa busied herself in the contents of her purse.

Decker was in. Marge said, "There's some weirdo named Genoa Greeves asking to speak with you."

"Genoa Greeves?" Decker stood up and put on his suit jacket. "Where is she?"

"In the squad room." Marge was taken aback. "Should that name register something?"

"She's the billionaire who reopened the Little case."

"Well, that explains the 'tude."

"Strapp will want part of this. You want to call him for me?"

"He's not in."

Decker made a face. "Not good. Find out where he is and get his ass over here ASAP. Otherwise, he's going be pi-issed." He spotted his target and walked over with an extended hand. She graced it with a two-fingered dead-fish shake. "I'm Lieutenant Decker, Ms. Greeves. I'm the one who's doing most of the work with the Little case. Let's talk in my office."

Genoa followed him. As Decker closed the door, she said, "Not much of an office. I hope that doesn't reflect your competence level."

Decker smiled as he pulled out a chair for her. "This is about as big as they make them around here. And I'm sure you didn't travel all this way just to talk architecture. What can I do for you?"

"Where's your captain?"

"I'm sure he'll be here momentarily. If you want to talk about progress on the case, you're better off talking to me."

"He shunted the case to you?"

"Captain Strapp is running the precinct. He did you a supreme favor by assigning the case to me. I've worked hundreds of homicides, and I'm much more familiar with handling cold cases."

"Are you good?"

"I'm terrific."

"When I googled you, it said you were a sergeant."

"I got promoted. That shows you how good I am."

"Do you have any suspects?"

"We call them people of interest. A few."

"And how far away are you from solving the murder?"

Decker regarded her. Expensive clothes, but they didn't sit properly. Her face was made up, but she was clearly not used to using cosmetics. Her hair was shoulder length and recently styled. It was her dark brown eyes that said it all. Cold, calculating, piercing. "I'm hoping weeks or months. It could be years."

"Or it could be never."

"Absolutely."

"Would offering individual bonuses for those who solve the murder increase the incentive to work harder?"

Decker thought a moment before he spoke. "Downtown L.A. is filled with cold cases. People just like Ben Little . . . shot down, killed, no one ever apprehended for the murder, no one brought to justice. There are thousands of grieving families that have no idea about the last minutes of their loved ones, no idea if the monster who killed their wives, their daughters, their husbands and sons is still out murdering others. If we had a lot more people, we could do more with those cases. But we don't have the manpower, so ninety-nine percent of the cold cases remain cold. That's just the way it works."

Genoa was annoyed. "I'm not here for a sob story, Lieutenant. Only results."

"And I'm not giving you a sob story, so please just hear me out. Normally, a cold case wouldn't be assigned to an active lieutenant running a detectives division. But for Dr. Little, I got word to do it personally because you've promised a large sum of money."

"If the case is solved."

"Exactly. If the case is solved." Decker paused. "Believe me, we can use money. I can use money.

And you can promise me more money if you want. And if I solve it, I'll take the money. I like money. But I swear to God, Ms. Greeves, I can't work any harder than I'm working on it already. And frankly, I don't need any kind of incentive. The solve is my incentive. I don't like unfinished business."

Genoa stared at him with steely eyes. "You're blowing me off."

"I'm telling you the truth."

"I bet you were a real bully when you were a kid."

"And I bet you don't know a thing about me, although you probably figured out that I played high school football because of my size. Would you like me to bring you up to date on the case? Maybe if I tell you a couple of things, you can even start remembering Ben Little and your past and help me out."

The woman held his stare, but then finally blinked. "All right." She made herself comfortable in the chair. "What do you have?"

"Would you like some water or coffee before I start? It may take a while. I'm sure you'll have questions."

"Water would be nice. Normally, I carry around a backpack with all my staples." She smoothed her skirt. "Normally I dress in jeans and a T-shirt. I don't know why, but I felt impelled to dress up for this occasion."

"Not for LAPD's sake, I hope." He gave her a

genuine smile. "It's been a long time since you've been back in Southern Cal."

"I hate it here. It's only bad memories." She regarded him neutrally. "You seem pretty sharp. I suppose I shouldn't be antagonizing you."

"I've had a lot worse. Honestly, I'm a pretty nice guy." He presented her with a plate of Rina's cookies. "Want one? Freshly baked by my wife."

"Your wife is the milk and cookies type?"

Decker laughed. "If only life were that simple. Help yourself. I'll get your water." When he had returned, she was on her second cookie. By the time Decker was just about done with his recitation, Strapp made his entrance. The captain appeared cool and collected, but Decker knew the man well enough to see the nervousness. Strapp held out his hand. "I'm sorry I missed you, Ms. Greeves. Next time, if you'll tell me when you're coming, I'll be sure to be here."

"That's precisely why I didn't tell you," Genoa answered. "I wanted to see what's going on before you had a chance to prepare for me. Your lieutenant here was just bringing me up to date. He's working hard but as of yet, it hasn't produced much. Maybe you could get him more help in locating Rudy Banks."

"I'll look into it," Strapp said.

But his eyes were blanks. The captain only had a vague notion as to what was going on with the case. He had no idea who Rudy Banks was or how he fit into the picture.

Decker said, "I was just explaining to Ms. Greeves that since we found blood in Mr. Banks's apartment, Hollywood had become interested in his disappearance."

"Because the place is in their division and because of the Ekerling case," Strapp ad-libbed.

"Exactly," Decker said. "I've contacted Ekerling's girlfriend. She had Primo's old toothbrush. We're in the process of extracting the DNA. But even if we find something, the case will probably go to Rip Garrett and Tito Diaz. They're the primaries on Ekerling."

Strapp nodded.

Genoa said, "And what about the thugs behind bars for the Ekerling case?"

Decker said, "They claim they're innocent of everything except the car theft."

"And what do you think?" Genoa asked.

"Honestly, I haven't decided yet. I'm looking into them, but I have to do it discreetly. Ekerling is not my official case."

"That's ridiculous. You people should be working together, not worried about territorial claims."

"It is ridiculous, but the structure was in place long before I arrived," Decker said. "We do what we can."

Genoa rolled her eyes. "Would it help if I promised Hollywood some financial incentive if they cooperate with you?"

Decker smiled. "As well intentioned as that

might seem, Ms. Greeves, it might build a little resentment. Would you mind if I tried it my way a little longer?"

Genoa shrugged. "Suit yourself." She stood up and faced Strapp. "I'll check back in a few weeks. I offered your division more money for a quicker solution, but your lieutenant claims to be working as hard as he can."

Strapp's eyes twitched. "I'm sure that's true."

"Also, I've had a chance to look at your computer system. It's a dinosaur."

"We get castoffs," Decker said.

"I'd like to redo your entire computer system. It would be good publicity for me, and it might even help you solve cases better."

"I'm sure it would," Decker said. "Any help you could give us would be terrific."

"Really appreciated," Strapp answered.

Genoa took out her sunglasses and put them on. "Your lieutenant seems to be a man of principle, Captain Strapp. In my dealings, that's very rare. The last man of principle I knew was Dr. Little. Look what happened to him."

26

Strapp scratched his head. "Whatever you did to calm her down, could you work your magic on the upstairs brass? They're riding my ass something fierce."

"Tell them that you got on her good side," Decker said. "And to underscore the point, you can point to the promise of a new computer system."

"They're not going to like the favoritism. You know how the politicos work."

"She makes an offer, we can't turn it down. It would hurt her feelings, and she might rescind her whole reward thing."

A hint of a smile. "Yeah, tough shit for them. Who the hell is Rudy Banks?" After Decker brought him up to date, Strapp said, "You need a couple of extra guys to hunt him down, I can do that."

"First, let me see if I can get a bead on Banks before you start allocating men."

"Keep me posted." Strapp waited a beat. "You handled Greeves well, Pete. If I need to interface with her in the future, I'll want you around." As the captain left, he almost collided with Marge and Oliver as they were walking into Decker's office. He looked them over. Oliver was in a blue suit and Marge wore dark slacks and a sweater. Appropriate, clean, functional . . . Strapp approved, although Oliver was always too much the dandy for his taste.

"Sir," Oliver said.

"Hello, Detective." A nod to Marge. "Sergeant."

They waited a few moments until Strapp had left the squad room. Then Marge said to Decker. "How'd it go with Genoa? Good, bad, neutral?"

"Good." Decker smiled. "She's going to redo our computers."

Oliver was impressed. "How'd you arrange that?"

"She offered." He pointed to some chairs. "What's up?" After Marge and Oliver recapped last night's conversations with Jared Little and Delia Defoe, he said, "What's the next step?"

Oliver said, "I got off the phone with Nick Little about ten minutes ago. He reacted almost identically to his brother. Yes, there had been occasional arguments between Mom and Dad, but what couple didn't argue? Unlike Jared, he was vague about the contents of their disagreements. It was clear that although he doesn't have much of a relationship with his mother, he's not about to implicate her in anything bad."

"Ben was in charge of her trust money," Marge explained. "That has to build resentment."

"Enough to murder?" Decker asked her.

"I don't know. Her mom said that she always wanted to marry money. Not only didn't she marry money, but the money she was promised wound up being controlled by her husband."

"If she did a murder for hire, the money had to come from somewhere," Decker said. "You say the bank accounts are clean."

"She blazed through her insurance policy," Oliver said. "We all think she gambled most of it away, but maybe some of it went to pay off debts for a job well done."

Decker said, "I still don't see what she had to gain by bumping him off. If she wanted money, she was better off keeping Ben alive. It was clear that her parents weren't going to give her control over her money. With her husband holding the purse strings, she had more of a chance of getting something out of the deal."

No one spoke.

Decker said, "Until we have more information about Melinda's personal spending habits at the time of the murder, let's not push too hard. Go over her finances again and get a clearer picture of where her insurance money went."

Oliver said, "I'll see what I can do."

Marge said, "What about Phil Shriner, Scott?"

Decker said, "I thought he told you that he didn't know her until after the murder."

"That's what *he* said," Marge told him. "Neither one of us saw him as entirely truthful."

Oliver said. "I still think they were boffing."

Marge shook her head. "That's the one thing I *don't* see. Melinda is just too . . . I don't know. He's so old for her."

"If you're desperate for money, Marge, your taste goes out the window." She conceded the point. "I'll try to set up an appointment with Shriner some time this week." He turned to Marge. "How busy are you?"

"I have a couple of court appearances, plus, I'm still hunting down Jervis Wenderhole. If I can't make it, go without me. It might even be better, talking to him man to man."

"All right. If necessary, I'll fly solo," Oliver told her. "Who's Jervis Wenderhole?"

"Arlington's bud," Decker said.

Marge said, "Actually, I think I found him. There was a gang counselor at the Lynnwood Youth Center by that name, but he doesn't work there anymore. The secretary has no idea where he went. I'm checking out youth centers."

"And you want to talk to him because . . ." Oliver said.

"Because I think Darnell Arlington is hiding things. If I can trip him up . . . find a link between him and Rudy Banks or Primo Ekerling, then maybe I can wrest the truth from the dude."

"Sounds like a plan." Decker checked his watch. "I'm off to Cal Vitton's memorial in Simi Valley.

Arnie Lamar gave me the rundown. He said he's coming along with some of the old-timers. Also, Shirley Redkin, the primary on Cal's suicide, will be there. Maybe she can fill me in on the latest coroner's report."

"Any relatives?" Marge asked.

"Cal's ex-wife is also coming, even though I heard from Lamar that their divorce was nasty. When Arnie spoke to her, he said that she sounded genuinely broken up."

Oliver thought about that for a moment. "I suppose my ex might even cry if I ate my gun."

"God forbid," Marge said.

Decker said, "Cal's sons are coming. The oldest, Freddie, is bringing in his family from Nashville. Cal Junior and his partner, Brady, are also going to make an appearance."

"Where's the shindig taking place?" Oliver asked.

"Church of the Good Shepherd, wherever that is." Decker checked his watch again. "I might need a few extra minutes to find the place. And who knows what the parking situation might be. It might be a bit of a crowd."

"Sounds like a full house," Marge said.

"I certainly hope so. It would be sad to hold a memorial and have no one show up."

The place was immense, built at a time when land was cheap and so were construction costs: hand-hewn stone façade, majestic ceilings, stained-glass windows, a pipe organ worthy of Bach. Cal Vitton couldn't have asked for better surroundings to make a final stand. Good Shepherd was nestled in the foothills surrounded by oak, sycamores, and eucalyptus. The wildflowers—poppies, lupines, daisies—were in bloom but withering fast as the days grew longer and the sun shone hotter.

About fifty people had shown up, huddled together at the front of the altar, leaving behind a sea of walnut pews. It was immediately clear to Decker, who had been to hundreds of funerals and memorials, that the minister hadn't known Cal. The eulogy seemed canned and impersonal—something from a clergymen's cheat book—but it was delivered with a stentorian voice. Afterward was open mike. Anyone who wanted to speak about Vitton could do so.

Freddie was first at bat. Slim and tan, he had dark curly hair, a round face, and soft features. His emotion seemed genuine, as he stopped several times to compose himself. He spoke about his father's work ethic, touched on his dad's sense of justice, and talked about his father's loyalty to his fellow officers.

Cal J went next: dry-eyed and stoic. He re-iterated many of his brother's themes, calling his father a great investigator, a tireless worker, and a constant pursuer of justice. The ex didn't speak, but several of his fellow cops did. Perhaps Arnie Lamar had the most to say and even that wasn't too much. All of Vitton's accolades dealt with

Suicide still is everyone's number one choice. But I'll keep my ears open for contrary evidence."

Decker said, "Maybe I should start thinking about what drove Cal Vitton to suicide rather than if it was a suicide or not. Thanks for your help, Detective Redkin. And if you do hear anything, please let me know."

"Not a problem." Shirley checked her watch. "As fun as it was, all good things must end." A smile. "See you later, Lieutenant. Or maybe not."

Decker watched her go, then stopped by the food table. He was grabbed by Arnie Lamar, who offered to introduce him to his group of retired detectives. In rapid succession, Decker met Chuck Breem, Allan Klays, Tim Tucker, and Marvin Oldenberg—men, like Arnie, with veined hands, liver spots, and varying degrees of baldness. Their eyes were still sharp, though, taking in everything, forever wary.

The first five minutes were spent listening to "the way it was back then." The next ten minutes consisted of war stories with the usual suspects— dealers, thugs, bums, pimps, and hookers. Decker had heard it all before and didn't make much of a pretense of being interested. He blatantly checked his watch, his eyes shifting between Freddie Vitton and younger brother, Cal J. Lamar took the hint.

"Hey, guys, I'm gonna introduce the big man to the boys," Lamar said. "Keep the meter running. I'll be back." He steered Decker toward Freddie and when the time was right made the introduction.

261

Vitton's eyes sized him up. "You were a friend of his?"

"No, I came to his house to talk about one of your father's old cases."

"Bennett Little," Lamar chimed in.

Vitton's eyes drifted. "Bennett Little. We all knew him as Dr. Ben. The one that got away. That's what Dad used to say."

"Did your father talk about the case a lot?"

"No, he didn't. He didn't talk much, period. It's not that I was estranged from my father, but we respected each other's privacy. We saw each other maybe once or twice a year for holidays: Thanksgiving, Christmas, and birthdays. Overall, and Arnie can back me up on this, Dad wasn't a chatty guy."

"One hundred percent," Lamar said.

"I gathered that from your eulogy," Decker said. "You spoke very well."

"Thank you. What new information did you have about Little?"

"Nothing," Lamar broke in.

Decker said, "Arnie, I think your friends are missing you. They keep making some obscene gestures behind your back."

"I get the hint," Lamar said. "See you in five, Freddie. We're still on for dinner?"

"Absolutely." The son turned to Decker. "I'm surprised Dad agreed to talk to you about Little. After he retired, he was through with police work."

"He didn't want to talk to me. I had to press him.

262

But he did agree to see me. That's why I was so surprised to find him . . . gone."

"Do you think there's a connection between your phone call and his death?" Freddie let out a soft chuckle. "Of course you do. Why else would you be bringing it up? Do you think Dad was murdered? Is that what you're saying? The death was ruled inconclusive. That means they're not sure, right?"

"It means he may have been murdered but they don't know for certain. I'm wondering if there's something about the Little case being reopened that might have driven him to suicide."

"What specifically were you trying to find out from my dad?"

"At that time, I was just gathering information. Since then I've come across a few things. Does the name Rudy Banks ring a bell?"

"Of course I know Rudy Banks. He's a con artist. He rips off everybody, and when they protest, he makes their life miserable and sues them. Everyone in the industry hates him. But I also have a personal vendetta. Rudy spent four years torturing my brother. If it hadn't been for Dr. Ben's intervention, I think Cal J would have killed himself."

Decker gave himself a moment to breathe in the information. He took out his notepad. "Torturing him because he was gay?"

"Of course. But also because Rudy could get away with it. Not when I was in North Valley. Rudy was a few classes behind me, and the one time he tried to bully my brother when I was around, I cleaned his clock. After that, he had to wait until I graduated to start his reign of terror. He's a shithead."

"He's missing," Decker said. "He moved out over the weekend and no one has heard from him since."

"He's not really missing then. He probably messed with the wrong people and now he's running away."

"Was he physically as well as verbally abusive with your brother?"

"He punched him, he kicked him, he shoved him, he tripped him: that was just the warm-up. I believe the most treacherous thing he ever did was throw acid on his lower back in PE."

"Jesus! Was he arrested?"

"My brother wouldn't press charges. Cal was lucky. He had turned around at the last moment. I think you can figure out where the acid was supposed to land."

"What did you father do about it?"

"Nothing, because my brother never told my father."

"Surely your father knew something was wrong."

"I'm sure he did, but Dad wasn't a person who delved into emotions. Even if Cal J said something, I could see my father telling him to 'take it like a man.'"

"There's a difference between exchanging punches and getting acid burns."

"You're right. Maybe Dad would have done something about it if he had known about that specific incident."

"Did your dad know that Rudy was bullying Cal?"

"Don't know. I found out about the acid incident after the fact. I came home from college break and saw the burned skin. My brother said he had an accident. When I pressed him, he told me the truth. I was ready to confront Banks and beat the shit out of him, but my brother begged me not to. He said that Dr. Ben was handling the situation. I respected Dr. Ben. Lucky for Rudy. Otherwise I would have sliced his balls off."

He was kneading his hands.

"Look, I know you're here to find out information, but please don't bring this up with Cal J. It took him forever to get over the trauma. Not only Rudy, but coming out to my father. He seems all right now. He's got a good job and a nice boyfriend. I don't want to see him in any more pain. I mean, who'd want to talk about that?"

Decker nodded. "I heard Rudy left high school in eleventh grade."

"He was expelled."

"Because of your brother?"

"That and probably a million other reasons."

"Who kicked him out? Dr. Ben?"

"Probably the entire administration. What does this have to do with my father's death?"

"I think Rudy's involved in Little's death, but I

can't figure out how or why. This is compounded by the fact that Rudy had been out of the school for at least five years before Little was murdered, so why would he wait so long to murder Little? Did your father ever suspect Rudy in the Little case?"

"My dad didn't discuss that case with me. I was gone by then. But if there had been a reason to arrest Rudy, I'm sure my father would have done it. He hated Rudy and not just because of Cal. Rudy was always getting into trouble."

Decker said, "So you're saying that Banks probably didn't have anything to do with the Little case. Otherwise your father would have arrested him right away."

"Maybe he suspected him, but he didn't have the evidence. All I'm saying is, if there had been evidence, Dad would have gone for the jugular. He hated Rudy."

"And Rudy hated your dad?"

"Rudy hated everyone."

"Including Ben Little?"

"Most certainly Ben Little. Little was always on his case, for good reason."

"The murder had the earmarks of a professional hit. Any way that Banks could have arranged it?"

"Sure. Banks used to run drugs in high school. He'd have a lot of access to unsavory people."

"Did he have money to pay for it?"

"When Little was murdered, the Doodoo Sluts had some big hits. He would have had money."

"I understand most of that money went up his nose or in his lungs. That's what one of his band-mates told me."

"I'm sure some of it did. I wouldn't know."

Decker's brain started clicking. "How do you know Rudy used to run drugs?"

"People I knew used to buy pot from him."

"Did you ever know a boy named Darnell Arlington?"

Vitton shook his head. "That name isn't familiar. Who is he?"

"He went to North Valley, but he's younger than you by a lot. He was one of the black kids voluntarily bused into the school. He was one of Ben Little's charity cases."

"Sorry. I never heard of him."

"He also ran drugs. Maybe he knew Rudy Banks. Was Rudy still pushing drugs after he graduated?"

"Honestly, Lieutenant, I don't know if he was or if he wasn't. I got the hell out of Dodge and never looked back."

27

Between the memorial and his impromptu meeting with Genoa Greeves *and* all of his other regular duties, Decker was a bundle of nerves; his mind was whirling with ideas and theories combined with worries about scheduling problems as the months marched into summer vacation time. When he reached home, all he wanted to do was strip his clothes off, take a hot shower, eat, and go to bed.

Rina, on the other hand, was dressed up—a short-sleeved pink sweater and a brown suede skirt. She had put on jewelry and makeup. But the tip-off was the kitchen. It was aroma free and dark.

"Hannah's sleeping over Aviva's. I thought we'd go out." She regarded him. "Or maybe I can whip something up."

"No, no, no." Decker managed a smile. "We'll go out, and we'll go somewhere nice."

Rina smiled back. "I made reservations in the city, but if that's too far, I can change it."

"No, I don't mind driving. I'll take a shower and then we can go."

"You're being a good sport about this. You really look tired."

"A good cabernet and a steak will wake me up."

"More like put you to sleep."

"Then you can drive home."

What woke Decker up was hearing about Rina's day—the kids, the school, her gardening, her latest seed acquisitions, a new dish she was planning on making for Shabbos, Hannah's choir practice, Sammy's applications to medical school. Decker enjoyed hearing the melody of her voice. He loved looking at her. He savored her touch as they held hands across the table. Being other-directed prevented his brain circuits from going into overload.

After working through a sushi roll appetizer, he realized that he was genuinely hungry. He ordered a thick-slab prime rib cooked on the bone and prepared medium rare and it went down very well. They passed on dessert but took their time sipping tea.

Rina eyed him through the steam of her chamomile. "What's new with you?"

"Nothing much."

"That's a fib."

"Yes, it is." Decker rubbed his forehead. "Well, this morning I was greeted by a spontaneous visit from Ms. Moneybags Genoa Greeves."

"The tech billionaire who got the ball rolling."

"In person. She proceeded to tell me that because my office was small, I was probably incompetent."

"No!"

Decker smiled. "Something along those lines. We spoke a little and she thawed—but only slightly. By the time we were through talking, she promised to update our computer system for free."

"The charmster at work, you sly fox, you. What did Strapp have to say about that?"

"He was as political as ever."

"Figures. How'd you get her to do that? I'm assuming it was you and not Strapp."

"That's correct. Honestly, I think she appreciated my candor. She tried to offer me money to solve the case, and I told her she could offer but it wouldn't help."

Rina chuckled. "You had to say that."

"Pretty moronic, huh?"

"You're a man of integrity."

"A man of stupidity."

"How was the memorial?"

"Sad."

"Did you find the information you needed?"

"I found out that Rudy Banks used to torture Cal Vitton's son."

"The music producer in Nashville."

"No, that's the older son. Banks used to bully the gay one."

"I didn't know Cal Vitton had a gay son. What did Rudy do to him?"

"Aside from the usual bullying, the worst thing Banks did was throw acid, aimed at the kid's genitals, but he missed and instead the acid landed on Cal Junior's back."

"That's monstrous!" Rina was aghast. "I hope he did some jail time."

"Nope. Nothing. Cal J never told his old man."

"But surely his dad knew something!"

Decker shrugged.

Rina was taken aback. "C'mon. When you found out about Sammy and Jacob, you were ready to tear the SOB apart!"

"Vitton is the 'walk like a man' type of guy."

"Acid on the *genitals*, Peter?"

"If Vitton would have known, I'm sure he would have arrested Banks."

"That poor boy—Cal J. How did he stand such humiliation and physical abuse?"

"I think Dr. Ben came to his rescue and Rudy was expelled."

"So Rudy had a reason to hate Little."

"True, but Little wasn't murdered until five years later."

Rina thought about that. "If Little got involved in Cal's welfare, he must have said something to his father."

"I'm sure he did. I'm sure that Cal Senior hated Rudy. He just didn't have enough of anything to arrest him."

"Acid on the genitals . . . how could *any* father stand for that?"

"I'm sure he didn't know, Rina."

"Talk about emasculation . . ." She thought a moment. "Did Vitton suspect his son was gay?"

"According to Lamar, Cal J hadn't come out in high school, but everyone knew."

"Is Cal really, really gay or just like . . . gay."

Decker smoothed his mustache. He knew she was asking the question for a reason. "Uh . . . he's not overly flamboyant, if that's what you mean. He was definitely effete, but I've known guys like that who are married. I didn't get a chance to say more than a couple of words to him. He's not leaving until Saturday. Maybe I can catch him tomorrow."

"What did Cal Senior think about his son being gay?"

"According to Lamar, he dealt with it by denying or not talking about it."

"Hmmm . . ."

"What does hmmm mean?"

"How should I put this?" She tried to organize her thoughts. "I once knew a very religious family. They lived in one of the ultra-Orthodox sections of Brooklyn. Anyway, the family had quite a few sons and one was gay. He died of AIDS. The mother was broken up . . . just devastated. As for the father . . . he couldn't wait to be done with shivah. I would have thought it was my imagination, but I wasn't the only one who noticed."

"I'm sure your perceptions are accurate."

"Maybe, maybe not. Now it could be that the

man had deep, deep feelings for his son, but he sure didn't show it. What he projected was being repelled by his son's makeup."

"Okay. So, yes, maybe Cal was repelled by his son's gayness, but I would bet that Cal Senior didn't want anybody beating up on his son."

"Of course not. I'm not saying that at all. If he would have found out about Rudy and the acid incident, I'm sure he would have arrested that jerk with glee. I'm just wondering . . . not that he approved of the bullying, not that he even knew the extent of it. Just like I'm saying that I'm sure the father didn't pray for his son to die of AIDS. Still, his reaction was blunted . . . something was off. And just like that father, I can't help but wonder if deep down inside, there wasn't a little part of Cal Senior that agreed with the gay-bashing sentiment."

The bottom of his morning coffee mug had just touched his desk when the intercom squawked. "Good morning, Lieutenant; a man named Liam O'Dell is here to see you."

A stroke of luck. He'd been meaning to call him, anyway.

"Thanks. You can send him in."

A minute later, the Mad Irishman was standing at his door. Over his shoulder stood a well-built Hispanic uniformed officer whose eyes were pinned on the back of O'Dell's neck. He said, "He didn't make it through the metal detector, obviously.

I patted him down for weapons, but didn't do a strip search. It's your call."

"Thank you, that won't be necessary." After the officer left, Decker said, "You're up early."

"I didn't go to sleep."

That could explain why he looked so bad—droopy red eyes, blotchy skin, in dire need of a shave and ripe to the nose.

"Banks is gone."

"Would you like a cup of coffee?"

O'Dell became agitated. "Did you hear me?" he yelled. *Banks is fuckin' gone!*"

Decker got up and closed the door. "Yes, I heard you and you better lower your voice or any second you'll be on the ground, spread-eagled, with your arms cuffed behind your back. Now sit down!"

O'Dell turned quiet and plunked his rear end on a chair.

"I repeat," Decker said. "Do you want some coffee?"

Liam nodded. "Thank you."

"No problem." Decker buzzed for another cup of coffee. "Banks moved out Saturday. I don't know where he went. We're looking for him. I was going to call you anyway, so I'm glad you dropped by. What are you so pissed about?"

"He owes me money. How am I ever going to get what rightfully belongs to me? Primo's gone. Ryan's as good as gone. I'm all alone in this now, and I can't even find the bastard. I'm screwed!"

"The voice, O'Dell."

"Sorry."

The coffee arrived. The caffeine paradoxically seemed to have a soothing effect. Decker said, "Why don't you just put out your own 'best of' album. If for no other reason, it might flush Banks out of the woodwork."

"Where the fuck am I going to get money for that? To do anything in this bloody business, you need a backer."

"I'm sure there are some Doodoo Sluts fans who might give you support. From what I understand, you had quite a crowd of admirers—male and female."

"That was a century ago, mate. Rudy took them all. He probably fucked them over." He took another gulp of the hot liquid. "I was really counting on the lawsuit. Not for me, but for Ryan. The guy lives like a junkyard dog."

"I know. I went to visit him. His brother's a doctor."

"He told you that?"

"About ten times."

"That sounds like Ryan."

"Does his brother help out?"

"He does . . . he's a good man, Barry is, but he can't afford to put Ryan in the kind of home he needs."

"Ryan said he was a lung doctor. They do pretty well."

"He works at a university."

"Aha." Decker sipped. "Any idea where Rudy

could have gone—a favorite club, a bar, a restaurant, a casino, maybe a massage parlor?"

"I'm in the dark, mate. I don't know where he went or who he hung with. Whenever I went to see him, I tried to pick him off at his apartment."

"Pick him off?"

"Y'know what I mean, mate."

"Who is Rudy's lawyer, O'Dell?"

"What?"

"Rudy's attorney. You're in a lawsuit with Banks. You have a lawyer. He must have a lawyer. Judging by the amount of lawsuits the guy generated, he probably has several lawyers."

"He usually did his own defending. He's a lawyer."

"He's got way too many suits to do it alone."

"I suppose I could call me lawyer about it."

"Please do." Decker handed him the phone.

"Now?"

It was a little after eight. Decker said, "Even if your lawyer isn't in, call and leave a message. If anyone knows where Rudy is, it would be his lawyer."

"His lawyer won't tell us, mate. Confidentiality."

"I know that. I'll deal with that later. For starts, I'd like to find out if Rudy's alive."

O'Dell made a tiny O with his mouth. "You think he's dead?"

"That's an open question."

"Nah, he's not dead." O'Dell brushed Decker off. "He's just runnin' from his creditors."

"Or from his dealers?"

Again, O'Dell paused. "That could be. Rudy used to deal, y'know."

"Yes, I found that out. I think he might have used a kid named Darnell Arlington as one of his runners. Back then, he was around sixteen—tall and black. Built like a basketball player."

"Name doesn't ring any bell in me head. I didn't buy the drug, Lieutenant. Rudy did. Rudy was the supplier for the band, the roadies, the girls, especially the girls."

"What kinds of drugs?"

"From pot to H and anything in between. When we weren't doing drugs, we were drinkin' by the fifth. I don't remember the kid, but I don't remember much from those days at all. Not even the girls. That's what really pisses me off. I don't even know if it was good or not."

"Where did Rudy get the money to buy the drugs?"

"Probably skimmed it from the band's profits. He was in charge of the money. We were idiots for letting him do it, but we were also too stoned to care."

"Ekerling seemed to be aware of things. How'd he let Rudy get away with handling the finances?"

"That's what broke us up, mate. The money. When Primo started getting sober, he realized what was going down. The more sober he got, the more he and Rudy fought. When Rudy left the band, the Sluts wasn't the Sluts. We tried to pick up the pieces, got a new lead vocalist, but it just didn't click. And the times were changing. Grunge was pickin' up and everyone wanted to sound like Kurt Cobain. I hate Seattle."

"Does the name Jervis Wenderhole sound familiar? His street name was A-Tack."

"Don't know him, mate, but I don't know everyone." He finished his coffee. "So you think that Rudy's dead?"

"He moved and we can't find him. That's all I know. Sure you don't have a clue about where he might be?"

"Rudy always talked about moving to Mexico . . . money's cheap and so are the women. That's what he used to say."

"Does he own property in Mexico?"

"I hope so. It would be something I could sell for cold hard cash."

"Liam, if you think of anywhere he might be . . . if you find him, please call me right away. I found some blood drips in his apartment. More than a cut finger's worth."

"Oh bloody hell!" O'Dell looked grave. "Is it Primo?"

"It wasn't Primo. He was O positive. The blood was B positive. There's a nameless body out there, and Banks knows something about it." Decker paused. "Was he mad at anyone specific?"

"No one specific, mate, just the world."

28

Decker handed Marge a slip of paper on which was written a name, an address, and a telephone number. "One of Rudy Banks's lawyers. Go over and find out if she's had contact with Rudy in the last few days."

Marge flipped hair out of her eyes. Dressed in blue slacks, a white shirt, and a cardigan sweater, she could have stepped out of a Ralph Lauren ad. The name on the note was Hillary Mackleby, and the address was in the city. "You can't find out this information by a phone call?"

"She's not going to tell us anything about Rudy because of confidentiality issues, but a clever detective will be able to interpret her facial expression once you tell her that he's been missing since Saturday. If she seems calm, he isn't missing. If she seems alarmed, then maybe he hasn't contacted her."

"Where is this place?"

"Wilshire between Crescent Heights and La Brea."

Marge sat down. "No problem. It's convenient, anyway. I have to go into the city. I've found Jervis Wenderhole."

"A-Tack."

"I found out why they called him that," Marge said. "His full name is Jervis Attarack Wenderhole. Attarack . . . A-Tack. Anyway we set up the appointment by phone tag. Since I'll be going into the city, I'll stop by the law offices and try to speak with Mackleby in person."

Oliver knocked on the open door, then stepped into the office, wearing a brown jacket, white shirt, and a gold tie. Marge looked at him. "You look like you're headed for Vegas."

"I'll take that as a compliment." He pulled out a chair and sat down. "How'd the memorial go?"

"Freddie Vitton was a wealth of information. Rudy Banks used to torture Vitton's younger brother, Cal Junior, when they were in school together. Banks went so far as to try to throw acid on his genitals—"

Marge said "Jesus" and Oliver said "Ouch" at the same time.

Oliver said, "What did Cal Senior do when he found out?"

"Apparently, Big Cal man never found out about the bullying," Decker said.

"C'mon." Marge looked up from her notepad. "He had to have known something."

"According to Freddie, he probably did know *something*, but Cal J never confided in his dad, so Cal Senior never did anything. Freddie did mention that his father hated Rudy and if Rudy would have been implicated in Little's death, Cal wouldn't have hesitated to haul him in. Rudy was a punk and had run-ins with the law."

"I don't buy that. Big Cal knew about it. A good parent knows when something's wrong."

"He wasn't a very good parent," Decker said.

Marge said, "But how would Freddie *know* that his father hated Rudy if Junior never mentioned the bullying to his dad? And if Cal Senior hated Rudy because he was a local punk, why would he be talking about Rudy to Freddie?"

"Good point," Decker said. "Freddie also told me that Ben Little was intervening on Cal J's behalf. Maybe that's why Cal Senior didn't intervene. And eventually the situation was taken care of. Rudy was expelled. Since Arnie Lamar said that Big Cal wasn't that comfortable with his son's homosexuality, I could see Cal Senior letting someone else deal with the situation."

Oliver said, "If Little expelled Banks, then Banks would have a reason to hate him."

"But Banks had been out of North Valley for five years," Marge told him. "He was already a punk rock star. Why would he wait so long to kill Little?"

Decker said, "Maybe he had finally amassed enough money to pay for the hit."

Marge was making diagrams. "Banks torments Cal J, Little expels Banks. Then Banks kills

Little . . . and then fifteen years later, Cal Senior commits suicide?"

"Oh, I spoke to Detective Shirley Redkin about suicide. The death was ruled inconclusive." When both detectives looked up, Decker explained, "Off the record, she thinks the ME wanted to keep the options open just in case other information came in."

The room was quiet for a moment. Oliver said, "Is it possible that Rudy found out about the reopening of the case and murdered Cal Senior?"

Decker shrugged.

Marge shook her head. "You know, we've never even interviewed Banks face-to-face."

"I talked to him."

"For how long?"

"About five minutes."

"I rest my case," Marge said. "We seem to be making him our convenient fall guy."

Oliver said, "His name keeps showing up."

"How about this?" Decker said. "Freddie also told me that Rudy used to be the drug dealer for the school. I just talked to Liam O'Dell and he said Rudy was the drug supplier for the group."

"Banks was a drug runner and Darnell was a drug runner," Oliver said. "That's how the two were connected. When Arlington was arrested for drug dealing, Ben Little found out about the operation. He somehow managed to sweep Arlington's arrest under the table because he liked Arlington, but he had no such love for Banks. He became a threat to Rudy's operation, so Banks had him murdered."

Marge said. "You're assuming that Rudy still worked North Valley when Darnell came to the school."

Oliver said, "The turf isn't that big, and Darnell would have been perfect for the job. Then Darnell got caught and Little became a threat. Rudy told Darnell to fix the situation. Now by then Darnell had moved away, but he still had friends. Maybe he hired one of his dawgs to do the shooting."

Decker looked skeptical. "Wenderhole and Josephson were interviewed. They had alibis."

Marge said, "And why didn't Vitton arrest Rudy if he suspected him of selling drugs?"

Oliver said, "He probably didn't have the evidence. Just like *we* don't have the evidence."

Marge held up a finger. "Or maybe Rudy had something on Cal Senior. Something big enough to make Cal Senior back off."

"Like what?" Oliver said. "That Cal J was gay?"

Decker said, "Freddie implied that even before Cal J came out, it was pretty clear that he was gay."

"It was common knowledge?" Marge asked.

Decker said. "I got the feeling it wasn't spoken about, but it kinda hovered over Cal Senior's consciousness."

"Have you spoken to Cal J?"

"I'm going to try to talk to him before he goes back to San Francisco. By the way, the blood I found in Banks's apartment doesn't match Ekerling."

Marge made a face. "So we've got *another* body to deal with?"

"I wish we had another body," Decker said. "All we have is blood drips. I have no idea who the blood belongs to or how old it is. When are you going to meet with Wenderhole?"

"This afternoon."

Oliver said, "If Darnell hired Wenderhole to ice Little, he's going to lawyer up. You're not going to get anything out of him."

Marge said, "I left messages that I wanted to talk to him about the Little case. If he was going to lawyer up, he had his chance. He agreed to meet with me. So I think our theory about Darnell hiring out his peeps is crap. Maybe it was Melinda Little who hired out. That insurance policy keeps tickling the back of my mind."

"You think Melinda hired Rudy to kill her husband?" Oliver said.

"Why are you so *obsessed* with Rudy?" Marge asked.

"Because he keeps lingering around like a bad fart."

"But we keep blaming everything on him. It's like the Democrats in '08. Every ill that had befallen the country—from terrorism to global warming—was George Bush's fault."

Oliver smiled. "Ooooh, she's getting all political!"

"I'm just saying Banks right now is easy

dumping ground. We need to consider other alternatives. And by the way, you should hear Will if you think I'm a fascist."

"But he's from Berkeley."

"Precisely why he's so right-wing."

"We'll know more once you've spoken to Wenderhole," Decker said. "Arlington had a known beef against Little. Let's see if we can explore that a little further. When you interview Wenderhole, make sure he doesn't feel threatened. Put the blame on Arlington if you have to."

"Agreed." She turned to Oliver. "Want to come with me?"

"Funny, I was going to ask you if you wanted to come with me this afternoon to interview Phil Shriner."

"Can't do it. We'll meet up later and exchange notes."

"Good idea," Decker added. "Maybe by that time I will have talked to Cal J."

Marge sighed. "So many suspects, so little time."

People never fail to surprise. Once there had been three teenaged thugs. Although it was true that Leroy Josephson had died from gunshot fire, the two remaining boys had turned the corner from back alley to upright. Darnell Arlington was a high school athletic coach, and Jervis Wenderhole was now on the government payroll as a gang counselor at a youth center in South Central. When Bennett Little was murdered, Wenderhole would have been around seventeen. That meant Wenderhole should be about thirty-two—a young man at the height of his strength.

If someone had told Marge that Jervis Wenderhole was fifty, she would have had no trouble believing it.

It could have been the wheelchair. Psychologically, people associated the apparatus with the aged. But it was more than just the confines of the steel chair. Wenderhole's bald crown was ringed with white, kinky curls. His deep-set eyes were dark and wary. His lips were pale; his mocha skin was blotched with white colorless patches. When Marge knocked on his open office door, he looked up, noticing her badge around her neck, and held up an index finger. He was talking to a tall teen who was clutching a basketball.

"I'll just wait outside until you're done." Marge slipped into the hallway and leaned against a faded yellow wall festooned with children's art. Somewhere there was an indoor gym reverberating with the sound of bouncing rubber, and mixed with the din was the pulsating thump of rap music. Marge had passed a TV room and a crafts room on the way in. Not a computer in sight.

The teen soon emerged, dribbling down the hallway. He turned left and disappeared. Marge showed her face in the door opening. Wenderhole was at his desk, writing some notes. Without looking up, he said, "Come in, Sergeant."

His wheelchair took up most of the space and

also served as his desk chair. No place for her to park her butt. She leaned against the wall. "Thanks for seeing me, Mr. Wenderhole."

"Jervis." He spun around and faced her. "Did you have a chance to look around?"

"Not much. Didn't want to disturb anyone."

"With all that racket going on I don't think anyone would notice." Wenderhole smiled. "What'd you think about what you saw?"

"I think that you're doing very well with limited resources."

The man nodded. "*Very* limited resources."

"My daughter goes to Cal Tech. She belongs to a group that reconditions old computers and gives them away to worthy organizations. Most of the time, we've been the recipients. LAPD is pretty barebones. But I can pass the word to her if you want."

"Thank you, Sergeant, but it won't do us much good. Anything we can't affix to the wall or floor winds up getting stolen. However, I wouldn't mind a laptop."

Marge smiled. "I'll let her know."

"Cal Tech . . ." Wenderhole shook his head. "She must be a genius."

"She is, but not thanks to me. She's adopted."

"Is she Asian?"

Marge paused before answering. "You assumed she's Asian because she goes to Cal Tech?"

Wenderhole smiled. "Racist, isn't it. Well?"

"Chinese. She was orphaned while a teen and I got lucky."

"Stereotypes come from somewhere." Wenderhole leaned back, his shoulders folding into his body. "Geographically, I haven't strayed too far from home. I was born about a half mile south of here. When I was a teen, the Los Angeles United School District had optional busing. The lottery put me at North Valley with Darnell Arlington and Leroy Josephson. We were a trio in misery—misplaced, mismanaged, and mistreated. After Darnell was relocated, Leroy and I didn't last too long. We both dropped out in tenth grade, but neither of us told our mothers because we knew a good deal when we saw one. Working in that white area, it was a whole lot easier to sell shit. We were the only show in town for a while."

"You sold drugs. So who was the supplier?"

"Darnell handled almost everything. Once he got caught—and moved away—Leroy and me were shipped back to the 'hood. Then Leroy was gunned down, and I was shot and paralyzed. I probably would have kept going if a bullet hadn't stopped me. I probably would have ended up like Leroy."

"How long did it take for you to make the transformation?"

"You mean from gangsta to solid citizen?" He thought a moment. "I've been doing this for seven years. Psychologically, it's taken me longer to adjust, and that's because I see myself in so many of the kids here."

Marge took out her notepad. "You said you were misplaced, mistreated, and . . ."

"Mismanaged."

"Yeah, mismanaged. No one tried to help you?"

"No one."

"What about Bennett Little? He seemed to have an outstretched hand."

Wenderhole stared at her. "Dr. Ben's project was Darnell, not me. I suppose I was hopeless in his eyes. Or . . . maybe he did try to help, but I didn't hear him—really hear him. His words were white noise."

"Why's that?"

"Because I was pissed off and on drugs. I didn't listen to my nana, my mother, my minister, my coach. I certainly wasn't gonna listen to no pissy-ass white boy." He smiled. "What a stupid jerk I was. Even with missing almost all of school, I scored almost 1100 on the SAT. If I'd been born a different color in a different area, I would have been a lawyer or a psychologist."

"There's still time," Marge said.

Wenderhole was taken aback. "Yes, you're right about that. I'm still making excuses. Patterns die hard."

"So you didn't have much to do with Dr. Ben?"

"I didn't have anything to do with anyone in North Valley. I only stepped inside a classroom when it rained because it was too wet and cold to hang. You know how often it rains in L.A., so you now know how often I was physically in school."

"What do you remember about Dr. Ben's death?"

"I was wondering when I'd have this conversation. I thought he might come up as soon as I heard about Primo Ekerling."

Stunned, Marge tried not to stare. "You know Primo Ekerling?"

Wenderhole scratched his stubble. "Close the door. I got a story to tell you."

29

Dressed in white pants, a yellow polo shirt, and a brimmed cap, Phil Shriner had just finished with his power walk around the grounds of his retirement home when he found Oliver waiting for him in front of bungalow 58. Inside, the space was still claustrophobic with furniture, although some of the hardwood floor was peeking through. Shriner took a pitcher of lemonade from the refrigerator and poured two glasses' worth. He opened the patio door, went outside, and leaned over the railing. Oliver stood next to him and Shriner handed him a glass. The retired detective's backyard overlooked the number 6 fairway. He checked his watch. "I'm due to tee off in a half hour."

Oliver sipped the lemonade. "But I told you this might take some time."

"I don't have anything to add beyond our first encounter. I don't know why you bothered coming out at all."

"Then I'll make it quick," Oliver said. "I think you're lying to me about Melinda Little."

Shriner's head snapped back. "Well, that was blunt. So I'll be blunt back. Frankly, I don't care what you think."

"C'mon, Phil. You know how it works. You don't want to make it hard on yourself. Just be straight and I'll leave you alone."

He stared at Oliver. "What's your problem? You're getting nowhere, so you're bugging people to see what drops?"

"Okay. Let me get this out. I think that Melinda Little's gambling problem predated her husband's death. She was flushing money down the toilet way before the murder. We suspect that you knew that, too."

"Maybe I suspected it, but I didn't know it. And why would that matter?"

"Because, Phil, if she was heavily in debt before the murder, she might have viewed Bennett Little's insurance policy as a ticket out."

"I wouldn't know. I told you I met her after her husband died."

"We have witnesses that put you two together before Little was murdered," Oliver fibbed.

"Then your witnesses are lying. I met her after her husband was already dead." Shriner gave him a steely glare. "She had been gambling heavily, and I gave her a shoulder to cry on. She was desperate and I was rock bottom. I joined Gamblers Anonymous first and convinced her to come to a meeting. That's the extent of our relationship. One forged in misery."

"So tell me again about this scheme you cooked up because she spent the insurance money."

"We're mining old territory."

"Indulge me."

Shriner finished the lemonade and put the glass on a patio table. "Melinda had blown most of the insurance money from her husband at the casinos."

"What was her choice of poison?"

"The card tables. She resisted joining GA because, like most addicts, she was convinced that she had it under control. It took a lot of prodding on my part, but she agreed to accompany me to a meeting. Then she went to another . . . and another. Soon she realized the extent of her problem. The money was almost gone and if she didn't get it together, she'd be destitute. She needed to borrow money to tide her over until some bond interest came due, and her parents were the only ones who wouldn't do a credit check."

"But they knew she had the insurance money."

"Exactly the point. She *couldn't* tell them the truth about her gambling. She felt they wouldn't understand her psychological state."

"Or maybe they were tired of giving her their hard-earned money."

"That's why she was petrified to face them. She told me that if she admitted her gambling to her parents, they'd try to take away the kids. So she asked me if I could think of something to help her out."

"So you lied for her."

"Not completely. I said she could tell her parents that she spent the insurance money on a private detective. I'd back up her story."

"Did they call?"

"Of course. I could tell that they liked Ben. Money spent for the case would be acceptable."

"What did you say?"

"That I was looking into the case and was in contact with the detectives. They accepted that."

Oliver said, "According to Melinda's mom, she knew it was not."

"Then she didn't let on to me."

"Which detective did you speak with?"

"Arnie Lamar. Both he and his partner thought it was a carjacking. He also told me they suspected Darnell Arlington but couldn't pin it on him because he had an ironclad alibi. That's why I called Darnell up. And like I told you the first time, he seemed broken up about Little's death."

"Why did Lamar suspect Arlington if the kid had an alibi?"

"Because Arlington was a black kid and had a beef against Little. For a while, he and his partner were working on the assumption that Arlington got one of his friends to do it, but that went nowhere. Arlington didn't seem to have much contact with his friends once he moved, and he certainly didn't have any hit money to do the payoff."

"Maybe they did it as a favor."

"Lamar said that according to the phone records, there wasn't a lot of back and forth contact between Arlington and his old friends. Maybe Darnell kept in communication by carrier pigeon, but I didn't have any way of exploring that option." He checked his watch again. "Oliver, things were cold when I stepped in. And while I'm a good detective, I don't like to work for pennies. I wrote up a report and covered her butt so that she could save face with her parents."

"And you two were never sexually involved?"

"She wasn't interested in me, and I didn't want to push it. I was separated from my wife at the time, so it wasn't a moral thing. I suppose I didn't think it was a good idea for two gamblers to hook up even temporarily. Also, it would have destroyed any chance of reconciliation with my wife. For once, I was trying to act smart."

He sighed and looked longingly at the golf course.

"I'd really like to catch that game."

Oliver ignored him. "Let me ask you this, Shriner. If you knew that Melinda had been gambling all through her marriage and was in debt, do you think that she, in her darkest hour of despair, would kill for insurance money?"

"She didn't kill him."

"How can you be so sure?"

"Because I know, Oliver. We were in GA together for over a year. You admit a lot of things to yourself and to the group. You get to know people pretty damn well."

"She wouldn't admit to murder."

Shriner came in from the patio, went into the closet, and took out a bag of golf clubs. "I'm not saying she was an angel. She probably wasn't a very good mother. She probably wasn't a particularly good wife. She probably drank too much and maybe she ran around a little, but I don't think she's a murderer."

"*Ran around* a little?" Oliver let go of a smile. "Why would you think she was loose if you two didn't fuck?"

Shriner's face grew pink. "She wasn't loose. I don't know why I said it."

"What is it? Did she come on to you?"

"You think I'd turn her down?"

"I don't know. Maybe you would."

"I gotta go."

Then it dawned on Oliver. "She admitted things in Gamblers Anonymous. That's part of the program, to admit your past mistakes. Things like having an affair. So if she didn't fuck you, who'd she fuck?"

"You know I can't divulge confidences."

"Shriner, I'm trying to solve a murder."

"I can't divulge confidences!"

"Okay, don't tell me who she fucked. Just give me a list of possible names."

"No—"

"Just a first name. How about that?"

"Oliver, give me a break. I can't divulge confidences. And if you go to her and tell her that I told you about an affair, I'll sue your ass off."

"Did she have an affair with one of Little's students? Sometimes women get a kick out of that. Sticking one to the old man who had time for everyone except the wife. Did she have an affair with Darnell Arlington?"

"Oh, Christ, Oliver, the kid was seventeen when he left."

"And a seventeen-year-old can't get a hard-on? There are teachers getting it on with twelve-year-olds. Seventeen is practically legal. And probably a lot better than her old man, right? Maybe that's why Little had him expelled."

"You have an evil mind. She didn't fuck Arlington. I'll tell you that much."

"How about a *former* North Valley student. He would have been about twenty-one or twenty-two at the time of Little's death. Does the name Rudy Banks ring a bell?" And there it was . . . that millisecond pause. Oliver clapped his hands. "Holy shit, it *was* Rudy."

"I'm leaving now."

"He's missing by the way—Rudy is."

That stopped Shriner for a moment. "What do you mean?"

"He moved out of his apartment last Saturday."

"So he moved. That doesn't mean he's missing."

"We can't find him, there's no forwarding address, and the neighbors never saw him with the movers. Plus we found blood in his apartment."

Shriner grimaced slightly. "I can't help you there. I haven't thought about Banks in years."

"But you thought about him at one time. Did you ever consider him a suspect in Little's murder?"

"I can't say anything."

"We're not talking about Melinda Little, we're talking about Rudy Banks. Did you ever consider him a suspect in Bennett Little's murder?"

He sighed. "His name came up."

"And?"

"That's it. I mentioned him to the police. I'm not in the business of solving murders. I'm in the business of passing along information to cops who are supposed to be solving murders. If they don't choose to act on it, there's nothing I can do about it."

"Why did you mention him to the police? What made you consider him a suspect?"

"I can't get into that without breaking confidences."

"Do you know what Banks had against Little?"

"Banks felt Little had disrespected him, but Rudy felt everyone disrespected him."

"You told your suspicions to Arnie Lamar?"

"No, Lamar wasn't in. It was the other one."

"Calvin Vitton?"

"That's the one."

"And you never followed up on it?"

"No, I never followed up on it. I am not in a position to arrest anyone. If the police didn't think he was worth looking into, who am I to step on toes."

"All right," Oliver tried to contain his anger. "You can't solve everyone's problems, But why didn't you tell me that you suspected Rudy Banks?"

"You never asked."

The travel brochure featured an inland cruise to Alaska: seven days of sailing and port stops leaving from Vancouver, British Columbia, and ending up in Anchorage. Cindy said, "The best part is that it goes from Sunday to Sunday so Shabbat isn't a problem."

Decker skimmed the information.

It was Cindy's day off, and when she called to get together, it came at an opportune time. Cal Junior had canceled their appointment, deciding that Los Angeles was too much for him and he was too emotional to talk, anyway. If Decker wanted to talk to him next week, he'd probably be calm enough for a conversation. And while what Cal J said was probably true, Decker suspected that Freddie Vitton had had a long talk with his brother, steering him away from the interview.

Win some, lose some. In the meantime, he was

sitting with his beautiful daughter at a local café not too far from the station house, sneaking glances at Cindy with her flaming hair bundled up in a scrunchie. A few loose strands blew in her face and she kept sweeping them away with graceful fingers. She wore jeans and a green T-shirt. Since she hadn't put on makeup, her face was splattered with freckles.

He smiled. "It sounds great. When were you planning on making the voyage?"

"Last week in August. Oddly enough, that's your vacation time, too." Decker was silent. "Didn't you say something about always wanting to go to Alaska?"

"Don't recall it."

"Doesn't it sound like a fabulous trip?"

"I told you, it sounds great."

"And the problem is?"

"We need kosher food."

"Dad, I've talked to the people in charge. There are always plenty of fresh fruits, vegetables, and vegetarian entrées."

"Rina doesn't eat cooked food, Cindy, unless it's kosher."

"They always have tuna salad and egg salad. Plus they're happy to supply new plates and cutlery. They even said it isn't a problem to buy a new set of knives for our family and cut up a whole salmon just for us. They'll cook it in foil or buy a new sauté pan. Dealing with kosher food is nothing they haven't done before. They get vegetarians, they get Muslims only eating halal, they get kosher, they get low salt, low fat, diabetic, high blood pressure. They work with hundreds of people with dozens of dietary needs. Plus, you have the option of TV kosher dinners—"

"That sounds charming."

"It's a cruise, Daddy. Food is never a problem. And when all else fails, there's always ice cream."

She was probably right. Besides, dietary restrictions weren't a bad way to control the gluttony. He had heard that people gain massive poundage on these kinds of jaunts. "Let me talk to Rina."

"I already have."

Decker made a face. "Thank you for running my life."

"I called just to ask her if it was even feasible. Once she said it was feasible, she told me to talk to you." Cindy lifted her cappuccino. "Hence, my presence."

"I think Sammy and Jacob will be home that week."

"Great. You know how much the boys love Koby."

Decker was already looking at the rates. "This is going to cost a fortune. There are seven adults."

"Only five. Koby has agreed to work in exchange for our fare."

"That doesn't seem very equitable. Our playing while he's working."

"It was totally his decision and we're going whether you go or not. It's something we both want to do. I'm asking you to come along, not to wangle money out of your pocket, but because we'd really love to do this as a family. Last year, Mom and Alan took us to Mexico for a week. We had so much fun that I thought I'd like to do it with your side. Alaska seems like your kind of place, Daddy. And look at all the excursions we could do when we go to port."

Decker started reading, and despite his reticence, he became excited. Among the activities listed were canoeing, white-water rafting, hiking, kayaking, salmon fishing, panning for gold, and taking a helicopter ride to a glacier. And then he noticed the fine print. Optional excursions were not included in the price of the cruise.

Well, he didn't have to do *every* activity.

"What did Rina say when you broached this with her?"

"I told you. She said she was game, but of course it was up to you."

Decker thought a moment. They never went anywhere when he had vacation time, other than to visit the boys back east. If the kitchen was willing to make accommodations, it sounded like a good thing to him. Unpack once and enjoy the open seas, even if the average age was probably around seventy.

Seventy didn't seem that old anymore.

Mostly he felt extremely touched that his daughter wanted to include him in her vacation plans. This was the dream of most parents: relaxing

302

and laughing with adult children. "This seems like something I could get behind."

Cindy's smile was radiant. "You're considering it?"

Decker laughed. "Is that so unusual?"

"Yes. Usually when I suggest something, it just . . . I don't know. It never works out. I'm so happy!"

"First I have to talk it over with Rina. Then I have to check my schedule again. Then we have to deal with the boys. I'll try to make it happen, Cindy. It actually seems like something that everyone could enjoy. And I'll pay for you two. It isn't going to send me to the poorhouse."

"Absolutely not. Koby would never agree to it. But if you want to pay for the helicopter ride so we can walk on the glacier, I won't object."

Decker raised his espresso to his lips. "This was an expensive cup of coffee."

Cindy reached into her pocketbook and took out several pieces of paper. "You didn't think I came all this distance just to talk you into going to Alaska."

That's exactly what he thought. "What do you have?"

"I've been doing a little background check on Travis Martel and Geraldo Perry."

"With or without Rip Garrett's permission?"

"I didn't ask for his blessing, but if he found out, I wouldn't care. Both of the boys have a long sheet: drug offense, theft, B and Es, D and Ds, GTA, soliciting, illegal possession of firearms." She looked at one of the pieces of paper. "Here you go. For your files."

"Thanks." He already had them, but why make her feel bad.

"I've also done a little bit of investigating beyond the obvious. Perry is from Indiana, so I don't know too much about his youth, but Martel is a local boy. He went to L.A. High for about a year before he dropped out. I found his yearbook. He was in the rappers' club."

"They have a rappers' club in high school?"

"Clubs are a reflection of the student body's interests. All you need is a sponsor and some kids for membership. Anyway, his being in a rappers' club makes total sense because when Martel was booked, he listed his occupation was 'aspiring rapper.'"

"As in he's never made a record."

"That's not entirely true, and we really don't say 'made a record' anymore, Daddy. It kinda sounds like classic vinyl."

"Cut a CD?"

"These days you don't need a label and a producer to get your song out, since you have the Internet. Do you know about MySpace?"

"It's a networking website."

"Exactly. It's actually a social networking website as opposed to a professional one. One of the things it's known for is sharing material. Anyone who has a MySpace account can surf and look at your websites unless he or she is specifically blocked. Lots of bands and singers without contracts use MySpace to showcase their material. It's specifically geared toward downloading music. So I started surfing to see if either Perry or Martel had a profile."

"And you found something."

"I wouldn't be here if I didn't." She turned pink. "I mean, I love spending time with you, but I know you're busy and I don't like to bother you—"

"You're never a bother. What did you find?"

"Travis has a MyFace profile under his nom de rap." She looked down at her notes. "He has several of them: Rated-X. Travis-X, X Marks the Spot, or plain X. I downloaded whatever songs he uploaded. I thought maybe there's something in his lyrics that I would find interesting. He's really hard to understand. It took me a long time and slowing down the speed to get them all down."

She handed him several pieces of paper.

"Look at number three, second paragraph: 'All Bets Are Off.'"

"Which one?"

"'All Bets Are Off': paragraph three."

Decker read the doggerel to himself.

Take it all, take it all, that's my philoso-phy
This whole fuckin' world ain't got integri-ty
So mess up the ho' with the beasti-al-ity
It's me for all and it's all for me
Like music and the crime—the shit of B and E
You grab it for yourself and fuck etern-ity.

"Charming. What am I looking for?"

"Look at line five, Daddy. Like the music and the crime—the shit of B and E. Not just the crime of B and E. The *music* and the crime—the shit of B and E. Maybe I'm reading too much into it because I want to, but maybe he's not just talking about breaking and entering."

Decker said, "Banks and Ekerling."

"Maybe you should see Marilyn Eustis again."

"She knows that Travis Martel and Geraldo Perry were arrested for the murder. She told police she didn't know either one of them."

"Maybe she doesn't know them, but it could be that there's something in Ekerling's files about them."

"I'm sure the police went over his files. Besides, from what she told me, Ekerling didn't produce a lot of rap." Decker regarded the rap words again. "But it is worth another look. Thanks for the tip. Did you relay this information to Garrett and Diaz?"

"Not yet. I didn't want to step on anyone's toes, especially because you seem to be doing a good job of that. Besides, you're the one investigating homicides. Me? I'm a peon in GTA. And maybe B and E is just breaking and entering. Still, I'm passing it on to you. If you want to pursue it, fine."

Decker said, "It's worth a second look."

"That's what I thought. If it goes anywhere, you can pass it on to Garrett and Diaz so there won't be any hard feelings."

"Absolutely. Thanks, Cynthia, you're thinking like a pro."

"You're welcome. Let's hope when you pass the information to Rip Garrett and Tito Diaz, they feel like you do and thank me as well. When it comes to promotion time, let's hope they think of my ingenu-ity."

30

Wenderhole stroked the arms of his wheelchair.

"I know that someone was trying to do good by busing me into a white school, but there's a lot more to school than education. Darnell, Leroy, and I were tight, but it wasn't that we had so much in common. It was more like if we didn't hang together, we'd sink alone. When Darnell was caught dealing and shipped away to Ohio, it was down to Leroy and me and a couple of other flunkies. Darnell was hard to replace. Leroy was a nice kid, but frankly put, he was as dumb as a rock.

"As dropouts, we had no work ethic. We didn't have a lot of opportunities, either. We never saw education as a way out. That's what I try to teach the kids. You have options. If a washout like me in a wheelchair can earn his keep, think what you can do."

"It's a good message."

"If it gets through—and that's the problem. It's

just words to these kids, same as when I was growing up. They don't see education as a way out, either. It's either sink alone or gangs, and gangs mean running drugs. Nothing's changed. That's what we did. Run drugs for the white boy when we weren't trying to break in as rappers."

"You were A-Tack," Marge threw out. "Leroy was Jo-King."

Wenderhole laughed. "You've done some research."

"I like to come prepared."

"Leroy was Jo-King at first, then it became Yo-King." He smiled. "One day Leroy comes to us all puffed up after going to French class on a rainy day. He found out that Leroy came from Le Roi. That's how he became Jo-King."

"I didn't find anything for Yo-King. I've heard that you cut a couple of demos."

Wenderhole said, "I'm getting to that. This is a story. You've got to have patience."

"I'm all ears."

"Okay . . . in answer to your question, I did cut a few demos under A-Tack, but that wasn't until later. Back then we were thugs—legends in our own minds. While we were waiting to be discovered, we had to eat and we needed pocket money, so we sold to the neighborhood white boys who fed our delusions by thinking we was real cool. Darnell was the front man because he had the best social skills. He also had pipes, so if anyone was gonna make it in the music business, it would be Darnell. He said that he knew all these hotshot rock stars and producers and we should form a rap group. Not that Darnell really wanted a group—he's a solo man if ever there was one—but he needed me."

He took a breath.

"Darnell had the most talent, but I wrote the songs. Back then if you rapped it, you wrote it. Nowadays, these corporate producers have scores of people writing rap undercover for the bros. It's all soulless and it's all shit. Empty words 'bout bling and sex and hos and money because the shit is made to sell to whites. Nothing about social issues anymore. Whitey didn't like NWA, but they touched core issues in the community."

Marge just nodded.

"Like you care." He didn't try to hide his disdain. "I'm boring you."

"No, you're not and I do care," Marge retorted. "Every day that I work I'm acutely aware that there are victims who can't talk for themselves. I wouldn't be a homicide detective if all I wanted to do was bust heads. Right now my victim is Bennett Little and that's why I'm here. Did you ever record with Darnell?"

"I'm getting to that. Y'see, Darnell kept asking me to write stuff to show to the producers."

"Where'd he meet these producers?"

"I suppose he met them while running drugs, but I couldn't swear to it. He was higher up the ladder than Leroy and me. I never really swallowed the fantasy, and I was shocked when Darnell came through."

"Primo Ekerling."

He rolled his eyes. "Not yet, no."

"Sorry. I'll wait my turn."

He smiled. "Like I said, Darnell came through. We got some studio time to cut a couple of demos, but that was as far as we went because Darnell got busted and they shipped him off to Ohio."

"Who produced the demos?" Marge asked.

"We didn't have a producer, just an engineer who recorded the vocal track. We did some stuff together, and we did some stuff individually. He told us the percussion and instrumentation would be added later. It never went that far. After Darnell got busted, Leroy and I were sent back to the 'hood, and I spent most of our time getting stoned."

His eyes drifted from Marge's face.

"It was weird to be back. When you're black and poor and hopeless, you don't make plans, Sergeant. You don't see a future. You just go with the flow and that's what I did. But Leroy, dumb ole Leroy, he was the one who kept pushing for the fantasy. He kept knocking on doors, the crazy fool. I told Leroy to forget about the tapes, but he wouldn't give up. Then one day, I get this call . . ."

Wenderhole looked down.

"It's from Leroy and he don't sound so good."

Marge nodded.

"He don't sound so good emotionally, but I was

311

also having a hard time hearing him. He was talking on a cell phone, and fifteen years ago, cell phones weren't what they are now. They were also really expensive. The only ones who had them were doctors and dealers."

"That's true."

"He had to call back a few times because the static was real bad and the call kept getting dropped. It was about nine or ten in the evening. He asked me . . . could I come pick him up and take him home. I asked him where he was. He told me Clearwater Park."

Marge's heart started slamming against her chest. "I see . . ."

"Yeah, we all see it now, but this was after the fact. I asked him what he was doing there. He said he had business. I asked him what kind of business. He said he'd tell me when I picked him up. I told him I didn't have a car and I wasn't about to drive twenty-five miles out to the Valley to get his sorry ass back where it should be."

"What did he say?"

"He started crying. That's when I knew something nasty had happened."

"Did you go?"

"Of course. I wasn't going to leave him in a bad situation. I didn't have a car, so I boosted my neighbor's Chevy. I figured I'd have it back before the old woman woke up. I drove the freeway out there, hoping that along the way, I wouldn't run into a cop itching to crack a black head. The good

Lord was with me. I made it to the park in record time and without any incidents.

"The place was deserted. The streets were deserted. The park is a big one, and there were spots where it was as dark as sin. It was just lucky that I found Leroy 'cause he was sitting on a bench. He was shaking and I could tell he was really scared about something. I asked him what happened. He pulled out some cash . . . a couple hundred bucks, which was a fortune of money. I asked him how he got it."

"What he'd say?"

"Dealing . . . he said he got it dealing."

"And what did you think?"

"I thought he got it dealing, but not by regular dealing. My first thought was that the fool ripped off a dealer. I got to tell you, I was scared shitless because as we left the area, I started seeing cop cars. One was enough to give me the shakes. Then I counted two and three." His eyes got wide. "I drove out of the area taking side streets with my headlights off."

"Again you were lucky."

"Don't think I don't know it. It wasn't until a couple of days later that I heard about Dr. Little. I wasn't in school no more, so I didn't get the lowdown until after the fact—the carjacking and the Mercedes being left at Clearwater Park. Leroy was in big trouble, and I was probably in trouble by extension. We met and we got a story together in case the cops came to us."

"And you never asked him what happened?"

"I didn't want to know, especially if the cops were coming after me and they was gonna give me a lie detector test . . . I wanted to pass."

"So what was your story for the cops?"

"We'd be each other's alibi. Before I left to pick up Leroy, my mom asked me where I was going. I told her to hang out with Leroy. She was talking to the minister and he heard me say it. She'd never imagine that I traveled twenty-five miles to pick up Leroy. I didn't have a car. Leroy didn't have a car. And why would we be there? Besides, why would we hurt Dr. Ben? We were never his special boys like Darnell. In North Valley High, we were invisible."

"But you were interviewed about the murder."

"Yeah, of course. Because of Darnell and the drug charges and we were his friends and were black. No one could believe that a white boy would hurt Dr. Ben. I was interviewed by some white cop named Vitton who came to my house. He talked to me. He talked to my mom. He talked to my minister. After that, he never spoke to me again."

"And Leroy?"

"His grandmother said that Leroy and me was home with her. She must have been about ninety at the time—deaf and blind. She didn't know if Leroy was home or not, but she wasn't gonna say anything to a bunch of cops."

He paused to reorganize his thoughts.

"About six months after Dr. Ben's murder, Leroy calls me out of the blue and tells me he's got some good news. He found some rock star who liked my songs and wanted to hear more of them."

Marge was quiet.

"Now's the time for Primo Ekerling."

"I didn't want to interrupt you."

Wenderhole gave her a fleeting smile. "Primo had been into the punk scene, but it was wearing thin. He was having trouble with the band, and he really wanted to be more behind the scenes. He liked my songs. We did a demo tape. Leroy somehow managed to get the tape played at a few of the alternative stations. I didn't make a dime off it, but, man, hearing yourself over the squawk box. It got me women. It got Leroy women. It got us welcome at all the clubs. Problem is, if you run around with shit, you get your hands dirty. And that's exactly what happened."

He patted the wheelchair.

"We were partying just like we always did, except one night some hyped-up bro went crazy and started peeling off rounds. Leroy caught it in the chest and head. I caught it in the back. When I woke up, I couldn't move my legs. I couldn't even *feel* my legs."

Wenderhole's jaw clenched as tightly as his fists.

"I wasn't allowed to feel that sorry for myself because at least I was alive. Leroy . . . he didn't have a chance." A beat. "It wasn't a wake-up call, it was a fuckin' time bomb going off in my brain.

For the first time in my life, I could be on drugs legally because the pain was so unbelievable."

"It must have been hell."

"If there was something worse than hell, I was in it. I swore that I was going to clean up my act and *do* something. It took me years, but finally I joined the human race. I started trying to better myself. I talked to other paraplegics. I realized that I was luckier than most because my dick still worked. I eventually did get some feeling back in my legs and toes. For a while, I could even manage on crutches. But you get older, it don't get better. I finally got tired enough to admit I needed a little more help. I can still swim like a fish, but I've been using a wheelchair for the last three years."

Wenderhole waited long enough for Marge to feel that it was okay to ask questions.

"Did you talk to Ekerling after you got shot?"

"I think Primo visited me a couple of times, then nothing. No market for a rapper in a wheelchair, and there was lots of others writing rap. He didn't have any use for me anymore."

"Did you think that Leroy's connection to Ekerling had something to do with Bennett Little's murder?"

"Why would I think that? Ekerling didn't come into the picture until way later."

"And you never questioned Leroy about Bennett Little's murder?"

"No. I didn't want to know nothing."

"And your only involvement in the incident was picking Leroy up from the park."

"That was it. You want me to make a statement about that, I will. That is part of recovery. I lied to the police. I fully admit it."

"When you heard about Ekerling's death—his car being jacked, the body being stuffed into a trunk and shot execution style—did you make a connection between his murder and Bennett Little's murder?"

"I thought about it only after I read about the two moronic dick brains that the police hauled in for the crime—that one of them was an aspiring rapper. That set off bells. That was me and Leroy fifteen years ago."

Marge was writing furiously. "Why would someone have wanted to shoot Bennett Little?"

"I don't know, Sergeant; I barely even knew the man."

"How do you think Leroy got involved with his murder?"

"I don't know if he was."

Marge said, "From what you've told me, there had to be other players in Little's murder besides Leroy. Any ideas who might have set the thing up?"

"No."

"What about Darnell? Could he have called the shots? He had a reason to hate Little."

Wenderhole was circumspect. "Darnell was angry, but I can't see him being angry enough to arrange a hit. And where would he get that kind of money?"

"He might have saved up something from running drugs."

Wenderhole smiled bitterly. "You've never been a runner. All you get is pocket change. Everything you make goes in your mouth, up your nose, or into your lungs. Darnell didn't have money to pay Leroy."

"And you have no idea who paid Leroy to murder Little?"

Wenderhole hedged. "I don't know if Leroy killed Little or not."

Marge tried a different tactic. "When you worked with Ekerling, did you meet any of his former bandmates?"

Wenderhole thought for a minute without speaking. Then he went into his file, pulled out a folder, and began to rummage through it. "Here is my former life as A-Tack: old clippings, PR pieces, and the few reviews that I got. I saved them all."

"Can I see them? They might be helpful to the investigation."

"In a minute . . ." He pulled out a yellowed piece of newspaper print. "Here . . ." He handed it to Marge. "Once I opened for Primo's group—the Doodoo Sluts. I think it was their last concert together. It was at a club in Hollywood. The place was packed, but not because of me. It was a bunch of white punkasses. I got through two numbers before they started throwing shit at me."

Marge read the review. The critic had good things to say about A-Tack but called the Sluts sell-out hacks. "Your two numbers must have been impressive."

"Sergeant, all I remember is trying to escape without being lynched. I was pissed off at Primo for setting me up like that."

"Do you think he did it on purpose?"

"No, not on purpose. Maybe he thought he was doing me a favor . . . giving me exposure. But a producer should know the audience for his performer."

"If you opened for the Doodoo Sluts, you must have known the members of the band."

"I didn't know them. I met them before the show. I liked the Irishman on the drums. And the guitarist was real good. I forget his name."

"Ryan Goldberg."

"That's right. Ryan. He was a big guy. Kinda weird, too, but friendly in that Lurch sort of way."

"What about Rudy Banks?"

"Rudy Banks . . ." Wenderhole paused. "I remember him best of all because he knew I'd gone to North Valley High. I asked him how he knew that and he told me that Darnell Arlington used to run drugs for him in North Valley. If that's true, I was running drugs for him, too, because I ran drugs for Darnell."

"He told you this after meeting him once?"

"The guy was a loudmouth. He said Darnell was a moron who blew the entire operation when he got caught. Even talking about it made him mad. I got the feeling that Rudy felt Darnell owed him something."

"You don't remember Rudy Banks from North Valley High."

"First off, I was never in school. Also, I think he was out by the time I got bused into the valley."

"He was out of school but that doesn't mean he wasn't still running drugs."

"*Still* running drugs?"

"According to some people, Rudy ran drugs while he was enrolled in North Valley."

"Don't surprise me."

"Did you ever call up Darnell to ask if he had run drugs for Rudy?"

"No, ma'am. By the time I opened for the Sluts, I hadn't spoken to Darnell in a long time. He had his new life. He didn't want nothing to do with Leroy and me."

"Maybe you hadn't spoken to him, but maybe Leroy had."

"I already told you that Darnell didn't have money to pay off Leroy."

"But Rudy had plenty of money to hire Leroy."

"I don't think Rudy ever met Leroy."

"Was Leroy at your show when you opened for the Sluts?"

"Yeah, I see what you're saying. He might have been backstage with me and met the band. But this was way after Dr. Ben's murder."

"And after the show, the Doodoo Sluts broke up?"

"More or less. Primo went into producing full-time. I don't know what happened to Rudy, Ryan, and the Irishman. As for me, I was living the high life until a hype flushed the dream down the toilet." A heavy sigh. "I keep tellin' myself that it was for the best. Maybe one day I'll believe it."

Marge let the words hang in the air. Then she said, "What was Leroy Josephson's role when you were recording with Primo? After all, he was the one who set you up with Ekerling?"

"Leroy acted as my manager. He'd push the demo to the radio stations."

"Did he and Ekerling work together to promote you?"

"Now that's a good question." He thought a moment. "The few times that Leroy came to the studio, Ekerling shooed him out. Leroy was pissed, but he understood. Mostly they did their things, and they did them separately. Leroy did the legwork . . . talking people into listening to the demo. And we were finally getting somewhere." His face darkened. "We was just in the wrong place at the wrong time."

Marge regarded the newspaper clipping again. "I want to go back to Rudy Banks because his name keeps showing up in our investigation. You told me that Rudy was pissed at Darnell for getting caught. Was Rudy also pissed at Ben Little for busting open the operation?"

"I don't know if there even was an operation. Rudy just told me that Darnell used to run drugs for him. This was a year or two after Little's death. I certainly wasn't going to call Darnell and ask if it was true. I didn't care if it was true. I was doing my own thing and I'm sure Darnell was doing his own thing and that was that."

"This is all coming at me very fast. We're going to have to go over this again . . . and again."

"I figured that. I can't give you much more time today, but like I said, I'll come in and make a statement to the police. I'll accept the consequences for my actions, but I'm not going to implicate Darnell in anything. As far as I know, he didn't do anything."

"I've talked to him. He's hiding something."

"If he is, I don't know about it. All I did was help a friend, and now he's dead. I've carried some kind of queasy guilt in me for a long time. I'm ready to get rid of it and move on. That's the key to living in peace, Sergeant, the ability to recognize your mistakes and then to move on."

31

The call was from Marge.

Going sixty-five on the freeway, Decker had reservations about driving while connected even though he had a hands-free option: too many people distracted for a nanomoment with dire consequences. The closest off-ramp was a mile away and would drop him deep in the Santa Monica Mountains. Reception would be challenging.

He skipped over Moraga Drive and passed up Sunset Boulevard—nowhere to pull over and park. His first opportunity came with the Wilshire off-ramp, but as soon as he got off, he realized he made a mistake. The major thoroughfare was clogged with traffic and lined with high skyscrapers that prevented any kind of clear reception. He waited until he had crawled through the corridor that bled into the main shopping district of Beverly Hills.

There were no big buildings to interfere with

phone waves, but the congestion remained horrendous. He sat and sat while cars inched along, wondering if he should call back or park or wait until after he talked to Marilyn Eustis. At the last minute, he pulled his clunker onto Rodeo Drive and parked in a loading zone. He took out his notepad, rang up Marge, and was about to settle back for a phone conversation until he heard a knock on his window. A BHPD uniformed motorcycle cop with white hair and a walrus mustache was peering inside, his expression partially hidden behind shades. The scowl on his face was obvious.

"I've got to call you back," Decker said when Marge answered. He rolled down the window. "I'm an LAPD police lieutenant and need to return a phone call for official business. Can you give me a minute?"

"You have a badge?"

"I have a badge and I also have a gun," Decker told him. "I'm going to pull back my jacket to show it to you, reach into my pocket, and get you my identification, okay?"

"Go slow."

"You bet." Decker fished out his ID. The mustachioed man regarded it and nodded. "Try to make it quick. The merchants start screaming when access to their stores is blocked. You're not going to take the heat, but I will."

"I understand. I'll be done in a moment. Thanks."

After revving the handles of his motorcycle, the cop drove off. Decker redialed Marge. "What's up?"

"Where are you?"

"On my way to see Marilyn Eustis."

"Great. So you must have found out what I found out. Who told you?"

"Who told me what?"

"That Primo Ekerling used to produce Jervis Wenderhole under the name A-Tack."

"He did?" Decker took out his notepad. "When was this?"

"About a year after Ben Little's murder." A pause. "So why are you going to see Eustis?"

"To find out if Primo Ekerling had recorded or had dealings with Travis Martel."

"Travis Martel? The guy who's in jail for Primo's murder?"

"Yes."

"Didn't Marilyn Eustis tell us that she didn't know Martel or Perry?"

"Yes, she did, but that doesn't mean that Ekerling didn't know him." He explained Cindy's downloading of Martel's rap song and the B and E lyrics.

"Ordinarily I'd say that's reaching, but maybe not." She recapped her conversation with Jervis Wenderhole. Decker had been sitting for around twenty minutes, taking notes and talking theories, when he was interrupted by a small, dark-complexioned man banging on his window. The chap was middle-aged with slicked black hair, and dressed completely in yellow. Even his croc boots had been dyed deep gold.

"Hold on, Marge." Decker rolled down the window.

"You have to move right away," the man yelled out in accented English. Out came Decker's badge. "I don't care if you're the president, you have to move!"

Bossy dude, but he was in the right. Decker said, "One minute—"

"One minute!" The man screamed. "You've had twenty!"

"You've been timing me?"

"You bet your— . . . you need to move! I have a very important client coming any moment. This is a big space and he has a Phantom Rolls-Royce."

Decker told Marge, "I have to call you back. I have to move. I'm blocking a space for a very important customer—"

"Client."

"Excuse me. Client." He hung up the cell and started the motor. "Sorry. You're right. This is your space and you're entitled to it."

"That's okay." The man calmed down. "That's okay." As Decker was about to pull out, the little yellow gnome held up his hand. "Hold on." He ran into the store and came back with a bag. "My new aftershave. No hard feelings. I just need the space. Besides, it's smart business. Who knows?

Maybe someday you'll be rich and you'll be a very important client."

Ekerling's former office room had been reduced to a generic couch, a bare coffee table, a couple of club chairs, a clear desk, and a filing cabinet. The shelves, however, were still triple stacked with CDs, but gone were the multitude of cardboard boxes and with them, probably any evidence that Ekerling had worked with Travis Martel.

Marilyn sat on the couch, her legs crossed with the right one extending up and down at the knee like the arm of a railroad crossing. She had a cigarette in one hand and a Coke Zero in the other, periodically flicking ashes into the pop-top opening. The blue-eyed blonde looked fetching in black latex jeans and a scoop-necked tee. "I'm taking over Primo's clients."

"I didn't know you were a producer." Decker had settled opposite her in a chair.

"I'm not. I'm talking about being an agent. I can probably do it as well as anyone else, considering the client list." She shook her head. "Poor Primo was a good guy, but he didn't exactly burn up the airways with success stories."

Decker pointed to the bookshelves. "He seems to have amassed a lot of CDs."

Marilyn craned her neck to look at the jewel boxes, and then turned her attention back to Decker while puffing on her cigarette. "You're impressed by that?" A roll of the eyes. "Ninety-nine point nine of them puppies went to the pound and were never heard from again. And the point one percent who had some success left Primo as soon as they could. Don't confuse quantity with quality. Demos are cheap."

"I didn't know that Primo was an agent."

"There you go. Yes, he was an agent, but not a very good one. Talent and charisma don't just show up at your doorstep. You've got to go out and chase it. When you're numbed by alcohol and shit, ambition and hard work seem like dirty words."

"How far back do these demos go?"

"I dunno. I haven't gotten to them yet."

"Are you going to chuck them?"

"I'll go through them to see if any of them have promise. What I should do is box them all up and take them to my place. The lease here is up in a couple of weeks and I'm not going to renew it. I can work from home. All I need is a CD player and a good set of ears."

"How long do you think it'll take you to box them up?"

"I dunno. It took me a long time to sort through his paperwork. Gawd, it was tedious." A flick of the ashes in the can. "You didn't come here to listen to my woes. What do you need?"

"Well, for one thing, I'd like to go through those CDs."

"What are you looking for?"

"For anything by a rap artist named Rated-X,

Travis-X, X Marks the Spot, or just plain X. Anything of those names sound familiar?"

"Primo didn't do a lot of rap."

"That doesn't mean he didn't get rap demos."

"That's true, but the guy doesn't sound like a client." She knitted her brow. "But the name isn't foreign. Should I know this guy?"

"Travis Martel used those names when he rapped."

"Travis Martel?" Marilyn took a deep drag on her cigarette. "The guy who's in jail?

"Yes, ma'am."

"You're kidding! You think this punk and Primo worked together?" Another puff. "C'mon. While I don't know all of Primo's clients, I'd know if that fucking murderer worked with him."

Decker was quiet. His silence made Marilyn turn red with fury.

"Why would Primo work with a punk like that?"

Decker pointed to the CDs. "All sorts of people sent him demos."

"And with all those demos, how many do you think Primo actually contacted?"

"I don't know. Maybe twenty."

"How about three?"

"So maybe that's the issue, Ms. Eustis. Maybe Travis Martel sent in a demo and when Primo didn't get back to him, Travis got pissed."

"How do you even know if Travis went beyond taking a rap name? A lot of these assholes who call themselves aspiring rappers don't even rap. They just like the titles and the idea of rapping."

"Travis posted his music on his MySpace."

"Him and every other loser."

"In one of his pieces, there's a line that refers to 'the music and the crime—the shit of B and E.' That could be a reference to the crime of breaking and entering, but it also could be Banks and Ekerling."

"Wait a minute, wait a minute." She uncrossed her legs and leaned forward. "What does Rudy Banks have to do with any of this?"

"This is just conjecture, but what if Primo turned Travis down, Travis went to Rudy Banks. Maybe Rudy promised Travis a recording contract if he'd murder Ekerling."

Marilyn's eyes got wide. "That's incredible."

"It's possible that Banks had done something like it before—hiring punks to knock off his enemies." Decker liked his theory, but Marilyn's expression was highly skeptical.

"You're telling me that somehow Rudy found out that Travis Martel had been turned down by Primo. So he hired the punk to kill Primo?"

"Maybe he didn't even need to hire him. Maybe all he needed to do was encourage Travis. Being the punk that he is, he then acted on his own. What intrigues me is now Rudy Banks is missing. I'm wondering why."

"Missing?" She smiled warmly. "With any luck, he'll show up dead!"

"Ouch!"

Marilyn dragged on her smoke again. "Okay. Maybe that was harsh. All I'm saying is, it would be a lot easier on the two remaining guys of the Sluts if he was."

"Liam O'Dell and Ryan Goldberg."

She nodded.

"I've talked to Liam a couple of times. He said he initiated the lawsuit for Ryan's sake."

"First of all, it was Primo who initiated the lawsuit."

"With Liam's blessing."

"Of course. Maybe there is some altruism in Mad Irish, but he's also doing it for himself. The guy's a washout."

"He seems at peace with himself."

"Yeah, and I'm going to be a famous actress!" She puffed mightily on her smoke. "Let me tell you something. Once you've been infected by the fame bug, the germ is like herpes, always there lurking in your system, waiting for that chance."

"After a while I would think that you get realistic."

"You would think and you'd be wrong, Lieutenant. That's what happens in the thrilling journey of ninety-nine percent of rock stars: from fame to obscurity before they're thirty. A few talented souls are able to tread water by doing something else in the industry, but the rest drown. It's brutal, but in a youth profession, you can't be onstage for all your life. Primo knew it, so did Rudy."

She paused to smoke. "Where do you think he is? Rudy, I mean."

"I don't know. I was going to ask you the very same question."

"I don't know anything about his personal life. When I met Primo, he and Rudy had already been involved in a number of lawsuits, mostly for money that Rudy owed Primo when they produced together."

"How did they meet?"

"They were in the L.A. music scene together. Two rebel guys just hanging and doing a lot of drugs. Then they met Ryan and Liam. The personalities meshed and the band clicked—meteoric rise, meteoric fall. Ryan freaked, Liam faded into obscurity, and Rudy and Primo tried to parlay their fame into something a little longer lasting."

"They worked together on a couple of projects before the partnership went south," Decker said. "What happened?"

"Rudy's a psycho, that's what happened." She shrugged. "A band is one thing. Business partnerships are quite another. See, what I don't understand is why would Rudy suddenly kill Primo if they've been involved in lawsuits for years?"

"Maybe the opportunity? In the form of Travis Martel?" Decker smiled. "I've got a dandy supposition but nothing to back it up. That's why I wanted to look through Primo's papers and find out if he ever produced the kid. But it looks like you threw away most of Primo's old papers."

"I shredded them to little strips. About a quarter of the pieces are in my mulch pile at home. You're welcome to dig through it, but I must warn you it's a bit stinky and about four feet high."

"A mulch pile." Decker chuckled. "My wife has one. She's into gardening in a big way."

"Flowers?"

"Everything."

"Tell her they have a new variety of tea rose: lemon kiss. It's bright yellow and has a pungent citrus smell. It's gorgeous."

"I'll pass it on to her. And, no, I don't want to dig through your mulch pile. But if you wouldn't mind, I'd like to go through the demo CDs and old tapes just to see if I can find something by Travis Martel."

"Be my guest. Lots of them have photo pictures on the covers so that may help."

"Thank you very much for being so cooperative." Decker gave her a closed-mouth smile. "It'll probably take me a while. Is that going to be a problem?"

"Nah, just close the door when you leave." She stubbed out her cigarette. "Why don't I do this? I'll bring out some boxes. After you're finished with the cases that you don't need, instead of putting them back on the shelves, just pack them up. As long as I'm being so cooperative, you might as well help me clean up."

32

By the time Decker arrived home, Rina was dressed in flannel pajamas and in bed, the duvet's pattern obscured by dozens of brochures and travel books. She looked up from her makeshift desk and smiled. "Don't mind me. I'm just having a fantasy."

"A fantasy without me?" Decker said.

"Not that kind of fantasy, although I suppose that in my fantasy I can include that kind of fantasy."

Decker laughed. "I found a turkey sandwich with coleslaw and potato salad on a plate wrapped with Saran in the refrigerator. Is that for me?"

"Yes, it is."

"I am starving. I'm also dirty. Do I shower first or do I eat?"

"You shower, I'll set your dinner up on a tray and you can eat it in bed while I read and pretend."

"Sounds like a plan."

Twenty minutes later, the bed had been cleared, the books and brochures stacked on

Rina's nightstand. A tray held his dinner and two cans of diet root beer. Decker bit into the juiciest turkey sandwich he had ever tasted. The rye bread was very fresh and Rina had slathered it with mustard and mayo. She also added some cranberry sauce. He was in heaven.

Rina gave him a few minutes of peace to eat his dinner. Then she said, "Good day?"

"Long day?"

"The two aren't mutually exclusive."

"You're right. It was a long day and a pretty good day. It ended better than it started."

Rina brightened. "You found Rudy Banks?"

Decker gave a sad smile. "See, that's why I said it was a pretty good day. Finding Rudy would be a very good day." He polished off one can of soda and opened the other. "No, I didn't find Rudy, but I found a connection, albeit a weak one, between Primo Ekerling and his alleged murderer, Travis Martel."

"That's good." Rina paused. "What's the link?"

"Martel had sent several demos to Primo Ekerling. One actually included a note that said: 'Yo. Here's more. Let me know when it's happening.'"

"What's happening? A record deal?"

"That's what I took out of it." After finishing his sandwich, he methodically devoured the potato salad, washing it down with the second soda. "Primo dated every song demo he got."

"Compulsive guy."

"Thank goodness. The date on this particular jewel box was over a year ago. I don't think a record deal ever happened."

"So you think Travis Martel murdered Primo because he couldn't get a record deal?"

"Maybe. Or maybe somebody put him up to murder. Somebody who didn't like Primo anyway and took advantage of Travis's own anger at Ekerling."

"Rudy Banks hired Travis Martel to murder Primo Ekerling?"

"Maybe."

"Do you have a link between Travis Martel and Rudy Banks?"

Decker took another swig of root beer. "No. My next step is to talk to Martel. See if I can squeeze something out of him . . . if Hollywood will even let me near him."

"Didn't you initially have your doubts that Travis did the murder?"

"I did. I thought that Martel and Diaz just boosted the car not knowing that Ekerling was in the trunk. Because who would drive around the city in a stolen Mercedes with a body in the car? Only somebody very stupid, right?"

"Right."

"Now I'm thinking it might have been a murder for hire. It's possible that Hollywood has the right kids sitting in jail. So if I'm now on the same page as Garrett and Diaz, maybe they'll give me a chance with Martel." He finished the coleslaw and his root beer. "Enough about me. What did you do today besides conspire with my elder daughter about how to spend our money?"

"No conspiracy, we just talked." She handed Decker a brochure. "I normally wouldn't have thought of a cruise . . . especially one that isn't kosher specifically, but I talked to the office directly. They've made accommodations for kosher clients umpteen times before."

"Where does the number umpteen fall in the ordinal scale?"

Rina ignored him. "Food is not going to be a problem. Even if we had to eat cold, there's plenty of cottage cheese, lox, tuna salad, and egg salad for protein and a vast cornucopia of fruits and veggies. I could always bring some cold cuts for those needing a meat fix."

"Sign me up for the turkey. The sandwich was delicious."

"I suppose I could cook a turkey, freeze it, then have the kitchen warm it up in tinfoil."

"We're not going to schlep a turkey on vacation. That's ridiculous."

Rina smiled. "Anyway, even if we don't feel comfortable with their food, we can always catch our own. One of the side excursions is salmon fishing."

"Call me Papa Hemingway." Decker wiped his mouth. "All teasing aside, I think it might be fun, albeit expensive."

"What else is money for?"

"Food, clothes, education, car insurance, house insurance, property tax, health coverage—"

She hit him. "When was the last time we actually took a real vacation, not a trip back east to see the boys?"

"The last time was maybe . . . very long ago."

"Or maybe never."

"We went to Hawaii."

"That was before Hannah was born."

Gads, had it been that long? Decker told her, "Call up Cindy, call up the boys, arrange everything, do all the packing, and don't tell me how much it cost. Just put me on the boat, and I promise I won't jump off."

"You also have to promise that you won't say a word about money, not even a hint of a word. We can afford this, Peter, without breaking the bank. That's all you need to know."

"Fair enough. You arrange everything—the food, the transportation, the side excursions—and I'll show up and won't complain the entire trip. Just point me in the right direction."

"I'll lead you in the right direction," Rina told him. "I'll even hold your hand."

Each CD was encased in its own plastic bag, both of them sitting on top of Decker's desk with the same photo of Martel's sneering visage gracing the front of the jewel boxes. Marge picked one up by the corner and read the name. "You get these from Marilyn Eustis?"

"I found them on the shelves in Primo Ekerling's office. Eustis told me I could keep them."

"Better still. A direct chain between Ekerling and Martel." She yawned. "You're having the lab dust them for prints?"

"Yes."

"Hoping to find Travis's print so he can't say that someone else sent them in without his knowing or that you planted the boxes."

"Exactly."

"Although even if they had Martel's prints, he could still say that."

"Maybe with one jewel box, but it's harder to explain away two of them. Plus in one of the jewel boxes, there's a note. I've called in a handwriting expert to try and match the note to Martel."

"Great. Have you informed Hollywood yet?"

"I'd like to pull up a print before I call them." Decker rolled his shoulders in an attempt to loosen his muscles. "What I really want is a crack at Travis Martel, get him to admit some involvement in Ekerling's murder."

"Why would Travis do that?" She yawned again.

"Didn't get much sleep last night?" Decker smiled.

"None of your beeswax." Marge pulled up a chair and sat down, crossing her legs at the knees. Her black slacks rode up, exposing her ankles, and to her horror, she noticed one black sock and one navy sock. She quickly uncrossed her legs. "I repeat. Why would Martel implicate himself in a murder if his defense is boosting a car and joyriding?"

"Maybe I can convince him that if he doesn't tell us the truth, Rudy Banks is more than willing to tell lies about him." Decker explained his theory about Rudy Banks hiring out thugs to do his dirty work. "Trouble is, we don't have a link between Banks and Martel other than the lyrics of his rap song saying B and E." He smiled. "That's where my smooth lies and my superior interviewing skills might come in handy."

"And you think Hollywood will let you interview Travis Martel?"

"I think so, especially if I find Martel's prints on the CD box. Garrett and Diaz will be delighted to have a connection between Travis and Ekerling. It punches a hole in the story that the punks just boosted a random car and had no idea who Ekerling was and that he was in the trunk."

"And when are you going to tell them the news?"

"As soon as I have news. I'm waiting for the techs to come and dust the boxes."

Oliver walked into the office and took a chair. "I tried calling both of you last night . . . several times. Where were you?"

"I was inside an office building sorting through hundreds of CD demos," Decker told him. "The reception was bad and by the time I got your message it was past twelve."

Oliver turned to Marge. "What's your excuse?" She blushed. "Never mind."

"You didn't leave a message," Decker said. "I figured it wasn't that important."

"It's not the type of thing you leave on voice mail."

"What's going on?" Decker asked.

"You first." After Decker told him about the demo CDs found in Ekerling's shelves, Oliver straightened his purple tie. It blended perfectly with his matching purple shirt. "It's nice of you to solve Hollywood's murder. How's that going to translate into solving Bennett Little's murder?"

Marge said, "I can help with that." She spoke about her conversation with Jervis Wenderhole, aka A-Tack. "We have Wenderhole picking up Leroy Josephson from Clearwater Park. We have Leroy with a wad of cash in his possession. We have Leroy crying and acting upset. Then six months later, Wenderhole gets a call from Ekerling and he records a CD demo with Ekerling."

"So that ties Ekerling to Wenderhole and possibly to Leroy Josephson," Oliver said. "This would be great news if we were thinking that Ekerling murdered Little. Are we thinking that?"

"No," Decker answered. "But I do think Rudy Banks is connected to both Little and Ekerling."

Marge said, "History repeating itself: Banks hired Josephson to whack Little, and he hired Martel to whack Ekerling. I mean, why else would Martel whack Ekerling?"

"Yeah, about that," Oliver said. "Why would

Banks whack Ekerling? They've been in lawsuits for years."

Decker said, "Like I told Marilyn Eustis, maybe the opportunity finally presented itself in the form of Travis Martel."

"Banks randomly offered Martel money to whack Ekerling, and Martel accepted?"

"Maybe there's a little history," Decker said. "Maybe Martel thought that Ekerling was going to offer him a contract. After all, the note does say, here's more, when is it happening? But a contract never comes through, and Martel moves on to Banks. While he's with Banks, he complains about Ekerling. Finally Rudy sees an opportunity."

"I know what he's saying," Marge told Oliver. "If we could establish murder for hire between Banks and Travis Martel, it would help us establish a history for a grand jury to charge Banks with murder for hire of Bennett Little using Josephson."

"Correct me if I'm wrong, Marge, but didn't you just tell us that Josephson is dead?"

"Josephson is dead, but Wenderhole is very much alive. And so is Darnell Arlington. I think it's possible that Rudy hired Darnell to whack Little and since Darnell was out of town, he hired Leroy as the hit man."

"But Wenderhole is saying that Darnell didn't kill Little. He isn't even saying that Josephson killed Little."

"That's why I need to go back and talk to Darnell

Arlington. I think I can shake things up now that I've spoken with Wenderhole." She turned to Decker. "Can you get me the funds to fly back to Ohio?"

"If you get Wenderhole to write an official statement, I could justify another trip."

"Wenderhole is willing to state that he picked up Leroy from Clear-water Park, that Leroy had a lot of money, and that Leroy was very upset. And then around six months later, Ekerling came to him to record some demos."

"Exactly. Ekerling came to *him* to do some demos. Ekerling, not Banks," Oliver said. "The whole tie-in with Rudy is nonexistent."

Decker said, "Scott, it's just a theory. But the blood in Banks's apartment isn't a theory. It's fact. That's why I want to talk to Martel: to see if he knows Rudy. If he does, I'll tell him that Rudy is blaming Ekerling's murder exclusively on Martel and Perry. Maybe that'll offend Martel and he'll say something dumb."

"He'd have to be real dumb to start admitting he knew Ekerling," Oliver responded.

"And he'd also have to be real dumb to ride around in a car with a body in the trunk and leave his prints all over the place."

Oliver said, "And what if Martel shoots back that he's never heard of Banks?"

Decker shrugged. "Then you're right. We've helped Hollywood buttress their cases against Travis Martel by establishing a connection between

Martel and Ekerling. But we'll be no further along in the Little case."

"Maybe I can drag something out of Arlington," Marge said. "Especially if Darnell thinks that Wenderhole knows way more than he does."

"Or maybe he'll be smart and keep his mouth shut," Oliver told him. "Or maybe he's totally innocent."

"Correct on both possibilities." Marge smiled. "This is where my superior interviewing techniques might come in handy."

Decker laughed. "Did you get a chance to speak with Banks's lawyer and find out if she's heard from Banks this past week?"

Marge said, "She wasn't in yesterday. I left my card and she called me back last night. I'll call her in about . . ." She checked her watch. It was close to nine. "Maybe in fifteen minutes and try to set up an appointment today." She addressed Oliver. "Your turn. What happened with Shriner yesterday?"

Oliver straightened up his shoulders and knotted his tie closer to his neck. "What I have is good because it actually has something to do with the Little case. Last I heard, we were working on that and not on Ekerling."

"You're annoying me," Decker said. "Go ahead."

"Rudy Banks was having an affair with Melinda Little."

"Wow!" Marge was impressed. "That's good."

"Damn right," Oliver said.

"The affair happened before or after Ben's murder?" Decker asked.

"Before."

"Man, Banks has had his dirty little fingers in just about everything," Marge said. "How'd he manage to bag Little's wife?"

Oliver said, "Well, we know Melinda was gambling behind her husband's back. She probably needed money. Why not get it from Rudy?"

"Where'd Rudy get expendable money? Were the Doodoo Sluts that big?"

Decker said, "Marilyn Eustis told me they had cash, most of it spent on drugs." He turned to Oliver. "How'd you find out about the affair?"

"Phil Shriner implied it."

Marge stared at him. "What do you mean, *implied* it?"

Oliver shrunk back a tad. "He couldn't actually tell me yes, because it was said to him in confidence, but—"

"So you don't know if it's true?"

"It's true, Marge, he just won't admit it because Melinda confessed her sins at one of those GA meetings where everything is confidential."

"So how did you get it out of him?" Decker asked.

"I just made the leap and he didn't tell me no."

Decker said, "Scott, go over to Melinda Little and lie to her. Tell her that Shriner told you about the affair and what does she have to say for herself."

Oliver shrank back again. "Uh, I'd like to get some independent corroboration first. Shriner told me that if I approached Melinda Little and told her that he blabbed the affair, he'd sue me and the department. I can pump Melinda on it and try to get her to admit it, but we need to leave Shriner out of it."

"Back it up for a second," Decker said. "Oliver, did Phil Shriner find out about the affair before or after the Little murder?"

"Melinda was in GA after Little died, so he must have found out about it afterward."

Marge said, "If he's to be believed."

Abruptly Oliver hit his forehead with his hand. "I'm going senile. Shriner told me that he passed Rudy Banks's name to Cal Vitton as a possible suspect for the murder."

"He passed Banks's name to Cal Vitton?" Decker was taken aback. "I didn't see anything in Vitton's note indicating that he interviewed Rudy."

Oliver said, "So maybe Cal checked Rudy out and he couldn't hold him."

"Or maybe he didn't even try to hold him," Marge said. "I'm still thinking back to Pete's conversation with Freddie Vitton, about Cal Senior not coming to his son's rescue when he was being bullied."

"Maybe he didn't know."

"I don't believe that. Now Oliver says that Shriner passed Rudy's name to Cal Vitton, giving Cal an opportunity to haul in Rudy's ass. But he doesn't do it."

Oliver said, "Rudy had something on Cal."

"I still think it had something to do with Cal J's homosexuality," Marge said.

Oliver said, "Freddie V said that just about everyone knew that Cal J was gay."

Marge said, "But that doesn't mean that Cal Senior would want it advertised. Maybe Cal didn't have anything concrete on Rudy, so he decided not to look too hard if Rudy kept his mouth shut about Cal J's sexuality."

"He might let some things slide," Oliver said. "But not murder."

Marge looked at him. "But maybe Cal didn't know that Rudy was a murderer. All I'm saying is that we're familiar with a certain breed of cop who'd rather have their own sons conveniently disappear than to admit to the world that their offspring are homosexuals. They think it reflects on their machismo."

"Not just cops," Decker said. "It's a certain breed of man."

Oliver said, "Can we get back to Melinda Little for a moment? We have several reasons why she would want Little dead. The insurance money and maybe she was in love with Rudy and wanted to go off with him."

"There's divorce for that," Marge said.

"But then she might lose her trust fund money."

Marge said, "Or maybe Rudy wanted Melinda and ordered a hit out on Little."

Decker said, "First we need a way to verify an

affair between Rudy and Melinda. Scott, you need to lean on either Shriner or Melinda Little."

"Shriner's an immovable object," Oliver said. "He's out for now. I could go to Melinda Little, but I'd like more ammo before I shoot."

A thought hit Decker's brain. "Maybe we don't need Shriner to verify the affair. Give me a few minutes and I might even have an idea."

33

Venice Beach spanned the socioeconomic spectrum in a ten-block radius: from the multimillion-dollar architectural homes on the canals to the gang-riddled roads of the Oakwood area. In between were a number of California ranches, Pasadena-style Greene and Greene houses with wraparound porches and wood-sided shingles, and old Victorians, some restored, some not.

The beach part in Venice usually referred to the "walk streets"—little alleyways that connected Ocean Park Boulevard to the sand and grit deposited by the blue Pacific. These lanes were lined with the gamut—from shacks to three-story statements—with the main draw being the proximity to the ocean. Decker didn't know if O'Dell owned or leased, but if he had been bright enough to purchase, the ex-Slut was living the good life in an appreciating asset.

The address corresponded with a one-story, side-by-side Cape Cod duplex painted bright blue with white trim. O'Dell's unit was the left side and the door was open, the smell of grease wafting clear down to the sidewalk. Decker knocked on the screen door frame, then stepped inside a stuffy, dark room with worn, planked floors and cracked plaster walls. The ceiling beams were half-painted, half-exposed wood and sported a mounted fan on full blast. The artwork consisted of Doodoo Slut posters, lots of framed pictures with babes in bikinis, and a gold record in a shadow box. The furniture was mismatched and looked to be secondhand stuff. The window curtains had been drawn, blocking out most of the natural light.

Decker was sweating under his jacket. He loosened his tie and called out to O'Dell. When he didn't get a response, he drew back the curtains and the beams streamed in, highlighting the dust and the must. "Liam, are you home?"

"In a minute. Have a seat."

"Thanks." Decker took off his jacket and draped it over the sofa. He opened one of the windows and a saline breeze sifted through the screen. O'Dell emerged as a surfer dude in a Hawaiian shirt, cutoff shorts, and sandals. An apron fell down to his knees. His eyes were squinting.

"Did you find Rudy?"

"Not yet."

"Balls. What the hell is taking so long?"

"I don't know where he is. Do you?"

"No, but it's not my job to look for the bastard. That's what I'm paying me taxes for." He was still squinting when he noticed the open window. "Who the hell pulled the curtains?"

"Mea culpa," Decker said. "Is it a problem?"

"Bloody hell, yes, it's a problem. What time is it?"

"Around twelve." Decker started to close the curtains, but O'Dell stopped him. "S'right. Just leave it. I'm frying clams. Want some breakfast?"

"No thanks, I'm good." A pause. "I thought you were a vegan."

"Clams don't count."

Decker could hear a sizzling pan in the background. "Why don't you finish up your cooking and then we can talk."

"That'll work. Want a beer?"

"No thanks."

"Something stronger?"

"How about a bottle of water?"

"I've got tap or a diet 7UP."

"Diet 7UP is fine. I can drink it out of the can."

"That's good because the glasses aren't clean. You can take off your tie. It's like a bloody sauna in here."

"Might cool things off if we opened all the windows."

"Go ahead. I'll be back in a jiff."

After getting some decent ventilation, Decker sat down on the sofa. O'Dell came in with a plate of clams drenched in malt vinegar and tartar sauce. He tossed Decker a can of 7UP and then took a swig from a bottle of Heineken. He ate sans utensils, popping clams into his mouth and licking his fingers afterward. "Delicious. Sure you're not interested?"

"Thanks, but I'm fine."

Another healthy gulp of beer. "So you haven't found Rudy. You think he might be dead?"

"Don't know," Decker said. "I'm interested in the time you got along with him."

"That would be never."

"You were in a band with him for years. You must have gotten along a little bit."

"Nope, never." He ate another clam. "If we didn't break into fistfights, it's only because we were too blasted to care. Whenever I was sober, which wasn't too often, I never liked the son of a bitch."

"But you two weren't overtly at war *all* the time."

He thought about that. "I suppose there were a few times that I could be in the same room with him."

"Rudy wrote most of the songs for the band?"

"Yeah, like I told you before—Rudy and Primo. That's why me and Ryan got the raw end of the stick, mate." Another clam. "The band may fold but the songs live on. Just not for me."

"I know the band went through lots of women." A smile on O'Dell's face. "In addition to the groupies, did Rudy have a special girlfriend?"

"I don't know, mate, we wasn't close. Is this going somewhere?"

"Does the name Melinda Little sound familiar to you?"

O'Dell thought a moment. "Melinda . . . Melinda . . . Melinda was mine, til the time . . ." Recognition in his eyes. "There was a Melinda."

Decker perked up. "Melinda Little?"

"Melinda something." Decker described her and O'Dell said, "Could be."

"What can you tell me about her?"

"Not much. It was a fog. She was around thirty?"

"More like thirty-five."

O'Dell slowly nodded. "If me memory is intact, I think she was one of 'em who made the rounds."

"Meaning?"

"What do you think?" O'Dell finished his clams and put the plate down on the coffee table. "Something's clicking in the airspace." He pointed to his brain. "I remember something about her being married. She liked to fuck. I don't think she was getting too much at home."

Decker nodded.

"For some reason, I remember . . ." He picked up the plate and took it into the kitchen. When he came back, he was holding another bottle of beer. "I remember that Mudd fell in love with her." He looked at Decker. "Ryan used to fall in love with whoever he fucked. He was a sucker." Another pause. "She liked money."

Decker took out his notepad. "Melinda liked money."

"I mean, who doesn't like money, but most of the girls we screwed did it to say they screwed us, or for the party scene or for the drugs. Melinda liked money. I remember talking to Mudd about it. Ryan used to give her money. It's all coming back."

"Take your time." Decker wrote as he collected his thoughts. "So Ryan gave Melinda money? How much?"

"Too much." Liam took another swig of beer. "I used to tell him, 'Mudd, you can't be fallin' in love with every bird you screw. It's just ass, mate. You can't be givin' it all away for ass. You gotta use your head.' I musta told him that twenty times a day; the idiot kept fallin' for one bird after another."

"Ryan was in love with Melinda?"

O'Dell sipped beer. "Ryan couldn't . . . it wasn't like a mature love. More like a teenage crush. Melinda was squeezing the bloke dry. I forgot who told him. Maybe me, maybe Primo. We finally told Mudd she was married. I think she even had kids."

"She did . . . she does."

"Yeah, she had kids. It was clear to us that she was just foolin' around. We told Mudd she was married, that she wasn't gonna leave her husband, that she wasn't gonna leave her kids. That she was only interested in a good screw and money and that he should forget about her."

"Did he?"

"He had no choice. We all saw what was happening. We took control of Ryan's spending cash. When he ran out, she stopped coming around."

"That doesn't mean he forgot her."

"Mudd moved on to the next bird, probably a normal one who liked drugs."

"Do you remember when Melinda started coming around?"

"Like a date?"

"Even a year."

"Between the time we formed the band and before we broke up. That was a three-year period."

Decker mentally noted it was the three-year period in which Little was murdered. "And you don't remember Melinda's last name?"

"I don't remember it as Little . . . why does that sound familiar?"

"Because Melinda Little's husband, Bennett Little, was murdered during that three-year period."

O'Dell looked confused. "Murdered?"

"You don't remember it? It made big news, Liam. That's why I'm looking for Rudy. He went to the high school where Little worked."

"I thought you suspected Banks in Primo's murder . . . which is ridiculous."

"Why? I've heard stories about Banks trying to throw acid on someone's balls."

O'Dell scratched his cheek. "Yeah, I could see Rudy doing that. But not killing someone. He didn't like blood."

"Could he have hired someone to kill Primo?"

"Kill Primo or kill this Little guy?"

"Either."

O'Dell threw up his hands. "I dunno."

"And if Banks didn't like blood, why is there unexplained blood around the baseboard in his apartment?"

"Dunno." A shrug.

Decker said. "What about Mudd? Could you see him murdering Bennett Little, hoping to snag his wife?"

The suggestion made O'Dell laugh. "Mudd? No way, no how. Not Mudd. He was as soft as soapsuds."

"You guys were flying most of the time. Your judgment gets whacked."

"Yeah, but not whacked enough for Mudd to kill someone."

"Lots of bad things can happen on drugs, Liam."

"You know, you tell me that you think Rudy's a killer, now you think Mudd's a killer. Make up your mind."

"I'm handling *an investigation*, O'Dell. That means I'm *investigating*. Like you said, it's your tax dollars at work."

"And you still can't find Rudy. The only thing you do is ask a lot of questions." He pointed to his chest. "Am I next in your line of killers?"

"Why would I think that, Liam?"

"You seem to be thinking a lot of strange things. Like Mudd doing murder. He would never kill someone. Rudy yes, maybe even Primo. Maybe even me. Not Mudd."

"So let's do him a favor," Decker said. "Why

don't we both go over to his place and ask him about Melinda Little?"

"He's not gonna remember her."

"Indulge me."

O'Dell looked as if he'd swallowed vinegar. "I need another beer."

"Take a whole keg, if you want," Decker said. "I'll drive."

The drive to Goldberg's place was an hour of crosstown hell. First it was a bumper-to-bumper freeway crawl because some semi had jackknifed, blocking three lanes of the 405 West. Decker got off at Bundy and tried Olympic, which was moving but at a tortoise's pace. By the time he weaved over to Sunset, the air had turned filmy, the temperature had risen, and the sun was piercing his windshield like a bullet. It was almost one-thirty and Decker was sporting an ogre headache.

The Hollywood Terrace was still ugly and depressing and maybe it was Decker's mood, but the entire day seemed to have dissolved into a muck pile of smog and heat. Decker parked and they both got out of the car without speaking. O'Dell pushed the button to Goldberg's apartment, and when he didn't get a response, he pushed it again.

"Does he go out a lot?" Decker asked.

"No!" O'Dell spit at the ground. "Fuck!"

Liam was concerned. Decker said, "Last time I was here, his TV was playing at top volume. Maybe he just didn't hear the buzzer." Decker pushed the bell to a random apartment. He kept doing this until someone opened the glass door to the lobby.

They entered and hurried to Goldberg's apartment. O'Dell tried the handle but it was locked. He jiggled it several times hoping to prod it open, and when it didn't budge, he said, "You still got those picks?"

"A good detective comes prepared." Decker took out a credit card and snapped the lock. "Always go simple first."

They went inside. The place appeared undisturbed and as tidy as Decker remembered. The flat-screen TV was still there, as was Goldberg's Dreadnought Martin. Liam picked it up and strummed a few chords.

Decker gave the one room a once-over and shrugged. "Everything looks okay."

O'Dell was visibly relieved. "I'm gonna stick around until Mudd gets back."

"I'm going to go grab a bite to eat," Decker said. "I'll be back in twenty minutes. Can I bring you back something?"

"Nah." He started picking some licks. "This baby is beautiful. He shouldn't keep it here. He's gonna get ripped off and then what? Maybe I'll buy him a repro and put this in a vault or something."

Mad Irish seemed lost in thought. Decker took the moment as an exit cue. He found a vegan storefront about two blocks down. It was relatively clean and had received an A rating. He took a chance, filling his stomach with a burrito of beans, rice, and tofu cheese. As promised he was back at the apartment in twenty minutes.

Still no Mudd.

O'Dell was still playing the Martin.

Decker said, "How long are you going to wait?"

"I've got a TV and a guitar. I'm a happy man."

"Do you have a cell phone?"

"Am I alive in the twenty-first century?" O'Dell gave Decker his number. "You go and I'll wait. It's fine."

"Call me when he comes back."

O'Dell nodded and stopped playing. His face was etched with worry. "What if he doesn't?"

"Then especially call me."

34

The Hollywood substation of the LAPD was a cinderblock bunker about two blocks from Ryan Goldberg's freestanding prison cell. Luck was in the air, and Cindy was back from the field at her desk, filling out paperwork, when Decker called and set up the desired meeting. He waited for her at the same A-rated, storefront vegan restaurant where he had eaten a burrito that had gone down fairly well. He marked time by sipping a soy chai tea and listening to the black-haired Goth waitress with multiple pierces argue over the cell phone. The heated conversation was still going when Cindy came in twenty minutes later wearing dark slacks, a green short-sleeved blouse, and rubber-soled flat shoes. Her hair was tied in a ponytail.

Without a word, Decker handed her a padded envelope that contained the two CDs extracted from Primo Ekerling's shelves, the jewel boxes secured in plastic evidence bags and still black with dust powder. The note to Ekerling was in a separate evidence sack, as was the fingerprint analysis report. As Cindy gingerly lifted one of the bagged Lucite cases, Decker told her about his meeting with Marilyn Eustis.

"The download was a good tip," he said. "Whatever the B and E meant, it got us thinking in the right direction. You're going to make Tito and Rip very happy. It provides a link between Travis Martel and the murder victim."

"Especially the note," Cindy said. "Did you have it matched to Martel's handwriting?"

"No, I'll leave that up to Rip and Tito. I'm sure Hollywood has its own experts."

"But you dusted the boxes for Martel's prints."

"Yep. We got lucky and found Martel's right thumb and right index finger."

"You can bring in the envelope yourself, Daddy." She pulled out the scrunchie from her hair, gathered up her locks and remade her ponytail. "Fortuitously, I think Rip is at his desk."

"Nah, you do it."

"You're being silly. It doesn't matter to me."

"But it was your tip."

"But you did the work."

Decker finished off his chai tea and held up the teacup. "I'm having another. Do you want something to drink, princess?"

"I'll take what you have."

Decker signaled Ms. Goth for two more chai teas. "I think there's a Jewish saying that taking

361

credit for someone else's accomplishments is akin to stealing. I won't take credit for your detection, but I would like a favor from you."

"Name it."

"I'd like to meet with Rip and Tito before they question Martel. Could you ask one of them to call me right away? It's important. I think this case might be related to Bennett Little's murder."

"Dad, why don't you just come into the station house and talk to Rip yourself? After what you found, they'll be in a very good mood."

"Cin, I don't think it'll do much for your reputation if we walk in together like some kind of wayward crime-fighting team showing up the primary investigators."

"You're absolutely right. I will talk to Rip and pass along your request."

"Be sure to say that I found the CDs based on your download of Martel's lyrics."

"Dad, I know how to sell myself."

"I'm just trying to help."

"I know, Dad. I appreciate it. Thank you. Anything else?"

"No." Decker stood up and so did Cindy. "I should be back in my office at around four. If they have a moment, give me a call."

"I'll pass it along. That's the best I can do. By the way, I hear that Alaska is a go."

"Not up to me. Rina's in charge."

"I know she's in charge. That's why it's going to happen."

Decker acted offended. "I make things happen."

"When you want to."

"What does that mean?"

"It means that . . . how should I say this? You get distracted." She kissed his cheek. "But never with work. That's why you're the man."

O'Dell called as Decker was pulling into the station house parking lot. His voice was agitated. "He's not back. I don't like this at all. I called up his brother."

"The lung doctor," Decker said.

"Yeah, Barry. He's coming down to drive around and look for Ryan. I'm gonna wait at the apartment and hope that Mudd just got adventurous."

"Does Barry the lung doctor know anything about Ryan's habits?"

"I asked him about Mudd taking off like he did. Barry said that if Ryan goes out at all, it's in the morning for a few groceries. It's almost four, mate."

"Maybe he took a small vacation."

"He wouldn't just pack out and go. And he wouldn't leave behind his guitar."

"He might if he figured he'd just be gone for a few days."

"Where would he go, mate? I'm telling you, this ain't right or good."

"I just pulled into the station house's parking lot. I have to check my messages and make a couple of calls. Then I'll come back and help Barry look for Ryan. It'll take me about an hour and a half. If Ryan does return, call me right away."

"I'm a little queasy about this. Rudy's missing . . . Ryan's missing." Anger in Liam's voice. "Why'd you mess things up, mate? Why didn't you just let well enough alone?"

"Wasn't my doing, O'Dell. It's the ghosts of murder past who stirred things up. I'm just the translator for the dead."

He was just about to lock up when Marge and Oliver came through the door of the squad room. Decker flagged them down and beckoned them into his office, plunking himself back down on his desk chair and rubbing his eyes. "Sit."

The detectives sat.

He turned to Marge. "I got an allowance for the trip to Ohio."

"Great."

Decker's tired eyes drifted to Oliver's. "*If* the trip's necessary, I'll send both of you. Don't call up Arlington yet. We have other business first. Ryan Goldberg's missing."

"Who's he?" Oliver asked.

"The guitarist of the Doodoo Sluts. The one who had a psychotic break."

Marge said, "I'm sorry he's missing, but is he relevant to our case?"

"He is, and I found out this afternoon just how relevant. Not only did Melinda Little screw Rudy Banks, she fucked the whole damn band."

"Oh my!" Marge said. "Busy gal our Melinda is."

"I talked to Liam O'Dell—the drummer for the

group. He was a font of information." He recounted his afternoon with Mad Irish.

"How'd you even find O'Dell?" Oliver wanted to know.

"By accident. Liam's involved in a lawsuit with Banks. I met him at Banks's place when he was trying to track Rudy down just like I was doing. O'Dell remembered a Melinda who seemed to fit Melinda Little's description, although he didn't remember her surname."

"Maybe she was using her maiden name," Marge said.

"That's a thought." Decker looked at his detectives. "So there's your source of independent information about Melinda Little and Rudy Banks. Arrange another interview with Melinda. Let's concentrate on her before we spend money tracking down Arlington." He raked his hands through his hair. "I want some answers. I'm tired of this fucking investigation dragging on and taking people like Ryan Goldberg down with it."

"Maybe *he's* involved and he's running," Marge suggested.

"I've talked to Ryan. The guy doesn't have enough brain matter left to plan his dinner, let alone a murder."

"But he wasn't always like that, Pete," Marge said. "He was in love with Melinda, and people do weird things when they're in love."

Decker blew out air. "You're right. I've been surprised before."

Oliver held back a smile. "So Melinda Little was a groupie?"

"Sounds more like Melinda Little was a woman desperate for money."

"How believable is O'Dell?" Marge asked.

"He's got nothing to gain by lying." Decker thought a moment. "I believe that they all screwed her, but Ryan Goldberg was the only one unbalanced enough to fall in love with her. He gave her money, and when the rest of the band found out about his largesse, they turned off the cash tap. Eventually she stopped coming around."

Oliver was already taking notes. "When did all this happen?"

"Sometime during the period when the band was together. Liam couldn't get any more specific because his memory was fogged by drugs. But even if he didn't remember exact dates, I'll bet that she does. Pounce on her. Press for details. Tell her you're going public unless she tells you the damn truth." Decker glanced at the wall clock. "I'm going back to hunt down Ryan before someone else gets to him."

Marge said, "You think Rudy Banks is behind his disappearance?"

"Maybe Rudy . . . maybe Melinda. In his present state, Ryan Goldberg is certainly naïve enough to go with either of them and not question their motives."

"What *motives* are we talking about?" Oliver asked.

Marge said, "Maybe Melinda hired Rudy to kill her husband, and Rudy hired out Goldberg to actually do the murder. If Goldberg was a little off to begin with and he loved Melinda, he'd have a reason for wanting Little dead. Then maybe once Rudy got wind that we were reopening Bennett Little's investigation, he killed Goldberg to keep him silent about Little."

Oliver scratched his head. "You were hot on Leroy Josephson as the bad guy just a few minutes ago."

"He still could be," Decker said. "If Wenderhole is believable, Leroy was the one at Clearwater Park with a wad of cash in his wallet. And it was Leroy who was crying and sobbing like he did something wrong."

"So where's the link between Josephson and Goldberg?"

"Maybe through Rudy," Marge said. "I'm thinking that Josephson must have had some help to pull off the murder and that help was Goldberg."

Oliver said, "Didn't you just say that you thought Darnell Arlington had figured into Josephson's involvement?"

Marge was thinking out loud. "Maybe Rudy called Arlington, his former drug runner, and told him to call up one of his buds to help out Goldberg."

Oliver said, "Rudy's doing all this murder for hire, putting himself on the line. What would be in it for Rudy?"

"Insurance money," Marge suggested. "Melinda promised him a bundle."

"Rudy already had money from the band," Oliver said.

"Maybe Rudy loved Melinda," Decker suggested.

Oliver gave him a sour look. "The woman screws his entire band and you're telling me that Rudy Banks, a psycho by everyone's definition, falls in love with her?"

"A bad boy liking an even badder girl."

Marge laughed. "Badder?"

Decker smiled. "Maybe Rudy loved Melinda or maybe he hated Bennett Little. Or maybe both. The only good thing I can take out of Ryan's disappearance is that perhaps it means that Rudy's still in town."

Marge said, "If Rudy's still in town and kidnapping people, do you think Melinda Little's in danger?"

Decker said, "You might want to bring that up when you talk to her. It'll no doubt make her more amenable to the truth."

It was almost six before Decker made it back to the city and over to Goldberg's apartment. O'Dell was still sitting on the couch, strumming the Martin. Barry Goldberg was pacing the tiny floor, which was about as effective as swimming in a fish tank. He had barely taken three steps before he reached a wall and turned around in the opposite direction. The lung doctor appeared to be in his early thirties at most. He was stocky and had a baby face—smooth red cheeks and dimples. When he addressed Decker, he spoke in urgent tones with a respectful manner.

"The police won't consider him missing until he's gone for forty-eight hours."

"I know that. I'll stop by Hollywood to see if I can't speed things up."

"I tried to explain to them that Ryan isn't just your ordinary missing person. But no one was hearing me."

"I'll see if I can light a fire—"

"He is a severely compromised individual who has managed on his own only by living in a circumspect circle," Barry broke in. "He eats, sleeps, watches TV, plays a little guitar, and occasionally shops for food. I do all his banking, his laundry, and most of his shopping."

"You're a nice brother," Decker said.

"Yeah, well, guess who put me through medical school?" Barry stopped cold. "I'm not accomplishing anything by yakking with you two. I'm going to go comb the streets again. Liam, you'll be here for a little while?"

"I'll be here as long as you want, mate." He looked at Decker. "I'm gettin' a little hungry. Can you run me up some food?"

"What do you want?"

"I had me fried clams. Now it's time for me veggies. And a beer wouldn't hurt."

"I can do that." Decker turned to Barry. "I'll walk you out." When they reached the entrance to the complex, he said, "What about you, Doctor? Can I pick you up some food?"

"Can't eat right now. I'm too nervous."

"I'll go over to Hollywood Police now and I'll see if I can get the message out to a couple of local cruisers. When I'm done, I'll hunt around myself."

Goldberg nodded. "Thanks."

"No thanks necessary. It's my job."

"Well, you look sincere. A lot better than those guys behind the desk I talked to."

"They care. Their hands are tied. You don't look for an adult male for forty-eight hours unless there are definite signs of foul play."

"Yeah, but he's not just any adult male."

"I know. He's psychologically impaired. That's why I think I can do something."

Goldberg's eyes became moist. "It's too bad you never knew Ryan before he decompensated. He had a poet's soul and was so incredibly talented. It was all those fucking drugs. It took him to a place he couldn't handle. It pushed him over the edge."

Decker nodded. "It must be hard for you."

"I've made peace with it. The Ryan I knew and loved died a long time ago. The Ryan that now exists is just a shell."

Tiptoeing in at midnight, Decker saw that the light was off in his bedroom but shining through the crack of his daughter's private space. He knocked gently and went in after receiving permission to approach from the queen. Hannah was sitting cross-legged on her bed, garbed in candy-striped pajamas, her bright red hair flowing past her shoulders. The TV was on, but muted. Her computer was in her lap, and she was talking on her phone while highlighting something in a textbook.

She put down the phone. "Hi, Abba."

Decker said, "Did you hang up the call?"

"No."

"Why don't you tell your friend you'll call back in a minute? Better yet, why don't you get some sleep?"

Hannah picked up the phone. "I gotta go. Bye." She looked at her father. "What's up? You look tired."

"I am tired."

"Why don't *you* get some sleep?"

"I will in a minute." He sat down on the edge of her bed. "What's going on in your life?"

"Nothing."

"How are your friends?"

"Fine."

"How's school?"

"Okay."

He smiled. She smiled. Decker said, "Well, it's been nice having this chat with you."

Hannah said, "I don't have anything to say. You're the one in the exciting job, but you never talk."

Decker was about to respond defensively but held himself in check. "What do you want to know?"

"What was your day like?"

"Long and fruitless. I spent the majority of my evening hunting around for a psychologically compromised man who seems to have suddenly disappeared."

"That's sad. Does he have any relatives?"

"He has a brother who is very concerned." Hannah looked upset, so Decker added, "It could be he didn't disappear. Maybe he just decided to take off."

"Why would he do that?"

"I don't know. It's my job to second-guess people, but often I'm wrong."

"Anything *good* happen?"

"Uh, yeah, actually." He smiled. "I spoke to a couple of detectives in Hollywood and they brought me on board a case they're working on. It was very nice of them considering I poked around their business without asking."

"What case?"

"The murder of a record producer that might be related to a cold case I'm working on."

"The one involving the Doodoo Sluts?"

Decker tried to hide his initial surprise. "Uh, yeah, we spoke about that, didn't we? See, I do talk to you about my cases."

"You didn't talk about the case, just the band."

"Did you find out anything about them?"

"Nothing big. The founding members are . . . hold on . . ." She ticked away on her laptop. "Rudy Banks and Primo Ekerling. They met in the L.A. punk scene and started performing as the Jerkies at underground clubs, but it was as the Doodoo Sluts when they got a following. They wrote most of the songs and went on to be record producers. The other two main members were . . . Ryan Goldberg and Liam O'Dell. They seem to have dropped out of sight."

"For Ryan Goldberg, he's literally dropped out of sight," Decker said. "He's the man I've been looking for."

"Oh . . . so I guess you know all this stuff about the band."

"I didn't know that Rudy and Primo performed as the Jerkies. Where'd you find that out?"

"I think I read it in an old interview online."

"That was smart."

"So who's the record producer who got murdered? Ekerling or Banks?"

"Primo Ekerling."

"Oh . . ." She was quiet. "That's too bad. I feel like I kinda know the guy now."

"That must feel strange."

"A little. Who killed him?"

"Hollywood Homicide arrested two punks for the murder," Decker told her. "Your sister found some damning evidence against one of the suspects."

"Who are the suspects?"

"Two thugs. Look it up on the Internet if you're interested in them."

"Fair enough." Hannah played with her computer for a moment. "I didn't know that Cindy is in Homicide."

"She's not. She was helping me out. I saw her today. That was the high point . . . until this moment."

"Good save."

"It's not a save; you are the high point of this long and dreary day."

Hannah stifled a smile. "How's Cin doing?"

"Working hard."

"What would you do if I decided to become a cop?"

Decker was momentarily stunned. "Please don't do that. Your mother would divorce me."

"You didn't answer the question."

"Is this a true question or are you just being provocative?"

"Maybe a little of both."

Decker sighed. "After I was done screaming at you, I suppose I'd support you."

Hannah leaned over and kissed her father's cheek. "That was a very good answer. You passed the dad test." A quick smile. "I still have some work to do."

"It's after twelve."

"That's why I sorta need to stop talking to you and get studying."

"You were talking on the phone when I came in."

"I was talking to Sara and we were going over the material together."

"With the TV on?"

"It's muted. I like the occasional image."

"And you're IMing."

"I'm talking to some of my friends in Israel. It's the only time I have when we're both up."

"You have an answer for everything."

"Multitasking is the hallmark of brains in my generation." She kissed him again. "I love you, Abba. Close the door on the way out."

35

By the time Decker made it over to County Jail and went through procedure to gain entrance, Rip Garrett and Tito Diaz were already in the interview cell, sitting on metal chairs, drinking coffee from paper cups. Both of them had on typical detective dress: dark suits, white shirts and dark ties, rubber-sole oxfords. With a single swoop of the eyes, Decker did a quick overview of Diaz. His most prominent feature was a thick neck, followed by a strong chin, broad forehead, black hair, dark eyes. More muscular than Garrett but he sat shorter. Decker introduced himself with a hand-shake, and by the time Martel was led in by the guards, Decker had a coffee cup in his hand.

Travis appeared to have beefed up since his mug shot taken on the day of his arrest. His chest seemed wider under jail blues, and his arms were thicker. His hair had grown even longer, wavy tresses hanging down his back. In person, Decker could discern Asian influence in Martel, demonstrated not only by the black hair but also by the slight tilt of his brown eyes. His skin was coffee and cream, his cheekbones were prominent, his lips were thick, and his teeth were big and white.

His arms were shackled for transport, but the jail guard took off the cuffs when they seated him inside the interview cell. Martel regarded Decker. "You my lawyer?"

"No, Mr. Martel. I'm Lieutenant Decker from LAPD."

"So you the boss?"

"I'm a boss but not the boss over Detective Garrett or Detective Diaz."

Diaz said, "Are you comfortable, Travis? We have our coffee. You want something to drink?"

The jailbird thought. "How 'bout a Red Zing."

"No alcohol, Travis. You know that."

"Then how 'bout a Pepsi?"

"That we could probably do—"

"And a smoke would be good."

Decker took a cigarette out of his pocket and gave it to him. He lit the smoke with a lighter, then regarded the thug as he puffed. Furtive eyes. So what else was new? A paper cup with Pepsi came a few minutes later. He finished it in a single gulp. "I'm a little hungry."

"Lunch is in an hour," Garrett said.

"I'm just be sayin' I'm a little hungry."

Decker said, "You want to know why we're here?"

377

"I ain't have to be curious 'cause you're gonna tell me."

Decker's face was flat. "We're here, Mr. Martel, because we all have something interesting to relate to you."

Martel's eyes narrowed as he finished up his first cigarette. He dropped it in the paper cup. "Like what?"

Garrett leaned forward. "First I want to remind you that you can ask for a lawyer whenever you want. You don't have to talk to us because we still could use what you say against you and your case."

"Just like the first time, it's your right to have an attorney present when we talk to you," Diaz said. "We'd like to keep it simple, so just hear us out."

Travis asked for another cigarette. Decker complied. Martel sat back and puffed for a moment without speaking. He had their attention and he was going to milk it. "Now y'all be sayin' that you want me to talk without my lawyer. And I sayin' to you that mebbe I don't want to talk with you without my lawyer, nomasayin'? But mebbe I do wanna hear why y'all here. I'm decidin'."

Decker said, "That certainly is your right, Mr. Martel. So let me give you a hint. It has to do with the new evidence that could affect you."

"How's it gonna infect me?"

"It links you to the murder of—"

Martel levitated out of his seat. "I ain't done no murder!"

"Sit down," Diaz told him.

"Why you be tellin' me the same shit you tole me before?"

Diaz stood up and appeared very tall. "Sit down now!"

"It's cool." Martel sat back down and held out his hands palms up. "I ain't be throwin' shades at you, bro, I just be axin' a question."

"Throwing shades?" Decker asked.

"Dissing," Diaz said.

"Beaning you with sunglasses," Garrett said.

"Ah." Decker regarded Martel. "I'm doing this for your benefit. Do you want to hear what I have to say?"

"Yeah . . . course."

"And you are waiving your right to have an attorney present?"

"I don't need no lawyer if all I be doin' is listenin', nomasayin'?"

"I agree." Decker gave him a few seconds to relax. "I was talking to Detective Diaz and Detective Garrett about your case. You told them you've never met Primo Ekerling."

A swift shift of the eyes. "Who?"

"The guy you're accused of murdering, Mr. Martel."

"Oh, yeah . . . him." He sat back in his chair and spread his legs apart. "I didn't whack that guy. I don't even know the dude."

"Yes, you told us that," Garrett said. "That's what Lieutenant Decker is saying. That you don't know Primo Ekerling."

"Tru' dat."

"You've never met Primo Ekerling?"

Another shift of the eyes. "Sayin' I don't know him be meanin' I never met him."

"Never talked to him?"

"I don't know the dude!" Martel repeated. "This is what you come here to yak about, I ain't hear nothin' that interests me."

"You don't know Primo Ekerling, you never met him, you never talked to him, you never communicated with him, you've never even heard of him before you were arrested for his murder," Decker said. "Is that what you're telling us, Mr. Martel?"

"Yeah . . ." Again he slumped back in his chair. "That's what I be tellin' you over and over. Are we done here?"

"That's real interesting." Diaz laid the bagged jewel boxes on the table. "Do these look familiar, Travis?"

Martel picked up one of the plastic sacks. "Course they do. They're mine. Is this a trick question or somethin'?"

"Know where I found them?" Decker waited for Martel's attention, specifically eye contact, because when Martel was talking, he was looking at the floor. "I found them on Primo Ekerling's office shelves."

Martel's eyes skittered back and forth. "So what? How do I know how Ekerling got my demos? Maybe someone thought I had talent and sent them to him."

Garrett said, "We dusted the jewel boxes, Travis."

"See, that's why they're all dirty with black powder," Diaz said.

"We got a couple of perfect prints, Travis. You sent those jewel boxes out, and you sent them to Primo Ekerling."

Martel's eyes made a swipe at Garrett's face. "So what's the big D? My shit must have went to a million producers."

"You sent out your stuff to a million producers," Decker said.

"Yeah. That's whachu gotta do to get your foot into the door, nomasayin'?"

"You sent them out?"

"Yeah, that's what I said . . . to a million people. I don't be rememberin' who I have sent them to and who I have not sent them to."

"When you sent them out, you addressed the envelopes," Decker said.

A pause. "You gotta talk to my manager," Martel said. "He's the one who have sent out the CDs to the producers, y'all. I don't remember no names. Why don't you axe my manager?"

"Who's your manager?" Garrett asked him.

"I ain't gonna tell you shit, man, if y'all gonna start accuzin' people."

"We don't have to ask your manager if he sent them out or not, because the handwriting on the envelope was yours." Decker's lie was smooth. The envelopes containing the jewel boxes were long gone.

Another shift in the eyes meant another shift in strategy for Martel. "Like I tole you, I have sent them out to 'bout a zillion producers. How am I gonna remember one name or the other? I thought you are here to tell me somethin'. So far all you be tellin' me is a lot of shit that you throwin' my way."

Decker said, "Travis, if you knew Primo Ekerling . . . if you had a business deal with him, it's better if it comes out now."

"This is the only chance that you're going to have to explain the relationship to us," Garrett said.

"I don't know what you be talkin' 'bout."

"Sure you do," Decker said. "We're talking about your relationship with Ekerling. Those jewel boxes will be entered into evidence at your trial. So explain to us why Ekerling had your jewel boxes. If you don't, some state prosecutor will provide his own explanation and make you look like a fool."

"I ain't got no relationship with Ekerling. That's whack! I did not know him and I did not have no deal with him!"

Diaz said, "Travis, we're trying to help you, and you're not helping yourself!"

Garrett told him, "Only way we can help you is if you tell the truth."

"I'm tellin' you the tru'."

"No, you're not; you're telling us smack."

Diaz said, "Help yourself out because everything's going to come out."

Garrett said, "The best thing you can do is to stop playing games and admit that you knew Primo Ekerling."

"Truth is easier to remember, Martel. What's the big deal telling us that you knew him?"

Travis dug his heels in. "'Cause you're tryin' to make a connection and there ain't none there. I don't know him—"

"Now how do you think that's gonna play?" Garrett said. "You keep on saying you don't know him and then we show the jury the envelopes in your handwriting addressed to Primo Ekerling—"

"I tole you I sent the CDs out to a billion producers."

Decker said, "Did you also send out a billion CDs with handwritten notes, saying: 'Yo, here's more. Let me know what's happenin'?"

Eyes darted from one face to another. Martel looked down, then up, then anyplace except Decker's face. "I don't know what you're talkin' about."

Blatant denial was best countered by blatant evidence. Diaz put a copy of the original note on the table. "Two experts have matched this note to your handwriting."

Decker said, "What happened, Mr. Martel? Did Ekerling go back on the recording deal?"

Martel's eyes scanned Decker's face. Then he became defiant. He shoved the note away. "Someone must be copyin' my handwriting, nomasayin'? There weren't no deal, and I don't know Ekerling and that's all I gotta say."

Decker said, "With all this evidence and the witness we have, you're going to look very bad in front of a jury. He's not saying nice things about you."

"Wha' witness?"

Now was not the right time to mention Rudy Banks. First Decker wanted Travis to admit that he knew Ekerling. "You know who I'm talking about."

"You mean Gerry?" Martel shook his head and smiled. "Shit, Gerry ain't telling you nothin' he hasn't tole you before. Talk about smack, man. That's total bullshit!"

"Who said it was Geraldo Perry who's talking?" Decker looked at Garrett and Diaz. "Did I say anything about Geraldo Perry being a witness?"

"Nah, you didn't say anything about Geraldo as a witness," Diaz said.

"Perry wasn't even part of the Ekerling hit," Decker said. "He didn't know what was flying. You just took him along for an alibi or maybe to help you chuck the body."

"You be makin' shit up, I don't have to be here."

"You want to go back to your cell?" Diaz asked him. "I can have someone take you back."

"Or you can stick around a little longer and smoke another cigarette," Garrett told him. "Up to you."

Martel didn't answer.

"If I've got it wrong, then tell me what happened," Decker said. "But tell the truth."

"I tole y'all like a million times, we boosted the car, we didn't know nothin' about no body in the trunk."

Decker told him, "No one is going to believe that, Travis, especially once we show the judge and jury these CDs and your note to Ekerling in your own handwriting."

Diaz said, "You knew Ekerling, Travis. That's very clear."

"What happened, Mr. Martel?" Decker asked. "Did Ekerling tell you he was going to produce your CD and then did he back out?"

"Y'all talkin' shit and I ain't got no more to say."

Decker had a lot more to say. But first he needed Martel's admission that he knew Ekerling. Six Pepsis, a pack of smokes, and three hours later, the magic moment came.

Martel kept raking his hands through his black strands, sweat pouring off his nose. "You keep hammerin' at me."

"We need the truth if we're going to help you," Garrett said.

"Hep me?" Martel sneered. "You ain't gonna hep me. You ain't gonna do shit for me. If you be heppin' me, I wouldn't be in my cons, man."

"Of course we want to help you," Diaz said. "That's why we're here. Do you think we'd be wasting our time, talking to you, if we didn't have something in mind?"

Garrett said, "We know that you're not going to talk to us unless we help you. But we can't do anything for you, Travis, as long as you continue to lie."

"Once you lay off the bullshit and start telling us the truth, then maybe we can help you out."

Decker said, "Because we know that you knew Ekerling. Just get it over with and tell us that you knew him and then we can begin helping you."

"Don't deny the obvious facts, Travis," Garrett said.

Decker said, "That's just plain stupid. It's stupid when you say you didn't know Ekerling when obviously you did."

"So what if I knew him!" Martel blurted out. "Don't mean I pinched the dude. I be havin' nothin' to do with his murder!"

The glory hallelujah words took a few seconds to sink in. Decker broke the silence. "Great. That was step one . . . that you finally admitted that you knew Primo Ekerling."

"I didn't be *knowin'* the mofo." A long pause. "Mebbe I have had met him once or twice."

"See, that's smart," Decker said. "To admit that you knew him . . . that's smart. Because we knew that already."

"I said I didn't *know* him. I just be meetin' him a couple of times."

"Met him where?" Garrett asked while looking at his hands.

"I don't remember," Martel told him.

Decker took a chance. "Travis, you were at his office. We've got your prints in his office."

Martel's eyes skated across the jail cell. "Mebbe I was at the mofo's office once."

"Maybe?"

"Okay, I had been there just once. Mebbe ten minutes. In and out. The bitch at the desk wouldn't let me get pass no door. She kept saying he wasn't in."

Garrett said, "Why'd you go to Ekerling's office?"

"'Cause I had not heard from the dude," Travis said angrily. "He wrote me that he liked my shit and I sent him more shit, nomasayin'? But then I never had heard from him again. He coulda called. How long would that have took?"

"About one minute," Decker said. "Must have pissed you off."

Martel waved him off. "You gotta get past the bullshit if you want to be big, nomasayin'? You don't got a thick skin, you ain't gonna make it." He looked around the interview cell. "If I didn't have a thick skin before I had came here, I got one now. Fuckin' mofos here dig my shit, though. Once I get out, I got my credentials, nomasayin'?"

"Nice to be appreciated," Decker said.

"True dat."

"Must have pissed you off when Ekerling went back on his promises."

"'Course it pissed me off, but that don't meant that I whacked him!"

"Then it's too bad that we have someone who is saying that you did."

Finally Martel made eye contact. "Say what?"

"That you whacked Ekerling."

Martel squirmed in his chair. "For the last time, I didn't whack Ekerling."

"We have someone who said you did," Decker said again.

"Then he be lyin'."

"Interesting that you don't ask who we have as a witness against you," Diaz said.

Decker pulled the trigger. "C'mon, Travis. Tell us the whole story. Somebody set you up. You're taking the rap for someone who isn't worth it. Who set you up and why?"

"If you got a witness, why don't you axe him?"

"We have asked him," Garrett said. "We've heard his side, and it doesn't look good for you."

Diaz said, "Now we want to hear your side."

Martel folded his hands across his chest and looked smug. "You're total bullshittin' me, man. You ain't got no witness!"

"We've got a witness," Decker said.

"Yeah?" Another sneer. "Who?"

"We know who set you up, because you've told the world in your download on MySpace." Decker leaned toward him. "'Like music and the crime—the shit of B and E.'"

Martel's head snapped back. He attempted to recover and tried to stare down the cops, but he couldn't pull it off. He finally figured out that the best way to combat undesirable information was to remain silent. Decker started to reel him in.

"B and E," he repeated. "Very clever. To anyone not in the know, it's just breaking and entering, right. But we know what the real crime is."

Martel remained silent.

"Once we arrested him, how long do you think it would take Mr. B to start talking against you? Do you want to talk about Mr. B? He's sure as hell talking about you."

Martel didn't answer. Decker kept at him without mentioning specifics.

B and E.

B and E.

The music and the crime—the shit of B and E.

The shit of B against E.

It took another hour before Martel's cracks began to appear.

Martel opened and closed his mouth. "Mebbe I know whachu mean, mebbe I don't."

"We need more than a maybe if you want us to help you," Garrett said.

"Mebbe I know, mebbe I don't know."

"So which is it?"

"If it be the same dude, mebbe I met him once or twice."

"Once or twice, Travis?" Garrett questioned.

"Somethin' like that."

Decker said, "Mr. B liked your music?"

"That's what he said." Martel talked under his breath.

"He wanted to do a record deal with you?"

"That's what he said."

"But only if you'd whack Primo—"

"I didn't do no whack and if Banks be sayin' that, he's lyin'! That's whack!"

Yes, Decker said inwardly. The name has been verbalized! He wanted to play the video back just to make sure that it was recorded for posterity. The only thing lacking was the first name. He still wanted Martel to call him Rudy before Decker mentioned the name. "So what was the arrangement between you and Banks?"

"I didn't do no murder! And if you pootbutts don't know righteous from smack, that ain't my problem, nomasayin'?"

Decker's brain was firing snippets of past and present. Using the parallel from Little to Ekerling . . . Leroy Josephson is to Little as Travis Martel is to Ekerling. If his assumption was true, it made sense that Banks used Travis Martel in the same way as Leroy Josephson—either to do the hit or to dispose of the body and car.

He said, "Banks said you whacked Ekerling . . ." When Martel tried to protest, Decker held his hand up to silence him. "That's his side. If you didn't pull the trigger, tell us who did."

"That's what I'm tryin' to tell y'all," Martel cried out. "I don't know who did it cuz I wasn't there. All I did was boost the whip, you got it?"

"Okay, Travis, let's have it your way," Decker said. "All you did was to steal the car. So how did that work?"

Martel thought long and hard. For a minute Decker thought he lost him. Then Travis made eye contact. "First I want to hear what Rudy be sayin' 'bout me."

There it was. The first name. Rudy . . . Banks. He had said them both.

Decker said, "You know what Rudy's saying." He fired an imaginary gun with his fingers. "That's what Banks is saying."

"I didn't whack Primo!"

"So what happened, Travis?" Garrett said. "Just tell us the truth and maybe we can help you out."

Decker said, "Don't go down for capital one murder if all you did was boost a car."

"That's what I'm tellin' y'all!" Travis was hot with frustration.

Garrett said, "If all you did was boost the car or help out as accessory after the fact . . . then let's hear it all. But let's hear the truth. Then maybe we can help you out."

Martel looked away. "I need a smoke."

"I ran out," Decker said. "I'll get you another pack just as soon as you tell us what happened."

"I don't zackly know what happened cuz I wasn't there."

"Just tell us what you know," Garrett said.

Travis started out very slowly. "Banks be sayin' that he wanted to produce me, nomasayin'?"

"Yes."

"That he thought my shit was real good. The man had plans. He tole me his plans. He could do stuff."

Decker said, "Rudy is a successful producer."

"Yeah, that's what he tole me."

The three detectives waited. Martel said, "I need a smoke."

Decker made a show of patting down his pockets. He found a cigarette and gave it to him.

A few drags later, Martel began to talk more quickly. "Rudy tole me that there was a problem with Ekerling. Y'see, Ekerling had my shit, and Banks tole me that I had gave permission to Ekerling to produce the CDs."

"How did Rudy know that Ekerling had your demos?" Decker asked.

"I tole him when I met him. I tole him how the mofo dissed me, nomasayin'?"

"You told Rudy Banks that you had a deal with Primo Ekerling?"

"There was no deal. Ekerling blew me off. But Rudy sez that he can't do my shit because Ekerling has the rights to the CDs and he weren't gonna give us the permission back."

Decker said, "Rudy Banks told you that he wanted to produce your songs but Ekerling owned the CDs and wouldn't give you your rights back?"

Martel's eyes clouded. "Yeah, zackly."

"Why would Ekerling own your CDs?"

"'Cause Rudy said that it *looked* like we had a deal."

"Okay," Decker told him. "Go on. So you need Ekerling's permission, but he isn't giving it to you."

"Yeah, zackly." Another drag on his smoke. "So Rudy said that he would fix the problem if I would give him permission to fix the problem. So I sez, 'Yeah, I give you permission to fix the problem.' I don't know what he means by fixin' the problem, nomasayin'? I thought he just be talking as one producer to another. Maybe he get a lawyer or somethin'."

"Makes sense," Garrett said. "That makes total sense."

When Travis stopped talking, Diaz prodded him to continue.

"Then . . . mebbe it was about a week later after we had had the conversation . . . yeah, it was about a week." A pause. "We're at the Bitty Bit party over in Hollywood at Citizen recording studio. Man, everyone was there. Everyone and everybody. Mo' fine-lookin' ladies than I ever saw in my whole life. Wearing fur and bling and . . . everyone was there." His eyes got far away. "I'm eatin' all this fancy shit, I'm drinkin' all this free drinks, I'm chattin' up the biggies . . ." A smile. "People listenin' when I talk . . . it was fine." He landed back on earth.

"Rudy comes over to me and sez he got somethin' big to do and he be back later to pick me up."

Decker said, "How'd you get to the party?"

"Rudy took me. That's why he come over to me and sez he'll pick me up later."

"Ah. Makes sense. So Rudy came over to you and said what . . . he had something big to do?"

"Yeah. He had somethin' big and he pick me up later." Martel scratched his cheek. "It must be like three hours later—the party's still on and I'm havin' a real good time. Rudy finds me, pulls me over, and tells me we got a problem."

The detectives waited.

"I was drinkin' lots, nomasayin'? I don't be rememberin' too clear."

"Tell us what you remember," Diaz said. "Rudy comes over to you and tells you that there's a problem."

"Yeah, that we got a problem." Martel nodded. "He tells me that he went over to Ekerling to talk to him and get the CDs but there was a problem."

"Rudy tells you this," Diaz clarified.

"Yeah, Rudy. I'm talkin' to Rudy. Rudy tells me that Ekerling was being a real motherfucker and wouldn't be givin' him no permission to produce my own CDs."

"Okay."

"Rudy was sayin' that it was my CDs and Ekerling wasn't being righteous, not givin' me my own CDs back."

"All right."

"Then it all kinda gets a little fuzzy . . . I was drinkin' . . . mebbe doing some other shit."

In other words, his brain was fried with mind-altering materials.

Martel said, "Rudy be sayin' that Primo got all wired. Then bam! Primo starts coming at him with a blade. He starts swipin' at him. So Rudy defended hisself."

"What did Rudy tell you he did to Primo?" Garrett asked.

"That he shot him in self-defense. 'Cause Primo kept comin' at him with the blade."

Decker said, "I'm confused. Who shot Primo?"

"Rudy shot Primo. They was only the two of them."

"Got it," Decker said. "Rudy told you that he shot Primo in self-defense."

"Yeah." Martel tried the story on for size and liked it. "That's what Rudy tole me. That he shot Primo out of self-defense. But now there was a problem, nomasayin'?"

"What was the problem?"

"That he had to get rid of the body and that I had to help cuz it was my fault that it happened in the first place. Cuz this was all about my CDs and that's the way a white jury was gonna see it."

The detectives nodded encouragement.

Martel sighed. "So Rudy tells me he parked Ekerling's Benzene a few blocks away. He had gave me the keys and told me to dump the car somewhere in the 'hood. And for my efforts, he gave me a couple hundred bucks. And he sez if anyone axe me where I got the money, just tell 'em from drugs, nomasayin'?"

Decker said, "Weren't you curious why he had Primo's Mercedes-Benz and why he wanted you to ditch it?" When Martel just shrugged, Decker said, "C'mon, Travis, you must have figured it out. Which 'hood did he want you to drop the car in?"

"Huh?"

"Did he tell you to dump the car in Hollywood or South Central?"

"He sez to dump it in my 'hood at Jonas Park. That it would look like some nicca boosted the whip, made a deal down there, and left the car cuz it was hot."

"Lots of drug deals at Jonas Park?" Decker asked.

"Whatever you want." Martel paused to organize his thoughts . . . or to concoct a plausible story. "So I call up Gerry from someone's cell at the Bitty Bit ho'down and I tell him I gonna pick him up and we gotta go dump a Benzene somewhere in the hood."

"Okay."

"So I go pick up Gerry and we go cruisin' in the whip and then we go to dump it in Jonas Park. But then we don't got anyone to take us home, nomasayin'? I ain't gonna ask no runner for a hike."

"Let me see if I understood you correctly, Travis." Decker tried to keep his face even. "Rudy gave you the keys to Primo Ekerling's car."

"Yeah."

"Where was the car parked?"

"Down the block."

"Down the block from the Bitty Bit party."

"Yeah."

"So you took the car with Primo Ekerling's body in the trunk of the car and called up Geraldo Perry—"

"No, first I call up Gerry and then I took the car."

Decker said, "Yes. Sorry. First you called up Gerry using someone's cell at the Bitty Bit party and told him you had a Mercedes-Benz with a body in the trunk that you had to get rid of and you were going to pick him up."

"I didn't know there was no body in the trunk. Just that I had to dump the whip."

"Whose phone did you use?" Garrett asked.

"Wha?"

"You said you called up Gerry at the Bitty Bit party. Whose phone did you use?"

"I don't remember. Some ho." He seemed annoyed by the question.

Decker said, "So you picked up Gerry and you two are riding around with Primo Ekerling in the trunk of the car and . . . then what happened?"

"We take the whip to Jonas Park to leave it there. But once we there, there ain't no one to get a hike from. So Gerry sez we got the Benzene, let's cruise and have some fun. And I figure, the man is dead, it don't make no difference now."

Travis Martel had just contradicted himself with the admission that he knew about the dead man in the trunk.

". . . we take the whip back to the Bitty Bit party, but by then it was almost two in the morning and all the food's gone and all the liquor's gone and Gerry . . ." He leaned forward. "See, we be riding around for over two hours, so Gerry's hungry and tells me he's in the mood for pancakes. So we get back into the whip and ride around until Gerry sees Mel's. So he sez, 'How 'bout Mel's?'"

"Gerry's hungry and says how about Mel's?"

"Zackly," Martel said. "So we dump the car 'bout a few blocks from Mel's. We still don't got no hike home since we left the car a few blocks away, so I call up Rudy on the number he gave me. But I musta copied it wrong cuz it ain't working."

"Maybe he gave you a wrong number on purpose," Garrett said.

"Yeah, I thought about that."

"So you're stuck without a ride home. What happened next?"

"Gerry calls up a whoadie of his and tells him we'll buy some pancakes if he come pick us up. And his whoadie sez okay but he's with a bro so we has to buy him some pancakes, too. So Gerry sez okay, he'll buy everyone pancakes. So we wait for 'round an hour and then Gerry's buds come in Mel's and I buy everyone pancakes with the money that Rudy gave me. I bought everyone pancakes and eggs and bacon and shit. It comes to like a hundred dollars. But that's okay cuz I still had about two hundred left over even with buyin' everyone breakfast. So we all ate pancakes and eggs and shit and then we went home."

Martel shrugged.

"That's it."

The cell was silent.

Decker said, "Let me recap this very briefly. Rudy told you that he went to Ekerling's office to get your CDs back."

"Yeah."

"Rudy said there was a problem. That he and Ekerling argued."

"Yeah."

"That Ekerling came at Rudy with a knife and Rudy shot Ekerling and stuffed him in the trunk of the Mercedes."

"Yeah."

"So you knew about the body in the trunk, Travis."

"He was dead. I checked it out with my own eyes. He was already dead."

"I understand that."

"I didn't do no murder."

"I know," Decker soothed. "Rudy said he needed you to get rid of the body. He gave you the keys to the Mercedes and told you to dump it in the hood."

"Yeah."

"You picked up Geraldo Perry and went to Jonas Park to get rid of the car. But then you realized that you had no one to pick you up from the park. So you took the car *all* the way back into Hollywood to dump it."

"Yeah. Like I tole you, Gerry wanted to go to the Bitty Bit party, anyway. And I figure why not cuz Ekerling be already dead."

"Got it," Decker said. "So you drove the car back to Hollywood, to the Bitty Bit party, but by that time, the party was over and Gerry was hungry. He wanted pancakes."

"Yeah, that's why we dumped the Benzene where we did. We saw Mel's and figured we'd get some pancakes. We bought everyone pancakes."

"Why didn't you tell us all of this in the first place?" Diaz asked.

"'Cause Rudy tole me that if somethin' happens, that I shouldn't talk. That he'd get me a white-assed lawyer and everything would be fine."

"And you believed him?"

"He's a white boy," Travis said. "He sez he's a lawyer."

"That much is true," Decker said.

"He knows the system. Besides, I knew that he weren't goin' be producin' my shit if I ratted him out."

Garrett pushed over a yellow legal pad. "You want to write your story down for us? Then maybe we can talk to the district attorney and help you out."

Martel regarded the paper and pen and then Garrett's face. "All this talk about food . . . it's way past lunch. I'm starvin'. I need something to eat."

"Start writing and I'll order in some food," Diaz said.

"I don't want jail shit," Martel insisted. "I be heppin' you out, I deserve a good lunch."

"What do you want?" Garrett asked.

"All this talk about pancakes . . ." Martel shrugged. "How 'bout some pancakes?"

36

Decker had been operating on casino time—protracted periods under artificial lighting without any sense of the passage of hours. He had arrived at County Jail at nine in the morning. By the time he was back in the West Valley, it was almost six, the sun still in the sky but the shadows long. His cell's voice-mail box was full, and there was a stack of telephone pink message slips in his in-box.

After parking in the lot at the station house, he had entered through the back door, winding his way through the halls to get to his private space. The door to his office was open, the light was on, and a wonderful aroma was wafting into the squad room. His desk had been covered with a red-checkered tablecloth and set with paper plates and plastic utensils. Rina was sitting in his chair, absorbed in a novel.

"Good book?" he said.

She looked up. "Very good." She stood up and kissed his cheek. "I was in the mood for a picnic."

"We're indoors."

"We can open a window and pretend."

Decker smiled and drew his wife into his arms. "You don't know how wonderful this is. I'm starved."

"Then shall we dispense with the pleasantries and get down to business?"

"Absolutely." Decker drew up a chair on the opposite side of the desk. "What have we?"

Rina opened a picnic basket. "Corned beef on rye or chicken salad on whole grain?"

"One of each."

She handed him two wrapped sandwiches. "I have cucumber salad, Waldorf salad—"

"Just set them on the desk and stick a fork in it."

"Will do."

Decker wolfed down the corned beef, then helped himself to the salads. "Where's Hannah?"

"In a study group. She told me that she spoke to you last night."

"I did."

"She said you two had a nice discussion."

"Interesting. It's hard to tell if she enjoys my company or finds me annoying." He looked up from his sandwich. "I feel like I'm a litmus test. Depending what kind of mood she's in, I'm either way too acidic or way too basic."

Rina laughed. "How was your day?"

"Really long but very profitable." He gave her a brief recap of his eight hours in a cell with Travis

Martel. "So now that Banks seems to be involved, Hollywood can justify even more manpower to hunt him down."

"Even *more* manpower? They were looking for him previously?"

"Yes, they were, but not with this newfound intensity." He explained to her about the blood splotches he had discovered behind the newly painted baseboard in Rudy's apartment. "The blood's not Primo Ekerling's."

"So whose blood is it?"

"A very good question. We got the DNA back. We know it was a woman. Once we locate Banks, maybe we can even get an answer. The good part is that with Hollywood looking for him, I don't have to concentrate my efforts toward finding him. Plus, I got them to post a couple of guys to look for Ryan Goldberg."

"The missing Doodoo Slut."

"Exactly." He put down his sandwich and picked up a pile of message slips. "Sorry. I just want to see if any of my messages are from Liam O'Dell."

"Take your time. I'll just eat my sandwich and read my book."

"What are you reading?" he asked absently.

"A biography of Eric Clapton."

"I didn't know you like that kind of thing."

"It has its moments. All celebrities are a might off, but rock stars are uniquely nuts."

"You're telling me?" Decker continued to sort through the messages. "Just the little acquaintances I've made with D-list people have made me realize that. And yet the wannabes keep on coming like locusts during the dry season. Doesn't matter who steps on them, who squashes them and mashes them under their heels, there's always more. Travis Martel was willing to sit in jail and risk a life sentence in prison for a crime he probably didn't commit, just on the off chance that if he ever came out of the pen, Rudy Banks would get him a recording contract. Now how crazy is that . . . ah, here we go." Decker picked up the phone and dialed Liam's cell. "This shouldn't take long."

O'Dell answered on the third ring.

"It's Lieutenant Decker. What's going on?"

"Nothing." His voice was tense.

"I've managed to secure a couple of Hollywood police officers to look for Ryan."

"Bully for you."

Decker ignored his anger, knowing where it was coming from. "I spent the entire day at County Jail talking to Travis Martel. He had some interesting things to say." He summarized eight hours of master interrogation for Mad Irish. "It seems Rudy promised Martel a record contract if he'd either murder Primo or just get rid of the car."

"And you believe him? Martel?"

"I believe that he was involved, and I believe that Rudy was involved."

"Nice to have Rudy's neck in a noose, but right now I'm thinking about Mudd. If the police crap out, we're thinking about a private eye. Know anyone?"

Certainly not Phil Shriner, Decker thought. "I know some Valley people . . . not so many city people." A beat. "I've heard good things about a West L.A. PI named Aaron Fox. He used to be with LAPD but we never crossed paths. I'll get you a number. Again, let me know if you hear from Ryan."

"Ditto." Liam cut the line.

"Everything okay?" Rina asked.

"One step at a time," Decker opened his chicken salad sandwich. "Wow, this is just terrific. Thanks again."

Rina opened another box. "Hannah baked cookies for the squad room. You can have one. They're pareve."

"Tell her thank you. To what do we owe such benevolence?"

"She was baking cookies for her friends, and I said as long as she had the bowls and cookie sheets out, she should bake for you guys."

"What did she say to that?"

"She said okay, but clearly wasn't keen on the idea. Then I told her you'd write her a note and the school would probably give her credit for community service. That brightened her outlook considerably. It means she won't have to do her after-school hours this week."

Decker popped a cookie in his mouth. "Delicious. I should be offended by my own daughter's tepid response to baking for me and the crew, but I'm not." He took another and made short work of it. "Let's face it. No one works for free."

The morning was clear and bright, the sunlight tumbling out from the cloudless, blue ether. The drive to the Palisades was free moving. Decker was behind the wheel with Marge sitting shotgun drinking a mocha latte and Oliver in the back mocking her coffee choice, railing on about suckers who paid three dollars for something that probably cost twenty-five cents to make.

Marge broke into his rant. "If you don't shut up, I'm going to pour this over your head."

"Let me just ask you a question," Oliver said. "Does Will drink any of that shit?"

"Will's a coffee drinker."

"I'm a coffee drinker, but that's not what I asked you. I want to know if Will drinks any of that mocha, chocolate, whipped, foamed, soy, nonfat—"

"Occasionally he does, for your information. Now if you'd kindly save your obnoxious aggressive streak for Melinda Little, I'd be much obliged."

"I bet she drinks mocha, whipped, foamed—"

"Can I kill him?" Marge asked Decker. She turned around to the back. "You know, if you would have ordered a plain coffee and gotten some caffeine in your system, you wouldn't be bitching at me."

"I don't pay two bucks for something I can make for ten cents."

"Scott, you don't own a coffeemaker. You don't even own a jar of instant. That's your problem. You show up in the morning and wait for someone in the squad room to make coffee, then you mooch off the common pot. This morning, no one bothered to make coffee. Now you have a friggin' headache and we have to put up with your chemical withdrawal. It's not fair." She rummaged around in her purse. "Here. Take a Motrin. Maybe it'll take the snarl off your face."

Oliver wanted to sneer, but the pain got the better of him. "Do you have something to wash it down with?" Marge handed him the last of her mocha latte. "Thanks."

"You're welcome." She looked out the window, at the billows of white foam barreling across the cobalt marine expanse. "Sure is pretty around here . . . especially without the excess noise."

Oliver held his head and grumbled from the backseat.

Decker said, "How the other half lives."

Marge said, "I wonder how Melinda—with two kids and probably a lot of debt—managed to snag a multirich guy like Michael Warren."

"She's a beautiful woman," Decker said.

Marge said, "There are lots of beautiful women in L.A."

"My guess is that she's hot in the sack," Oliver said.

"There are a lot of women who are also hot in the sack," Marge said.

"But probably not many who'll do *whatever* the guy wants."

"What makes you say that Melinda's that kind of gal?"

"She had a gambling problem. She fucked the Doodoo Sluts for money. When you whore, you do whatever the client desires, and in the punk scene, I bet they desired some pretty strange stuff."

37

The woman looked as if she had just stepped off a yacht. The reality was that Melinda Little Warren was just about to step onto one. She wore a blue-and-white-striped top, white capri pants, and white wedge sandals. Gold bangles along with a diamond watch encircled her wrists, and pearl drops hung from her earlobes. Her blond tresses were loose and wild.

She made a point of looking at her watch. "I don't have time for this. I have to be at the marina in an hour or else I hold everyone up. What do you *want* from me?"

"I want to find out why you lied," Decker said.

She blinked her eyes several times. "I've already told you. I lied about Phil Shriner because I was embarrassed about my gambling problem. I didn't see the point of bringing up my past issues when I don't have them anymore."

"Not that lie," Decker said. "I'm talking about the lie about not knowing Primo Ekerling. The record producer who was murdered in a manner similar to your husband. I asked you if you knew him. You told me the name didn't sound at all familiar."

Melinda was silent.

"Mrs. Warren, you're a very bright woman. You knew that we were assigned to investigate and we were going to investigate. You should have known that the lie was going to come back on you—"

"Shriner told you!" Her face was purple with outrage. "That bastard broke confidence. I'm going to sue—"

"It wasn't Shriner, it was Liam O'Dell." Melinda's mouth opened and closed. "You should have known we'd speak to all of them because Ekerling's murder was similar to Ben's. Didn't *you* think that there might be a connection?"

"When I read about it in the papers, I thought it was odd, but . . ." She stopped and tears pooled in her dark eyes. "Am I going to need a lawyer?"

Oliver said, "Why don't we ask you a few questions and then you can decide that for yourself."

"I shouldn't need a lawyer." Her cheeks reddened with anger. "I didn't do anything wrong."

Decker said, "All we're trying to do is get the truth. Maybe we should all sit down and start from the beginning."

Melinda glanced at her watch. A big dramatic sigh. "I guess a relaxing day on the ocean is not going to happen for me." Another hostile glare. "I need to call up my husband and tell the group to go without me. You have to give me a moment to compose myself. If he hears tension in my voice, he's going to come home and I don't want him knowing about any of this."

"Fair enough."

After taking several deep breaths, she made the phone call. Her voice was smooth and her lies were silken. Something about meeting an old friend who's in L.A. for only a day. When she hung up, her eyes were wet. "Happy?"

"Your misery doesn't make us happy, Mrs. Warren," Decker said.

"You could have fooled me."

She changed from the sailor's getup into jeans and a T-shirt. The bracelets had come off as well as the diamond watch. She had scrubbed down her face, and without any makeup, she looked like the fifties-plus woman she was. She made a pot of coffee and served it with some nuts and candy. She sat in an oversized chair with her legs tucked under her body, sipping coffee and letting the steam tickle her face.

Oliver put his mug down on the coffee table and took out a small notepad. "When you read about Primo Ekerling's death—and its similarity to your husband's murder—what did you think?"

She licked her lips. "It was odd, but I didn't think it had anything to do with Bennett's death. Fifteen years apart. Why would it have anything to do with Ben's death?"

"But why not?" Oliver said. "The similarities were right in front of your face. And if I may be blunt, Primo was one of your former lovers."

Her laugh was derisive. "When my husband was murdered, that psychotic episode of my life had been long over."

Decker said, "Let's go back a little bit. How did that psychotic episode happen in the first place?"

Her eyes moistened. She put down her coffee cup and kneaded her hands. "Do you know what it's like to be married to Jesus?" When there was no response, she continued. "Bennett was a saint and everyone told me so . . . how lucky and fortunate I was to have bagged him. My parents preferred him to me. So much so, they gave him *my* money."

"Your trust fund?" Decker said. When Melinda gave him a quizzical look, he said, "We talked to your mother."

"She hates me." Her voice was matter-of-fact. "The woman is so incredibly narcissistic that she was jealous of any attention not focused on her."

Marge said, "Must have been hard having to live up to your husband's image and dealing with a hurtful mother. Then as a topper, Mom gave away your trust fund to your husband."

"Oh, you got that right, sister!" She got up and started to pace. "Can you imagine the betrayal? Trusting a stranger over her own daughter? I wanted to kill her!"

"What about your husband?" Oliver asked.

"What?" Face flushed with anger, she turned to him. "My husband? What about him? I'm talking about my mother!"

Oliver pulled back the rhetoric. "I was just wondering if you were as angry at your husband as you were at your mother."

She stopped walking and let out an exasperated sigh. "Ben tried to be fair. He spent the money on things that he thought the whole family would enjoy. I wanted the Mercedes as much as he did. I don't know. Maybe I was a little pissed at Ben for setting up the arrangement with Mom."

"Like they were colluding against you?"

"What choice did Ben have? Either it was that or nothing. My mom was ready to take the money back and put it in trust for the kids. Ben was trying to act the peacemaker. But it was really hurtful."

Marge said, "Is that when you started having affairs?"

"Maybe . . . I don't know." She shook her head and sat back down, looking at the ceiling as she spoke. "Ben was never around. Always doing something for someone else. For the kids, for the school, for my parents, for the community. I was always last."

"Did you ever tell him how you felt?" Decker asked her.

"Tell Jesus what to do?" She pointed to her chest. "Moi?" She rubbed her eyes and looked away. "I got pregnant while we were engaged. The kid wasn't his. I got an abortion and he married me anyway. Saint Ben. My first mistake. I shouldn't have gone through with it. My mother loved Ben. I thought she might like me better because I chose someone she liked."

Silence blanketed the room.

"Did you like Ben?" Marge asked softly.

"Sure I liked him. I loved him." She slouched back into the oversized sailcloth chair. Her voice dropped to a hush. "I don't think he liked me all that much. I mean, what kind of man marries a woman who fucks around on him?"

No one answered.

"You want my opinion? He filled his life with all these obligations to avoid me. To avoid sex. I don't think he liked sex. At least not with me."

"Maybe he was gay," Oliver said. "Why else would he avoid sex with someone as gorgeous as you?"

That got a genuine smile. Every so often Oliver would do something like that and Marge remembered why she worked with him.

Melinda said, "I thought about that. I doubt if he had someone on the side—man or woman. His work and his extracurricular activities took up all his time."

"Could he have been lying about some of his activities?" Marge asked her.

"He was always available for my phone calls. And he always left me his schedule—just in case. When I phoned him, he took my calls right away. Maybe he was wrestling with his sexual demons.

Maybe that's why he scheduled himself so tightly . . . so he wouldn't have time to fool around."

Marge said, "And in the meantime, you were home alone with two little boys making demands and no help. I'm a mother. I know it's not easy."

"Especially because I was on a very tight allowance . . . because of my 'problem.'" She made quotation marks around the word with her fingers. "I had to beg for every dollar just like a kid. It was demeaning!"

"Who controlled the purse strings?" Decker asked. "Mom or Ben?"

"Both. Ben did the weekly grocery shopping, he bought clothes and supplies for the boys, he paid the bills, he paid all the expenses." She gave a wry smile. "I was allowed to shop for my own clothing, but Ben had to account for every dollar spent or else Mom would take away my trust fund. That didn't give me lot of latitude for my recreation."

"By recreation do you mean gambling?" Oliver asked.

She picked up her coffee and took a gulp. It was lukewarm by now. "Everyone was so afraid that I couldn't control my gambling that I started gambling just to prove them wrong. That's when I got into deep debt."

"How'd you pay it off?"

Melinda turned to Decker and raised an eyebrow. "I was creative. A couple of times I managed to forge Ben's signature and withdrew my own money."

"Did Ben find out?"

"If he did, he didn't tell me about it. Maybe he was secretly glad. All this responsibility of taking care of me . . . I think it was a burden. And every so often, I'd win big at the tables and refill the coffers."

Decker jumped into the touchy subject. "So when did you meet the Doodoo Sluts?"

The name caused her head to jerk back. "That part of my life was completely over before Ben was murdered. At least a year before."

"I believe you," Decker said, "but I need you to answer the question."

"I met Primo first . . . at one of the poker casinos. I was about to bust and he bought me some chips. That night I won and Primo and I celebrated." Again, she looked up at the ceiling. "Ben had taken the boys on a camping trip. No one was home. It wasn't my first time being bad, but I hardly knew this guy."

The room was silent.

Melinda said, "He drank, Primo did. He was loose with a buck. I liked that." A shrug. "That's it."

"And how did you move on from Primo to the others?"

Her eyes became steely. "I don't see the relevance between my psycho past and my husband's murder."

Decker said, "Let me tell you why we think it is relevant. We know for a fact that there's a common link between someone in your past and a prime suspect in Primo's death."

Melinda seemed confused. "But they have Primo's murderers behind bars. Punk kids. Certainly I don't know them. The paper said it was a carjacking."

"It was way more than a carjacking, and we're just beginning to put all the pieces together. But there's a key player, and I think we both know who that key player is."

"I don't know who you're talking about."

"Figure it out," Decker said. "We believe your husband's death can be traced back to someone in the Doodoo Sluts. Primo's dead. That makes three members left. Go down the list."

She remained silent.

"Melinda," Marge said, soothingly. "You've held in this terrible secret for so long. Get it off your chest. Unburden yourself. Tell us your side of what happened to your husband—"

"But I don't know what happened!" She cried out. "I don't know what happened! If I thought it had something to do with the Doodoo Sluts, don't you think I would have said something a long time ago?"

"Maybe you were too scared to talk," Marge said. "But now it's all going to come out. This is your one chance to tell us everything you know."

"I'm in the dark!" Melinda cried out. "Can't you get that through your heads? Why would one of the Doodoo Sluts murder my husband? Who are we even talking about, by the way?"

Decker said, "Rudy Banks is missing. And we've

got a witness who has implicated him in Ekerling's death."

"*Rudy?*" Melinda gasped. She seemed genuinely shocked. "I . . . I . . . Rudy murdered Primo? I can't believe . . . *Rudy?* They were friends!"

"They haven't been friends for many, many years," Marge said. "For the last ten years, they've been involved in multiple lawsuits with each other."

Melinda shook her head. "I didn't know. I walked away from those bad boys about a year before my husband was murdered, and I haven't seen any of them since."

Decker tried a different tactic. "Why'd you break away from the group?"

Melinda blew out air. "Because I felt tremendously guilty. It felt good for a while, and then it felt very dirty. I wasn't getting any affection at home, but I didn't care anymore. I just wanted out."

"Especially after the band stopped giving you spending money," Decker said.

She turned daggers onto his face. "Yes, especially after the band stopped giving me money. Don't be so damn smug, Lieutenant. I've paid for my sins in more ways than you could count. After it was all over, I was haunted by a lot more than just nightmares."

"Haunted by what?" Oliver asked. "That Ben would find out?"

"Uh, yeah, that, too. Look, guys, I'm exhausted. I can't deal with this anymore. You've got to go."

Something clicked inside Decker's brain. "You weren't afraid of Ben finding out, you were afraid of the band. And not the entire band, only one member. He was stalking you."

Tears leaked from Melinda's eyes. Decker gave Marge a barely perceptible nod.

"Tell us about it, Melinda," Marge cooed. "Unburden yourself."

When Melinda finally spoke, her voice was so soft Decker had to lean forward to hear her. "He'd show up as soon as Ben left for work and the kids were in school. And when he wasn't bothering me in person, he'd phone me ten times a day. He was a big guy. I was terrified."

Decker said, "You mean Ryan Goldberg. Mudd. He was obsessively in love with you, wasn't he, Mrs. Warren?"

"He was crazy!"

"And it never occurred to you that he had something to do with your husband's death?"

"Maybe . . ." The tears were streaming down her cheeks. "Even if I knew he did it, I wouldn't have said anything."

"You were afraid he'd come after you?" Marge asked.

Melinda wiped her eyes. "He was big, he was strong, and he was psycho! He thought I was going to leave my family and run away with him. I was petrified that if I implicated him in Ben's death or even mentioned him to the police that my sordid past would come out, but even more important,

I was scared that Ryan would come back and finish off the kids!"

Decker regarded her flushed face. Yet, he wasn't totally satisfied. "So you *did* think that Ryan might have done it."

She dabbed her eyes. "I thought it was a possibility, even though he told me he didn't do it. He swore that he didn't lay a finger on Ben."

Decker said, "So he was still coming around after Ben was murdered?"

"He came a couple of times. That's when he swore he didn't do it."

"And you believed him?"

"I don't know what I believed," Melinda said. "All I know is he finally stopped showing up at my doorstep. I had to convince him that if he didn't leave me alone, the police would think he murdered Ben. I told him that, for his own sake, he had to hide out for a while and that I would contact him when it was safe."

"And he agreed to that?"

"All I know is he stopped coming around and we never had any more contact."

"Did you wonder why he stopped seeing you, stopped trying to contact you?" Decker asked her.

"No, I didn't wonder why. I was just relieved. After Ben died, I was so stunned. I was scared, I was broke, and I was crazed. I had two kids to support, and I had no one to turn to. I suppose that I assumed that Ryan got bored waiting for my phone call and moved on to another woman.

He was an easy mark. A little flattery and he'd give you anything he had."

"He gave you money."

"He gave me lots of money until the other band members took over his bank account."

"You were angry at them?" Marge asked.

"Of course. I was furious. But it was the best thing that happened to me. It made me realize how low I'd sunk. I tried to call it quits with Ryan, but then I realized he was in love with me."

Oliver said, "So why didn't you just dump him?"

"Because I was afraid he'd say something to Ben. And I felt a little sorry for him . . . he seemed like a gentle giant until he started showing up at my house ten times a day. Then all pity flew out the window."

"So you think if anyone murdered Ben, it was Ryan?"

"I don't know." She threw up her hands. "It's over. Ben's dead. I've moved on."

Decker said, "What was your relationship with Rudy Banks like?"

"It was torrid and it was brief. Rudy was a good-looking guy and a total psychopath. We had an affair and then poof, it ended, which was fine for both of us."

"Did you know that Rudy was a North Valley student and that he knew your husband?"

Melinda looked confused. "I don't . . . I seem to recall him being a local."

"Rudy didn't like your husband," Marge said.

"He claimed that your husband got him expelled from high school."

"News to me," Melinda said.

Oliver said, "Your husband also busted up Rudy's drug business."

"Rudy had a drug business?"

Her surprise seemed real. Decker said, "Rudy sold drugs to North Valley High. He used ghetto kids as runners because they were easy targets. One of his runners was Darnell Arlington. When Darnell got suspended, the whole business collapsed."

Melinda said, "I didn't follow what went on in my husband's school."

"But you knew Darnell Arlington."

"I knew that my husband had a special interest in him. And I knew that Darnell had a grudge against Ben when he got expelled. But he had an alibi and that was that."

"Rudy never mentioned anything about knowing your husband?"

"No, of course not. I wouldn't have gone with him if he had. When I met him, he was pure punk—lots of drugs, kinky sex, and angry music. He was young, he was really good-looking, he was wild, and for a while, he was very exciting. Then it got boring. When he stopped giving me cash, I hooked up with Mudd, who was very generous. Why else would I have a fling with Ryan? It certainly wasn't his dashing looks."

Decker could see the calculated shrew inside

the respectable woman. He said, "Where did Liam O'Dell fit into the string?"

"You don't need to know all the sordid details, okay? It ended with Ryan. I did *not* murder my husband and I *don't* know who did!"

Decker raised a finger. "You cheated on your husband. You stole from his bank account. You resented his time away from you and his disinterest sexually. So tell me why I should believe that you had nothing to do with your husband's murder."

"How about this!" Melinda snapped back. "The police spent hours checking me out. They checked out my story on the evening of the murder and it was all true. They checked my phone records. They checked my financial records. They checked insurance policies. They checked if I had ever purchased any weapons. If I was cheating on him at the time . . . which I wasn't, by the way. I had come to appreciate how much I had. I truly loved Ben."

She became suddenly angry.

"Look, I've been cooperative. I've told you everything and I've talked without a lawyer. What more do you *want* from me?"

Oliver said, "Really quickly . . . you were interviewed at the time by Arnie Lamar and Cal Vitton. They're the ones who cleared you?"

Melinda rolled her eyes. "I don't know who cleared me, but they were the primary investigators in my husband's case and, yes, I spoke to both of them many times. If you don't believe me, go ask them."

"I can ask Lamar; Vitton is dead." When she didn't react, Oliver added, "Suicide."

She flinched. "When was this?"

"Right when we reopened your husband's investigation," Oliver said.

"Interesting timing," Marge added. "Do you think his suicide might have had something to do with your husband's demise?"

"How would I know?" She began to tap her foot. "Can we wrap this up?"

Decker said, "Rudy Banks moved out of his apartment about a week ago. Since then, no one has heard boo from him. And his disappearance also neatly coincided with our reopening the case."

"Didn't you tell me that you had a witness who implicated him in Ekerling's murder? Or was that utter bullshit?"

"No, it's absolutely true. We do have a witness."

"Then maybe he felt you were closing in on him and he took off."

"It doesn't worry you?" Decker asked. "Vitton's dead and Rudy's missing?"

She didn't answer.

"Well, how about this?" Decker said. "Probably one of the reasons that you stopped hearing from Ryan Goldberg is that he had a serious mental collapse. His breakdown was so serious, he underwent shock therapy. I spoke to him a couple of weeks ago. He's completely decompensated."

425

"Did he bring me up?" Melinda asked.

Decker digested the question. Talk about narcissism. Or maybe it was fear. "No."

"Why'd you go to see him?"

"Initially I went to get some information about Primo Ekerling. Then Rudy went missing and I went back to Ryan for information about Rudy—and to make sure he was okay. Now Ryan appears to be missing as well."

Melinda's reaction was slow shock. "*Ryan's* missing?"

"Maybe he's lost, maybe he packed out. We can't locate him."

She bit her thumbnail. "Should I be worried?" When none of the detectives answered, she cursed out loud. "God, this is just terrific . . . just fucking terrific! Ekerling is dead and two maniacs are missing plus the police are breathing down my neck. I think it's time I hired a lawyer!"

"Sure, do that," Decker said. "And while you're at it, you might also consider hiring a bodyguard."

38

Decker tossed Marge the keys to the Crown Vic. "You drive. I need to think."

No one spoke for the first ten minutes of the ride back to the Valley. Oliver put his hands behind his head, lay back, and closed his eyes. Decker had popped open a can of root beer and was sipping it while reviewing his notes and making diagrams. He said, "Okay, let's have a go at it. Melinda Little Warren. Lying or not lying about her involvement in her husband's murder?"

"Even though she is a liar, in this case I vote not lying," Marge said. "She spoke to us without a lawyer."

"To play devil's advocate, maybe she knew that once a lawyer was involved, her current husband would find out about her past and dump her."

"True, but if she was in real trouble, I don't think she would hesitate to hire the best legal mouthpiece in the country. She certainly could afford it."

"Or at least her husband could. How much money does she have on her own? And what if her current husband is like her past husband? What if he holds all the purse strings and she knows he'd be reticent to hire a lawyer to defend her?"

"All true, but the fact that she did speak without a lawyer to me means either she thinks she's clever enough to beat the system or she doesn't have anything to do with Ben Little's murder. Plus she was checked out thoroughly by Vitton and Lamar, and they couldn't dredge up anything against her except Ben's insurance policy. I think Ben was worth more to her alive than dead. He allowed her to tap into her trust fund. And, as a woman, I think part of her really liked her husband."

"Ditto," Oliver chimed in with his eyes still closed.

"Are you agreeing with him or me?" Marge said.

"You." Oliver straightened up. "Melinda's arrogant, and a liar and a thief. She could even be a murderer. But I don't think she murdered Ben Little. I believe her when she said she had enough of the sex, drugs, and rock and roll. I think she was grateful to get out of the scene with her marriage intact and get rid of those losers."

Decker said, "You think she was happy in a loveless marriage?"

Marge said, "Some women can deal with passionless marriages, especially if they occasionally get it

428

from an outside source. Melinda seems to me to be one of those."

Oliver said, "I also don't think that she set up Ryan Goldberg to murder Ben. She wouldn't be involved with a loser unless she was planning to whack him afterward. Otherwise he'd be an albatross around her neck."

Marge said, "I agree with that as well."

Decker said, "May I remind you two that Goldberg is missing? Maybe she did have him whacked."

"If she was going to whack him," Marge said, "she would have done it long ago."

"Then how about Ryan murdering Ben on his own?" Decker asked.

Marge was noncommittal. "Melinda told us that Goldberg swore he didn't do it."

"That's meaningless."

"You met Goldberg, Pete. What do you think?"

"At first glance, he seems too compromised mentally to pull off a murder. But like you said, I didn't know him then, and I don't know him now. He could be a gentle giant ninety-nine point nine percent of the time. It may be that point one percent that we should be concerned about."

Oliver made a face. "He stalked Melinda. That's not a passive guy."

Marge said, "But he stopped after Ben Little died."

"That fits with what Liam said about Ryan moving on to someone else," Decker commented on. "Goldberg was a serial romantic, falling in love with the women he screwed. On the other hand, Mudd had a major breakdown. Maybe his crack-up was precipitated by his murdering Ben Little."

Oliver said, "And from talking to Melinda, you could tell that she really was frightened by him. So scared that she didn't even report him to the police."

Marge said, "Was Ryan so out of it that he could have thought that murdering Ben Little was the only solution to getting Melinda?"

"Maybe," Decker said. "But if he murdered Ben with the hope of snagging Melinda, why did he suddenly disappear from her life after Little died?"

"How about this?" Oliver said. "Ryan murdered Ben with or without Melinda's okay. But now she's stuck. She tells Mudd to lay low. He did, and while he was hiding out, he felt so guilty that he had a breakdown and forgot about Melinda."

Decker nodded. "Sure, although I'm not certain I see him as a premeditated killer. If he did kill Ben, it was probably heat of the moment or an accident. A hulking guy who's not aware of his strength in an argument that got out of hand."

"Like Lenny from *Of Mice and Men*," Marge said.

Oliver said, "Let me remind everyone that Little was shot execution style in the trunk of his own car."

"He had help, Scott," Marge said. "We know Leroy Josephson was involved. Maybe Rudy Banks wanted Little dead and didn't want to do it himself.

He hired out Leroy Josephson but knew that Leroy needed help. That's where Ryan Goldberg comes in. Rudy puts the two of them together: two men he could manipulate."

"All that's fine," Decker said, "but what's Rudy's motive for wanting Little dead?"

"Maybe Rudy found out about Little's insurance policy," Marge said. "Ben might have been worth more to Melinda alive, but Ben wasn't worth anything to Rudy Banks. Rudy hated the guy. With him gone, Rudy gets rid of a guy he detests, plus it frees up Little's insurance policy."

Oliver said, "But why would Melinda give Rudy any of the insurance money?"

"To keep her past a secret," Marge said.

"We could postulate or we could actually try to do something," Decker said. "What's your schedule like tomorrow, guys?"

"I'm not sure," Marge said.

"I think I'm pretty light," Oliver said.

"Book a trip to Ohio. It's time to revisit Mr. Arlington. Let's go back and talk to the link we have left. Arlington wasn't in town when the murder went down, but maybe he set something up. Darnell and Rudy ran drugs together. Darnell had a reason to be pissed at Ben Little. You two go back to the station house, get your tickets and between now and tomorrow, think up a plausible scenario involving Rudy and Arlington that culminates in Little's murder. Then take your theory, splash it in Arlington's face, and see what he says."

"Got it," Oliver said.

"What about you?" Marge said. "I thought you wanted to go with us."

"Rudy's missing, Ryan's missing. I think I need to be in town for a spell."

The coach was dressed in black jogging pants and a collared, striped black-and-white ref's shirt. A whistle hung from around his neck. Multiple basketballs were bouncing on a wooden gym floor as his boys were going through drills. "I don't have to talk to either of you." Darnell's voice was molten metal. "I hope you realize that!"

"We appreciate your cooperation," Marge told him.

Oliver said, "It's very important that we talk to you. Why else do you think the government would allocate our travel not once, but twice?"

Arlington was still angry, but he held it back. He blew three sharp punches on his whistle, and the dribbling stopped. The big gym echoed as he spoke. "Twenty minutes free practice time. Work on whatever you want, just as long as you're working. I'm going into my office. I can see what you're doing. Anyone who shirks is gonna incur my wrath."

Coach led Marge and Oliver into a glass-walled office that looked over the gymnasium. The floor space was ample—about four times the size of the Loo's office with shelving that sagged under the weight of trophies. The walls were plastered with certificates of honor as well as black-and-white photos of Polk High winning athletic teams past and present. Arlington's desk was tucked into a corner, but he elected to stand at the window and watch his charges work.

"You have quite a legacy," Marge told him.

"Wrong," he said. "I'm creating a legacy."

Oliver took out his notepad and quickly glanced at his outline of the story that he and Marge had invented to link Darnell with Rudy. Then he regarded Arlington. "We're just trying to get at the truth about Ben Little. The guy went out of his way to help you. What are you so angry about?"

"Get off it," Darnell shot back. "I know how you guys operate. You don't get what you what, you make shit up."

Away from his wife and children, Marge could see the drug runner in Darnell. "I want to talk to you about Rudy Banks."

"I told you I hardly remember him—"

"Now who's making shit up?" Oliver accused. "You ran drugs for him, Darnell. You and Jervis Wenderhole and Leroy Josephson—"

"Leroy's dead, Jervis is working as a community counselor for the underprivileged, I'm working my ass off trying to bring home another trophy so I can keep my damn job and feed and clothe my kids. I had nothing to do with Dr. Ben's death."

He spun around and glared at the detectives.

"Sergeant, after you left *my* home, I thought of Dr. Ben and I cried. As an adult, I can finally see what that poor man was trying to do for me."

His eyes got moist and he looked away.

"I never got no opportunity to thank him. Just a simple phone call to say, hey, your faith in me was not for nothin' . . . look at me now. I'm doing fine."

"I believe everything you just told me, Darnell," Marge said. "But that doesn't change the fact that you and Rudy ran drugs for North Valley High. It doesn't change the fact that when Ben Little found out about it, he shut down the entire drug operation and expelled you from school."

Arlington's steely voice had returned. "If y'all got it so figured out, why wasn't Rudy arrested for drug peddling at the time?"

"C'mon, Darnell," Oliver said, "You know what happened. Rudy's walking was probably part of the deal that Ben made so *you* wouldn't get sent to Juvenile. If the operation would quietly cease, Rudy would disappear without charges and you'd be shipped off to Ohio with nothing on your records."

Marge said, "It probably worked for a little bit. But you know Rudy, Darnell. You know that he wasn't about to walk away from a cash cow. He went back to work using Josephson and Wenderhole."

"And then Ben Little found out," Oliver told him. "He was furious. He thought that you and

Rudy were still running drugs behind his back. This time he was going to whack you hard, Darnell. Rudy said that Little had to be stopped and if you didn't help get rid of him, Ben was going to expose you and this time you'd go to jail."

"Must have really pissed you off," Marge said. "You'd finally gotten your shit together, and Dr. Ben—the same man who expelled you from high school—was about to mess you up again—"

Darnell pivoted around, his face wet with fury, his eyes on fire with indignation. He spoke with a hiss. "You two jackasses ain't worth a penny of what they're paying you if that's the best that you can come up with."

"That's what Jervis Wenderhole told me," Marge pushed. "He said he got his information directly from Leroy Josephson. Rudy Banks promised Josephson and Wenderhole a recording contract if he'd help them out with the Little problem."

"You're feeding me total horseshit!"

"Like hell I am," Marge shot back. "Rudy arranged some studio time for you before you were busted and sent to Ohio. You thought that Banks was going to make you a star. So tell me how that's bullshit."

"After I got expelled, I didn't talk to any of them again!"

"You just looked away from me," Marge told him. "Now who's feeding who horseshit?"

Oliver said, "This is your chance to make it

right, Mr. Arlington. We're open to your side of the story. We're just telling you what Jervis—"

"Jervis didn't tell you nothin' about me." He zeroed in on Marge's face. "He called me after he saw you, Sergeant." He scrunched up his face in pure hatred. "We were bros, man! We were tight! I know exactly what he said to you. And I ain't saying anything more, because you'll turn it against me." Arlington checked his watch. "I've got to get back to the kids in ten minutes."

"We can meet you after practice," Marge said.

"What I got to tell you won't take more than thirty seconds. I didn't know anything about what happened to Dr. Ben. And I never bothered to find out because when he was killed, I wasn't on good terms with anyone back in Los Angeles."

"Dr. Ben tried to call you," Marge stated.

"Yeah, couple of times. But I was pissed as hell at him, so I didn't take his calls. And I couldn't take calls from Jervis and Leroy because Nana monitored the phones and wouldn't let me talk to no one from L.A., including my own mother."

A pause.

"I was pissed at her for that at first, but she was right. I had to start from scratch if I was gonna start over. Nana sent me to an intercity Catholic school that had a pretty good track record with its students. I was there and I had a clean slate. I could either fuck up again—there was lots of opportunities to do that—or turn it around. So I decided to give it a shot. And that's what I did.

I tried out for the team and made it. I wasn't the tallest, but I was fast with my hands and feet and, just as important, I began to work! I was being scouted by some local colleges to play on their teams. Now why would I fuck up my last chance to succeed to do something two thousand miles away to a man who tried to help me?"

"Because you were angry."

"Not *that* angry." Arlington checked his watch again. "I gotta go."

Marge lowered her voice until it was at a silken pitch. "Yeah, you can go, Darnell. We can't stop you. But this has haunted you for fifteen years. And I'll guarantee you that it's going to keep haunting you until you get it off your chest."

"Nothin' on my chest."

"You have two little girls, Darnell. Could you imagine your girls growing up without their daddy? What do you think happened to Ben's little boys? Don't they have a right to know?"

"I wasn't there!"

"I know you weren't there. You were right here in Ohio playing basketball. And you can keep on insisting that you don't know anything about it. Maybe I'll even believe you. But you can't lie to your conscience."

No one spoke. Darnell continued to look out the window, at his boys going through their workout. Suddenly his eyes moistened. "Leroy Josephson . . . he called me about six months after Dr. Ben died. I hadn't heard from him since I left

L.A. so his call was unexpected. Nana wasn't home and I answered the phone." His face began to unfurl. "I shoulda hung up. I knew he was bad news. Leroy was always gettin' himself into one kind of fix or another . . . but Leroy was Leroy and we had a history." Arlington flinched. "You must know some friends like that—all take but no give. You like the dudes, but deep down you know that they're bums."

"I know about twenty guys like that," Oliver said. "In fact, some people might say I'm that kind of friend."

Arlington raised his eyebrows. "So Leroy's on the phone, and suddenly I'm back in L.A. and I'm all ghetto. Yo, bro, whaddup . . . shit like that. Leroy's crowing about some recording deal that he got for A-Tack . . . Jervis Wenderhole."

"I know Jervis is A-Tack, and I know he cut a CD for Primo Ekerling."

"Yeah, exactly. Leroy's goin' on that Jervis cut a CD and is gonna be a big pimp and Leroy was gonna be Jervis's manager and they already got gigs opening for bigger pimps and shit like that. And that I should get my ass over to L.A. and Leroy would make me a pimp and that if I didn't have no money to come out, Leroy would give me some because he was flush."

"Did he say how he earned the money?"

"Nah, he didn't say. I assumed he scored big on some B and E."

"Not drugs?"

"Nah, you don't make much money running drugs unless you are up at the top. All the soldiers get is pocket change and maybe some free shit—whatever you can steal from a rock or a bag." He licked his lips. "Now I knew Leroy was full of shit, but he sounded true. I was just about to say yes, I'm in. I was working my ass off in school and still bitter about being shipped off. And with Dr. Ben out of the way . . . I figured that I could maybe even pick up where I left off . . . selling to North Valley and doing some rap.

"But the good Lord must have been looking over my shoulder. I meant to tell him yes, but what came out of my mouth was a no. He starts trying to up me, and suddenly I'm back in his face, besting him. I told him that I was a star basketball player and I was being looked at for the bigs, which was a total lie, but hell if he was gonna do better than me, know what I'm saying?"

Oliver nodded. "So how did Leroy respond to that?"

"Just by tellin' me what a fool I was. And then he said that it was probably a good thing that I said no because Rudy was still mad at me for botching up the operation. So then I told Leroy, it wasn't me who botched the operation, it was Ben Little."

No one spoke.

Arlington said, "Then Leroy sorta laughed. You know . . . snickered kinda. Then he said to me . . . he said, 'We don't have to worry no more about

Ben Little.' And I said, 'I know that. He's dead. Someone shot him.' And he said, 'I know all about that, Big D'—that's what he used to call me. Big D. Then he says . . . he says . . . 'You know, I was there when it went down.'"

Another moment of silence.

"I got mute. Like Leroy just sucker-punched me. I felt sick just like when I first found out about the murder. I mean, I didn't even know that Leroy and Dr. Ben knew each other. But I suppose that Dr. Ben knew everyone. So I said . . . I said, 'You did it, Yo-King? You snipped Dr. Ben?' Then Leroy was acting all defensive. He said, 'I didn't do no snippin', I just said I was there when it went down.' Then he said, 'I didn't know they was gonna take him down. Things just got bad.' And I say, 'Who took him down?' And Leroy say, 'Don't matter who done it. It wasn't me and it wasn't Jervis and it wasn't even a brother. And now it's over.' Then he asked me do I want to be a major pimp or no. So I say, 'No, I don't got time to be no pimp.' And that was that. He never called me again, I never called him again."

Arlington swallowed hard.

"I never even thought about calling the police. I had no proof that Leroy was talking true, and even if he was, I would never pigeon a friend." Another beat. "It turned out that Leroy wasn't just blowing smoke about turning A-Tack into a pimp. He did cut a CD and Leroy sent it to me, being all smug. At that time, I was burning with envy. Just burning! I was determined to do better. I figured I really fucked up myself by not going back and joining Leroy. I kept playing the CD and saying, 'I could do better than that. I could do way better than that.'"

Silence.

"If you know what happened to Jervis and Leroy, you know what changed my mind."

Marge asked, "How'd you hear about the shooting?"

"My mama told me." He looked away. "She called me up all excited and told me about Leroy dying and Jervis being paralyzed."

"What did you think?"

"What did I think?" A beat. "I was sick. I got down on my knees and thanked Jesus for my salvation." He blew out air. "I tried not to look at Leroy being shot as God's justice for Dr. Ben, but you think what you think. I didn't know why it was in God's plan for Jervis to be hurt. Hell, if Leroy would have called me to pick him up, I would have done the same thing.

"The shooting turned Jervis's life around. He told me that since he was in a wheelchair, he had lots of time to think about things. He found Jesus and never looked back. That's what he told me."

"Did Jervis try to contact you again after you left California?"

"Nah. We faded out of each other's life for ten years. Then out of the blue, he sent me a Christmas card . . . telling me what he's doing. So I wrote him back, telling him what I'm doing. We've been exchanging cards now for about five years but nothing more than that. I was happy he found his life, and he seemed happy that I found mine. I hadn't actually talked to him until last week, when he called to tell me about the interview he had with you." He looked at Marge. "That's when he told me that he had gone to Clearwater Park to pick up Leroy. He also told me that Leroy was real jingly, and Jervis knew that something bad had happened. Then I told him about my phone call with Leroy six months after Dr. Ben died. I told him that Leroy said he was there but never admitted to doin' nothin'"

Arlington stared at the window.

"Maybe Leroy snipped him, maybe he had help. We're never gonna know because Leroy's dead."

"And you're sure that Leroy never mentioned Rudy Banks in connection with the killing," Oliver said.

"Leroy didn't tell me any names. I know that the police talked to Leroy after Dr. Ben's murder. If they couldn't get the truth out of Leroy, I figured why should I do their job for them?" He turned to the detectives. "I suppose if you're determined to arrest me, you'll do it no matter what I say."

"We're not going to arrest you," Marge said. "But we're not at that point yet where we have to be concerned with legal matters. We're just trying to solve an old crime. We're trying to speak for Ben Little who can't speak for himself. Thank you for talking to us again. We'll probably have some follow-up questions if you don't mind."

Arlington opened the door to his office and blew the whistle. "Back in formation. I want to see you practice going down the lanes. Keep it smooth." He turned back to Marge and Oliver. "You can go ahead and ask your questions. And I'll answer them. But do me a favor, Detectives. Next time you want to talk to me, use the phone."

39

Decker leaned back in his desk chair and regarded his two detectives. A dedicated duo, they had come straight from LAX to work. "So Leroy Josephson told Darnell Arlington that he was there when Bennett Little was shot?"

"Leroy 'saw it go down' was the quote," Marge answered. "Leroy made a point of telling Darnell that he didn't murder Ben, just that something bad had happened and Little was killed."

"And that was about the extent of his details," Oliver added.

"Yeah, it seems that everyone that we've talked to is involved and connected, but none of them murdered Little," Marge remarked. "And equally as convenient, the supposed guilty ones are either dead or missing."

Decker said, "And both of you found Darnell to be credible?"

Oliver rubbed his eyes. He and Marge had been up since four in the morning to make a six-thirty flight out of Ohio to get to work by ten. Going cross-country east to west was always disruptive. True, he gained three hours, but his internal clock was so discombobulated that it hardly mattered. Even full-strength coffee wasn't helping. "Right now, I don't know. When we left, I felt like he was telling the truth."

"I did, too." Marge was wearing drawstring pants, a loose-fitting T-shirt, and an unstructured jacket. Comfortable traveling clothes that went anywhere. "If you think it's necessary, we can set up lie detector tests to rule out Wenderhole and Arlington. But even if they came back as being deceptive, we don't have anything that ties them to the crime—no witnesses, no physical evidence, just a lot of hearsay."

Oliver yawned. "I agree with Marge."

Decker said, "You look tired, Scott."

"I'll wake up eventually. I have to. I have a court case this afternoon."

"Lester Hollis?"

"Yeah."

"What about you?" Decker asked Marge.

"Other than a mound of paperwork, nothing too pressing."

"At this point, do we have any new reason to think that Melinda Little, Jervis Wenderhole, and Darnell Arlington were directly involved in Bennett Little's murder?"

"I don't know about involved," Marge said. "I don't think any of them were actually there when Little was murdered."

"Agreed."

"Do we think Melinda, Wenderhole, or Arlington commissioned Bennett Little's murder?"

"After talking to Darnell, I don't think that he had anything to do with Little's murder," Oliver said. "He wasn't in town, he had no money to commission a murder, he was turning his life around, and phone records don't show any contact between him, Rudy Banks, Jervis Wenderhole, or Leroy Josephson directly after the murder."

Marge said, "There were some phone calls to Arlington from both Josephson and Wenderhole before the murder—after Darnell left L.A.—but those calls could have been the ones that his nana intercepted. They certainly didn't last long. After Little's murder, no contact between the boys until around six months later, when Josephson called him. Then there was nothing in the way of any communication for a long, long time. I think Arlington is in the clear."

"What about Wenderhole?"

Marge said, "He freely admitted that he picked up Leroy at Clearwater Park, so he was involved. But he insists that was the extent of what he did. He admitted that he did wrong, and he's willing to take a polygraph to clear him of the murder. I believe Wenderhole's telling the truth."

"So let's save the department the expense of a polygraph until we have more reason to think that Wenderhole was directly involved."

"In his condition, he's not going anywhere."

"So that brings us to Melinda Little. She was home when her husband was murdered. Do we think that she hired someone to kill him?"

"She's the joker in the deck," Oliver said. "She could have hired Banks, she could have hired Goldberg, she could have even talked Goldberg into doing it for free. But for all the reasons we said before, I don't think she did it."

Marge said, "Also, bank records don't indicate any large transfers of money going in and out of the account immediately before or after the murder. Even after she got the insurance money, the amount of cash taken out was steady—no big lump sums paid in cash or suspicious-looking checks."

"It looked to both of us like the money was slowly being drained to pay for her gambling habit," Oliver said.

Decker said, "So with those three out of the picture and with Leroy Josephson dead, I think we've taken this as far as we can. Hollywood has more immediate reasons for wanting to find Banks. They're also looking for Goldberg, since the MP report was filed in their division. Until we can locate one or both, all we can do is wait."

Waiting usually meant for someone to make a mistake. That could mean a day, a week, a month, a year, or never. After two weeks had passed with nothing to propel the case forward, Strapp told Decker to call up Genoa Greeves and give her an update.

Strapp said, "Make it sound like we're on top of it."

"We are on top of it," Decker said. "We're just at a standstill."

"Don't tell her that. Tell her an arrest is right around the corner."

"I'll handle it."

"See that you do."

The woman came down two weeks after Decker's phone call. This time, she was all casual, dressed in jeans, a white T-shirt, and sneakers. Her face was free of makeup, she was unadorned by jewelry, and her hair was braided. No purse, just a briefcase. She extended a hand to Decker. "You'll have to excuse the informal dress. I just got off the plane."

"Traveling is hard enough without having to worry about how you're dressed. No matter what the airlines say, it just seems to get worse and worse."

"I flew privately," she said.

"Ah . . . of course." He ushered her into his office. "Thanks for coming in."

"No problem."

"And thanks again and again for redoing the station house's computer system. We at West Valley are the envy of the rest of LAPD."

"All this advance technology doesn't seem to help you solve cases," she said.

"It does, but not in Bennett Little's situation. Eventually it's going to break open, but I don't know how long eventually is. I'll tell you what we've done."

Genoa took her laptop out of the briefcase. "Go ahead." As Decker recounted the case, her fingers clicked away. She was fast at the keyboard and seemed to be taking down every word he was saying. When he had finished, she folded up the laptop and stowed it neatly into her briefcase. "I'll review what you said later. How are you trying to locate Rudy Banks and Ryan Goldberg?"

"We're talking to everyone who knew them. Goldberg is hard to get a handle on because he was such a loner." When she didn't comment, he continued. "His brother and a former bandmate have hired a private detective to try to find him, but so far he hasn't had much luck."

"What about Rudy Banks?"

"We've determined that his furniture is in storage here in L.A. The name and address on the rental application is phony. So is the driver's license number. The rental unit was paid for in cash for two years. We have set up a camera in front of the bin. So far, no one's been there."

"So you are saying that no one has *been* at the *bin*." She smiled at her joke.

Decker smiled back. "No one has been at the bin. We've made arrangements with the people who work there to call us if they have any kind of contact with anyone associated with the bin. We haven't been able to determine who moved the furniture out of his apartment and into the bin. All the standard moving companies have been ruled out, but we're still checking out van rentals like U-Haul and Ryder's."

"What about Rudy's friends and business associates?"

"Rudy doesn't seem to have much by way of friends. He does have people who he's done business with. They haven't heard from him. What seems to be especially troubling is that his lawyers haven't heard from him. The man has at least a half-dozen lawsuits currently filed. I frankly don't know whether he's dead or alive."

Genoa's face was passive. "And Goldberg . . . you don't know if he's dead or alive, either."

"Yes, ma'am, that's correct."

"Would it help if I put some private detectives on the case?"

"It might complicate things. But I can't stop you."

She paused. "You're under a lot of pressure with this case."

"It's not pressure." A pure lie. "When I get involved, I work it hard, but I've backed off a little. Right now, Hollywood Homicide really wants to find Banks. They actually have a witness who can implicate him in one of their murders."

"The Primo Ekerling case."

"Exactly. We've sent out a BOLO for Rudy's car—"

"A BOLO?"

"Be on the lookout."

"You actually use that phrase?"

"We do."

Genoa smiled. "You've done some work, but the case is far from solved."

"That's true, but we're still on it. No one has thrown in the towel."

A pause. "I once learned in psychology that partial reinforcement increases behavior. Do you know what I'm saying?"

"Yes, I do, Ms. Greeves. Reward a little for each successful step and the person will keep working for the next reward."

"Exactly. I suppose you deserve a partial re-inforcement."

"Not me, ma'am, the police department. I'm just an employee."

"See, that's what I abhor about the government. There is no personal incentive."

"I have plenty of incentive, Ms. Greeves. My job is very important to me. My reward is getting the bad guy behind bars."

"You're telling me that you don't work for money?"

"No, I wouldn't work for free."

"So what's wrong with my giving you an extra incentive?"

"It just doesn't work that way. But I certainly don't want to discourage you, if you want to do something for the police or for the community. I know Captain Strapp is waiting to talk to you. Ask him what we need."

"I don't like that man. He's not sincere."

"He is sincere. He's just nervous around you."

Genoa smiled. Then she grew serious. "Out of all the people in the case, you know who I identify with?"

"Who's that?"

"Ryan Goldberg. His fate could have been mine if it hadn't been for Dr. Ben." She stood up. "All right. I'll meet with your captain and throw him a bone. Keep me informed if something new happens."

"I will."

"Let me know if you find Rudy or Goldberg or if you find Rudy's car. I would think while it might be hard to find a person, it shouldn't be so hard to find a car."

"Think how hard it is to find your keys when you've misplaced them in your own house."

She considered his words. "Yes, that is a good point, although I have a thirty-thousand-square-foot house."

Decker smiled, but she failed to see the humor. "The car could have been repainted, it could have been chopped up, it could be holed up in a garage, or it could be right under our noses. America's a big country, Ms. Greeves. There's lots of space to get lost."

The pillow began to vibrate: little tiny fingers massaging his cheek. Without opening his eyes, Decker pulled the covers over his head, reached underneath, and extracted the phone.

"Decker."

"This is what I got, and I don't know how reliable it is."

The voice jolted him awake. His heart began to pound.

"Hold on." Decker slithered out of bed and tiptoed into the walk-in closet. On the second shelf, he kept two pencils and a pad of paper. "I'm here. I'm listening. What do you have?"

"There's a small inn near Ocean Boulevard in Santa Monica called the Sand Dune. It rents by the hour. Ladies go in and ladies go out."

"Aha."

"My sources tell me that the guy you've been looking for has been there recently. Different name, different hair, different clothes, but it's probably him. They say that he pays in cash and they say he's a chubby chaser. Whether any of it is true or not, I don't know. I'm just passing it along. Don't bother saying thank you; your friendship is all I ask for."

"By friendship you mean almost killing me?"

"If I wanted to kill you, I would have. Besides, you always hurt the one you love."

"By any chance, do you have a direct connection with this fine law-abiding establishment?"

"Me? Never. Why would you think that?"

"You've been known to help the ladies."

"I'm a generous guy. I help everyone."

"I assume that a certain lady told you all this. I'd like to talk to her."

"Can't help you there, but I won't do you bodily harm if you go down to the establishment and talk to people. Just be polite."

"Donatti, it's a murder case. I *need* to talk to her."

"Who knows if she even exists? And if she does, who knows if she's telling the truth. People say all sorts of things to get on my good side."

"You've got a good side?"

"I do. I just don't use it too often. My bad side's so much more fun."

The uncertainty factor.

What if Donatti got it wrong?

What if Donatti was deliberately misleading him?

What if Rudy Banks didn't show up?

What if he showed up and something went wrong?

What if he showed up, everything went according to plan, but he wasn't involved in Ben Little's death?

What if, despite Decker's best efforts, the case was never solved?

For the moment, the "what if" was pushed aside to deal with the "what needed to be done". Talking to the owner of the Sand Dune motel was a chore. It took a lot of cajoling before Mr. Craddle was thoroughly convinced that the detectives involved were from Homicide and not from Vice. At last the proprietor figured out that to help the police would benefit him in the long run.

Hollywood placed rotating decoys at the front desk of the Sand Dune. Sometimes it was a man, sometimes a woman. Since security cameras had already been set up, Decker, Diaz, and Garrett reviewed the most recent tapes, trying to see if they could recognize Banks from the hundreds of grainy shots of furtive men. Since the quality wasn't sharp, it was hard to make out features, and even when they did, they noticed that a lot of men purposely hid their faces or turned their backs toward the camera aimed at the desk. Several additional security cameras were installed, courtesy of the police, so that it was easier to capture faces from different angles. Old cameras were upgraded. Everything was in place.

So they waited.

And waited.

And waited.

40

Patience was not only a virtue, it was a necessity. As months passed and there was no sign of Rudy Banks, the Hollywood brass became disenchanted with Decker's tip. They pulled back the decoys at the Sand Dune and allocated them to other operations. Every week, Diaz or Garrett or Decker or Marge or Oliver or some other Hollywood Homicide detective went in to check the tapes and replace them with clean cartridges. No one was surprised when the contents revealed nothing significant—just sneaky johns and call girls. But that was detective work: hours of mind-numbing tedium followed by that compensatory, glory-hallelujah, once-in-a-blue-moon, shot-in-the-veins adrenaline rush.

Marge was in her living room drinking coffee, flipping channels via remote control when she received a call from newly minted Detective Cindy Decker Kutiel.

"Do you know where Dad is?"

"Have no idea." Marge pressed the mute button. "You can't reach him on his cell?"

"It's turned off."

"Maybe he and Rina are watching a movie."

"He usually has it on vibrate."

"Maybe the battery is low. What's up, Cindy?"

"I'm here at Hollywood doing Sand Dune tape duty. I've put in a call to Rip and Tito, but I figured that maybe someone from your neck of the woods might want to come over as well."

Marge sat up abruptly, almost spilling coffee onto her lap. "You *found* him?"

"I *think* so. Actually, I didn't find him. I was reviewing the tape when Petra Conner came in to help me. Do you know Petra?"

"I met her at your wedding. She's from Homicide. You two are in a bowling league together."

"Exactly. Petra's also an artist. Her eye is particularly well trained to notice nuances in faces. I don't know why we didn't think of her before."

"I'm calling Oliver and we'll be right over."

"Good . . . I'm getting a call. I think it's Dad. I'll see you later."

Once they determined that it was most likely Rudy's face, they discovered that he'd frequented the place before, one time with a bald head—probably a head cap—and another time with a blond wig. The most recent visit—three weeks ago—showed him wearing a baseball cap with a bomber jacket.

"This one . . ." The clerk hit the photograph with the tips of his fingers. "He likes them with meat." The clerk was Cecil Dobbins: fifty-eight, five six, two forty with a raging potbelly, white hair, and milky blue eyes.

It had been a slow night and Dobbins was in a talkative mood. He had been under Mr. Craddle's employ for the last year and a half. The work was okay, a little boring. The hardest part was keeping a clean establishment, making sure that whatever went on was legal and lawful and between two consenting adults. "Mr. Craddle don't want any problems. That's why he's cooperating with you."

"We appreciate it," Marge told him.

"Just keep your eye out for this guy," Garrett said. "If you see him, don't try to apprehend him yourself. He's dangerous."

Decker added, "Just don't let on that you know who he is."

"You need a flat face to do my work." Dobbins spoke as he filled in a number in a Sudoku puzzle. "Nonjudgmental like, know what I mean? Lot of nervous men here. The more bored you look, the calmer they are. Besides, I play cards in Gardena every weekend. I got a good poker face."

"You ever win?" Oliver asked.

"I win just enough for me to keep coming back. I could probably save a little more if I stopped, but what's life without a little risk?" Dobbins went back to the numbers grid. "You don't have to worry about me letting on. I'm one smooth guy."

Garrett said, "You see this man, give a call."

Diaz said, "Immediately."

"Yeah, yeah," Dobbins said.

Marge said, "Any time and any day. Call one of the numbers we gave you."

Decker said, "And if you don't have the numbers in front of you, just call 911 and ask them to patch you through to one of us."

Dobbins said, "We ain't talking brain surgery. I know how to deal with the customers." He finished the puzzle. "Stop worrying."

Diaz said, "Just don't try to take him down—"

"I got it, I got it."

With nothing more to add, they left Cecil Dobbins to his dreary job. He picked up the paper and began to fill in letters in the daily crossword.

Monday: nine p.m.

Garrett to Decker. "We got him!"

Decker was at home in front of the TV. He couldn't believe what the voice on the other end of his cell was telling him. "You got Rudy Banks?"

"He's in our sights. Came into the Sand Dune about ten minutes ago. I'm about twenty minutes away: Tito's bogged down in traffic and is about thirty minutes away."

Decker gathered his keys and his wallet, then went over to his gun safe, spinning the combination dial, trying to steady his hands enough to align the correct numbers with the wheel notch. "Who's watching the place?"

"I've called up Santa Monica and asked them to send some unmarked units. They're starting to block off the perimeter area with cruisers, but I emphasized to make sure that nothing was visible. I don't know how many people are in the motel, but it's not empty."

"The last thing we need is a hostage situation," Decker said.

"Agreed. Last time I checked, there were two plainclothes units in the vicinity."

"That's good. Where should we meet?"

Garrett gave him an address. "He ain't gonna slip away this time."

The safe door popped open, and Decker slipped his Beretta into his shoulder harness. "I'll be there in a half hour to forty minutes."

"Let's hope it's all over by then."

As he pulled out of the driveway, he called Marge and brought her up to date. "I'm on my way. Call Oliver and tell him what's going on."

The traffic gods weren't with him. It took over an hour just to get off the freeway, and as soon as he exited, Decker knew there was trouble. All lanes were at a standstill. He punched in a news channel and when he heard the headlines, he hit the dashboard. "SHIT!"

Click, click, click, click . . .

"No one knows how many people are in the

Sand Dune or how many, if any, have been taken hostage. There have been several unsubstantiated reports of at least one gunman—"

Decker turned off the radio and tried Garrett's cell phone. When no one answered, he tried Diaz's cell phone. Still no answer.

He turned on the news station a second time.

". . . reports of the gunman keeping at least three women hostage."

His cell rang. It was Garrett. "How far away are you?"

"Five minutes."

"You heard?"

"Yeah, I heard."

"So we're meeting in front of the Sand Dune. See you in a few."

Decker took out the top dome light and ran the siren. Even with the bells and whistles, it took another fifteen minutes to weave through snarled lanes and pissed-off drivers. When he finally reached the destination, he flashed his badge to Santa Monica Police and was allowed to proceed.

Ocean Avenue had become a stagnant pool of chrome: SMPD patrol units in white and light blue, LAPD's cruisers in black and white, unmarked cars, ambulances, fire trucks, and acres of news vans. Decker parked wherever he could and slowly inched his way closer to the hot spot, walking behind the protection of steel that the cars afforded. He darted his way over to Tito Diaz and

Rip Garrett. Garrett had dressed in a suit and tie, but Diaz was still in jeans.

Decker said, "What the hell happened?"

Garrett was seething. "I asked for unmarkeds to the scene. When I got here, I saw cruisers. I thought at first that SMPD fucked up, but then I found out that they were responding to a 911 call from someone inside who was shot—"

"Holy moly—"

"Tito and I have just spent the last twenty minutes bringing SMPD up to date. They're not happy with us right now."

"We conferred with them every step of the way," Decker said.

"Yeah, but I don't think they believed that we were on to anything. That's why they gave us permission to operate in their vicinity."

"Who made the 911 call?" Decker asked.

"I haven't heard the voice, but it was a man."

Diaz added that he had heard it was Cecil Dobbins.

"How bad is it?"

Tito shrugged. Decker looked at the dilapidated building in front of them. It was probably a beautiful private home in the 1920s—a three-storied, white-wood-sided Greene and Greene bungalow style with a wraparound porch. Decker could imagine a family lolling about on a summer's eve like tonight, enjoying the cool sea breezes.

That hadn't happened for a very long time.

The place hadn't seen a paintbrush in decades.

Even with the minimal outside lighting, he could make out peeling paint flaking off like snow. Historically, it was great that the building retained many of its original leaded windowpanes. For their purposes, the cut glass hindered sharpshooters' visibility.

Garrett said, "SMPD has sent out for a hostage negotiator."

"What about a back door?" Decker asked. "He can't guard two portals at once."

Garrett said, "SMPD managed to get a few people out through the rear, but then he started shooting."

"Didn't hit anyone," Diaz said.

"And it's definitely Rudy Banks?"

Garrett said, "One of the women that SMPD rescued identified him from a picture. She also told us about the hostages."

"We think he has three women locked up," Diaz said. "Maybe even Dobbins."

Garrett added, "We know the cell number of one of the ladies."

Diaz said, "I think SMPD is just waiting for the negotiator before a call is placed."

Decker felt his pocket buzz and answered his phone. The voice over the line had a strong Irish brogue. "I'm flipping the bloody channels and a picture of Rudy in a blond wig flashed across my screen—"

"Fuck!" Decker turned to Garrett and Diaz. "TV's flashing a picture of Rudy Banks over the airwaves."

"Oh shit!" Garrett mumbled. "He's probably watching our moves right now."

Irish said, "What the fuck is going on? Is Mudd involved?"

"I don't know, Liam, I have to go." He hung up, but his cell sprang to life a few moments later. It was Cindy. "Daddy, I was listening to the news, and apparently Rudy Banks is holed up at the Sand Dune with some hostages."

"I'm already down here."

"I'm coming down—"

"Don't . . ." Too late. She'd hung up. Ah, fuck it! It would probably be over by the time she made it through traffic. Ten minutes later, Marge and Oliver arrived after having slogged through almost two hours of traffic. She was wearing sweats, but somehow Scott had found the time to put on a glen plaid sport jacket and a pair of brown slacks. It took Decker just a few minutes to bring them current.

Diaz said, "We've been asked to stand by. Right now, we're just accessories."

Garrett said, "Turf war."

"That's ridiculous," Oliver said. "We included them in every step of the operation."

"True, but if there's a homicide, it's gonna fuck up their statistics, not ours."

The media started coming their way: just in time for a live report on the eleven o'clock news. There was a woman from ABC, a man from CBS, a man and a woman from NBC. There were people from the local networks, people from Fox, people from CNN and MSNBC. The print media—Internet as well as newspapers—was equally eager for answers. Big headlines sell. If Rudy Banks had expectations of regaining his bad boy spotlight, dormant for the last decade, now was his chance.

The detectives were barraged with questions.

All the respective media got for their efforts were legitimate shrugs of ignorance. The press kept at them for a while, then moved on to another group in hopes of snagging something more interesting. By then, it was eleven-thirty.

Decker's cell rang again. It was Liam again. "How can I get over to you? I can't get through this bloody mess."

"Go home, Liam. You can see all the action better on your own TV set."

"I'm already seeing it on TV, mate. There are about a hundred people with laptops. Another hundred with video cameras."

"O'Dell, I have to go."

"If you don't talk to me, I'll start talking to them. Lots of bloggers out there, mate."

"Don't do that, Liam!"

"Where are you, mate?"

"You tell me where you are." Decker listened and then said, "I'll send someone to get you." He hung up and said, "Liam O'Dell is threatening to talk to the media unless we pick him up and let him watch at close range."

Marge said, "I'll find him."

Decker called Rina, telling her it looked like a long night. After he had hung up, his eyes focused on five men in dark suits stepping out of a black town car. "Special Ops . . . or maybe feds."

Oliver said, "It's not a federal case."

"Maybe SMPD requested the help," Decker said. "Maybe FBI has a field office close to here. Or maybe the hostage negotiator lives nearby."

"Too many people around," Oliver said. "We should go home. We're not doing anything here, and by morning it'll probably be resolved."

"You can go," Decker said. "I'm sticking around."

Marge managed to find her way back with Liam O'Dell in tow. He wore a sweatshirt and jeans with slippers on his feet. "Any sign of Mudd?"

"I don't know a thing, O'Dell," Decker shrugged. "We're just watching, same as you."

"Who are all those guys?"

"FBI or Special Ops," Decker said. "Can't tell without a scorecard."

O'Dell pursed his lips. "Shouldn't we go over there or something?"

"No, O'Dell, we should stay right here," Decker said. "If the men in black want to talk to us, they'll come get us."

"What're they doing?"

"If I had to guess, they're probably figuring out how to establish phone contact with Rudy."

"How long is that going to take?"

Decker slapped an arm around O'Dell. "Liam, my friend, the wheels of justice grind *very* slowly."

Cindy showed up a half hour later with a laptop, a large keg of coffee, and a pile of paper hot cups. She poured some java for all to share, and then she logged on to one of the local networks.

The group sat around watching themselves sit around.

It was after midnight, and the crowd hadn't thinned a whole lot. Since L.A. usually shut down by eleven, Decker figured he had provided the city with its late-night entertainment.

A half hour passed, and the suits deigned to come their way. The agent who spoke looked to be around forty. He was well dressed with a chiseled chin and an angry expression. He was chomping gum. "Who's Decker?"

"It's Lieutenant Decker and that would be me. Who're you?"

"Special Agent Jim Cressly of the FBI. What do you know about this?" Decker told him everything he knew. "So you have a prior relationship with Rudolph Banks?"

"I told you I spoke to him once over the phone. What's going on?"

Cressly said, "He wants to talk to you."

"Who does? Rudy?"

"Yeah, Rudy. This way." When the group of detectives started to surge forward, Cressly held up his hand. "Uh-uh. Only Decker."

"I'll be back." Decker rolled his eyes and spoke in his best Governator voice. Cressly led Decker into a police mobile unit van set up with phone lines, then introduced him to Jack Ellenshaw, the FBI hostage negotiator. Ellenshaw was around forty with a long face and a prominent chin. Neatly dressed and neatly trimmed just like Cressly. The FBI liked them a certain way. Advancement could be based on an inch of hair length.

After Ellenshaw gave him a two-minute lecture on the electronics, he asked, "Have you ever done anything like this before?"

"Actually, I have."

"One time, two times?"

"Two."

"Were you successful?"

"I never lost a hostage," Decker said, "One time the shooter died, one time the shooter lived."

"Let me handle it. I'll write down what you need to say on a pad of paper. Just stick with my lines and you'll be okay."

Decker didn't answer. He had no intention of adhering to a script. He was an ad-lib-as-needed kind of guy. "Do you know how many people he has with him?"

"Three women and Cecil Dobbins."

"The clerk, you mean?"

"Yes."

"I heard he was injured."

"He was shot in the arm. We need to get a move on."

"How about the women? Names? Ages?"

"Amber Mitchell, twenty-six, Lita Bloch, eighteen, and Pamela Nelson, twenty-one."

"Any of them have a medical condition?"

"We're trying to find that out right now."

"And you sure there's no one else except those five?"

"Not sure of anything."

"Whose line are you calling to get to Rudy?"

"Pamela Nelson. We need to get started."

"Call him up." Decker felt surprisingly calm until he heard the line ringing. When he heard the voice, his heart started beating full force.

41

"Who the fuck is this?"

If Decker hadn't recognized the timbre, he sure would have recognized the hostility. "It's Lieutenant Peter Decker, Rudy. You asked for me." Silence. "How are you doing?"

"How the fuck do you think I'm doing? All of a sudden, I'm looking down the barrel of the fucking U.S. Army. What the motherfucking hell is going on?"

The negotiator was writing like mad and pointing to his pad. Decker ignored him. "I'm not sure. I just got here."

"What the fuck did I do?"

"Who said you did anything?"

There was a pause. "Then why is some fucking cunt on the news flashing my picture on TV and saying I'm wanted for murder?"

"I have no idea," Decker told him. "Why don't you fill me in on what happened?"

"Why don't you ask one of your fellow morons

what happened? Don't you idiots talk to each other?"

"All we're doing is trading ignorance. Only you know the real story."

"Fucking A right about that! Why were you interested in talking to me in the first place, Decker?"

"I was stuck with a cold case. We were routinely interviewing everyone who was interviewed at the time. I told you that the first time we spoke."

"Who the fuck remembers? What cold case?"

"Dr. Bennett Little."

"Nobody ever interviewed me for Bennett Little's murder. I told you, I barely remember it."

Decker said, "Well, your name came up somehow. Who the hell knows? We haven't made any progress on it, so we're shelving it again. What's going on inside there, Rudy?"

"Assholes. A guy can't even fuck in peace anymore. How the hell did you find me?"

"Find you?" Decker paused for effect. "I didn't know you were missing." A beat. "What's going on, Rudy? I was rudely awakened from a sound sleep and told to get my ass down here. I'm getting all kinds of conflicting information. I want to hear from you."

"Don't give me that fucking sincere jackass bull-shit! What you want is for me to step outside so you can shoot my ass off."

"If that's what you think, don't step outside."

The negotiator was gesticulating like a wild man.

Decker looked down at the notepad and promptly passed up his suggestion. "Hey, Rudy, you called me." A beat. "Talk to me, man. Maybe I can help you."

"You tell those motherfucking, asshole pricks that if I go down, I'm going down in a blaze of glory! You fucking assholes don't know who the hell you're dealing with!"

Decker began to improvise. "Rudy, everyone knows who you are. The Doodoo Sluts went platinum, buddy. We all know who we're dealing with."

"Who put you up to this?"

"To what?"

"To looking for me?"

"I told you, Rudy, I wanted to talk to you about Bennett Little. But that case is dead—"

"You talked to that bitch, didn't you? Fucking cunt thinks I had something to do with her asshole boyfriend's death. I was nowhere around! I was at a party."

"Which woman are you talking about?"

"C'mon, c'mon. I don't like games. You play me for a fucking fool, I fucking blow holes in these bitches' heads!"

Decker took a chance. "I don't know who you mean. Do you mean Melinda Little?"

"Melinda Little?" A pause. "What does she have to do with it?"

"I told you, I was working on the Bennett Little case. She's the only woman I know."

"Not Melinda Little. Marilyn Eustis."

"Who's she?"

"You're shittin' me."

"No, I'm not. Who is she?"

"Primo Ekerling's girlfriend."

"Ekerling isn't my case, Rudy." Decker hoped his lie was smooth. "It's Hollywood's case. The only thing I know about it is what I've read in the newspaper. I know you two were business partners, I know you two were bandmates. I had no idea that Hollywood wanted to talk to you."

There was a long pause.

Decker said, "What's going on, Rudy?"

"What's going on is that piece of fat lard shit came after me with a gun! Suddenly I'm surrounded by a bunch of fucking Nazis! What'd I do except try to defend myself!"

"Rudy, they tell me that the lard ass has been shot. Is that true?"

"I was trying to defend myself."

"I know, and I completely believe you. But if the asshole was shot, it would be good if you sent him out here so the paramedics can take a look at him."

"Paramedics, my ass. You fucking assholes want to storm-troop the place."

"How about this, Rudy? I'll stay out on the front lawn with my hands up in the air. You send out Lard Ass while you keep a bead on me. If you think I'm trying to snow you, shoot my head off."

"I don't even know what the fuck you look like?"

"I'll be the only one standing in the middle of the lawn with a helmet on my head and my hands in the air."

"How can I shoot your head off if you're wearing a helmet?"

"Aim for the chest."

"You're probably going to be wearing a bullet-proof vest."

"Absolutely, I'll be wearing a bulletproof vest. The point is, you'll have the gun but I'll be unarmed. You have the advantage, and I don't want to die."

"And while I'm keeping a bead on you, trying to decide where to plug you, some motherfucking sharpshooter has a bead on me."

"Rudy, I have no idea what room you're phoning from."

"And I have no idea where you're phoning from. I don't see anyone out there on the phone."

"I'm in a police mobile unit. But I have my cell phone. How about this? I'll walk into the center of the lawn with my helmet and my vest and call you from my cell."

"Don't call me, I'll call you." He cut the line.

The Kevlar vest and a helmet were waiting for him. The vest fit, and although the helmet was a little tight, he could get it over his skull.

Cressly said, "Try not to get picked off."

"I'll do my best."

"We've got guys from all angles—SMPD, LAPD, and our sharpshooters."

"I appreciate it."

"Good luck."

"Thanks." Decker thought about being shot, and his mind immediately raced back to the few times he actually had been shot. Banks was a psycho, but on the psycho scale he was nowhere near Hersh Schwartz, and he was universes away from Chris Donatti. He left the van and walked into the middle of the front lawn. Flashbulbs were popping in his face . . . bursts of light like tracers. When his cell rang, Decker jumped. With shaking hands, he answered the call. "I take it you see me?"

"Yeah, I see you. You look like you're ready for Iraq."

"I'm just a cautious guy."

"Either you're a real dumb ass or I'm a real dumb ass."

"How about if none of us are dumb asses and you let Mr. Lard Ass out."

"Your hands aren't up."

Decker wedged the cell between his cheek and his shoulder. Then he raised both hands in the air. "Okay?"

Rudy didn't answer.

"Hello?"

"I'm still fucking here . . . as long as the fucking phone company allows my nighttime minutes."

The two of them went on for a few more minutes. Decker's arms began to ache. "I've got to put my arms down, Rudy. I'm going to move very slowly. Don't get any bad ideas." Bit by bit, he lowered his limbs until they were at his side. His feet were cold and tired, but he soldiered on. "See? I'm still harmless and still talking to you. Open communication. How about letting Lard Ass go?"

"How about not?"

They continued to talk for another hour. Decker's patience was rewarded when Cecil Dobbins came out huffing and puffing, holding his injured arm. Immediately the paramedics went to work.

Decker said, "That was really smart, Rudy. Really, really smart. Do you mind if I back away?"

"Afraid I might get Itchy Finger?"

"The thought occurred to me."

"Why do I need you? I've got three in here for target practice." As Decker started to back away, Banks said, "Stay where you are."

Decker stopped abruptly. His feet were like two blocks of ice. It had been hot in the Valley, but the beach was always ten to twenty degrees cooler in the summer. His shoulders were throbbing, brought on by the extra weight of the vest, the tension in his muscles, and the chilled saline spray carried over by the ocean breezes.

Rudy said, "I like seeing you."

Decker said, "Fine. I won't move. I just want to shift positions. My balance is off."

"Move slowly. If you make a wrong move, you're dead."

"I hear you." Decker rocked on his feet until he evened his weight distribution. "Thank you."

"You're welcome."

Decker couldn't believe the bastard had actually said something nice. Rapport, rapport. "So what's going on?"

"You fucking tell me."

"I wish I knew all the facts. You asked to talk to me, I'm here. You tell me to stand in the middle of the lawn, I do it. You're in control right now."

"Fucking A right about that. You tell Hollywood Police that I had nothing to do with that bastard's death. I'm glad that he died, but I didn't kill him."

"Not to be dim-witted, but are you talking about Primo Ekerling?"

"Fuck yeah, I'm talking about Ekerling. They have the guys who did it. Frankly, I'd like to give them a medal. The son of a bitch was a lousy drunk and a real bad bass player. Fucking bunch of no-talents. If it hadn't been for me, they wouldn't have gotten anywhere."

"Rudy, everyone knows you were the group." Another twenty minutes passed as Decker continued to praise Banks while Banks swore back in agreement. Finally Decker took a step forward. "We all know you're a smart guy, Rudy. You let out Lard Ass. That was smart. Be smart again and let someone else go. Why bother with three bitches when it's easier to keep an eye out on only one."

"'Cause in case one escapes, I got one for backup."

"Okay, so let one of them go."

"Which one?"

"You decide."

There was sudden noise in the background, women screaming. Decker's heart was doing a steeplechase, and it took all his nerve not to rush the building. Since he didn't hear any guns firing in the background, he willed himself to stand still. Five minutes later, a naked young woman came running out of the building, holding a shirt against her chest to cover her breasts. Immediately, she was scooped up by the waiting paramedics.

One down and two to go. Decker said, "That was really smart, Rudy. You keep being smart, I'm going to get you out of this mess."

"Don't fucking bullshit me!"

"I'm going to do my best."

"Start by telling all those cops to get the hell out of here. Once they're gone, I'll come out. Then we'll talk, just you and me."

"I can probably get them to back off a little."

"Not back off. I want the motherfuckers to leave!"

"They're not going to do that. Not until you send out the hostages. Once you do that, I can probably get them out of here."

"If I send out the bitches, they're going to fucking rush me. I can stay holed up a long time, Decker. I got food, I got women. I'm an independent kind a guy."

He had to sleep, Decker thought. Some time within the next twenty-four to thirty-six hours, his adrenaline was going to deplete, and fatigue was going to get the better of him. He said, "I'm not rushing you. You tell me what you want, I'll try to get it done."

"I want the fucking circus out of here!"

"I can get the news vans away. The paramedics are going to stay. So will the fire trucks."

"I'm not burning anything down." Decker didn't answer. Banks said, "Get the cops out of here."

"Let me see what I can do. I'm going to back away from the house, Rudy. I have to talk to people if you want me to get it done. It might take a little time. Call me if you have questions, okay?"

"Okay." Rudy cut the line.

Decker backed away until he was out of range, then he ran into the police van. He took his helmet off and rubbed his aching temples. "My feet are freezing, and I've got a monster headache. I need a thick pair of socks, Advil, and some caffeinated coffee. I've got to get back."

Cressly handed him a bigger helmet and said, "Get the lieutenant what he needs."

"Thank you." Decker tried on his new head protection. Much better. "Banks wants the heat to back off. Make a show of doing something while I think of my next move. Any advice?"

Ellenshaw said, "No advice. You're doing fine."

Cressly said, "We'll try to pull as many cars off as we can, but we don't want to leave you naked in the wind."

"Just do something to give me some credibility."

Decker downed the tablets and poured himself a giant cup of coffee.

A few minutes later, Cressly got off the phone with SMPD. He said, "We're taking away some of the visible units. He's not stupid, though. He'll know we're still out there."

"Yeah, but sometimes seeing is believing." Decker had wolfed down two muffins and had chugged two cups of coffee. He tightened the chin-strap of his helmet and adjusted the bulletproof protection across his heart. In addition, he had put on a double-ply pair of gym socks and a bomber jacket. He was sweating. "I should be getting back."

"Good luck," Cressly told him.

"Thanks."

Decker jogged back out to the front of the lawn as black-and-whites began to retreat from the front of the house. Five minutes later, his cell rang. "Decker."

"That's the best you can do? There's still a fucking army out there! Lemme count . . . one, two, three, four, five . . . I count at least a half-dozen cars in my sight. I know they've probably got about twenty surrounding the place."

"What's the least amount of cop cars you can deal with?"

"None."

"How about two?"

"Start with two."

A half hour later, two lone cruisers sat in front

of the Sand Dune. Decker said, "I did what I could for you, Rudy. How about showing some good faith and letting another gal loose?"

It took another half hour of prodding for a second naked woman to emerge from the seedy motel.

Two down, one to go. "That was smart, Rudy."

"I was a fucking moron to let her go. As soon as the last bitch is out of my hands, I'm dead."

"Rudy, I know you're going to think that what I'm saying is pure bullshit, but no one wants to shoot you." Decker paused. "What if I come in and the three of us go out together?"

"I'm a fucking moron but not that big of a fucking moron."

"What's making you nervous?" Decker asked. "I'll strip down buck naked so you can see that I'm not hiding weapons."

"How many snipers do you have out there, Decker?"

"I'll walk in front of you. They won't shoot me to get to you." Decker raised his eyes. "At least I hope they won't do that!" No answer. "I'm just trying to make this as easy as I can. But if you want, you can hole out there for as long as you want."

"Fucking A right about that!"

The next hour was chitchat. It was a little past three in the morning. Despite the socks, Decker's feet remained cool if not cold and ached like hell from standing so long. The rest of his body was bathed in sweat. Exhaustion was overtaking him, and he had to fight to keep awake and alert. Finally, he said, "Rudy, you can stay where you are as long as you want, but I'm going to need some sleep."

"So lie down and go to sleep."

Decker said, "Let me come in there, and we'll all go out together. You put the girl in front of you, I'll walk behind. We'll surround you until we get you safe and sound."

"And arrested."

"If all you did was shoot Lard Ass in self-defense, the only thing you'll be charged with is illegal possession of a firearm."

"Bullshit."

"I'll guarantee it," Decker said.

"You don't have that kind of power!"

"I got the cops pulled back, didn't I?"

"I'm not a fucking moron; you don't have that kind of power."

Decker repeated himself. "If all you did was shoot Lard Ass in self-defense, we can only charge you with illegal possession of a firearm. Can you live with that?"

"Of course, I could live with that, but you assholes are going to charge me with attempted murder."

"You shot him in the arm, Rudy. Not the chest, not the head, not the stomach. In the *arm*. Every one of us knows you weren't aiming to kill."

It took time to convince Rudy of Decker's sincerity,

but he finally agreed to some kind of surrender plan. More time passed as Banks went back and forth on how to handle giving himself up.

First Decker had to take off his bomber jacket and strip down to his vest. Then Banks told Decker to take off his shoes, show his ankles, and turn his pants pockets inside out. He managed to sneak a glance at his illuminated watch. It was almost five in the morning. The sun would be up within the hour.

Banks said, "I'm taking the bitch down to the lobby. I'll tell you when you can come in."

"You've got it." He waited over the line as he heard a female voice plead for her life. She was sobbing and mewing and Decker wished she would just shut up. He didn't want Banks to become unnerved. Finally, Rudy's voice came through his cell. "You can come in. Do it slowly."

Decker inched his way into the dark lobby. As his eyes adjusted, he saw the woman first, then the gun at her head, then someone taller in back. Curly dark hair with burning eyes. A square chin and high cheekbones. The same Rudy Banks he had seen on the Web, but with the look of a feral animal.

Rudy talked softly. His voice was surprisingly calm. "I just thought of something. If you're in back of me, what's stopping you from jumping me?"

"I won't jump you. But if that plan makes you nervous, let the girl go and put the gun to my head."

"Hard to do when you're wearing a helmet."

"I'm not going to take off the helmet. Let me repeat. You have the gun. I am unarmed."

"You're a big man. As soon as I let her go, you're going for my gun."

"If I was going to charge you, I would have come in with ten sharpshooters. I also know what it feels like to be shot. I'm not anxious to experience it again."

"You've been shot before?"

"Twice." Decker waited to hear his next move.

No one spoke for what seemed like eternity. Rudy weighed his options.

"I'm not going to let go of the girl. She's the only protection I have against getting my head blown off."

Decker tried to be as calm as he could. He didn't know which girl Rudy had in his clutches. Not that it mattered. All Decker saw was the terror plastered across a frightened child. "Do whatever you want. For what it's worth, I think it's better for you if you let her go. Less chance for something getting fucked up. But you're the boss."

"Fucking A right about that."

Decker's mind was racing with a single thought: how to get the gun away from the girl's head without either of them getting shot. If Banks got shot, while that wasn't ideal, Decker could certainly live with that. He could make out the girl's eyes—dilated and awash in fear. "What's next, boss?"

"Down on your knees."

That was not going to happen. Decker said, "If you're going to shoot me, you're going to shoot me standing up."

"I'm not going to shoot you, but how do I know when I let her go, you're not going to try to swipe the gun away."

Decker took five steps backward. "I'm way out of your reach."

After what seemed like hours . . . more like a few moments . . . Banks let go of the sobbing girl and she ran out of the lobby. Decker was now staring at the barrel of a Glock 11mm semi-automatic. "Just you and me, boss."

"Turn around."

Decker said, "You've got to keep your eyes on me, but I've got to keep my eyes on you. If you get cranky and start peeling off rounds, I need to be able to duck."

Silence.

"I'm not moving on you, Rudy."

Banks's arm was starting to shake. He propped it up with his free hand.

Decker said, "You'll notice that we've been in here for what . . . five minutes and no one has stormed the place. It's still just you and me."

Rudy didn't answer.

"All I have to do is phone and tell them we're coming out," Decker said. "That's all I have to do. I promise you that none of our people want to fuck this up. Once you're out of this sketchy situation, you'll get your lawyer, you'll get your bail, and you're home drinking Scotch and watching the game on TV."

"I fucking hate sports."

"C'mon. You know what I'm saying. You're a savvy guy, Rudy. You know how to work the media." Decker tried to keep condescension out of his voice. "Show these stupid kids what badass really is."

More silence.

The gun still aimed at his face.

Finally, Rudy whispered, "Make your call."

"Smart," Decker said. "Very smart." He tried to work as quickly as he could before Banks could change his mind. "All set."

Banks said, "We walk out slowly!"

Decker was shivering and sweating at the same time. "You better believe it."

"You're an idiot for coming in and making yourself a human shield."

"I'm sure my wife would agree."

"I think I'm a bigger idiot for trusting you."

"At this point, the only option we have is to trust each other."

"Are you going to get some kind of promotion for this?"

"Maybe I'll get a bonus."

"If we walk out alive."

"Yeah, if we don't, maybe my wife will get some insurance money."

"Fuck, fuck, fuck, fuck, fuck! How the fuck did this happen?"

"I don't know, Rudy. Hollywood called me down and told me you wanted to talk to me. That's all I know."

"You tell Hollywood that they're fucking lunatics if they think they can slap me with Ekerling's murder."

"I will relay the message with all your sentiments."

Banks exhaled, signifying resignation and/or fatigue. "Okay, let's get this over with. You go first."

"Rudy, you're going to have to ditch the weapon. If they see the gun, they're going to get nervous."

Slowly Banks lowered the gun. Decker heard himself exhale audibly. "Smart. Put it down on the floor. Don't kick it over to me. We don't want anything to go off. Just gently put it down on the floor."

Time crawled into second-hand ticks, but eventually Banks complied.

"Put your hands up and step away from the weapon."

"I can't believe I'm doing this."

"It's almost over," Decker soothed. "Raise your hands over your head, and we'll walk out together."

Banks cooperated.

"Perfectly done. You see, I'm not charging at you, I'm not doing anything stupid. I'm moving very slowly."

Rudy didn't answer.

Decker said, "You go first, but I'll be right behind you."

They inched their way out of the Sand Dune and stepped onto the porch. They were so close in proximity that Decker could smell Banks's sour breath, hear his frantic pants with each intake of air. Dawn was palpable. Outside it had turned from black to gray. Visibility was a plus.

Seconds from victory. Just a few more steps.

They hadn't gotten more than two paces forward when the single shot rang out. Immediately Decker dropped, covering his head and neck, trembling like a windblown aspen, not sure if the pain he felt was from the fire of a bullet or from his helmet knocking hard against the cold ground.

A surge of cops converged on him. He heard his own voice. It kept repeating, "I'm okay, I'm okay, I'm okay, I'm okay." He shook off the bodies around him. "I'm fucking okay! Leave me alone!" Trembling from fear and adrenaline, he rubbed his arms and waited for his eyes to focus. He was still viewing his life with rods instead of cones. A slew of paramedics were kneeling on the lawn, working frantically at the spot where he had stood a few moments ago.

"What the fuck happened?" he heard his voice ask.

"Someone shot the bastard," a disembodied voice told him.

"How the fuck did that happen?" Decker spun around and was staring at Cressly. "I was inches from the bastard. Whoever the fuck shot at him could have gotten me!"

"It wasn't one of us—"

"Then who the fuck was . . ." It was then that Decker noticed a commotion off to the side. The cops wrestling someone to the ground. He ran to the spot.

Ryan Goldberg was facedown with a cop on his back, a gun to his head, and twenty cops ready to beat the shit out of him if he moved. His hands had been drawn behind his back and secured with a plastic tie. A pistol lay a few feet away from where he had been tackled.

Decker was rendered speechless.

Somehow Liam O'Dell had made it through the yellow tape and over to the scene. He was frantic, waving his arms and shouting over and over: *"Why'd you do it, Mudd? Why'd you do it? Why'd you do it?"*

Ryan answered. "Because Rudy is bad."

The cops hoisted Ryan to his feet and pushed O'Dell aside. He tripped and almost fell on the ground. As he got up, he shouted. "Fuck, Mudd! Now you're going to jail. You're going to jail!"

Ryan turned around and smiled beatifically. "Irish, I've been in jail for the last fifteen years. Wherever I'm going, it's got to be better."

"Oh Christ!" Liam tried to run after him, but the cops held him back, threatening him with jail if he didn't get the fuck out. He shouted, "I'll get you a lawyer, Mudd."

"Call my brother," Goldberg shouted back. "He's a lung doctor."

42

It took a full week for Rina to even speak to him, and when she did, her conversation ran monosyllabic.

"I'm sorry!" Decker told her for the umpteenth time.

"It's fine, Peter."

"It was stupid. I admit it. It was stupid, stupid, stupid. It'll never happen again."

"I said it's fine. I know you were just doing your job." Rina tightened her robe. "I'm very tired. I'm going to bed."

He heard the door close a little harder than it needed to. He sat at the dining room table in his pajamas, looking down at his dinner plate. The meat loaf had congealed and the vegetables were wilted. When he looked up, Hannah was looking at him with pity. "Not too hungry?"

"Not really."

"I'll wash your plate."

"No, I'll do it." He checked his watch. "It's almost ten."

"Top of the morning," Hannah said. "She'll get over it."

"Eventually, I suppose she will." Decker said.

"She has a point. It was stupid, Abba."

"Et tu, Brute?"

Hannah came over to him and hugged his neck. Decker patted her arm. "Thanks, Hannah, I needed a hug." When he turned around to look at her, she was in tears. He took his daughter into his arms and embraced her tightly. She was wearing flannel bottoms and an oversized sweatshirt and looked so forlorn and vulnerable. Just when he thought his guilt level had topped out, it went up another notch. "I'm so sorry, pumpkin. I'm so, so sorry."

"I was so *scared*!"

"I know, pumpkin. It was wrong for me to do something so dangerous."

"Weren't you scared?"

"Of course."

"Then why did you do it?"

"It's hard to explain, Hannah. The situation just kind of ran away from me. I was so focused on saving those women, I didn't see anything else."

She was silent.

"I had on a bulletproof vest and a helmet."

"Your job isn't supposed to be dangerous enough to need those kinds of things."

"Mostly it isn't."

"Except when it is." She broke away from him and folded her hands in front of her chest. "You were already shot twice. What are you trying to prove?"

Decker sighed. "I'm not proving anything. Like I said, the situation just got away from me."

"That's no answer," she harrumphed. "Well, it is an answer, but it's a lame answer."

"It is a lame answer, but it's the only one I have." Decker tried out a smile. "Please don't be mad at me."

Her face softened and the anger melted away. "I love you, Abba. I know that sometimes I can be difficult." Her lip quivered. "I do appreciate you."

"I know you do, Hannah, I know you do." He held out his hands and she fell into his arms again. "Love you, pumpkin pie. Can I tuck you into bed?"

"I'm not ready yet. I have to sign off, I have to organize my backpack, I have to brush my teeth and hair and put on my acne medicine."

"Tell me when you're ready."

"It may take a while."

"I'm not all that tired. I'll wait."

Dressed in a coral silk blouse, a white pleated skirt, and white sneakers sans socks, Genoa Greeves looked a step away from the tennis court. Her legs were bare, her calves strong and muscular. Again, she had her laptop and took notes as Decker recounted the probable trail of events.

Ryan Goldberg had fallen madly in love with Melinda Little. Egged on by Rudy Banks, Goldberg had decided to be a man and confront Bennett Little. But being as Goldberg wasn't quite right in the head even back then, he had asked for Rudy's help—could he arrange the meeting and also come with him just to make sure things didn't get out of control?

Decker said, "Ryan made a lot of mistakes . . . falling for the wrong woman . . . the wrong women. There were others. But this was a real bonehead thing to do."

"Like inviting the fox into the henhouse," Genoa said.

Decker continued.

Rudy arranged the meeting, but he knew that Bennett Little would never have agreed to meet with him. Little didn't trust him, didn't like him. As a matter of fact, Little had been so angry at Rudy Banks because of Darnell Arlington's expulsion that he wouldn't even talk to Banks on the phone.

"That much we got out of Goldberg. This is where conjecture comes in. I think Rudy did some improvising."

"Go on."

"If I had to lay out a scenario, it would probably be this. Rudy Banks called up Leroy Josephson, promising him a career as a rapper if he would just waylay Ben Little and bring him to a spot where Goldberg could talk to him. When Josephson asked how to do that, Banks probably gave him a gun and told him to use his imagination.

"Now, Little would never have met with Banks, but Little couldn't resist a student in trouble. Just after he had phoned his wife to tell her that he was on his way home, I'm thinking that Leroy Josephson flagged Little down just as he exited the civic center parking lot. Probably Little stopped for him, they talked, and eventually Leroy got into the Mercedes. Maybe Leroy was invited into the car, maybe he forced his way in. Then Leroy pulled the gun on Little."

"Why do you assume that?"

"Why else would Little have driven all the way out to the foothills? That was the designated spot where Ryan Goldberg and Rudy Banks were waiting for them. Also, Leroy had the gun drawn when he and Little got out of the car."

"That's awful."

Involuntarily, Decker rubbed his neck. "Goldberg told us that all he had wanted to do was to talk to Little, to find out if Ben loved Melinda as much as he did. He told us that Little was patient with Goldberg's pleas. He also remarked that Little didn't seem surprised by the affair, he didn't even seem upset by it. In the end, Little told Goldberg that it was up to Melinda. He couldn't make that decision for her."

Decker shifted in his desk chair.

"This part is where Goldberg's memory got murky. Rudy was telling him things and Leroy was telling him things and Little was telling him things."

"What things?" Genoa asked.

"Something like . . . are you just going to take that? Come on, Mudd, show him who's boss." A pause. "It appears that Rudy wanted a confrontation between two guys who weren't anxious to fight. But words got heated. Mudd remembered someone coming after him, and he threw a punch. The next thing that Mudd remembered was Little lying on the ground. Rudy went over to Little and felt for a pulse. He told Mudd that Little was dead."

"From a single punch?'

"Mudd was a big guy. Rudy also could have been lying. Rudy told Mudd to put Little in the trunk of his car and he'd take care of everything. Mudd complied. Then shots rang out. Mudd claims he didn't know who did the shooting. Just that Little was dead."

"Hmmm . . . sounds like a convenient time to forget things."

"Could be Mudd's lying, but remember also that Mudd wasn't too focused to begin with. He admitted being stoned. He was always on one kind of drug or another."

"That seems convenient, too."

"Agreed."

"Go on."

"Mudd said he went crazy after the shooting. Rudy managed to calm him down and get him into his car, but before they left, he remembered

Rudy with his hand on Leroy's shoulder, talking to him. Goldberg couldn't hear what he was saying. Ryan also seemed to remember that Rudy gave Leroy money. That would fit with Wenderhole's version of Leroy carrying around a lot of cash. What I think happened was that Ryan and Rudy went home while Leroy drove Little's car to Clearwater Park. Then he called up Wenderhole to pick him up."

"I see. And Goldberg just let the incident go without a protest?"

"Apparently he did. Mudd must have read about it in the papers. He must have been scared. But he swore that after that night, he never talked about it again . . . except to tell Melinda that he didn't kill her husband."

"But you're not so sure about that."

"No, I'm not. What I am certain about is that for fifteen years, Mudd lived with the guilt."

Genoa said, "But if Mudd lived with the guilt for fifteen years, why did he suddenly snap?"

"Again, no one knows for sure," Decker answered. "This is my theory for what it's worth. When I visited Mudd that one time, he said he called up his old bandmate, Liam O'Dell, to ask questions about why I was there. Liam made the mistake of telling him that I was looking for Rudy, probably in regards to Ekerling's murder. I think my investigation unleashed something inside of him. He told his doctors that he suddenly wanted to find Rudy himself and take care of something that should have been taken care of a long time ago."

"How'd he find Rudy?"

"Not by any brilliant deductive powers. The standoff made the news. Somehow Mudd managed to find a secret spot with a good view of the Sand Dune's front lawn. He waited for Rudy to come out, and from there, we all know what happened. I thank God every day that Goldberg was an accurate shot."

"How'd he do that? Wasn't it pitch-black outside?"

"It was actually light gray. The sun hadn't come up, but it wasn't nighttime."

Genoa said, "I can't understand this. If Rudy was involved in Primo Ekerling's death, and you think he was . . ."

"Definitely."

"Then why did he dispose of Ekerling's body in the same way that he disposed of Little's body? Didn't he think that someone would put two and two together?"

"We were dealing with two deaths, fifteen years apart, in different parts of L.A. The principal investigators on the Little case had retired. Banks probably thought that no one would notice."

"I did."

Decker smiled briefly. "Yes, you did. And maybe Banks thought that even if the cops did realize the similarities, we'd blame the murders on Ryan Goldberg. He was the one who was unbalanced."

"But Ryan had nothing against Primo Ekerling. Primo was his friend."

"You're right, Ms. Greeves. I can't answer that question well. I don't know what went through Rudy's head."

"All right." She clicked on her laptop. "That's not a completely sufficient answer, but I suppose it's the best you can do." She typed away. "That's taken care of. Now what about Cal Vitton? Why did he commit suicide? Or was it murder?"

"We'll never know for certain. I think it was suicide."

"Why?"

"Okay, let me see if I can make some sense. Phil Shriner had passed along Rudy's name to Cal Vitton as a suspect in the Little murder. Shriner knew that Melinda had had an affair with Rudy and he thought that Rudy looked like a pretty good candidate for Ben Little's murder. But Vitton never followed through. Maybe he forgot about the tip or maybe he chose to forget about it. I think Vitton didn't want to antagonize Rudy because Banks knew that Vitton's younger son was gay."

"I thought you said that everyone knew that Vitton's son was gay."

"But Cal J hadn't come out of the closet. Big Cal was embarrassed about it and didn't want the information to be common knowledge. Big Cal was from the old school where homosexuality was an embarrassment."

"Vitton was embarrassed enough to hide a murderer?"

"Maybe. Besides, Vitton didn't know for certain that Rudy had anything to do with Little's death. I'm betting that he probably chose not to find out one way or the other. I do know that Big Cal had been so ashamed of his son's homosexuality that he didn't stop Rudy and other boys from bullying his own flesh and blood."

"That's appalling."

"Yes, it is."

"So why should Vitton have sudden pangs of remorse?"

"Maybe Vitton knew it was all going to come out in my investigation. Maybe he didn't want to be around to see his reputation crash. Or maybe he was just depressed. Then again, maybe Rudy slipped him some pills, aimed the gun at his head, and somehow had Cal pull the trigger."

"Cal pulled the trigger?"

"Yes, we're certain about that. It's the *why* that's a mystery."

There were lots of mysteries that they'd never know now that Rudy Banks was dead. Like whose blood was splashed under the baseboard of his apartment.

Win some, lose some.

"As far as Little's death, I can't say for sure who actually killed him, but I think we can safely narrow it down to three people. Two are dead, the other's in custody."

"Then I suppose I got what I came for." Genoa stood. "Although not entirely solved, I'm satisfied. And I intend to make good on my promise, much to the delight of your captain."

"Much to the delight of the entire police force."

"I understand that your captain is taking me to a dinner in my honor tonight. I'm meeting the commissioner and the police chief. I assume you'll be there as well?"

Decker's smile was tight. "No, ma'am, I have prior arrangements."

"And you can't cancel them?"

"Not unless I want a divorce."

Decker was in a suit and tie. Rina was in a black dress and black pumps and wearing pearls. Just as they pulled up to the valet, Rina said, "I'm not in the mood for this."

Decker was silent.

"Not that I don't want to be with you, I'm just not in the mood for a dog and pony show . . . nor the giant bill that will surely follow. I packed a picnic dinner. Let's find a nice spot at the beach and eat in the car."

If Decker never saw the ocean again, it would be too soon. "Sure. Where?"

"How about Sunset Beach?"

As long as it wasn't Santa Monica, it was tolerable. It took about a half hour to drive and find a good spot on a paved parking lot right off Pacific Coast Highway. Decker pulled the Porsche over and killed the headlights and the motor. Looking out the window . . . the two of them staring out at vast nothingness. No moonlight, lots of overcast fog, and tides rolling back and forth.

"The picnic basket is in the front compartment."

"I'll get it." Decker returned a moment later with the food. Rina might have still been pissed at him, but it didn't translate in her cooking. There were smoked chicken breasts on baguettes, brisket on rye, butter lettuce salad with macadamia nuts, potato chips, strawberries dipped in chocolate and champagne.

"I'm unworthy," Decker said.

"You're not kidding." Silence. "That was mean. I apologize."

"Why don't you just get it all out, and maybe then we can move on."

"There's nothing to get out." A pause. "I can't believe how little disregard you have for your loved ones and yourself."

Decker didn't answer.

"Well?" she asked.

"I have no response that isn't going to get me into more hot water, so I plead the Fifth."

"This is getting it all out?" When Decker remained silent, Rina said, "You want a brisket or chicken?"

"I want to get along."

"Am I fighting?"

"You know what I mean."

"What am I doing? I cook you dinner, I take care of your daughter, I make love to you—"

"That's for both of us."

"I do whatever you need."

"You're talking about me like I'm a house pet."

"I don't make love to a house pet," she huffed. "By the way, thanks for the flowers—again—but no more. The house is looking like a funeral home."

"It isn't?" Decker's attempted joke was met with silence. "Pass the brisket." After Rina handed him a sandwich, he said, "This is much too good to eat when you're not getting along. What do you want from me?"

"For you to promise that you'll never do something that blatantly stupid again."

"Done."

"I don't believe you."

"That's probably wise."

Rina hit him. "So you don't care about making me a widow twice?"

"I'd only be making you a widow once. As pissed as you are, you can't blame the first time on me."

"You're not funny."

Decker put down the sandwich. "The situation probably won't come up again, so the promise I made you will probably remain valid throughout my lifetime. I know it was stupid; people make mistakes. I love you. Can we move on, please?"

Rina was silent. She took out a chicken sandwich, said grace over her food, and bit into it. They ate in silence: a half hour of chewing and swallowing and an occasional grunt in between.

When Decker offered to open the champagne, Rina nodded.

They toasted to health.

Then more silence.

Decker finally said, "In a very weak and not so subtle attempt to get on your good side, I've upgraded our accommodations for the cruise. I've booked us a room with an outside deck and an adjoining room for Hannah."

"This is what it takes for you to get a deck—almost getting yourself killed?"

"A simple 'that's great, dear' would suffice."

"That's great, dear." Rina was silent. But then she smiled. "I'm excited . . . about the cruise."

Decker smiled back. "So am I."

"Eight days without any responsibility in pristine surroundings."

"It doesn't get any better than that."

"And you're sure you can get the time off."

Decker laughed. "After what I went through, that's not a problem."

"We'll go whale watching?"

"Sounds great."

"And canoeing and kayaking."

"I'll row, you take the pictures."

"Will you serve me breakfast in bed?"

"I will."

"Will you wear a black uniform and call me madam?"

"Pass the strawberries."

"I think you'd look cute in a butler's uniform."